PRAISE FOR LIFE'S A DRAG

'This is like an edgy Jilly Cooper – lots of eccentric characters and a lot of fun!' Katie Fforde

'Truly terrific … I love this book' Judy Astley

'High jinks and high heels … Imagine The Archers in drag, with a huge heart and lots of laughs' Veronica Henry

'Life's A Drag is escapism at its best' The Gutter Magazine

'I absolutely LOVE it! Such a great story, heartfelt and positive…fabulous' Richard Rhodes (aka Cookie MonStar)

D0533245

LIFE'S A DRAG

ABOUT THE AUTHOR

Life's a Drag is Janie's first novel.

Before putting pen to paper she was an actress for over twenty years, playing a variety of theatrical roles. She appeared in major venues around the UK (and a few which were not quite as major), in London's West End, and abroad.

In 2009 she and her husband – actor Michael Wilson – had a rush of blood to the head and moved to south-west France. They spent a year renovating an eighteenth-century house in a beautiful market town on the banks of the river Dordogne. In 2010 they opened Chez Castillon and began hosting retreats and writing, painting and photography courses. For more information go to their website:

www.chez-castillon.com

Janie is currently writing her second novel, Skye's The Limit

Life's A Drag

Janie Millman

THE
DOME
PRESS

Published by The Dome Press, 2017

Copyright © 2015 Janie Millman

A CIP catalogue record for this book is available from the British Library
ISBN 978-0-9956723-0-7
[eBook ISBN 978-0-9956723-1-4]

The Dome Press
23 Cecil Court
London WC2N 4EZ

www.thedomepress.com

Printed and bound in Great Britain by Clays., St. Ives PLC
This eBook was produced using Atomik ePublisher

This book is dedicated to
Dr Graham Field
1959–2007 RIP

CHAPTER 1

San Francisco

Smoothing the gold lamé over his hips he flirted with his reflection in the mirror. Not bad, he thought: dress and body both a little past their sell-by date but, on the whole and under subtle lighting, not bad at all.

He gazed at the image in front of him. Gold gleamed back.

Gold dress, gold glitter and glistening ginger curls. He adjusted his breasts and turned sideways to inspect his ass. The new push-up pant seemed to be doing its job. It hadn't come cheap but it was worth every penny and he gave a cheeky little wiggle.

Moving closer to the mirror he pouted at himself and smeared on a final coat of lipgloss, frowning at the dark rings under his eyes which no amount of make-up could entirely conceal.

Drew Berry was not a man given to deep introspection but recently he had been feeling under par. His nights were plagued by anxieties concerning the future of his club and his career. He couldn't imagine life without either and he was worried. He was sleeping badly and drinking heavily and the effects were beginning to show.

Maybe he was going through a mid-life crisis, he thought. After all, his half-century milestone wasn't that far away. Perhaps these things ran in the family. He grinned at the memory of his Uncle Pat performing a full striptease at his fiftieth birthday bash. His Uncle Pat had been morbidly obese; many people had been damaged for life.

'On stage in three minutes,' Elliot popped his head around the dressing-room door.

'Babette ain't showed up yet, why you hired her is a mystery to me. I told you I smelled trouble on her.'

'You smelled bourbon on her.'

'Same thing.'

'Give her a chance, Elliot, she's good, and besides she ain't had an easy life.'

'So what are we now, some sort of charity?'

'Any busier out there?' Drew asked.

'Not so you'd notice.'

'Hell.' Drew slammed his face powder down sending clouds of dust into the air. 'What the fuck is going on here?'

The two friends stared at each other in the mirror as the white particles settled on the surface. Neither bothered to try and disguise their worry, they knew each other too well for that.

'OK, coffee and cognac meeting in the morning and then we'll talk seriously.' Elliot placed his hand on Drew's shoulder. 'But right now we've a show to do and we're a drag queen short.'

'Being a drag queen short ain't a problem. I'll fill in. Being short of an audience, however, is one *heck* of a problem.' Drew stood up. 'But you're right, sugar, they still need entertaining and that's what we're here for.' He gave him a sudden smile. A smile that brought warmth, that lit up a room, a smile that promised much.

He held up his hand for a high five and suddenly the years slipped away and they were kids again, daring each other, egging each other on, believing with the confidence of youth that anything was possible.

'You with me, buddy?' Elliot repeated their childhood refrain.

'All the way,' Drew replied, and grabbing his large brandy downed it in one.

CHAPTER 2

Suffolk

Smoothing the gold lamé over his hips he flirted with his reflection in the mirror.

Damn, I make a bloody good woman, he thought, gazing with satisfaction at the image in front of him.

'Jamie, you look like a cocktail waitress in a Dolly Parton wig.' His wife stood behind him.

'I'm looking pretty good, sweetheart, don't you think? Pretty bloody good. Come on, admit it, you're jealous.'

'I'm alarmed. Is there the slightest chance that you may be taking this whole thing too seriously? It's just a daft drag competition at a small village fete.'

'Roz, my love, it's not just any village fete, it's *our* village fete. We've only been here a few weeks, it's very important that we make an impression.'

'It's important that we make the *right* impression.'

'And we will, Rosalind, we will. Now come and give your old man a hug in all his finery.' Hands on hips he gyrated his six-foot frame in front of her.

'A million miles from London, eh, sweetheart?' He murmured, squeezing the living daylights out of her.

'Yes,' Roz replied, not entirely convinced right now that this was necessarily a good thing.

'I've a few things to do then what do you say to a quick fortifier at the pub before kick off?'

'Absolutely.'

The thought of a strong gin and tonic was immensely appealing. She turned to follow her husband out of the bathroom but catching sight of herself in the mirror stopped short. A tired face gazed back at her, dark blonde hair pulled back into a pony tail, dark shadows under blue grey eyes and a smattering of summer freckles across her nose. Roz was shocked.

She'd always laughed at the notion that house moving was up there with bereavement and divorce but looking at her strained face she began to think it might be true. Jamie had been busy working, so the lion's share of the move had fallen upon her and clearly it showed. That and the stress of the events leading up to it. She felt a familiar prickling behind her eyes, and bending down to the sink angrily splashed cold water on her face. New chapter, new beginnings, she reminded herself, no looking back.

Straightening her shoulders she faced herself in the mirror. *I can't go out looking like this. Come on, girl, drastic action needed, you can't be outdone by your husband.* She tore the elastic band from her hair and reached for the make-up bag.

Twenty minutes and a total transformation later they were strolling up to the pub.

'Wouldn't it have been better to have come here in your civvies and then gone back and changed?' Roz ventured to ask as yet another wolf whistle followed them down the street.

'Sweetheart, stop looking so bloody worried, it's all a bit of fun. You were the one who said we needed to throw ourselves into village life.'

'I was thinking more along the lines of country walks, a dog and pub lunches, not sky blue mascara, vermillion lips and false tits.'

'Stop growling, the sky *is* blue, the sun is shining and the pub is only metres away.'

They rounded the corner and there indeed stood the pub at the top of the hill above the village green. To the left of the pub was a huge church and to the right was the infants' school, above which was placed a sign which read: 'Come little children, listen to me, and I will teach you the fear of the Lord.'

Not something guaranteed to gladden the hearts of the little mites as they skip through the gates, Roz thought.

The green sloped down towards the road. On one side was a row of beautiful pink thatched cottages that adorned every picture postcard of the village and on the other side a couple of modern houses that never adorned anything. At the bottom of the green was a lone telephone kiosk, a duck pond with no ducks and a tiny village shop stocking everything from Tia Maria to tampons.

'OK, you win.' Roz turned to Jamie with a wide smile. 'You're right, it's a glorious day, no more worrying, no more growling, just a double gin, please, and throw in a packet of pork scratchings.'

'That's more like it, my little sunbeam, that's more like the Roz I know and love.' He winked at her.

CHAPTER 3

San Francisco

'Ladies and gentlemen, welcome to The Honey Bees Nightclub.' Elliot threw out his arms. There was a small smattering of applause.

A couple made their way to a table and Elliot waved at them. The elder of the two was tall, with olive skin and long dark hair. Beautifully dressed in designer jeans and a white linen shirt, he looked as effortlessly cool and elegant as only Italians can.

His companion was of medium height, with blond hair and blue eyes. Pure Ivy League from the neck up, and pure unrestrained Liberace from the neck down, he wore a flamboyant frilly shirt, skintight red trousers and cowboy boots. Elliot did a quick double take before continuing.

'And now, ladies and gentlemen, I am proud to present the Queen Bee herself, the incomparable, the inexhaustible, the incontinent, the one and only Miss Honey Berry.'

Drew stepped onto the stage to his signature tune 'Kiss me, Honey Honey, Kiss me.'

There was no lip-synching for Honey Berry. Never knowingly

underplayed, Drew belted out the song. His voice was far from perfect but the power and audacity of the performance more than made up for that.

Most of the small audience were familiar with the routine but that didn't diminish their enthusiasm. They sang along and gave him a standing ovation at the end, cheering and whooping him all the way. What they lacked in numbers they more than made up for in volume.

Smiling and waving, Drew made his way down from the stage towards the bar where Saul the head barman would have his drink waiting.

'Honey, over here.' Drew turned in the direction of the couple.

'Hey guys, good to see you. Holy Mary, Mother of God, Bobby, what in the world are you wearing?' Drew looked at the young man, his eyes widening at the sight of the red and white ensemble. 'You look like a stick of candy.' He raised his eyebrows at the elegant Joe who grinned, shrugging his shoulders in resignation.

'Honey, take a look at what *you're* wearing.' Bobby replied indignantly.

'I'm a fucking drag queen, sweetheart, I'm supposed to look outrageous.'

'Tell Honey our news, Bobby,' Joe said gently, putting an arm around his partner's shoulder.

A radiant smile lit up Bobby's young face. 'We're getting married.' He punched the air.

'No way? You gotta be kidding.' Drew was delighted.

Joe smiled in confirmation.

'Well, sweet Jesus, how wonderful.' He flung his arms around them both.

From behind the bar Saul watched the group hugging and kissing each other and wondered what the celebration was. Drew waved at him and mimed the popping of a cork. Saul was just reaching for a bottle when he spied Babette walking into the club. She made towards the bar.

'Hi, Saul, how ya doing?' She leant across the bar, her eyes bright, her face flushed and her breath reeking of bourbon.

'You're late, Babette,' Saul said, trying to ascertain how drunk she was.

'Better late than never, sweetie,' she replied, blowing him a kiss.

He watched her weaving her way backstage and hoped to God the others would look after her.

'How is she?' Drew appeared at his shoulder.

'She's had a few but seems in control.' Saul replied. 'I guess she'll be fine.' But he spoke with more conviction than he felt.

'Jesus, Saul, is it any wonder folk ain't coming here? I wouldn't pay to see us, would you? We gotta face facts, buddy, we're in big trouble.'

'We'll survive.' Saul smiled calmly at Drew before turning to the young men making their way to the bar. 'What's the celebration?'

'We're getting married.' Bobby screeched.

'Well, that explains the outfit.'

'No, we're not getting married now.' Bobby was flustered. 'What's wrong with what I'm wearing? Why's everyone making such a fuss?'

'They're just jealous, sweetie, not everyone could carry that off,' Elliot said, strolling over to the group.

'Not everyone would want to.' Saul grinned.

'Why the champagne?'

'We're getting married.' This time it was Joe who responded.

Elliot whooped with delight. 'Congratulations.' He grabbed a glass. 'This calls for a serious party.'

'Babette's here,' Saul informed Elliot quietly.

'What sort of state is she in?'

'Unsteady.'

'I'll go backstage.' Elliot put down his glass. 'C.C. meeting tomorrow, Saul.'

'What the hell's a C.C. meeting?' Joe was intrigued.

'Coffee and cognac.' Saul laughed. 'We put the world to rights.'

'Well, we try.' Drew grinned.

Saul knew what the meeting would be about. He knew Drew was worried about the club and if Drew was worried then Elliot would be worried.

Saul took a more sanguine approach to life, he knew times were tough but firmly believed they would somehow get through it. They had no choice. The three of them had worked so hard to make The Honey Bees a success. They'd put their hearts and souls into it and Saul couldn't imagine a life without it. He had met Drew the very day Drew had taken possession of the Club.

Saul had been living rough. On the night he first met Drew he'd been hanging around a club where the barman was sympathetic and could usually be relied upon to put some food and drink Saul's way.

He had been there most of the evening watching the nocturnal activities and he saw Drew stumble out around two in the morning very much the worse for wear. He'd remembered him arriving earlier. He'd been on his own and had generously handed over a ten-dollar bill saying. 'You're in luck, pal, I've got no change.'

Saul watched as a young lad approached him. He couldn't hear what the lad was saying but it was clear that there was some sort of trouble and he was gesticulating towards a nearby alleyway. Drew placed an unsteady arm around his shoulder and let himself be guided towards it.

A sixth sense had kicked in and without stopping to think Saul ran down the alley. There were two of them and they already had Drew on the ground. Drew was a big man but he was drunk and had been taken unawares. He was no match for the teenagers. With a blood-curdling yell, Saul broke the bottle he was drinking from and ran towards them screaming.

The sight of a large, unkempt black man brandishing a broken bottle and howling like a banshee was more than enough for them. They turned and fled, dropping both the wallet and their dignity.

Saul chuckled and turned to help an astounded Drew to his feet. 'It's the noise more than anything that scares them.'

'Scared the shit outta me,' Drew said.

'Well the war cry was invented for a reason.'

'My name's Drew. Thank you, buddy, you just saved my skin.'

'The name's Saul and it was a pleasure.'

The two men shook hands and looked at each other.

'Well, I sure could use another drink,' Drew finally said, dusting himself down. 'That little episode seems to have sobered me up some. What do say, Saul? Could you use a drink.'

'I could always use a drink.' Saul replied.

'Saul, a man could die of thirst here.' Drew shouted across the bar, breaking into his reverie. 'We ain't got that many punters and we wanna keep the ones we have.'

'Sorry, folks, drinks coming up.' Saul dragged himself back to the present day and moved to where a couple of guys were waiting patiently at the bar.

'Ladies and gentlemen.' Elliot was back on stage. 'The latest addition to our beehive, she's tantalising, she's tempting, she's Miss Titty Titty Bang Bang.'

She bounced onto the stage: blonde ringlets, enormous tits, long legs and a Ra-Ra skirt. The music started and so did she. She had a fantastic voice. Slightly husky, sexy and inviting.

'Hi, I'm pretty Titty Bang Bang,

Pretty Titty Bang Bang,

I love you.'

The small audience went wild as she cavorted around the stage. Elliot glanced over to Drew and Saul and gave them the thumbs up. Despite loving the act, they'd been slightly anxious that the film *Chitty Chitty Bang Bang* may not be well known enough in America and the humour of the lyrics lost. From the reaction of the audience, however, this was clearly not the case.

'High, low or in a motorcar,

Oh what a happy time we'll spend…'

Titty sang on leaving little to the imagination. It was a smart and sassy routine.

'She's awesome.' Joe laughed. 'Where the hell did you find her?'

'Rolled up bold as brass last week and demanded an audition,' Drew replied. 'She's kinda special, ain't she?'

'She's hot,' Joe replied, earning himself a dark look from Bobby.

'Wait until you see her encore of "Truly Scrumptious".' Elliot said, coming back off stage in time to hear the last remark. 'It verges on the pornographic.'

'Pornographic or otherwise we sure could use a few more acts like her. She's vibrant and energetic, unlike some I could mention.' He glanced over to where Cherry Pye was lolling against the stage waiting to go on. Her whole demeanour was in direct contrast to Titty's exuberance. Lifeless plaits, a gingham pinafore straining at the seams and make-up that had been ploughed on in furrows. Dorothy was not a good look for a woman over forty. If it wasn't so sad it'd be funny, thought Drew. But sadly it wasn't funny.

He'd taken his eye off the ball and let things slide. They all needed a kick up the ass. In fact, everything needed an overhaul. He looked around the club. The whole place could do with smartening up. When it was crowded and buzzing, it had ambience and glamour, on nights like tonight though it looked faded and tawdry.

The old gold curtain hung raggedly on the back wall, the lighting was fashionably dim but only because half the bulbs needed replacing, the tables and chairs were mismatched and the wooden floor pockmarked with the imprint of stilettos. It needed a new look, but new looks cost money and that was the one thing they didn't have. They needed a minor miracle and they needed it fast.

'Drew, will you quit staring into space with that pained expression.' Elliot nudged him in the ribs. 'We're supposed to be celebrating here.'

Drew spun around, instantly repentant. 'Hell, you're right. Guys, I'm so sorry.' He grabbed the champagne bottle and topped up their glasses. 'I'm all yours, now tell me about the wedding plans.'

'They have been but you weren't listening.' Elliot replied. 'Joe was saying he wants to throw an obscene amount of money at the club and hold a lavish wedding party here.'

'Really?' Joe raised his eyebrows. 'Is that what I said?'

'That's what you meant.' Bobby grinned.

'I'll drink to obscene.' Drew lifted his glass. 'Keep talking, Joe.'

The final act of the evening was a group number dancing to Sister Sledge singing 'We are Family' choreographed by Drew and Saul. It was by no means the most polished or original of routines but the small audience once again responded enthusiastically and Drew was filled with a steely determination. They'd been successful before and they would be successful again. Against all the odds they had got this far and he sure wasn't about to let it go without a fight.

CHAPTER 4

Suffolk

The local pub was everything a country pub should be, with low beams, gleaming brasses and huge fireplaces. George the barman was rotund, cheerful and strangely camp.

He greeted them with a huge smile. 'Let's take a look at you, Jamie. Trashy but tantalising, I like it.' He turned to Roz. 'Makes a fine woman, doesn't he?'

Jamie looked triumphantly at Roz while George yelled over to the far corner.

'Frank, my boy, come and see this. You've serious competition this year.'

They both turned in the direction of Frank and gasped.

'Make that a treble gin, Jamie, and easy on the tonic,' Roz muttered under her breath.

Frank was short and square with bulging biceps and hands like shovels. His fat, hairy legs were rammed into a pair of pink wellington boots. He was wearing a pink tutu, long, pink gloves and a huge straw hat. He had a round angelic face with dimples.

'Frank is our local butcher, winner of the drag competition three years running.' George said.

'Freestyle butcher actually, good to meet you.' He held out an enormous paw.

'Jamie and Roz are actors, just moved in here. Proper actors you know, films and telly, Jamie's been in *Taggart*,' George beamed.

'Actors, eh? Well, we have a lot in common, similar line of work. What will you have to drink?'

'Gin and tonic, please,' Roz stammered before turning towards Jamie, a bemused expression on her face. 'Freestyle?' she mouthed.

'Similar line of work?' he whispered back.

Raising her eyebrows, she reached for the gin George was handing her.

'Cheers, Frank,' Jamie said, lifting his pint. 'Now, I'm very intrigued, what exactly is a freestyle butcher? Certainly not a term I've ever heard before.'

'It's all about having a vision, Jamie, using your imagination, letting the meat tell its own story, being creative. As I said, similar line of work to yourselves.'

'Aye, right, well, what an interesting way of looking at things. And, er, what sort of story does the meat have to tell?'

He was floundering, Roz reached for his hand and took up the gauntlet.

'Where exactly is your shop, Frank? We'd love to come and see you at work.'

'Well that's the beauty of the whole thing, Roz my love. I have no shop. I have a van and I'm therefore able to keep everything very simple.' He was delighted to have such a sympathetic audience and went on to describe the finer points of freestyle butchery in a mobile van to an increasingly bewildered Jamie and Roz.

Taking a surreptitious slurp of vodka, George watched the group with amusement. He loved events like this, when the pub was crowded with excitement and laughter. He'd been manager here for the last five years and this had become his life.

It had been a total change for him. In the past he'd been a bit of a rolling stone, travelling the world and picking up work where he could. On his return, a stint as a doorman in a seedy Peckham nightclub had led to a brush with the underworld, which in turn had resulted in a few months in jail. After jail he took refuge in a commune in Devon, where under the name of Wilfred Woolfe he made quite a name for himself as a basket weaver.

A chance encounter with his niece, who owned a string of pubs and bars across the country, had led him to this position. Going against the wishes of her family, she had given George the job of manager and he was determined not to let her down. He had reinvented himself here and, for the first time in his life, felt needed and appreciated. A shout from Jamie interrupted his thoughts.

'George, we need your help. Apparently every drag queen needs a name, what do you think mine should be?'

George smiled. They were a lovely couple and were obviously determined to enjoy village life. Jamie had admitted early on that he'd felt very anxious about moving to a small village. Village life, he'd confessed, was alien to him, but watching him now George thought he seemed very at home indeed. Roz he was less sure of, she was extroverted and vivacious but there was sadness there, a vulnerability that he couldn't quite put his finger on.

'Frank, what's your drag name?' Jamie demanded.

'Cynthia,' Frank said without hesitation.

Jamie looked surprised.

17

'My sister had a mate called Cynthia.' Frank explained. 'An upper-class snob with enormous knockers. She was hot.'

'Cynthia it is, then,' Jamie said. 'Now what about me?'

'Isabella, after your mother?' Roz ventured.

'Christ, no, I'd feel a touch incestuous. And don't even think about suggesting your mother's name.'

'My mother was called Brenda,' George said.

'It's not really that exotic though, is it?' Roz said.

'Was your mother exotic, George?' Jamie asked.

'Well, if you call a size eighteen with a forty-a-day habit and a penchant for gin exotic, then she was incredibly exotic.'

'Sounds like my sort of girl. Brenda it is, thank you, George.'

'Lovely woman, your mother,' Frank said.

'You never knew her,' George replied, looking puzzled.

'Doesn't stop her being lovely.'

A round of applause terminated the conversation as a gangly young man dressed in a leather miniskirt and fishnet tights entered the pub.

'Billy, good lad, you've done yourself proud again,' Frank yelled. 'Come over here and meet the competition.'

'Nice lad, very bright, bit of a loner though. Lives with his granny, never seems to have any mates,' Frank said in an aside as Billy made his way to the bar. 'Ah, Billy, meet Jamie and Roz, stars of screen and theatre, so they say, although I've never seen them in anything.'

'Nice to meet you, Billy,' Jamie laughed. 'We were just talking names, what's yours?'

'Um, Billy,' Billy replied, looking a touch perplexed.

'No, I mean your drag name, Billy. I'm Brenda and Frank here is Cynthia.'

'And I am Bernadette,' a deep voice interrupted.

Jamie turned towards Clive the postmaster. He was very tall and narrow. Long dark ringlets hung to his waist, he'd waxed his moustache for the occasion, and was wearing a black floor-length lace dress.

'Bernadette, you look like a cross between Morticia Addams and Cher,' George said.

'George, you've hit the nail on the head. Just the combination I was hoping for. Now, a Guinness for me, whatever anyone else would like and a pint of the usual for Ollie.'

Clive and Ollie, short for Olivia, had been amongst the first people to welcome the newcomers to the village. They made quite a pair. He was over six foot, bald as a coot with a large black moustache and she was a diminutive elf with bouncing salt and pepper curls and a smile that reached every part of her face.

Roz was delighted to meet them again. Ollie was trotting towards them, waving to everyone and talking animatedly.

'Here I am, darlings, pint of the usual, please, George. Fantastic day for the fete. Jamie, you look fucking gorgeous. Clive looks like a fucking freak.'

Roz and Jamie were aghast. Where was the sweet lady with the cut-glass accent who'd greeted them not long before with a pot of homemade marmalade?

'Ah,' Clive grinned at their expressions. 'Perhaps I ought to explain. When Ollie has had a few drinks she swears like a fishwife. We've all tried to cure her but to no avail. Nothing seems to stop her, it's a sort of drunken Tourette's.'

'My father was a bishop, I think this may be a latent rebellion against my strict upbringing.' Ollie added. 'Anyway, great to have you here, you're just what this village needs, some fresh blood to shake us up. We've become rather boring and stale.'

19

Roz was startled. Boring and stale? A village that was home to a freestyle butcher, a Jekyll and Hyde postmistress and a young Billy-no-mates in drag.

She glanced around the rest of the pub, her gaze taking in the Morris dancers lolling in the corner, a man dressed in a druid outfit and a couple of overweight Hells Angels. Boring and stale were not the words she would have chosen.

'Roz, I want you to meet someone,' Clive said, tapping her on the shoulder.

Roz wheeled around and came face to face with a young woman of astounding beauty. Gleaming dark hair framed a perfect heart-shaped face, gentle blue eyes twinkled and the softest pale pink lips smiled at her. Roz, who had never in her life had a lesbian tendency, felt the strongest urge to kiss her.

'Hi Roz, lovely to meet you, I'm Charlotte, headmistress of the local primary school.'

Bloody hell, thought Roz, half the male population must want to be back in shorts and a blazer. A quick glance at Jamie's face confirmed it.

'Do you have any children, Roz?' the goddess asked. She had a husky voice with a light Suffolk burr.

'No, actually, sadly, we were unable to, you see, so no.'

Would that ever get any easier to say, she wondered? No matter how many times she practised the sentence at home she always stumbled. She was saved from continuing by Clive suddenly booming out,

'We've got a daughter, well two if you count her girlfriend. Apparently they're getting married.' He ruffled Ollie's hair and continued without a pause. 'My fellow artistes, are we ready to saunter onto the green and strut our stuff? The competition is in about an hour, may the best woman win.'

'What is the actual prize?' Jamie asked.

'There is the pride and glory, of course, the coveted cup and a bottle of homemade vintage rhubarb wine courtesy of George here,' Frank said.

George bowed in recognition of his generosity.

'And, of course, you get to organise the following year's contest.'

CHAPTER 5

Suffolk

Outside, a young marching band were having the greatest difficulty maintaining any formation on the sloping green, but they battled bravely on and the crowd swayed gently to the music.

Roz took in the scene around her. Tattered bunting was looped from tree to tree and bales of straw had been scattered around to provide seating. A huge marquee stood in one corner and a bouncy castle in the other. A large metal trough had been converted into a BBQ and the smell was making Roz's mouth water.

'It looks great, doesn't it?' She turned to Jamie. 'Shambolic but charming.'

'It looks wonderful. Shall we have a look around? I fancy my chances at beat the goalie.'

'That's because the goalie happens to be about ten.'

The goalie was a good deal better than Jamie had anticipated and Roz stood by, helpless with laughter, as she watched Jamie struggle.

'Have they hired him in for the day from the Manchester United youth squad?' Jamie demanded. 'He can't possibly look that bloody young and be that bloody good. It's outrageous.'

'I don't think your dress helped,' Roz said giggling. 'Do you want to try your hand at the skittles or have you had enough humiliation for one day?'

'I think a burger may be in order. I need to build up my strength.' Jamie grabbed her hand and marched up the green.

From under cover of the beer tent, Frank appraised them. He thought they made a delightful pair and such a contrast to each other, Roz with her English rose beauty and Jamie with his dark Gaelic looks. He watched Jamie stoop to kiss her and felt a very small stab of jealousy. They were clearly very much in love and Frank couldn't help but wonder if he would ever experience anything like that.

Unknown to anyone except George, he had placed an advert in the personals column of the local paper but, apart from an obscene telephone message from a bloke called Perry, the results had proved disappointing.

George had helped him with the wording: 'Freestyle butcher with imagination seeks like-minded carnivore with GSOH for intimate relationship.'

George had not been that keen on the use of the word "carnivore" or indeed, if he was truthful, "freestyle 'butcher" but Frank believed in being honest and upfront. He was proud of his profession and would certainly never entertain the idea of an intimate relationship with a vegetarian.

Maybe these things took time. People were busy during the summer months. Perhaps he would have more success during winter when a girl might be more desperate. Maybe Roz had a friend who would fit the bill, or possibly Jamie had a far-flung Scottish cousin frantic for some southern action. Greatly cheered by these thoughts, Frank went to order another pint.

A thought struck him. Should he let Jamie win the competition this year? He had won for the last three years; perhaps it was time for new blood. Also, if Frank were honest, he hadn't done much about organising the contest and there was still only a sad line up of five. Each year he had great intentions, and last year had even gone as far as placing an advert in the parish magazine with the heading "Is life a drag?" He had been quite pleased with that but he hadn't followed it up. Jamie seemed dynamic and passionate; he would probably throw himself into organising the event with enthusiasm.

Frank made up his mind. He wasn't going to win this year, and with that thought he tore off his straw boater and discarded the pink gloves.

'If these are Frank's, then I'm all in favour of freestyle butchery,' Jamie said, biting into a fat sausage.

'Absolutely,' Roz mumbled through a mouthful of burger. 'This is gorgeous.'

'I may have to get another one,' Jamie wiped ketchup from his chin. 'Or would that be just too greedy?'

He was saved from having to make a decision by someone tugging at his sleeve.

'Excuse me, are you the new actor?' Jamie looked down to see a wizened old lady with lipstick smeared around her mouth and bright rouge on her cheeks.

'Yes, I am. My name is Jamie, and this is my wife Roz.'

'Oh, I'm so pleased to meet you,' she said, completely ignoring Roz. 'I just knew you would come. I've been looking forward to it for years.'

'Have you?' Jamie laughed.

'You see, I heard the message,' she whispered, patting the side of her nose.

'The message?' Jamie echoed.

'On the television. But I won't tell anyone, not a soul.' She smiled a toothless flirty smile and gently farted.

'Beer tent, quick march.' Jamie grabbed Roz forcefully by the arm.

'It's nice when people recognise you, isn't it?' Roz was killing herself laughing. 'You should have given her your autograph.'

'Look, there's Frank, Ollie, Clive and the beautiful headmistress waving us over,' Jamie ignored her.

'She's very lovely, isn't she?' Roz was looking at Charlotte in admiration.

'She's an absolute goddess, but fear not, I prefer my women more earthly,' he said, slapping her firmly on the arse.

'My round,' Frank said, as they approached the beer tent. 'What will it be? You have a choice of beer, cider or undrinkable wine?'

'In that case, I imagine a cider for Roz and a beer for me, please. Why've you abandoned your hat and gloves, Frank?'

'I have my reasons,' Frank replied enigmatically, as he departed for the bar.

'He's mad, isn't he?' Clive said. 'Just look at what he's wearing.'

'That's a bit fucking rich coming from a man wearing a moth-eaten wig and a floor-length gown,' his wife retorted.

'Ollie, I can tell from your language that you have been partaking of alcoholic beverages.'

A long-limbed, fair-haired man with the greenest eyes Roz had ever seen appeared in their midst.

'Leon, bloody lovely Leon, we've been looking for you everywhere. Fuck me, have you been stabbed?' Ollie pointed at a dark red stain down the front of his shirt.

'Red wine, Ollie, nothing more dramatic than that.' He wiped ineffectually at the stain.

25

'Let me introduce Leon, our local vet and the worst-dressed man in the village,' Clive said.

'Listen, mate, I'll have you know that mustard and lime green are absolutely this summer's colours and that flares are, indeed, making a comeback.' Leon looked down proudly at his wide trousers. 'The whole ensemble got the thumbs up from Hannah and you can't ask for better praise than that.'

'Is Hannah your wife?' Roz asked, liking him immediately.

'No, Hannah is my nine-year-old daughter and, therefore, a fashion guru.'

'Where is she?'

'She's practising her cheerleading routine over there.' He gestured towards a group of girls in sparkling leotards and short skirts.

'Which one is she?'

'The chunky monkey on the end, usually a beat behind the others.'

'Leon, stop calling her that, you'll give her a complex,' Charlotte said.

'Is your wife here?' Jamie enquired.

'No, Jamie, my wife hasn't been here for the last nine years. She scarpered soon after Hannah's umbilical cord was cut.' He grinned ruefully, 'Not what you'd call a successful marriage really. She thought I was wealthy and I thought she loved me, turned out we were both wrong. Still, she gave me Hannah, so all was not lost. And right on cue, here is my little chunky monkey,' he said, as his daughter rushed over. 'Hello, angel, how goes it?'

'Not great, Dad. I'm rubbish really.'

'Absolute nonsense.'

'It's true. I'm having fun, but I just keep dropping my pom-poms.'

'I'm going out tomorrow to buy myself a leotard and together we will practise pom-pom twirling until we are the most perfect pair of pom-pom twirlers the world has ever seen, and then we'll give a demonstration. How does that sound?'

'How does what sound?' Frank asked returning from the bar with a tray laden with drinks. 'Leon, I saw you arrive – it's hard to miss you in that outfit – so I got you a beer.'

'Now hang on just a minute, here I am standing next to three men, one of whom is wearing a pink tutu, the other an off-the-shoulder gold lamé number and the third a black lace gown, and yet you have the cheek to comment on *my* wardrobe.'

'But we're all wearing these outfits for a reason,' Frank said, handing round the drinks. 'You have no excuse.'

'When is the drag show?' Leon ignored Frank's comment. 'Are you the grand finale?'

'Not necessarily grand, but we close the proceedings,' Clive replied. 'In fact, ladies, we need to find the others and have a pow-wow. We need to work out our opening dance routine.'

Jamie choked on his drink. 'Christ, I didn't realise we took it that seriously.'

'Our public expect no less,' Clive said, grinning. 'See you all later and remember no favouritism now, you vote for the queen you think is most worthy, but if I don't hear you screaming for me, Ollie, there'll be trouble later on.' Clive threw his arm around Jamie and led him off.

Roz watched him go and felt a sudden stab of panic at being left alone. Jamie seemed to have slotted into village life with perfect ease but she was struggling a little. She'd expected to be the one helping Jamie to settle in, not the other way around. She loved it here but felt slightly overwhelmed at times. It seemed almost too good to be true.

For God's sake get a grip, Rosalind, she chastised herself. Stop being so pathetic. Enjoy the moment. And on this thought she spun back to the group with such force she knocked the beer straight out of Leon's hand and onto his shirt where it mingled with the red wine.

'This outfit doesn't seem to be very popular at all today, does it?' Leon looked down at the ever-increasing stain on his lime-green front.

'Leon, I'm so sorry. Let me buy you another one. Drink, that is, not shirt,' she giggled.

'You can buy me a drink later on, Roz, but for now I have to go and judge the final of the dog show,' Leon said. 'Who's coming?'

The dog show was a riot of noise and confusion. Roz adored dogs and longed to have a puppy. She determined to ask Leon if he knew of one going.

Fuelled by her glass of cider, she suddenly felt on top of the world. 'The laughter and gaiety surrounding her rendered her suddenly light hearted and the doubts and anxieties of a few moments ago disappeared.

Charlotte had captivated her completely with her warmth, beauty and wicked sense of humour. Watching her and Leon laughing together, it suddenly occurred to her that they would make a marvellous couple and she turned swiftly towards Ollie.

'Leon and Charlotte would make …'

'A bloody lovely couple. Yes, they would and everyone knows it except the silly fuckers themselves.'

'Perhaps they do secretly know it but are too scared to do anything?'

'Very profound, Roz. Clive says much the same thing; at least I think that's what he says.' She smiled, 'Personally I hate all this constant bloody analysing. In my day you leapt into bed, had a good screw and either saw each other again or didn't. All quite simple.'

'Oh Ollie, you're priceless but quite right too. We do over-analyse everything.' She raised her glass in a salute. 'My new resolution, less study more screwing.'

Strolling across the green, Jamie caught sight of Roz and Ollie laughing together and smiled with delight. He knew Roz had been looking forward to this move, but he'd been worried that she may have built her expectations too high. They'd been through a lot in the last few years and it had scarred them both.

Roz saw him and waved him over. 'Finished your drag queen summit?'

'Yes, we've decided on the line-up, and rehearsed a little number,' he said. 'You seem to be having a great time with Ollie. I saw you giggling like a couple of schoolgirls. It's good to see you happy.'

'You make it sound like I've been going around with a face like the grim reaper,' she grinned. 'But you're right, I'm feeling good. After all, what's not to enjoy?'

As if on cue, a voice blasted out over the microphone: 'Ladies and gentlemen, please gather round the arena for that eagerly anticipated annual event, the drag queen competition. They are brave but not necessarily beautiful. Ladies and gentlemen, boys and girls, put your hands together for the village drag queens.'

Jamie turned to kiss Roz. 'I won't let you down, sweetheart.'

'Just do your best, that's all I ask for,' Roz said, trying to keep a straight face.

As the men minced onto the green she turned to Charlotte. 'When we lived in London I could never get him onto a dance floor. Just look at him now.'

The five had taken up positions in the middle of the green and were blowing kisses and waving at the crowd. The music started and they began their hastily prepared routine to Madonna's 'Like a Virgin'. They whirled and gyrated on the uneven ground. Clive was in the middle of performing a series of bizarre leaps and turns, his arms waving like windmills above his head.

'He looks like a demented dragonfly,' Leon said, coming to join them.

'The others aren't doing much better,' Roz giggled, as she watched Jamie and Frank skip hand in hand. Thankfully, the music and dancing came to an end, and a young vicar stepped nervously into the arena.

'What's the vicar got to do with it?' Roz asked.

'He's the judge. Well, really it's down to the audience screaming out their favourite, but he oversees it,' Charlotte replied.

'This village gets more eccentric by the minute,' Roz shook her head. 'Poor vicar, he looks as if he'd rather be anywhere but here.'

The young man fiddled timorously with the microphone.

'He's a replacement,' Ollie explained. 'Reverend Priest is laid up with a slipped disc.'

'Reverend Priest?' Roz couldn't believe her ears.

'That really is his name,' Ollie laughed. 'Anthony Priest. A Priest. Bloody fantastic, isn't it? He should convert to Catholicism, I keep telling him that.'

'Put your hands together, please, for Cynthia, Bernadette, Billy, Rita and Brenda.' The young vicar was reading from a sheet of paper.

'What have I missed? I've not missed the sodding dance routine, have I?'

Roz turned around to see a breathless George arriving from the pub clutching a bottle of rhubarb wine decorated with ribbons and bows.

'I wouldn't have called it a routine exactly.'

'Now in time, I mean in the, um, tradition-honoured, tradition in time.' The young vicar stumbled through his lines. 'We will interview each of these ladies.' He hadn't looked up once from his sheet of paper but did so now, visibly upset by the sight before him.

'He's not exactly having the time of his life out there, is he?' George remarked.

'Give him time,' Ollie said. 'He may relax into it.'

'So let me start with this, er, this lady first.' The vicar took the microphone to Clive.

'What's your name?'

'Bernadette,' Clive trilled.

'And what would you do if you won, Bernadette, or may I call you Bernie?' He was desperately trying to get into the spirit of things.

'Oooh, you little flirt, you naughty little vicar,' said Clive, thwacking him over the head.

Petrified, the vicar leapt back. 'What, er what, I mean is what would you do if you won the title today?'

'Well, obviously, I would give all my money to charity, but in my case charity begins at home.'

'Too fucking right, Bernadette,' Ollie yelled.

The vicar moved swiftly on, sweat pouring down his face. 'Now, let's have a word with our ballet dancer,' he said, stepping warily up to Frank. 'And your name, please?'

'Show us your Nutcracker, Frank,' a voice from the crowd yelled.

The young vicar was near to tears. Anthony hadn't prepared him for any of this. He'd told him it was a bit of harmless, light-hearted fun and that he would enjoy himself. Anthony had lied. He couldn't ever remember a time when he'd enjoyed himself less.

After Frank, it was Rita, then Billy and then finally Jamie. 'And last but not least,' he was so relieved to have reached the end of the line, he nearly smiled. 'What's your name?'

'Brenda.' Jamie blew the vicar a kiss and fondled his boobs. The vicar averted his face.

'And, Brenda, are you, um, enjoying yourself?'

'I'm loving it, vicar. This is my first time here and I've made so many new friends, and you are simply gorgeous,' Jamie said, planting a smacker on his cheek.

The vicar turned ashen but gamely tried to carry on. 'Right, well, what would you do, Brenda? I mean, if you won, what would you want to do?'

Fuelled by several pints of beer, and forgetting that this was a family show, Jamie boomed into the microphone: 'I'd like to travel the world and have as much rough sex as possible.'

The vicar stood rooted to the spot, unable to believe his ears.

The crowd exploded with mirth and roared their approval. Charlotte and Roz were clutching each other, helpless with laughter.

'Fucking fantastic, what a fucking fantastic day,' Ollie squealed.

'Ladies and gentlemen …' The vicar was shaking. He got no further. The crowd were chanting. They had chosen their winner.

George strode onto the stage and gently prised the microphone from the young man's trembling hands. 'Ladies and gentlemen,' he yelled. ''Let's hear it one more time. Who is it you want to win?'

'Brenda, Brenda, Brenda!' the crowd yelled back.

'And the coveted title of Drag Queen of the Year,' George paused and smiled at Jamie.

'Is awarded to … BRENDA!'

CHAPTER 6

San Francisco

Elliot and Saul glanced uneasily at each other as Drew reached yet again for the cognac bottle and slopped out a generous measure. It was not yet midday.

'Bright suggestions welcome any time, guys, don't hold back. We need a miracle. We've never been this close to the brink. One small step and we're over the edge.'

'Drew, there's a recession, it's not just us, everyone's suffering …' Elliot got no further.

'God damn it, I don't care about anyone else, I care about us. We're in big trouble. You're the fucking accountant, you know the score.' Drew slammed his fist onto the table. It was an uncharacteristic outburst and Saul and Elliot were momentarily silenced.

Rudely awoken from his slumber in the sun, the dog looked up, quickly assessed the situation and quietly padded over to Drew. He sat by his feet and placed his head gently on Drew's lap. Drew looked down into the soft brown eyes and his anger melted away.

'Sorry, guys, tantrum over.' He grinned at them contritely and, pleased to see him back on an even keel, they nodded encouragingly back.

'OK, let's look at it calmly. What's lacking? Why've we lost the edge? Let's go through last night, for example. A line-up of five girls, not including me.' He reached once more across the table but this time lifted the coffee pot. 'Elliot, kick us off.'

'Babette,' Elliot said, without hesitation. 'We've a problem there.'

'Yeah, I know, but when she's on form, she's bloody good. Saul, what do you think?'

'Sure, she's been late a few times, but she's never yet missed a performance.' Saul paused to think for a moment. 'I'm with Drew here, she's good, she's gutsy and she's fun. I say give her a second chance.'

'And I say she's had her chances, she's a liability, and we don't need her.'

'Actually, I think we do need her,' Drew contradicted him. 'She's young and vibrant; she's just what we need. We're not in a position to be that picky and I agree with Saul, she brings something extra to the show.'

'Yeah, it's called a bottle of bourbon.'

'So, two against one, Babette stays but she gets a warning,' Drew said, ignoring Elliot's last comment.

'Next, our newcomer from the UK, Miss Titty Titty Bang Bang. I love her, she's original and very funny.'

'I second that,' Elliot agreed.

'She's good, she's very good,' Saul said hesitantly.

'But what, Saul?' Drew asked.

'There's something not right, she's hiding something.'

'She's a freakin' drag queen, Saul, of course she's hiding something,' Elliot said, and Drew howled with laughter.

'OK, two down, three to go. Who's next? How about Diana Dross?'

'Lived up to her name last night,' Elliot said. 'A tired and weary routine, the lip-synching was terrible and she ain't the only one.'

'The whole show was under par last night,' Saul agreed. 'We can do better. You said it earlier, Drew, the edge has gone.' He reached for the coffee, changed his mind and poured cognac instead. 'You're right, Elliot, the lip-synching is a joke. Cherry must've sung "Somewhere Over the Rainbow" more than a hundred times but I'm tellin' you there weren't no connection between her mouth and the music. A blind three-year-old could do better.'

'Don't you mean a deaf three-year-old?' Elliot grinned.

'Don't split hairs, you understand what I'm saying.'

'Point taken, Saul. Cherry needs an overhaul,' Drew said. 'But we gotta tread careful. We don't want to lose her; she's been with us from the start.'

'And so's her stuffed dog,' Saul said. But Drew was right, she had been around for a while; there could be no question of her loyalty. Drew inspired devotion, Saul knew; even the cleaning lady had been with them since the beginning. Drew trusted people, gave them a second chance, like he was doing with Babette, like he had done with Saul himself.

'Let's talk to Cherry about reinventing herself.' Drew pushed back his chair and stretched. 'Time she waved goodbye to Judy. Now that leaves Mama Teresa and myself.'

'Nothing is ever gonna change Mama T,' Elliot laughed. ''She's a law unto herself.'

'And besides which there ain't nothing wrong with her,' Saul said.

He adored Mama Teresa. In his opinion she was all that a lady should be. She was kind, gentle, refined and modest, and the fact that she was actually a "he" seemed irrelevant.

'OK, guys,' Drew smiled. 'Just one person left to discuss now and that's me.'

Saul and Elliot stared at him.

'I mean it, guys, I need to know. How am I doing?' Drew was serious. 'Have I still got what it takes? Or is it time to hang up the high heels?'

'Jesus, Honey, what the hell are you talking about? You're a bloody institution,' Elliot said.

'Yeah, but every institution sometimes needs a fresh lick of paint.'

'Drew, buddy, you're what keeps everyone going,' Saul said. 'You never give less than one hundred percent out there. Everyone loves you.'

'But you would tell me, guys?' Drew wanted to make sure. 'If the routine wasn't up to scratch, you'd tell me?'

'We'll be the first to shoot you, I promise,' Elliot said.

'I've never heard Drew talk like that,' Elliot said later on, as he recounted the meeting to Joe over a late lunch. 'I don't mind tellin' you, it kinda unnerved me.'

'Drew is your rock, if he starts to crumble then everything collapses. But I don't see that happening anytime soon. Just a moment of self-doubt, it happens, you know.'

'Not with Drew it don't, leastways, I've never seen it before.'

Joe watched as Elliot lit another cigarette and inhaled deeply. He did look shaken. Things must be pretty bad at the club. 'Coffee to finish off?' he asked.

'You know what?' Elliot said. 'Forget the coffee, let's get more wine, I wanna hear all the wedding plans.' He put his cigarette in the ashtray and stood up. 'I'm going to the bathroom and I'll grab Luigi on the way. Happy to stick with red?' Without waiting for a reply, he pushed back his chair and headed into the restaurant. Joe watched him go, a tall figure, threading his way gracefully through the tables, impeccably dressed as always, charming and flirtatious.

They were lunching at an Italian restaurant not far from Union Square where Joe had his own graphic design company. The food was fantastic, the wine list was varied and most importantly there were tables outside so that Elliot could smoke.

They'd first had lunch there when discussing some artwork Joe was putting together for the Club. One lunch had led to another and it had soon become a regular tradition. There had been a minor dalliance once, after a particularly boozy lunch, but although satisfactory for both parties it had never been repeated. There was a mutual fear that it could ruin what was fast becoming an important friendship for them.

Before Bobby had come on the scene, Joe had felt the odd pang of regret that Elliot's devotion to Drew rendered him incapable of having a relationship with anyone else. The irony was that even Drew had suggested on more than one occasion that he and Elliot would make a good couple. But that was water under the bridge now, and these lunches had become a firm and valuable fixture in their diaries. A chance to bare their souls and, as Elliot said, a damn sight cheaper than therapy.

'Wine is on the way, so let's talk wedding.' Elliot settled himself back in the chair and reached for his cigarette. 'Who popped the question? Was it you?'

'Do you think me completely mad?'

'Hell no, why would I think you mad?'

'Bobby is a young twenty-four, I am an old thirty-six and we've not been together for very long. Many people would think me mad.'

'Joe buddy, age has nothing to do with anything. As long as you're happy, that's the main thing. I take it you're happy?'

'Bobby can be demanding and childish, but he's also loyal, loving and generous. He makes me feel glad to be alive, so yeah, I think it's safe to say I'm happy.'

'That's sure good to hear. So have you set a date yet?'

'One step at a time, please.' The wine arrived and Joe poured them each a glass. 'Bobby is scouring the shops for wedding outfits, which is alarming enough.'

'Bobby wouldn't be Bobby without his appalling dress sense,' Elliot grinned. 'Drew's delighted that you're gonna hold the reception at the Club. I wish we could get a few more wedding parties; we sure could use the money.'

'I'd no idea things were so bad. Is it really serious then?'

'We need something to happen, otherwise your wedding may well be our swansong.'

'No wonder Drew's stressed. What's he up to this afternoon?'

'Buying cheesecake.'

Joe raised his eyebrows.

'Tomorrow is our old folks' afternoon.'

Joe continued to look puzzled.

'You know, we hold a tea dance every month,' Elliot explained. 'We've been doing it for years now. Drew's aunt used to love to dance so it's a sort of tribute to her. She gave him the money to start the club.'

'It rings a vague bell, guess I'd never really computed it before,' Joe said. 'What a cool thing to do.'

'We all love it,' Elliot smiled. 'As we speak I've no doubt that Saul and Drew are in The Cheesecake Factory spending a fortune on ludicrously rich cakes with no regard for money. I tell Drew to go to the supermarket but he insists on the best for them. He says they don't get many treats and it's a small price to pay for the pleasure it gives them.'

'He's a good man,' Joe said.

'The best,' Elliot agreed.

CHAPTER 7

San Francisco

As it happened, Drew was not choosing between velvet pumpkin or peanut butter chocolate cheesecake. He was doing what he always did when he felt tense; he was watching the seal colony at Fisherman's Wharf.

His Aunt Glenda had first taken him there when he was fourteen and he had fallen in love with both the seals and San Francisco. Aunt Glenda had been responsible for his love of performing. She had, in her own words, been a spectacularly unsuccessful actress, but this hadn't stopped her encouraging Drew. She'd been livid with him when he had gone to join his father in his law firm.

'You'll hate it, Drew honey, you'll be stifled. That ain't no life for you.' She was right, he had loathed it from the moment the office door first slammed shut behind him.

His father's death, a few years later, had freed him from his sense of duty and Aunt Glenda's death, a couple of months after that, had freed him financially. She'd left him a large legacy and a letter telling him to live his own life. San Francisco had seemed the obvious choice.

He stood in the sun among the tourists with his dog at his feet and waited for the seals to work their magic and for his anxiety to recede. He watched with amusement as the seals jostled for position, barking and growling, sudden spats breaking out and just as sudden reconciliations. They reminded him of his girls in their dressing room and the thought made him chuckle out loud.

A young woman with a camera slung around her neck turned around at his laughter. She smiled up at him. 'They are kinda cute aren't they?'

'They were reminding me of some friends.'

'Jesus, really? I'm not sure I'd wanna meet them.'

Drew laughed. 'Are you here to take some photos?'

'No, I'm covering the opening of a new restaurant,' she grinned. 'I'm a journalist. Yesterday, it was twins celebrating their centenary and the day before a three-legged dog up a tree. It's cutting-edge stuff, you know, they don't just send anyone.'

'And what paper is this?' Drew was enjoying this exchange.

'The *San Francisco Chronicle*.'

'One of the best,' Drew said. 'How long have you been working there?'

'Long enough for me to be doing more than this.'

'Who is doing the big stories and why them rather than you?'

'At the moment, we have Jason from the UK who's with us for a year as part of his degree. He's posh and handsome and considered a must for all the big stories.' She laughed. 'Then, there's India, with long legs and a sexy voice. Luckily she goes quite soon. And then, finally, they may realise the potential of a tubby five-foot-four-inch journalist with a mousy frizz.'

'They're fools,' Drew said. 'You are utterly captivating and delightful and I've no doubt that you're an excellent reporter.'

'I'm not so sure,' she replied. 'Look, in less than five minutes I've told you all about me and I know absolutely nothing about you, some investigative reporter that makes me. Maybe they're right to stick with Jason and India.'

'Don't put yourself down. I'll bet that while we've been bantering away you've been observing me with a sharp journalistic eye. Come on now, tell me what you see.'

'OK, let's have a look.' She put her head on one side and regarded him through large hazel eyes. 'Well, you're a powerful and handsome man. You've a characterful face, the face of someone who is used to getting their own way but also a very kind face. Like myself, you could benefit from shedding a few pounds. However, you look reasonably fit, so I imagine you must do some exercise, but you're not toned enough to be using the gym on a regular basis. There's no wedding ring, so you're either single or separated. You exude charm but there is no flirtation. Maybe you're gay. I don't know, I can't quite figure you sexually. Judging from some puffiness around the eyes, I'd say that you have been sleeping too little and drinking too much, which would indicate that all is not well with you. You have a strange-looking dog sitting lovingly and patiently by your side, which tells me that you inspire devotion. You have big hands, which surprisingly have been recently manicured, so you do look after yourself.' She leant closer to him. 'There is a slight whiff of expensive cigars mingling with cologne and, last but certainly not least, if I peer closely I'm sure I can see a hint of mascara around your eyes which maybe suggests something to do with performing. All in all, I find you most intriguing. There, how've I done?'

Drew smiled. 'Alarmingly and terrifyingly accurate. I knew you'd be a good reporter and you are.' He was impressed. 'Now that we've become so intimately acquainted perhaps we should introduce ourselves. Drew Berry, very pleased to meet you.'

'Fran Ferguson. Delighted to meet you, too. And who is this beside you?'

'This is Elvis. We called him that on account of his white bodysuit and dark shades.'

Fran giggled. 'He does look as if he's wearing shades.' She bent down to pat him. 'Hello, Elvis.' The dog held out his paw. 'Gee, he's just adorable. Where did you get him?'

'He just turned up one day and wouldn't go away.'

It was true. On the first morning that he and Saul had gone to see the Club, Elvis had been sitting outside. He was there the following day and the day after that. They finally gave in, took him home and he hadn't left their side since.

'Now, Mr Drew Berry, do I get to hear your story?' Fran asked, eager to know more about him.

'Fran, I've an idea. Here's my card, come to this address tomorrow afternoon around four. Bring your camera and some dancing shoes. I can guarantee you a much better story than a three-legged dog up a tree. Promise me you'll come?'

Fran was looking at the business card. 'The Honey Bees Night Club,' she read. 'Why do I get the feeling I'm not been given the full story here?' She looked at him puzzled. 'Sure, I'll be there, but I warn you I'm somewhat out of practice on the dance floor.'

'You'll be alright with this lot, trust me.'

Saul was having a coffee at The Cheesecake Factory waiting for Drew. He knew that he would be watching the seals. He knew exactly what they all did in times of stress. Elliot went into his beloved garden, although today he would be getting drunk with Joe. He himself would go to his old homeless centre where he now worked as a volunteer, and Drew would go watch the seals.

He remembered the night when he'd first met Elliot. It had been his suggestion to get him to come to San Francisco. Elliot's mother had just died and Drew was going back to be with him for the funeral.

'A crueller woman than Elliot's mother never lived,' he told Saul. 'She was a bitch from hell. Elliot will be the only one at her funeral and I just can't let him face that alone.'

Drew and Elliot had been best friends all their lives. They'd grown up together. They'd gone to school together, gone to church together, shared everything together. While Drew was hating every moment in his father's law firm; Elliot was hating every moment of his job as an accountant.

Saul sent Drew off with reassurances that he would oversee the building work at the club for as long as Drew wanted, but they both knew he would be back as soon as possible.

He was back after just four days.

'Did you ask Elliot to come here?' Saul asked on the evening of his return.

Drew looked at him in astonishment. 'No. Should I have done?'

'It strikes me that we could use an accountant right now,' Saul replied. 'At the rate we're going we'll sink before we're afloat.'

On the day of Elliot's arrival the three of them sat in the overgrown garden drinking champagne. Saul got up finally, saying: 'I'll go into the kitchen and leave you two together. I'm guessing you must have a lot to talk about.'

Elliot laid a restraining hand on his arm. 'Saul, I know everything there is to know about Drew Berry. I wanna get to know you.' He smiled his slow lazy smile. 'Let Drew go into the kitchen.'

Drew left them and the two men looked at each other. Normally laconic, Saul uncharacteristically spoke first.

'I've no idea how much Drew has told you, Elliot, but I've not been the most honest or law-abiding guy in the past.' He paused and Elliot waited for him to continue. 'I've done some time in jail and I've lived rough but that's all behind me now. Drew's given me a chance and he won't regret it. I swear to God I'll never let him down.'

Elliot lit a cigarette and took his time before replying.

'Saul, you've been honest with me and you deserve honesty in return.' He paused for a moment as if deliberating how much to say. 'I've been in love with Drew Berry for as long as I can remember. He loves me too but not in the same way. I've learned to live with that. Any friend of his is a friend of mine. I've a feeling we're gonna get along just fine.' He'd thrown back his head and laughed. 'You, me and Drew are gonna turn The Honey Bees into the best goddamn drag club in the whole of California.'

'Saul.' Drew was striding through the restaurant. 'Sorry I'm late. I've just had a real interesting encounter.'

'With a seal?'

'No, with a young reporter,' Drew grinned. 'Let's go buy cake and I'll tell you all about it. We'll ring Elliot and tell him to meet us. This could be good, buddy. This could be just what we need.'

CHAPTER 8

Suffolk

'You have no right to be looking so perky, no right whatsoever. You should be looking and feeling like rubbish, as I do.' Roz growled indignantly, walking into the kitchen to find Jamie merrily slurping a mug of tea and reading the Sunday papers. 'You mixed your drinks all day, you smoked several cigars, and yet here you are looking as fresh as a daisy. It's not fair.'

'Sweetheart, I'm Glaswegian, we feel no pain, we feel no cold, we suffer no hangovers but we feel sympathy for those who do. Sit down and I'll make you breakfast.'

'I don't believe it, you've even managed to get to the shop this morning. Just give me a strong black coffee and a dozen headache pills. Ye gods, I have said it before but rarely with as much conviction, I am never going to drink again.'

'Shame, I passed George on the way to the shop. He said that there would be cold roast pork on the bar at lunchtime courtesy of Frank, roast potatoes and a jug of his homemade "hair of the dog" famed the county over for its healing properties.'

Roz put her head onto the table and groaned.

George waved and shouted cheerily at them as they walked into the pub a few hours later. A nearby table turned to see who had come in and greeted them like old friends. Roz was startled but returned the greeting in what she hoped was a sociable and knowing manner before hissing out of the side of her mouth.

'Who the hell are they? Did we meet them last night?'

'Absolutely no idea, just keep smiling.'

'Two glasses of my famous brew coming up, help yourselves to cold pork and the roast potatoes will be arriving shortly,' George said as they approached the bar.

Roz eyed the green mixture with apprehension. 'What's in it?'

'Roz, my love, as the saying goes, "if I tell you I'd have to kill you".'

'I think I'd rather take my chances with you than drink this,' she laughed. 'George, who are those people by the door? Do we know them?'

'You were dancing intimately with them all last night.'

'Oh Lord.'

'Yes, I have to say that you two made quite a splash yesterday evening,' he chuckled. 'Jamie, you danced with such ferocity I'm amazed that you or indeed any of your partners are able to walk this morning.'

'Oh, they were loving it.' Jamie was unabashed.

George turned to Roz. 'For me though, the highlight of the night was your rendition of "On the Good Ship Lollipop".'

'I second that,' Clive said, arriving in time to catch the last remark. 'It was unexpected but charming nonetheless, especially the accompanying tap routine.'

For the second time that day, Roz put her head on the table and groaned.

'Not feeling too good, Roz darling?' Ollie staggered into the pub under the weight of two huge plates. 'George, I made some sage and stilton stuffing to go with the pork. Oh absolutely, yes please,' she replied in response to George lifting his jug of magic potion.

'You must all have iron constitutions,' Roz said. 'Is no one feeling the slightest bit worse for wear?'

'Drink the hair of the dog, Roz.' Jamie pushed the glass towards her.

Roz tentatively lifted it to her mouth and took a small sip and then another much larger one. It was all right. No, it was more than all right. It was delicious. She detected a hint of mint and chilli, an aftertaste of lime, something fruity, something woody, and more than an intimation of alcohol.

'George, you're a genius. I won't question further but I'd love to know the ingredients. You should market this. You could make a fortune.'

'Everyone tells him that but he says it would lose its magic if it were bottled.' Ollie rolled her eyes. 'Great evening last night by the way, George. I think everyone had a marvellous time. You two certainly did,' she said grinning at Roz and Jamie.

'I certainly did, but I'm not convinced about Roz. She's worried that we behaved badly,' Jamie said.

'Good heavens, no, you were the stars of the evening. Roz, I loved your Shirley Temple impersonation but the best part for me was watching Jamie's "Jumpin' Jack Flash."'

Roz looked at Jamie in consternation.

'She means his dance routine, nothing more sinister,' Clive chuckled. 'I think the whole day went off extremely well yesterday. There was a huge turn out.'

'And it will be even better next year. I'm already hatching big plans for the drag contest, just wait until you hear them.' Jamie was full of enthusiasm.

'I hate to dampen your spirits,' George said, 'but I've heard the usual voices demanding that it no longer be a part of the fete.'

'Why?' Jamie asked. 'I thought this was a long-standing tradition. Someone last night, no idea who, was telling me that she remembered her grandfather winning wearing his wife's wedding gown. What on earth have people got against it? It's just a bit of harmless fun.'

'Not everyone sees like that,' Clive said. 'We have some killjoys around who feel that it's demeaning and not quite what one wants to see in a village fete.' He smiled, 'Unfortunately I imagine your rough sex remark will have given them extra fuel.'

'Christ, I'm so sorry. I just wasn't thinking, I didn't realise anyone would be that offended.'

'Don't be daft, it made the day. You heard the reaction. They loved it, kids and all. It's not the normal village folk who object, just some pompous gits who think the whole thing is beneath them.'

'They make me so bloody angry. See, I'm swearing already and I've only had one drink. Make that two will you, George?' Ollie said, her eyes glinting in fury. 'The really annoying thing is that these people who profess to care so much about the village are the ones who never damn well attend anything.' She was on a roll now and there was no stopping her. 'They never come to the quiz night, the racing night, the comedy night. They don't join the cricket team or the bowling club. They don't even come to the pub that much, and yet they think they have the right to tell us what to do.'

'Who are these people, then?' Jamie asked.

'Snooty council members and rich city folk who live in barn conversions. They contribute nothing to the village, their kids go to the private school, they join none of the local clubs and yet they're trying to change our whole identity.' She paused for breath.

'Don't stop, Ollie, I'm loving it,' Jamie laughed.

'I know I'm on my high horse. Of course they're not all like that, but there is an element of truth. I came in here the other day to ask George something and that upper-class twit Fergal was here having a drink with Toby.' She turned to George. 'You remember, George, I smiled and said hello and they barely looked up. Unbelievably rude.'

'Shocking behaviour,' George agreed.

'His wife is lovely, though,' Clive said. 'Toby's wife that is, not Fergal's. I can't imagine that he's married. She's always very chatty when she comes to the post office, charming girl.'

'Yeah, she's sweet, Kate I think her name is, and the kids are cute, too. It's just her husband who's the problem.'

'Well, there's a village society meeting soon so I guess we'll know the fate of the drag contest along with the fate of village hall but in the meantime let's not spoil our day,' Clive said.

'What do you mean by the fate of the village hall?' Roz asked.

'The village hall needs a new roof, Roz. Well, it needs many new things to be honest, but as always it's a question of money, or rather the lack of it.' He reached for the jug and found it empty. 'Anyway, as I said, enough of all this. My wife seems to have drained the jug dry. George, may we pay for another?'

'The hair of the dog is on me today, Clive,' George replied. 'You've provided stuffing for the pork.'

'This pork is fantastic,' Roz said biting into a huge slice. 'I'm feeling more human by the minute. Where is Frank, by the way?'

CHAPTER 9

Suffolk

Frank was lurking in the kitchen on the pretext of overseeing the roast potatoes. In fact he was embarrassed to go and join the crowd. The truth was that he had developed a small crush on Roz and the previous day had become unusually flirtatious, going so far as to pat her bottom on several occasions. He had a disturbing but very vivid memory of planting a huge smacker right on her lips as a good-night kiss.

He knew that it was ridiculous and would lead nowhere and, indeed, didn't really want it to lead anywhere. It was like a schoolboy crush on a favourite teacher, someone unobtainable and therefore infinitely more desirable.

She had looked so appealing during the day, fragile yet wholesome and extremely sexy. He had loved her sudden craziness in the evening, her smudged mascara, her loose hair, the dress slipping off her shoulder and her endearing vulnerability while she sang that stupid song.

He had gone home with the sweet name of Roz on his lips but had woken up with the sour taste of beer and cigars and a feeling of shame and mortification that he had behaved in such a manner.

He would have preferred to have hidden quietly at home but he had promised George the roast pork and Frank was not a man to go back on his promises, so here he was skulking in the kitchen shaking like a frightened whippet.

He was jolted from his reverie by the sound of Jamie's deep voice. 'I'll go and search him out.'

His worst fear realised, he put the plate of potatoes on the worktop and braced himself for an encounter with a seething Scot.

'Frank, there you are,' Jamie smiled as he came into the kitchen. 'Listen, why don't we push the tables together outside so we can all sit around? What do you think?'

Relief rendered Frank speechless. He nodded and, beaming up at Jamie, thumped his back enthusiastically. If Jamie noticed anything peculiar in this effusive greeting he didn't comment.

'OK, why don't you take the potatoes through and then join me in the garden.' Jamie popped a potato into his mouth but spat it out rapidly. 'Shit, that's hot,' he grimaced. 'What are the names of the people by the door? Last night is all a bit of a blur to me. Roz remembers even less and we certainly don't want to offend anyone.'

Frank was so beside himself with joy at those words he positively skipped through the kitchen and into the bar. 'Careful with these, they're extremely hot,' he smiled at everyone.

'You certainly cut a very different picture today, Frank,' Roz said.

His joy evaporated and was replaced by fear once again.

'Don't get me wrong, Frank, I loved the tutu, but I much prefer you in your normal apparel,' she winked at him.

She had made his day and his smile could not have been wider. He went into the garden to help Jamie.

'George, this drink has cast a spell on me,' Roz said 'I feel like a different person from the one who walked in.'

George smiled to himself. They would never ever know the secret ingredient which made the drink such fun but he was a little worried that his stock was running low. He needed to make a few phone calls to his old Devon commune.

The pub door opened and Leon strolled in sporting a Hawaiian shirt, faded jeans and a huge black eye.

'Leon, look at you.' George was alarmed.

'Oh come on, this is cool. This is my beach boy look. It's class. You can't possibly complain.'

'I was talking about your eye. What's happened to your eye? You're right, for once the outfit is acceptable.'

'Ah the eye, yes well,' he smiled ruefully. 'Hannah and I had a little boxing match last night and, um, as you can see, basically I lost.'

'She must throw a powerful punch. It looks bloody painful.'

'She took me unawares,' Leon touched his eye gingerly. 'I have to say it hurt like hell.'

'She's obviously got a demon right hook. I'm going to keep my distance,' Clive laughed.

'Don't say a word about it, she was very upset, poor love,' Leon took the drink George was proffering. 'I thought my cover story in the vets tomorrow could be that I was ravaged by a Rottweiler. What do you think?'

'Savaged by a spaniel?' Ollie suggested.

'Pawed by a Pekinese?' Roz joined in. 'Bitten by a budgie.'

Leon looked at the hysterical pair. 'How long have they been here?' He turned to George. 'I've clearly got some catching up to do.'

'George, do you have any more parasols lurking … bloody hell, Leon, was there a fight?' Jamie appeared in the doorway.

'Yep.'

'How many?'

'Four, maybe five. I lost count.'

'Big?'

'Giants, each and every one of them.'

'Any survivors?'

'Nope.'

'Bloody brilliant,' he said and went to shake his hand.

'What happened?' he whispered.

'Hannah hit me.'

'Ah.'

The soft Suffolk sun bathed the lovely terrace in a gentle summer light. The tables had been grouped together and laughter and chatter mingled with the bees and the distant throb of lawnmowers.

To Jamie's mind everything seemed suffused in a pale buttery colour, from the sandstone slabs to the yellow fields in the distance. He wasn't entirely sure what was in these yellow fields, mustard perhaps, or rape, or even sunflowers. He hadn't a clue but it didn't matter. He felt totally content and in tune with nature.

Looking around the assembled company, he realised that everyone was smiling. It was like looking at one of Renoir's famous café scenes pasted on top of Van Gogh's sunflowers. He laughed at the thought.

'First sign of madness, Jamie, telling yourself jokes,' Roz was giggling like a kid and he was suddenly reminded of a previous time when she'd behaved like this. It had been at an Amsterdam café. It couldn't be mere coincidence surely. He said as much to George on his next trip to the bar.

'Ah, yes,' George said, 'I'm very fond of Amsterdam. It's a great place.'

'You know very well what I mean, George,' Jamie said but he was met with a bland smile. 'You'd make a bloody good poker player.' He conceded defeat. 'Come and join us outside, you can see if anyone comes in.'

'I was just thinking the same thing myself,' he came out from behind the bar. 'I want to see who'd be interested in a comedy night coming up. They've been before and they're good. Well, two of them are good and maybe the third has improved.'

'Sounds tremendous, count us in.'

'Count us in for what? I'm beginning to feel wary of what this village has in store for us,' Roz said, catching the last comment as they walked onto the terrace.

'Comedy night,' George replied. 'Ten quid a ticket, free jug of sangria and as much tapas as you can eat.'

'Sounds fantastic,' Ollie said. 'Clive, are we up for comedy next weekend?'

'Isn't that when the dykes are coming to talk weddings?'

'Yes, but they're not coming until the Sunday. Don't call them dykes, Clive, that's such an ugly expression.' She frowned at him. 'You're so damn rude about the kids.'

Clive laughed. 'You're the one who's rude. Last time you told them they looked like a pair of matching armchairs.'

Everyone howled with laughter, including Ollie.

'Did I really say that? Shit, how awful. I remember now they were both wearing sort of tapestry trouser suits.'

'Can't wait to meet them,' Jamie said.

'They're wonderful,' Clive said fondly. 'You'll get to meet them, don't you worry.'

'I'll be there for the comedy,' Frank was feeling on top of the world. His misdemeanours of last night appeared to have gone unnoticed and on reflection he couldn't remember why he'd been so worried. After all there had been no real harm done.

He caught his reflection in the window. He wasn't a bad-looking fellow. He was under no illusions about himself. He knew he was overweight, short and bald, but he wasn't badly overweight and he wasn't that short. Obviously there was no getting away from the baldness, but he was fit and strong and people always commented on his eyes. Someone had once told him he had smouldering eyes, to Frank they looked a mouldy grey but he would take smouldering any day.

The afternoon moved seamlessly into early evening. The pork and potatoes had been polished off and a general languor settled over the company. The chatter had lessened and been replaced by yawns and contented sighs.

'I can't quite believe that I've spent the whole afternoon in the pub again. This village should come with a health warning,' Roz said. 'But I have to say I feel marvellously mellow and a million miles away from the stress of London. Reminds me of that Keats poem, how does it go? Something something … "and a drowsy numbness pains my sense, as though of hemlock I had drunk". That just about sums me up right now.'

You're not far off the truth there, thought Jamie, raising his eyebrows at George, who returned his unspoken question with a knowing wink.

CHAPTER 10

San Francisco

'What did you make of that?' Drew asked Fran.

The last of the pensioners had been bundled off into the minibus. Elliot was clearing glasses and plates and, although it was strictly forbidden, Saul was feeding the last of the cheesecake to Elvis.

'Guys, that was so cool. It was such fun. Some of those old folk can really move. Saul, you were awesome. Where did you learn to dance like that?'

'Oh, just picked it up along my travels, you know how it is,' Saul replied. He'd actually learnt to dance in gaol but didn't feel it was the right time to go into all that.

'No, I don't know how it is, my travels have never taught me anything like that, but then again I haven't really travelled too much.'

'So, you think it'll make a good story?' Elliot asked.

'Are you kidding?' Fran laughed. 'A drag club hosting a tea dance for the elderly. Sure beats antique twins and a dog stuck up a tree. Let's just hope my editor will see it that way too.'

'There were a few antiques here today, and we could always shove Elvis up the yucca, then you'd have everything combined.'

'Shove Elvis up the yucca. That sounds like a euphemism for something rather rude,' Fran giggled.

Elvis looked up as his name was mentioned. Blissfully unaware that anyone was about to shove him up anything, he yelped his appreciation of the cheesecake and looked optimistically at Saul.

'No, Saul, no more,' Drew and Elliot both yelled.

Saul looked down at Elvis and, crestfallen, they turned away from each other.

'You don't, by chance, do roller disco for the blind and a puppet show for deprived kids? That really would be the icing on the cake,' Fran asked.

'Not a bad idea, not bad at all, but sadly not this week. However, we have volunteered to help paint the nearby homeless centre.'

'You're the sort of unofficial three amigos of San Francisco,' Fran said. 'I'm totally in love with each and every one of you, as well as that mad dog.'

'Are you coming to the show tonight?' Drew asked. 'Front row seats and the first drink on the house. Try and entice the delectable Jason and your editor along. The more the merrier.'

'I wouldn't miss it for the world,' Fran replied. 'My life has suddenly got rather exciting. Are you sure I can't stay for the rehearsals?'

'Sorry, sweetie, it's gonna be a rather painful truth session and I doubt the girls would appreciate a public whipping. We're fragile creatures, us drag queens,' he grinned at her.

'I understand. See you later,' she reached up to give him a kiss. 'By the way, what do I call you later on? Do I call you Honey?'

'Sure you do, sugar, because that's who I'll be.'

A couple of hours later Drew was sitting on the stage talking to his 'girls'.

'The Queen Bee attended by her hive,' Elliot whispered to Saul as they made their way to the platform.

'Thanks for coming, everyone,' Drew was saying. 'It's been a while since we had a get together. We seem to have missed out on some regular sessions, so I felt it was important that we have a chat today, especially as we have two new girls to welcome.' He turned to the newcomers. 'Babette and Miss Titty, we'd like to formally welcome you to The Honey Bees Night Club. I've put a couple of bottles on ice so that we can raise a toast to you when we've finished.'

Elliot and Saul exchanged glances.

'Now I'm gonna talk about the show and I'm gonna be frank and truthful. Everyone here has talent otherwise you wouldn't be working at The Honey Bees Night Club. You're all unique and you're all special, but here's the thing, the show has lost its sparkle and the routines seem kinda tired and weary.' He looked around at their faces. 'I'm not really including Titty and Babette in this but I'm certainly including myself. We can do way better than this. We need to kick ourselves up the ass and get the Honey Bees buzzing again.' He grinned, 'Corny, I know, but that's what I do best. This club is our life and you are like family and we care about you.' He took a gulp of coffee. 'We're going to start having regular rehearsals again. We work as a team; everyone can chip in, there ain't no room for spotlight whores here.' The girls giggled. 'Saul is gonna help work the lip-synching. In fact both him and Elliot are gonna have a word if I ever shut up and, after that, we're going to rehearse the final number. It's the last impression we make and it's the song they all go away singing.' He paused again before delivering his final morale booster. 'Sweet honey bees, let's make this the hottest damn drag show in town.' He punched his hands in the air and a cheer went up.

'That's a hard act to follow,' Elliot laughed 'There ain't a lot to add really. Honey has said it all. On a business note, I'm always open to any ideas you may have. We're goin' through hard times and we have to work that bit harder to pull in the punters. I think most of you heard the other night that Joe and Bobby are holding their wedding party here and if you hear of anyone else wanting to celebrate anything just point 'em in this direction.'

'Thanks, Elliot. Now, Saul, do you wanna say something about the lip-synching?'

'Yeah, seems to me everyone's getting real lazy.' There were a few murmurs of dissent but Saul carried on regardless. 'Remember it's not just your lips that you need to move, it's your whole face, practice in front of a mirror, practice every bloody day, you need to anticipate every entrance or you'll lag behind. You need to know the song better than the singer. It ain't easy and it needs constant work.'

Titty regarded the large black Rastafarian with bafflement. He mystified and unnerved her. What he said about the lip-synching made absolute sense but where the hell had he learnt it from?

She was intrigued by all three of them. Honey, the puppet master, charismatic, compelling and caring, a guy with a big heart and a waistline to match. Elliot, his right-hand man, debonair and sexy but, behind his silver specs and carefree manner, Titty sensed a ruthless streak. And Saul, this huge black man with hands like shovels and soul-searching eyes. Right on cue, he spoke to her.

'Did you hear what Honey was saying, Titty?' he asked, knowing full well that she hadn't. 'We've a reporter in tonight, from the *San Francisco Chronicle*, she may want to have a chat with you all, if that's OK?'

Titty felt the blood drain from her face. No, it sure as hell was not OK. She was not about to talk to any snooping journalist. She felt angry. She'd finally begun to feel settled. Why the fuck did it have to be ruined by some nosy columnist? She felt Saul's eyes boring into her. She needed a fag and she needed some fresh air. She ran her hand through her hair and managed a strained smile before excusing herself.

Once outside, she forced herself to take deep breaths. Calm down, Titty, she told herself. This has absolutely nothing to do with you. Of course they want the publicity, Elliot was just saying that they needed to get the punters in. You may not even get to talk to them. No one you know back in the UK is likely to read the bloody *San Francisco Chronicle*. You've made an exhibition of yourself, she thought, you've panicked for nothing.

'Everything OK out here?' Elliot appeared at the doorway.

'Yeah, fine, just having a fag and then I'll be in.'

'You're not having a fag, Titty. What you're having is a cigarette.' He chuckled. 'There is quite a big difference.'

Titty grinned weakly.

'Mind if I join you?' Elliot said, lighting up.

They puffed away in companionable silence for a few moments.

'Best thing I ever did was to create this garden,' Elliot said, looking around. 'I had no idea about gardening when I started and now I'm hooked.'

'It's a beautiful garden, Elliot.'

'You're nearer God's heart in a garden than anywhere else on earth,' Elliot said. 'No idea who said that and I don't believe in God but I kinda agree with the sentiment.'

'Dorothy Frances Gurney.'

'Well, ain't you something else.' Elliot was impressed.

'My mother's favourite poem,' Titty said softly and Elliot was surprised to see something like despair on her face.

'Titty, you know it's not compulsory to chat to the reporter. We're just hoping that an article may generate some publicity.' He smiled at her gently. 'But there's no pressure whatsoever.' He stubbed his cigarette out. 'OK, back to work. Honey is keen to get the finale rehearsed. She's delighted you've joined us, Titty, we all are.'

'I'm not so sure Saul is delighted.'

'It was Saul who sent me out to make sure you were OK,' Elliot replied, throwing an arm around her shoulders. 'See, sweetie, corny as it sounds, Honey is right, we're one big family and, like it or not, you're part of it.'

To her mortification Titty felt tears spring to her eyes and she glanced away hastily.

'Ah, Titty, right on cue, come and join us. We're just about to launch into 'We are Family'.' Drew beckoned her onto the stage. 'Saul, why don't you leave those glasses for a moment and take us through the routine, let's make this number really sharp.'

Elliot took over polishing the glasses and watched as Saul put them through their paces. He really was very good, he would have made a great drag queen and Elliot chuckled quietly at the thought of the muscular black man in heels and a wig.

The girls were doing OK; even Mama Teresa was managing to look vaguely coordinated. His own mother, a devout Catholic without a Christian bone in her body, had been a huge fan of the real Mother Teresa. He would've loved to introduce her to this one. He could picture her now, her pinched narrow face, lips permanently pursed in disapproval, hooded eyes and a tongue like a viper. Drew used to call her The Serpent.

She had loathed Drew; although to be honest she had loathed pretty much everyone. He would love to see her reaction if he was able to tell her that he was working with a man dressed up as Mother Teresa in a drag club owned by the hated Drew Berry. It would almost be worth bringing her back to life for one second and Elliot chuckled to himself again.

'Elliot, for the third time of asking, would you stop grinning like a baboon and put the bloody music on?'

'Sorry, I was miles away. I was thinking about my mother actually.'

'Jesus, that's not normally something that makes you smile.'

'Music coming up, are you all ready?' Elliot asked.

The routine was exuberant and flamboyant. Drew was right, thought Elliot, the presence of Babette and Titty did make a huge difference. The others seemed inspired by their energy and youth.

It was pure 1980s kitsch and by the time they had formed a chorus line for the last few bars Saul and Elliot were clapping along to the music.

'Yeah,' Saul yelled. 'Way to go, girls, do it like that this evening and they'll be dancing in the aisles. Sister Sledge would be proud of you.' He came to join Elliot. 'Was Titty OK?'

'Not really, she looked quite shaken and ready to burst into tears. We'll have to keep an eye on her tonight.'

'That seemed to go well.' Drew joined the two of them. 'Not just that last number but the whole rehearsal. We must do this regularly, it sure makes a difference.'

'Have you spoken to Cherry yet?' Elliot asked.

'Nope, but there's no time like the present.' Drew grabbed a couple of glasses of champagne.

CHAPTER 11

San Francisco

'Cherry, can I have a quick word?'

'Sure, Honey, course you can. Anytime.'

'Let's go and sit down, this body ain't quite as fit as it should be and frankly I'm bushed.'

They seated themselves on a couple of stools at the far end of the bar.

'Cherry, I've been having some thoughts about your routine and ...'

'It's garbage, ain't it?' Cherry butted in quickly.

'Course it ain't garbage, sweetie, it's a show-stopper,' Drew lied. 'No, the thing is I'd like to hear you sing in your real voice. No, no, hear me out,' he said as Cherry began to butt in again. 'You've got a great voice, real husky and sensual, obviously it's not right for "Over the Rainbow" but if we were to think of some new material you could be a real sensation.'

'Really?' Cherry was not sounding convinced.

'Trust me, Cherry. I've been giving this a whole lotta thought. You know you're one hell of a foxy lady, Cherry, but that just ain't coming over in your Dorothy act. I think we need a new image, something more, well, something more ...'

'Grown-up?' Cherry suggested.

'I was thinking mature but grown-up will do.' Drew laughed.

'I know what you mean, Honey, it's kinda too cute for me now, right?'

'I can just picture you on that stage, smouldering in a tight dress, singing in that smoky voice, teasing and tantalising the audience,' Drew smiled inwardly at the picture he was painting. 'How do you feel about it, Cherry? I want you to feel good.'

'It's kinda scary, Honey, a new Cherry Pye. You honestly think it will work?'

'Sure do. But I tell you what, I'm not so sure Cherry Pye goes with the new image. Maybe we should lose the Pye? What do think? It's your name, after all.'

'Just Cherry you mean? Ain't that a bit dull?'

'Let's have a think. Cherry, Cher, Cheri, Cherie, of course. Sugar, we've got it. Cherie is the French for sweetheart.' He smiled at her. 'Very chic and sexy. What do you think?' The name had come to him in a flash in the middle of the night.

'Cherie, yeah I like it, Cherie, kinda rolls off the tongue, don't you think? It's got a real nice feel to it. Maybe I should do a French accent?'

'Well let's not get too carried away,' he said, steering her rapidly away from that line of thought. 'One thing at a time. Let's put our heads together again in a few days' time when you've had time to think about it. You're gonna be just awesome as Cherie.'

'When do you think we should tell the others?'

'I'd say let's wait until we have the whole new look and the new songs and then we can unveil the new Cherie.'

Elliot clapped his hands. 'Listen up, folks. Two hours before curtain up so I suggest we finish here and start to get ready. Great rehearsal, let's make it a great show.'

This was one of Drew's favourite times, the moment when the club began to transform itself before his eyes. The lighting was dimmed and the candles lit, the daytime shabbiness disappeared and in its place was glitz and glamour. There was a sense of anticipation in the air, the promise of things to come, a delicious hint of wickedness and sin.

'How did it go?' Elliot asked Drew.

'Easy as pie. She can't wait to lose her Cherry.' And he chuckled with laughter at his own joke.

Elliot looked on shaking his head.' You worry me sometimes, Drew.'

'I worry myself, Elliot.'

Maybe it was the motivational speech beforehand or the fact that there was a journalist in the house but the show was about the best it had ever been.

Honey kicked the evening off in style and the others followed suit. Diana Dross, resplendent in a glossy new wig and a skintight dress, brought the audience to their feet with 'Baby Love'. Saul still had reservations about the quality of lip-synching but was happy enough for the moment.

Bourbon, for once, had not got the better of Babette and she strutted her stuff boldly to 'Jolene'. With her blonde wig and cowboy boots she was an immediate hit and even Elliot's qualms began to fade.

Cherry followed next and, perhaps knowing that she may not be performing this number again, gave it everything she had, and there wasn't a dry eye in the house.

Mama Teresa was her normal gentle and self-effacing self. As usual she started her act with a bona fide Mother Teresa quote. This evening the quote was: 'Let us always meet each other with a smile, for a smile is the beginning of love.' This was followed by her favourite song, 'Amazing Grace'.

Not your usual drag queen number but then Mama T. was not your usual drag queen. Neither Drew, Elliot or Saul could recall the day she had arrived; she just always seemed to have been there. She almost always chose religious songs and always quoted from her namesake. Ageless and mysterious, she had become a legend in San Francisco. The Honey Bees was not the only club she performed in but it was her favourite and she rarely missed a show.

Miss Titty was the only one not to perform with her usual exuberance and vitality. It was still a good routine though and the audience roared their approval but the others knew her sparkle was missing.

What the hell is the story there? Elliot wondered. She had confidence and she had balls. He smiled at his unintended pun. But there was a real vulnerability and more worryingly a real fear.

'Elliot, this is the fourth time I've caught you smiling like a Cheshire cat for no apparent reason, and you say you worry about me.' Drew appeared at his side.

'I'm just a funny guy, Drew, I make myself laugh. It's a particular gift, and not everyone has it.'

'Not everyone wants it,' Drew winked and turned to walk away. 'I'm going over to Fran's table, they seem in high spirits.'

'Yeah, I've been keeping an eye on them. Saul's kept them supplied with drinks and they look like they're having a ball. I'll go and have a word with Bobby and Joe then come and join you.'

'Bring them over too.'

Drew walked over to where Fran was sitting. She was looking flushed and happy and leapt up eagerly when she saw him, knocking the table and upsetting most of the glasses as she did so.

'What a fantastic evening! We've loved every minute.' She threw her arms around him and whispered in his ear. 'Honey, you look amazing. I barely recognised you.'

The other two were mopping ineffectually at the spilt drink. Fran turned towards them.

'Honey, let me introduce the rest of the party. This is my colleague, Jason, on loan to us from the UK.' Drew shook hands with an extremely handsome man in his mid-twenties.

'And this is our marvellous features editor, Corey Hayward.' Drew turned to greet a middle-aged man, lean faced with sharp, intelligent eyes.

'Sure glad to meet you, real pleased that you made the show.'

'Wouldn't have missed it for the world. Indeed I can't believe that I've lived in ignorance of this place for so long.'

'Lucky you have a bright young reporter to bring it to your attention and hopefully to that of your readers,' Drew said and Fran beamed at him.

Elliot approached the table brandishing a bottle of champagne, with Joe and Bobby behind him clutching yet another. The evening was clearly far from over.

Several hours later the three of them were relaxing with a nightcap in Elliot's beloved garden. Drew had showered and changed into a flowing kaftan. A friend had bought it in Morocco as a present and Drew adored it. He was lolling back on the bench with a large brandy in one hand and a fat cigar in the other; vestiges of lipstick and eye shadow remained, making him look decadent and dissolute.

Not many men could carry that look off, thought Elliot, gazing at him fondly. Drew caught the look and returned it with a slow smile.

'A good night, eh? We're not out of the woods, but an article in the *Chronicle* will sure help.'

'They definitely going to run with it then?' Saul questioned.

'Seemed pretty definite. They're gonna send over a photographer and Jason and Fran want to come tomorrow and interview us three and the girls. I made sure Corey knew that it was Fran's story, though. We don't want the delectable Jason, her words not mine, stealing the show.'

'Not all the girls may want to be interviewed. Titty looked far from ecstatic at the idea.' Elliot glanced across at Saul.

'Did you manage to find out anything?' Saul asked.

'Nope, but she looked shaken at the thought of talking to a reporter.'

'She's on the run from something. I've seen that haunted look too many times in gaol not to recognise it.' Saul paused to take a drink. 'I'm not saying she's a criminal but I am saying that, behind her bravado, this is one scared lady.'

'He's right, Drew, something is bothering her.'

'Let's see if we can find anything out,' Drew frowned. 'We know her real name. I'll do a bit of digging tomorrow. I don't mean to pry but if something's wrong with one of our girls I want to know why. OK, guys, one small one before bed?' He poured himself a large one. 'Where's Elvis? Ain't seen him all evening.'

Drew got up in search of Elvis and found him lying quietly behind one of the bushes paying dearly for his moment of cheesecake ecstasy. He tried to rouse himself when Drew called his name but the movement brought on another bout of nausea and once again he was violently sick behind the jasmine.

'Saul.' Drew glared at him accusingly.

'Yeah, yeah, I'm sorry.' Saul came to join Drew and hunkered down beside the poorly dog. 'Plain chicken and rice for you tomorrow, buddy. No treats for a long while or we're both gonna be in big trouble.' Elvis nodded his consent, already feeling better as the familiar hand caressed him softly.

CHAPTER 12

San Francisco

Fran was over the moon; both Jason and Corey had seemed delighted with her last night. Corey had praised her resourcefulness and Jason had said it was one of the best evenings he'd spent since arriving in San Francisco. She couldn't wait to write the article. She would phone Drew early today, get the interviews organised and thank him for the night before. He had been so cool, singing her praises and plying them with endless champagne.

She'd felt a sense of belonging at that club that she had rarely found anywhere else. Despite the fact that she had only been there twice she couldn't stop thinking about it. Her mind drifted back to the tea dance and she pictured Saul gently waltzing a wizened old girl around the floor. Drew holding a glass of champagne for a lady too shaky to hold the flute herself. Elliot wandering amongst them, guiding the gentlemen towards their partners, charming and attentive. Even that mad-looking hound Elvis had played his part, allowing himself to be endlessly petted and caressed albeit mainly in the hope of a crumb of cheesecake.

Fran had seldom encountered such kindness and generosity; the combination of that and the outrageous show in the evening was intoxicating. She had led a very isolated life. Her parents rarely went out and she could never remember anyone other than the gasman coming over to the house.

They loved her in their own way and she'd never lacked for food or warmth but she had been bored and stifled and had left home as soon as possible. She had worked hard to earn her place at the *Chronicle*. She knew that she could write, she was a good journalist, and now, thanks to Drew, she might finally have a chance to prove herself.

Drew, meanwhile, was busy in his office sitting at his computer searching for clues as to why Miss Titty Bang Bang would not wish to be interviewed. So far he was not having much luck.

Why didn't he ring Fran? Surely as a journalist she would have some ideas on how to investigate. Maybe when she came over to do the interviews she could glean a little more information from Titty. Pleased with himself, he picked up the phone then, glancing at his watch, smiled and replaced the receiver. It had been fairly late when they all finished last night, she might not thank him for a phone call at this time of the morning.

No matter what time Drew went to bed, he rose early. Sleep had never really come easily so he had learnt to exist on only a few hours during the night and a power nap in the afternoon.

His mother had said it was because his mind never shut off and she wished she could find a switch for him. Keen on homeopathy, she was forever blending various concoctions, but they were all in vain.

Elliot's mother had said that it was because the devil was talking to him and stealing his soul during the night, which was no surprise as his mother was a witch.

'She's just jealous.' Drew's mother had laughed when Drew had told her. 'Not even the devil himself would venture into her bedroom.'

Privately she had stormed over to the woman's house and told her that if ever she filled her son's head again with such evil thoughts, she would drug her with one of her potions, strip her naked, tie her to a lamp post and let the whole town witness her humiliation. Normally a mild-mannered lady, she had been shocked by how much she had enjoyed the look of sheer terror on that vicious bitch's face.

Drew got up and stretched, he felt stiff and his muscles ached. I really must get into better shape, he thought; maybe I should give jogging a whirl. But the thought did not appeal and the idea of returning to the gym was anathema to him.

Full of enthusiasm for his new life, he had signed up for a fitness club when he first arrived in San Francisco. He had paid a small fortune for a one-year membership, thrown himself into a thirty-minute induction with an anorexic redhead called Lulu and had never returned.

Maybe he should invest in an exercise bike? He could put it in the office and pedal as and when he wanted without the world witnessing his sad sweaty exertions. For now however, a brisk walk with Elvis followed by a coffee and a bagel in The Paws Café would have to suffice. Some fresh air would do them both good. Elvis was still looking a little green around the gills and Drew was starting to feel the effects of one cognac too many. He was just encouraging a reluctant Elvis out of the door when his phone rang.

'Drew? It's Fran here, I just wanted to say thank you so much for all you did last night, everyone loved it and you were so kind to say the things you said about me. I really think Corey may view me in a different light from now on. I'm just so excited. What time is good for the interviews? Would it be possible to do all the photographs today, do you think or do you need to give them more notice? Perhaps we could just do a few today and the rest tomorrow?'

'Jesus, Fran, slow down, kid, you're making me feel dizzy, I need a strong coffee before I can cope with an assault like that.'

'Oh gee, I'm so sorry, I hadn't realised the time. Are you still in bed? Did I wake you? I'm so sorry, shall I phone you back or do you want to phone me when you're ready?'

'Fran, take a deep breath.' Drew laughed. 'I'm just heading out the door with Elvis, do you want to join us for a coffee?'

She was a real nice kid, he thought, as he wandered along the sidewalk. Hard-working, bright and compassionate. He had watched her with the old folk yesterday, patient and understanding but never patronising. She had the makings of a good journalist, her enthusiasm and friendliness putting people immediately at their ease. He bet she would be able to draw information out of Titty without her even realising it.

I wonder if Saul is right, thought Drew. Is Titty running from something? She doesn't really strike me as a criminal. Will she even agree to an interview? Actually, it's going to be very interesting to see exactly what any of the girls will reveal. Drew knew more than most about their backgrounds but only on a fairly superficial level. No one was ever that keen to talk about their everyday lives, preferring to keep the two areas of their existence separate.

He arrived at The Paws Café to find Fran already seated outside in the watery sunshine.

'Sorry we're late,' he said, bending down to kiss her. 'Elvis has a delicate bowel due to yesterday's cheesecake extravaganza, so the walk took longer than usual.'

'Poor Elvis.' She patted the dog who, sensing sympathy, gazed up with sorrowful eyes.

'Don't indulge him, it's his own fault, well, him and Saul. They never bloody learn.' He sat down beside her. 'Are you eating anything? I can highly recommend the "Paws" speciality, blue cheese, bacon and avocado bagel. Without doubt, one of the most calorific on the menu and so all the more delicious. Although to be fair everything here is delicious, Gina and Antonia are awesome cooks.'

'Paws speciality it is, then. This place is neat. I've never been here before.'

'It's our hangout, isn't it, Elvis? Very dog-friendly, as the name suggests, and the girls are sisters of a friend of mine. In fact, you met him last night, Joe Giordelli.'

'Oh, he's gorgeous, and his boyfriend, whose name I've forgotten. Everyone was gorgeous. I'm on a real high today.'

Drew smiled. 'So, I take it last night was a success, then? You've earned street cred from Jason and respect from Corey.'

'You said it. Now I just need to do some shrewd and perceptive interviews and write an amazing article.'

'OK, let's talk about the interviews. Let's talk about the ones that may potentially be difficult, starting with Miss Titty. She ain't keen to be interviewed and we're not sure why. Saul is convinced she's on the run from something. If she does agree to an interview, try and do some gentle probing. I have her real name and I kinda hoped with your journalistic skills you could help me unearth some facts. I don't usually meddle or snoop but if something is wrong then I'd like know. We may be able to help.'

'OK, I'll see what I can do for you. You really do care for them, don't you? Elliot said you were like a family, and he's right.'

'Yeah, I care, but I have to admit I'm also a real snoop.' He sat back and grinned. 'I'm interested in people. I like to know what makes them tick. I'm always curious. Much like you, I imagine.'

'I guess.' She took a sip of her coffee and sat back. 'Do you have family, Drew?'

He laughed loudly. 'Nicely done, Fran, real cool. So my interview begins now, does it?'

'Do you mind?'

'Do your worst, kiddo.'

After an hour over bagels and coffee, Fran was more in love than ever with Drew. She found him enthralling and was fascinated by his life and background.

'I can't believe that you used to be a lawyer. What made you want to become a drag queen?'

'I guess it was always there, I just didn't see it. I loved performing, was always dressing up for shows and concerts, from high school right through university and beyond. Just never really figured it, too busy trying to fit in with what my folks and the rest of the world wanted.'

'And you were married?'

'For seven years.'

'Do you still see her?'

'Rarely, but we do talk. She's a special lady. I just couldn't give her what she wanted.'

'Has she found someone else?'

'She has and she's very happy.'

What Melissa had actually said to him was. 'There will never be anyone like you, Drew' but Robert is a good man. He's not gonna set world on fire but he loves me and he'll look after me.'

'She deserves to be happy.' He said.

'I'm sure she does.'

'To make up for being with me, you mean,' Drew laughed.

'No, not at all. I think you're wonderful.' Fran said. 'I guess I was just surprised that you were married. I just thought, well, I mean I sort of assumed, not that I know much about it, but …'

'You thought I was gay? I gave it a go, but it ain't really for me.' Drew winked at her. 'I'm not that interested in either sex if I'm honest. Not sure what that makes me, slightly peculiar, perhaps?'

'No, just unique.'

'Well hell, that's just about one of the nicest things anyone's ever said. Thank you, Fran.'

'I happen to believe it's true. Did you ever want children, Drew?'

'Melissa did, but it just never happened. Probably just as well the way things turned out. I imagine it might be awkward having a drag queen as a father.'

He stood up and drained his coffee. 'Now listen, sugar, I really have to go. I'll have the girls lined up in all their finery for you later on for the interviews and a photo shoot. Don't get your hopes up for too much information, unlike me they may be reluctant to expose themselves to a reporter.' He kissed the top of her head. 'Good to have a fellow early bird to drink coffee with. Thanks for joining us. Come on, Elvis,' he said, clicking his fingers at the dog, who obediently rose and trotted after him.

It amused her the way that they treated Elvis as almost human. She'd never had a pet and was unused to their importance within the family. Her coffee was finished but she was reluctant to leave. She sat thinking about what Drew had told her. What an extraordinary man. What an extraordinary life.

There were so many other things she longed to ask him. She was intrigued by his relationship with Elliot. From what he'd said they had been childhood friends, but what had brought Elliot to San Francisco?

Had they ever had a relationship? They clearly weren't in one now, at least not one of a sexual kind.

And what about Saul? Where the hell had he sprung from? He was obviously not gay but then again there had been no mention of a girlfriend.

She wondered about Drew's wife and bizarrely felt a very small pang of jealousy. She clearly meant a lot to Drew, how amazing that they could still mean so much to each other after all that had happened.

Fran had a limited experience of relationships. There had been a couple of guys at college but nothing very meaningful. There had also been a couple of one-night stands which she'd thought would make her feel like a woman of the world but had actually made her feel cheap and common.

Writing an article on The Honey Bees Night Club was evidently going to be more of an education than she had bargained for and she smiled at the thought.

CHAPTER 13

San Francisco

They weren't the only ones having an early coffee that morning. Titty was sitting on the terrace of a diner sipping her second large cappuccino. Plagued by terrible nightmares, she had abandoned her bed, showered, and headed out onto the streets.

Everything had been going swimmingly since her arrival in San Francisco. She loved The Honey Bees, had found a tiny bedsit, got some part-time work, and the demons that had been haunting her had finally taken a back seat, until now. Until this bloody reporter.

Her hand shook as she lit yet another fag. She drew deeply on it and then smiled as she remembered Elliot's correction of that word yesterday. She also remembered that he had specifically said that the interviews were not compulsory.

Stop feeling so anxious, she chided herself once again. It's the *San Francisco Chronicle* not the *Daily Telegraph*. No one from your past is ever going to read it and if they did they'd never associate it with you. You have a new life, Titty, you have new friends and they deserve your help. If giving an interview is going to help them, then damn well give an interview. End of story. Stubbing her cigarette out and gulping back the last of the coffee, she stood up filled with determination.

'Elliot?' Drew yelled.

'In the bar doing stock takes with Saul,' he yelled back.

Drew flew in, flushed and out of breath. 'Hell, I'm late. I'm meeting Chantal to talk about a show she wants me to host next week. I should be back before Fran arrives to interview the girls but, if not, tell them not to worry, I've spoken to Fran and she ain't gonna to ask anything too personal, just general stuff like how long they've been working here? Do they enjoy it? Tell 'em the answer to that is yes,' he laughed. 'If Babette shows up drunk then don't let her be interviewed. The photographer will be here, too, just a few group shots, oh, and of course, she wants to chat to you two. She already interviewed me.'

'When the hell did she interview you?'

'We met for an early morning coffee. OK, see you later.'

'Jesus Drew, you gotta slow down or you're gonna die.'

'We're all gonna die sometime, my little ray of sunshine.'

When Drew returned several hours later, he found the interviews in full swing. He stood in the doorway observing the action before he was observed himself.

Mama T. was being photographed on the stage and behaving in an uncharacteristically coquettish manner. Cherry and Diana were sat at a table in animated conversation with Jason, a half-empty bottle of champagne in front of them. Saul had clearly felt the need to calm any pre-interview nerves. No wonder we never make any profit, thought Drew.

Most pleasing of all was seeing Titty in earnest conversation with

Fran, the pair of them looking relaxed and comfortable. One person was missing, however, and his heart sank when he realised that he couldn't see Babette. He thought he'd made his concerns about her drinking more than obvious the other day, but maybe she'd not taken him seriously. Damn and blast, he thought, she's got so much potential but she's screwing her life up at the moment. He was more tolerant than most but even he couldn't fight her corner for much longer.

'Wonderin' where I was, Honey?' a Southern drawl interrupted his thoughts.

'Yeah.'

'Worried I may be out of it?'

'Yup.'

'I made y'all a promise, and I'm keepin' to it.'

'Sure glad to hear it,' Drew gave her shoulders a squeeze. 'Now, your turn in front of the lens, I think,' he said, as he saw the young photographer beckoning her.

He strolled over to the bar towards Saul and Elliot and did a double take. 'Holy Mother of God, just look at the pair of you.' Elliot was resplendent in a dark blue velvet smoking jacket and Saul had abandoned his usual loud shirt in favour of a white tuxedo and dickey bow.

'We thought we'd make an effort,' Elliot gave him a twirl.

'It's a knockout. I'm not sure that we shouldn't make this the permanent dress code. Everything going OK here? Seems to be a real buzz in the air.'

'Yeah, everything's cool. The girls are lovin' it. They're dressed to kill, as you can see. Even Mama T. has a new wig.'

'Odd but strangely appealing,' Drew glanced in her direction. 'Pleased to see Titty turned up for an interview. I'd love to be a fly on the wall; she and Fran seem to be putting the world to rights.'

Drew had been right in his theory that Fran was a good reporter. She had a flair for asking seemingly unobtrusive questions. She seemed to have gained Titty's confidence and, at that moment, Titty was unwittingly giving Fran the information she needed about where she had lived in the UK.

'Southern England? I'm crap at geography. Do you mean Devon?'

'No, that's south-west, I'm talking about south-east.'

'Ah, I get you, that's the big bubble that sticks out the right-hand side, right?'

'That's the one,' Titty grinned.

'Did you live there all your life?'

'Heavens no, sadly we were always travelling around. Never stayed longer than about two years in any place.'

'Gee, I just love your accent. The way you say "heavens", it's too cool for words. Travelling all over sounds so glamorous. So why are you sad about it? I was stuck in a one-horse town for most of my life.'

'Trust me, it's not glamorous. You never feel settled, you're constantly changing schools, it's impossible to make friends and it seems that you've only just unpacked before you're on the move again. I'd have much rather stayed in one town all my life.'

'Not in my town, you wouldn't.' She guessed that Titty's father must have been in the armed forces to warrant all that moving but some sixth sense told her to avoid asking. Instead she decided to concentrate on the present.

'How did you choose your act? I love it; it's so original. Where did it come from?'

'Basically it started as a bit of fun in a revue when I was a college student. I always knew Titty had a life but I guess I never realised it would be mine.'

'What college were you at?'

Titty looked uneasy and guarded, so again Fran decided to steer clear. 'Not that it matters, I guess most of our readers won't have a clue about British colleges. What did you study, though, just as a matter of interest?'

It was the right thing to say and Titty relaxed a little. 'Art, sex and alcohol.'

Fran laughed. 'Sounds like my sort of place. Well, actually, it doesn't sound anything like my place, but you know what I mean. So are you enjoying San Francisco? Are you going to unpack your boxes and stay here for a while?'

'You know I may just do that. It's a good city. People accept you for what you are.'

'Didn't they where you come from?' Fran asked, but again she sensed that she had gone too far. This was territory that Titty didn't want to get into. Fran saw the shutters coming down and made one last valiant attempt. 'Is San Francisco the first place you visited in the States, or did you go to other places before?'

'Oh, I travelled a bit, but I was always aiming for here,' Titty replied in a non-committal way.

Fran decided to call it a day. She didn't want to be in danger of alienating Titty and, after all, she'd gathered a fair amount of background information. 'I guess I'd better let you go, but it's been a real pleasure talking to you. Have you had your photo taken?'

'You know what, Fran, I really hate photos. I'll wait for the group one and then sort of melt into the background. Is that OK?'

'Sure, no problem. I hate photos, too, I always look terrible. My parents used to have a series of school photos on the mantelpiece. A hideous record of dimples, acne and puppy fat from the ages of five to fifteen. Those pictures haunt me still.'

* * *

Fran wandered over to where Drew was chatting with Elliot and Saul. 'All the interviews are done, Drew, save these two characters,' she said, motioning towards Saul and Elliot. 'Jason and I split up, I did Mama Teresa and Titty and he did Babette, Cherry and Diana. We thought it was less intimidating if there was only one of us.' She added quietly to Drew, 'I thought Titty might not like to talk to anyone from the UK.'

'That sounds great. Shall we get a couple of group photos? And then we can let the girls go, and you and Jason can chat to these two. Now where's your photographer?'

'Aiming his zoom towards Babette's tits right now. Wouldn't have thought he would have needed too much zoom, they ain't exactly hard to find,' Elliot laughed. 'I have to say, he's real easy on the eye.'

'His name's Diego. He's Brazilian.'

'Well, he can open his aperture ...'

'Everyone together for a group photo, please,' Drew yelled, cutting off Elliot with a warning glance. Unrepentant, Elliot grinned back at him.

Shaking his head, Drew turned to Saul. 'Have you seen ...' Anticipating his question, Saul nodded in the direction of the stage, where Elvis sat with a velvet bow tie and matching coat, looking sheepish yet strangely proud. 'What the fuck?'

'Ask Elliot,' Saul laughed.

'Elliot, you can't be serious, this is just so ...'

'Gay? I know, but darling, I am. And sometimes one just has to embrace it. No straight man would get away with that. Doesn't he look a picture?'

'You're in a very strange mood today, Elliot, very strange indeed.'

'So what brought you to San Francisco?' Fran and Elliot were seated at a table, while Jason and Saul conducted their interview at the bar.

'Basically Drew brought me to San Francisco. He was here, so it seemed only natural that I should be here too.'

'You two go back a long way, don't you?'

'We go all the way back, Fran, I don't remember a time when Drew wasn't in my life.'

'Did it come as a surprise that he wanted to run a drag club?'

'Nothing he did ever surprised me. He's always loved performing. Actually he was a good actor, a little over the top, but good nonetheless.'

'Are you never tempted to perform, Elliot?'

'Jesus, Fran, hell would have to freeze over before that happened. I admire them but it sure ain't for me.'

'I think I get the message,' Fran smiled. 'What did you want to do, or did you always want to be an accountant?'

'Sweetie, no one always wants to be an accountant.'

'So there was no burning ambition then? No hidden aspirations? Just a desire to be with Drew.' She wondered if she had overstepped the mark.

He gave her a sharp look. 'That's right, Fran. Just a desire to be with Drew.'

Jason was struggling with Saul. Not that he was being particularly unhelpful, just opaque. Saul was a master of deflection. After fifteen minutes of chat, Jason was no further forward than he had been at the start. He glanced down at his notepad while Saul went to serve someone. There was no story there at all.

Saul claimed that he and Drew had just bumped into each other one night and that he'd been with the club since the start. In response to Jason's question about what he had done before he'd been vague and elusive. There was clearly a story but Saul wasn't going to reveal it today.

He glanced over to where Fran was sitting. She had closed her notebook and was sitting chatting to Elliot. Maybe it was time to call it a day. Customers were arriving and they had more than enough information to make a cracking article.

He couldn't wait to exchange notes with Fran and learn what she had found out. He was more excited about this story than anything else since he had been out here. He must phone his dad and tell him.

His father had once been a journalist, indeed had even briefly worked for the *San Francisco Chronicle*, but now sat on the board of a large corporation. How that transition had been made, Jason never really knew, and he suspected that his dad still wondered, too.

He was always telling Jason that stories needed a personal angle. Jason had recently sent him an article he'd written on 'The Plight of the Homeless in California' which he'd been rather proud of. His father had said that while it was well-written it wouldn't hold anyone's interest because it was too general.

'You need a personal angle, Jay,' he'd said. 'Not just facts and figures. You need something that captures the imagination, the angle most people don't see.'

Jason smiled to himself. The Honey Bees Night Club would certainly capture the imagination. He couldn't believe some of the stories he had heard. As soon as it was written he would send his dad a copy.

CHAPTER 14

Suffolk

It was a glorious golden evening as Roz and Jamie strolled up the road towards the pub. They were experiencing a real Indian summer of the type that was frequently predicted but rarely arrived.

'It's very beautiful here, isn't it?' Jamie said. 'Our London life seems incredibly remote right now, don't you think?'

'Light years away. It's a bit weird really,' Roz stopped and pointed. 'Oh Jamie, just look at the sun shining on the roof of the village hall, it looks fantastic.'

They stood for a moment admiring the old building.

'They surely wouldn't contemplate knocking it down. It would be outrageous. It must be listed or something. And look at the huge oak tree in the car park. If the hall isn't listed that should be,' Jamie said.

'I don't know what they'd do without it. So much goes on here. Ollie says that almost every day something is happening.'

'Shall we go in? Let's see if it's open.' Jamie walked up to the entrance.

The door wasn't open so they had to be content with peering through the large windows.

'It's huge. Look at the lovely stage. It beats the hell out of some of the venues I've performed in,' Roz laughed.

'We should start our own theatre company here, perform weekly rep in the summer.'

'That would be fantastic. Let's face it, there's not that much else on the horizon at the moment, well not for me anyway. You've got some exciting film stuff coming up.'

'I would hardly call one small scene in a sub-standard sitcom "exciting filming".' Jamie frowned. 'Roz, are you worried? Do you think you've damaged your career moving here?'

'No, of course not. But it's a little worrying that it's so quiet on the work front. Although, if I'm honest, it worries me that I'm not more worried, if you understand what I mean.' She paused trying to rationalise her feelings. 'I feel like I'm in limbo at the moment, it's all a touch surreal. I'm so pleased we moved here, I love it – but in some ways it seems almost too good to be true.'

'Roz, you're never satisfied. We've moved to the country, which is what you wanted. We have a gorgeous cottage, we're making new friends, and yet you're concerned that it's all too good to be true and you're worried about not being worried about not acting. You crack me up.' But he wasn't exactly smiling as he said this.

'Clearly I'm certifiable. What about you? Any reservations?'

'None whatsoever. Thought I may have, but actually I've not given London a backward glance.'

He was right, she thought, as they headed towards the pub. Her reaction was odd. It was all that she wanted and more, so why these nagging uncertainties?

In the past, Jamie had accused her of being wild and abandoned. Maybe it was time to start behaving like that once more. With that thought, she strode in front of Jamie and flung open the pub door, knocking Billy – who had been standing behind it – off his feet.

'Billy, I'm so sorry. Are you OK? Let me give you a hand.'

'Yeah, I'm fine. No harm done, just, um, just took me by surprise,' he stammered as he dusted himself down.

'What on earth were you doing, Roz?'

'I was acting with wild abandon.'

There was a good turnout for the comedy show and it took them a while to thread their way to the bar.

'Some entrance, Roz,' George said.

'She's being wild and abandoned,' Jamie rolled his eyes.

'Just so long as we know,' George grinned. 'The show starts in about half an hour, tapas will be served in the interval and I've reserved a table for you by the window. Charlotte is joining you, and Clive and Ollie, of course.'

'That sounds fantastic. Cheers, George. How on earth do you manage to organise everything so well?'

'I'm very bossy. Now what can I get you both?'

'Pint of Adnams for me, please, George, and a glass of white for Roz.'

'Maybe we should get a bottle, Jamie?'

'See, I told you, George, no stopping her tonight.'

'Very funny. No, I meant for the table, does headmistress Charlotte drink white, George?'

'Headmistress Charlotte does indeed drink white, and after the week she has had she may not be stopping at one bottle,' Charlotte said, appearing by their side.

'Heck, they're both at it. Wish me luck, George.'

The first act was hilarious: a young comedian with a razor-sharp wit and some cutting-edge material. He had the audience in the palm of his hand and his session came to an end all too quickly with a standing ovation.

Sadly, humour did not come naturally to the second act which, as Jamie pointed out, was something of a drawback for a comic. There was more than a hint of desperation about his routine. Here was someone who was giving it one last shot, a middle-aged man having a mid-life crisis. His biggest round of applause came when he left the stage.

'This is such fun,' Roz said, seated in front of several plates of tapas during the interval.

'That first guy was seriously good. He'll go far.'

'Whereas the second one can't go far enough,' Charlotte giggled.

'Shall we get more drinks before the second half starts?' Clive asked.

'About to suggest that very thing myself. Same again for everyone?'

'I've beaten you to it,' Leon said as he arrived at the table bearing a tray.

'Leon, how fantastic. I thought you were at a birthday party.'

'I was. It was a dreadful, dreary affair – warm booze and wooden conversation. I'm afraid I used Hannah as an excuse to escape. On the way out I knocked over a whole tray of stuff, crisps and dips all over their cream carpet and down my shirt. They didn't seem too unhappy to see me go. I came here as quick as I could.'

'You've made a bloody good job of your shirt. I can hardly see anything, just a small stain down this side,' Ollie pointed to a circular dark patch.

'Ollie, I went home and changed the sodding shirt, that's part of the design.' Leon was up in arms and the rest of them were in stitches.

Billy was hovering near their table.

Jamie grinned at him. 'Sit yourself down, Billy, and join the party. I need your opinion on my advert for next year's drag competition. I've got a rough draft here so we'll grab Frank after the show and I'll see what you both think. I'm rather pleased about it but Roz has reservations.'

Billy sat down on the chair Jamie had dragged up for him. He felt rather shy, but at the same time flattered that he'd been asked to join the group. He normally liked to stay on the periphery of things. Small talk and socialising had never come easily to him and he often felt ill at ease and awkward, but Jamie was reassuring company.

His grandmother worried that he didn't have any close friends but he wasn't that bothered. Going out in a big crowd was not something that appealed to him.

'How long you had lived here, Billy?' Roz asked, breaking his train of thought.

'All my life.'

'And what do you think of these people who feel that the drag contest is degrading?' Jamie demanded.

'Jamie, you are becoming way too preoccupied with all this,' Roz was exasperated.

'I don't understand them,' Billy said, quietly but firmly. 'There's nothing wrong with it. I have pictures of my grandfather taking part. The tradition of drag goes back to Shakespeare, maybe even before that. It's a tradition as old as Morris dancing, and they don't have a problem with that.'

'Well said, Billy,' Charlotte was astonished. She'd never heard him talk like that before.

'How many years have you been taking part, Billy?'

'The last three or four. I enjoy it. I enjoy performing,' he surprised himself as well as the rest of the company with this revelation. It was true, though, he realised, he did love to perform. It was the only time he didn't mind being the centre of attention.

'Room for a little one?' Frank arrived at the table.

'There is nothing remotely little about you Frank but we'll squeeze you in. The third comedian looks warmed up and ready for action, come on love, bring it on.' Leon said leaning back in his chair.

The third comedian was a woman in her mid-thirties who spoke in a nasal twang. She started off well, before descending into a rant about menstruation and a diatribe against men and their failure in bed.

'Why does she do that?' Leon asked. 'Doesn't she realise she's alienating half her audience.'

He was not the only disgruntled customer; a voice from an old boy near the back rang out. 'I can get all this at home from the wife without paying ten quid.'

'Try paying her ten quid and you may get something different,' the comedian replied. The audience laughed and her act was rescued.

'Close shave, but she managed to hang onto it,' Jamie said when she had finished.

'You have to be pretty bloody tough to do that, I imagine,' Charlotte said. She turned to Roz, 'Would you ever fancy trying it?'

'Not in a month of Sundays. I need a script, a director, a lot more money than George is paying and a talent for comedy.'

'Useful but not essential, as we saw from the second act,' Clive said.

'Come on then, Jamie,' Frank said. 'Let's have a butchers at this advert of yours, no pun intended.'

'Let's go over to the bar, I want George's opinion on this.'

Roz was delighted that Jamie was throwing himself into village life but couldn't quite understand why he had chosen the drag competition to concentrate his energies on. He was like a man obsessed and, if she was honest, she worried that he might be making a fool of himself.

It was very black and white to him; the people who liked the drag show were the good guys and the ones who didn't were the baddies. She didn't think it was quite so cut and dried and was concerned that they could be alienating people unnecessarily. They hadn't been in the village long and she didn't want to make enemies if she could help it.

'Right, here goes, now pay attention,' Jamie was in full flow. 'I want you to picture the Lord Kitchener poster, the one where he is pointing and underneath is the caption "Your Country Needs You". Are you with me so far?'

'We all know the poster. Get on with it, Jamie,' Roz said sharply.

'OK, well, we change "Your Country" to "Your Village" and touch up Lord Kitchener a bit, you know, false eyelashes, lipstick, rouge etc and then, underneath, we have a poem. Here we go:

Are you man enough to dress as a lass?

Have you the balls to really shake that ass?

Don't cower in the corner, be bold and bright

Drag Queens of the World Unite!'

There was a moment of silence before the laughter broke out.

'Jamie, you're something else. Puts me to shame. I placed a pathetic advert stating the time and date of the event, that was all. Well done, I knew I was right to let you win,' Frank said, full of admiration.

Jamie was about to ask what Frank meant about letting him win, when the others joined in with their praise. Leon even went so far as to promise to take part.

'That's great, Leon. There's no going back, now. You have witnesses.'

'I think that deserves a drink on the house. What do you want? In fact, what does everyone want?' George was in an expansive mood. The last couple of weeks had been great fun. Jamie and Roz had added a new dynamic to the usual gatherings. 'Leon, you should have brought your guitar along, it's perfect party time.'

'A fellow guitarist? How wonderful, we must have a session,' Jamie was delighted.

'He also plays the trumpet and the piano. He's a sort of one-man band, except he can't sing. You should busk, Leon. Obviously no one would give you any money here, but they might in Cambridge,' Charlotte said.

'Anyone else play an instrument?' Jamie looked around.

'Clive used to be in a band. Didn't you. darling?' Ollie said.

'We were called "The Screech". I was known as Clive the Beat and was possibly the worst drummer the world has ever known.'

'It's true,' Ollie giggled. 'Not a rhythmic bone in his body.'

'Frank?' Jamie queried.

'I'm more manager material.'

'I make a damned good groupie,' Charlotte said.

'Can a responsible headmistress be a groupie?' Leon asked.

'Whoever said I was a responsible headmistress?'

Jamie took Roz's hand as they strolled back up the village.

'Another brilliant evening. London may be the capital, but Suffolk is clearly the place to be.'

'And to think we were worried about having to adapt to a quieter pace of life,' Roz laughed. 'Nothing could be further from the reality.'

CHAPTER 15

Suffolk

The evening had been anything but brilliant for a different young couple. It had begun yet again with a row.

'Kate, where on earth is the babysitter?'

'She'll be here in a minute, we've got plenty of time.' Kate came out of the kitchen. 'What wine do you want to take?'

'I've already chosen … Oh bloody hell, Kate, you're not even ready. What's the matter with you?' Toby exploded.

'For heaven's sake, Toby, calm down. I am ready. I've only got to grab a jacket and put some shoes on.'

'Are you going like that?' he asked, looking at her T-shirt and simple summer skirt.

'Yes, I am going like this. It's a casual supper, Toby, not a cocktail party,' Kate snapped, immediately feeling under-dressed and unattractive. 'I'll go upstairs now, grab my sandals and you can go and sit with the kids for a couple of minutes.' Upstairs, she hastily flung a scarf around her neck, reapplied lipstick and opted for a pair of shoes with a heel rather than the comfortable espadrilles she'd been planning on.

'Kate?' Toby screeched from the kitchen. 'It's nearly half past bloody seven. We're going to be late. Where the hell is this bloody girl?'

'It won't be the end of the world if we're a few minutes late, but we won't be,' Kate said, coming down the stairs. 'Vicki said to come between half seven and eight. Meg will be here any minute and then we can go. Give me the wine and I'll put it in a bag. Gosh, two bottles tonight? Wise move, we know Steve isn't exactly overgenerous,' she smiled in an attempt to lighten the mood.

'There's no need to be catty, Kate. They're supposed to be your friends, although I must say you're not exactly behaving as though they are.' All Toby's pent-up anger spewed forth. It was like a dam bursting and he felt powerless to stop. 'You never wanted to go tonight. You've been whining on about some ridiculous comedy evening.' His face was red and angry. 'And now it appears you're hell-bent on punishing me by making damn sure we arrive late and not bothering with your appearance. It's pathetic, Kate; it makes you look stupid and it embarrasses me.'

There was a moment of stunned silence, then something inside Kate snapped.

Toby saw it, knew he'd gone too far, and cursed himself. Why had he said that? It was a terrible thing to say, and it wasn't true. She looked lovely. She looked fresh and totally natural. What had possessed him to lash out like that? He turned away to escape the look of shock and hurt on her face.

To Kate, it seemed as if he couldn't bear to look at her any more. 'How dare you say that? How dare you treat me like this? They're not my bloody friends and they never have been. They're snobbish, overbearing and mind-numbingly dull, which is precisely how I would describe you at the moment, so it's no wonder you all get on.' She couldn't remember when she had last felt so angry.

'You're right, I never wanted to go tonight. I wanted to go and have fun with some normal village people, "the peasants" as your friends so sweetly describe them. But as usual I gave into you. As usual, my wishes weren't considered, they rarely are these days. But I wouldn't be so petty as to try and punish you, those would be your tactics, not mine. As for my appearance, I'm mortified that it offends you. I had no idea you were so ashamed of me.' She was shaking with fury and disbelief at his cruelty.

'Mummy?' Belinda stood uncertainly in the hallway. Her eyes were huge with anxiety and her pretty face was blotchy. Her younger brother hovered uncertainly behind her.

'Darling, don't cry,' Kate said, quickly bending down to hug her. 'Mummy and Daddy are just having a silly argument, all over now. What a pair of morons we are, eh?' She deliberately used their favourite expression and somehow forced herself to laugh.

With relief, Kate saw the fear fade from her young daughter's eyes. The doorbell rang. 'That will be Meg. Run and answer it, and you can tell her what you want to watch before bedtime.' She watched them as they scampered towards the front door.

'Kate, listen –' Toby began, but she cut him off.

'Not now, Toby. We don't have the time and I sure as hell don't have the inclination. Perhaps you could go and say goodnight to your children while I go and talk to Meg. Then we'd better go, otherwise your worst fears will be realised and we will indeed be a few minutes late.'

They strode up the village in stony silence, oblivious to the beauty of the evening, passing Jamie and Roz who were standing hand in hand staring with reverence at the village hall.

'I wonder what they're up to?' Toby smiled, desperate to establish contact.

'I doubt they are up to anything,' his wife replied tartly. 'In common with many of us, they're probably wondering how anyone could think of tearing down such a beautiful building.'

'Kate, the building is riddled with woodworm, every roof tile needs replacing and there is asbestos in the ceiling. It's simply not safe.'

'So they say.'

'Why would they say that if it's not true?'

'Because "they" want a swanky new health club in its place.'

'Well, wouldn't you like that? Would that be such a terrible thing?'

'It would, indeed, be a terrible thing. No one from the village would be able to afford it. It would be a club for the rich city boys and their stuck-up wives. It would destroy village life. I would certainly never go, although perhaps you think I need the exercise.'

He gave up, she was angry and he couldn't really blame her. He wished they weren't going to this bloody dinner party but then the alternative would be to sit at home arguing. What was happening to them? He took his glasses off and rubbed his temples, he seemed to have a permanent headache these days.

'Kate, Toby, how lovely to see you. Go through to the garden and Steve will bring some drinks over. What a pretty skirt, Kate,' Vicki said.

'Thank you. Toby thought it might not be smart enough.'

'Oh heavens, you know we don't stand on ceremony here,' she simpered, in her high heels and cocktail dress.

'How are the kiddies? Not long now before they'll be joining our two at The Lodge.'

'We're not sure about that. They seem to really love the village school,' Kate replied.

'Oh?' Vicki said, flustered. 'I thought it was all decided.'

'So did I,' Toby said darkly.

'Christ, Kate, you can't leave them at the village school.' Vicki's husband Steve joined the conversation. 'They need a decent education, and to mix with the right people not the local yokels.' He put his arm around her. 'Got to give the blighters the best chance in life. Send them to The Lodge. The fees aren't too disastrous and what else is the fat bonus for, eh?' He laughed and Kate had an overwhelming desire to knee him in the bollocks.

The evening did not improve. Kate was seated next to a domineering man called Hugh, while his wife Patricia – don't shorten it to Pat, darling, makes me sound like a barmaid – held court opposite.

The main topic of conversation was the wine. She watched Toby and Steve swirling their glasses around ostentatiously. Just drink the bloody stuff, she wanted to scream.

'So what do you think, Kate? Are you coming?'

Kate dragged her focus back to Hugh. 'Sorry, Hugh, coming where?'

'Big village meeting, decide the fate of the hall and finally quash that detested drag contest.'

'What's wrong with the drag contest?'

'Oh, come on, Kate,' he looked at her incredulously. 'A load of bloody faggots in frocks. Not the sort of thing we want to encourage. We all know it goes on, but not in our village, if I can help it.'

Kate glanced anxiously to see if Toby had heard this and saw with relief that he was still deep in wine conversation with Steve. Thank heavens, she thought, she certainly couldn't face opening that particular can of worms tonight. She looked around the table and realised that she simply couldn't stand another minute of their vile company. She had to get out.

* * *

Thirty minutes later, having feigned a sudden and not entirely false migraine, she was back in her own garden sitting under the stars, nursing a large mug of tea and letting her tears fall unchecked. The children were fast asleep and Toby was walking Meg back.

She'd been amazed that he had accompanied her back home after her precipitous departure. She had fully expected a look of disbelief and disgust and had resigned herself to yet another drunken row when he returned. But to her astonishment, he'd leapt to his feet when she'd announced her sudden illness and, if she didn't know him better, she could have sworn he looked almost relieved.

She heard the front door close but couldn't be bothered to move or to disguise her sadness. She felt tired and disorientated. She heard him pour himself a whisky and was aware that he was standing in the doorway watching her, yet still she felt unable to stir.

'Kate?' He cleared his throat.

'Toby, I don't want to talk. I don't know what to say and I don't know what to think. The only thing I know for certain is that I never want to spend another evening like that.'

He didn't respond. He didn't know what to say.

'Thank you for coming back with me,' she said unexpectedly, after a long pause.

'I could hardly let you come home alone when you felt so ill.' He smiled and came into the garden.

'I wasn't really ill.'

'I know that but I thought it would be better if I came.'

'I see. You mean otherwise it would have looked bad to everyone.' She stood up.

'No, I didn't mean …' But she had turned away from him and was walking back into the house.

'Shall we go for lunch tomorrow? You, me and the kids?'
She stopped but didn't look around. 'Where?'
'The pub?'
'Maybe.'

CHAPTER 16

Suffolk

Roz and Jamie sat at the kitchen table surrounded by the remains of a long lazy breakfast. The radio was playing in the background and the back door was wide open allowing the morning sun to slope in.

Roz wordlessly held out her mug as Jamie reached for the cafétière.

'Empty,' Jamie said.

'Well, put the kettle on.'

'I'll look silly.'

'Oh, Jamie, will you ever tire of that joke?'

'Never.'

She shook her head smiling, and then yawned and stretched herself back in the chair.

'Like the cat that's got the cream,' Jamie smiled.

'Talking of cats, Leon says he's on the lookout for a puppy for us.'

'Word association, what a remarkable thing,' he said to himself.

'What are you mumbling about? Aren't you excited?'

'Just marvelling at your train of thought. Yes, of course, I'm excited. What sort are we going to have? Did you specify a type?'

'Not really. I said we wanted an average-sized dog, but I didn't go into specific breeds.'

'Guess we'll wait and see what turns up.'

'Let's have a relaxing day at home today, Jamie,' Roz suggested. 'We've got that enormous chicken you bought from the farm shop. We can have that for lunch and then I can test you on your lines for next week before you mow the lawn.' She got up and walked to the door.

'I was happy up until the chicken lunch but then the day began to go downhill.'

'It really is a fantastic view,' she said, ignoring him and gazing down the garden to the river beyond. 'We've struck gold here. There's something so magical about standing at your kitchen door and hearing the sound of water.'

'That'll be the kettle boiling.'

'You've not got a romantic bone in your body,' she sighed as she went to make the coffee. 'Charlotte asked me last night if I'd be interested in helping the kids at school with their reading. It's just for an hour or so every Thursday. She also wondered if I could do some drama games as a bit of fun at the end of the session. I think I'll say yes, work permitting. What do you think?'

'Great idea, and if for some reason you can't go, then I could step in.'

'Really?'

'There are two of us who miss not having children, you sometimes forget that, Roz.'

'I didn't mean. I don't forget …' She was saved from further reply by the telephone ringing.

Leaving her to make the coffee, he went to answer and came back grinning.

'Oh no, what was that all about? Why are you laughing?'

'That was Clive saying that they are going to the pub to have a pre-lunch snifter with their daughter and her partner and would we care to join them?'

'What did you say?'

'I said thank you very much, but you wanted a relaxing day at home with a large bird.'

'What did he say?'

'He said we could have two large birds for the price of one, and that he'd see us there later.'

'God, this village is impossible,' Roz said, shaking her head in despair.

Kate and Toby were sitting at the bar. Toby's friend Fergal was ordering drinks for them. Kate had been furious when she saw him.

'I didn't know, Kate. I swear I didn't know he would be here,' Toby had whispered.

'The proper way to serve a gin and tonic is with lime. It should really be served with lime, George, and garnished with cucumber,' Fergal was saying. It was clearly not his first drink of the day.

'Is it indeed?' George was unimpressed. 'In the absence of a lime, will the humble lemon suffice, Kate?'

'The humble lemon will be perfect, George, thank you.'

'Two more of those, please, George,' Jamie said, striding up to the bar. 'Clive and Ollie are also on their way up.'

'Good God, it's that awful Jock in a frock,' Fergal stage-whispered to Kate and Toby.

There was a moment of awkward silence before Jamie turned towards him. 'You have the advantage over me, pal. Clearly you know who I am, but I'm in the dark about you.'

He held out his hand. 'I'm Jamie Forsyth and this is my wife Roz, but I'm happy to be known as the Jock in a frock, in fact, I quite like it.'

'Yes, we all know exactly who you are,' Fergal ignored the outstretched hand. 'Dancing around the village in drag, screaming obscenities down the microphone.'

'I would hardly call them obscenities. I just got a little carried away in the heat of the moment.'

'Well, I guess I should be thanking you. I think that was the final nail in the coffin for the drag show.'

'I thought that had yet to be decided. Isn't there a meeting next week?'

'A mere formality.'

'I wouldn't count your chickens just yet,' George stepped in. 'It's a very old tradition and people like traditions.'

'Shoving kids up chimneys was also an old tradition but we put a stop to that,' Fergal smiled smugly, rather pleased with himself.

There was another moment of silence before Kate spoke. 'Hi, I'm Kate, this is Toby and these are our kids, Belinda and Tom.' Kate was astounded by Fergal's behaviour and mortified that they should be associated with him.

'Pleased to meet you,' Roz smiled, placing a restraining arm on Jamie who she could feel was champing at the bit. She bent down to the children.

'Hello, you two. My best friend at school was called Belinda, it's a beautiful name.'

'My best friend is called Hannah,' Belinda said.

'Oh, I've met Hannah. That's Leon's daughter, isn't it? She's lovely. So, do you both go to the school here?'

'We do at the moment. Daddy wants us to go to The Lodge but we like it here.' Belinda glanced nervously at her father. The look confirmed her fears; he had a face like thunder.

'The school cat is going to have kittens,' Tom added, as if that should really be the deciding factor. 'We want one, don't we, Bell?' Belinda nodded but looked desperately uneasy.

'Well, if you're still there next term then I'll see you. I'm going to come and help you with your reading, if you need any help that is, and maybe do some drama with you. Does that sound like fun?'

'Ye gods,' Fergal said. 'How the mighty are fallen.'

'I beg your pardon?' Roz said, looking up at him puzzled.

'Bit of a come down for you, isn't it? Teaching drama at a village school.'

'Why on earth would it be a come down for me?' She stood up slowly.

'Rumour has it that you are a model turned TV star and were well on your way to Hollywood. Now you're planning to teach in a poxy village school? For someone who was hailed as the next Julia Roberts, I'd say it was a bit of a come down. What went wrong? How did you fuck up?'

'My, my, someone has been doing their homework,' Roz said in a steely voice. 'I'm terribly flattered to think that anyone should take such an interest in my career. I must return the compliment and google you when I get home.'

'That could prove tricky, you've no idea what name to call me,' Fergal was smirking at Toby.

'Trust me, I can think of a few names to call you,' Roz responded.

'I can think of a few too,' Ollie had arrived in time to hear most of this exchange.

'I imagine we all can,' Clive added, and the others murmured their agreement. 'What a great game. Who would like to start? Jamie, how about you?'

'I'd love to, Clive, but I'm afraid I wouldn't know when to stop,' Jamie said giving Ollie the giggles.

Fergal was livid. This was not how he had planned the conversation. He had somehow been made to look a fool and that was the one thing he couldn't tolerate. He was furious and resolved one day to get even with Roz. Slamming the glass on the bar he turned to the assembled crowd. 'Well, if you'll excuse me, I'll leave you all to your little game. Such infantile behaviour is not really to my taste.' He marched out in what he hoped was a dignified manner but in reality was more a petulant stomp.

'Roz, my love, you were bloody brilliant. Wasn't she brilliant, everyone?' Jamie said, planting a kiss firmly on her lips. She looked a little shaken and he determined to make light of the affair.

'Bloody brilliant, indeed,' Ollie hugged her. 'Large gin and tonic for Roz, please George, and the usual for us. Girls, what do you want?'

'Roz and Jamie, this is my daughter, Liz, and her friend, Carol,' Clive said, throwing his arms around two girls standing either side of him.

'Partner, Dad. Carol is my partner,' the large fair-haired girl by his side smiled. 'Although friend is an improvement, he normally refers to us as "the dykes".'

'Lovely to meet you,' Roz said, laughing.

'Mum said you've both livened up the village, and I must say all of that was most entertaining,' she beamed at her, with the same generous smile as Ollie's.

'Glad you enjoyed it. What an odious man.' Roz turned to her husband, 'I admit I've been thinking that you've become obsessed with this drag contest, Jamie, but I'll be damned if the likes of him think they can tell us what to do. From this moment on, I am one hundred percent behind you.'

'We're all one hundred percent behind you, Jamie,' Ollie said. 'But, come on, Roz, you have to spill the beans. What's all this about modelling and Hollywood? Is he right?'

'Sort of, I guess. When I was fifteen or sixteen, I did some work for a teen magazine called *Jacqui*. I suppose you could call it modelling but it was nothing very glamorous. Later, I had a major part in a TV drama, and on the back of that I was offered a part in a film. I had to pull out of because of a family crisis.' She shrugged, 'Hollywood isn't very forgiving of a family crisis; they tend to cost time and money and I was never asked back. I certainly don't remember being hailed as the next Julia Roberts, so God knows where he dug that up from. Odd that he's worked so hard finding all this out. It's freaked me out a bit.'

George, who had seen the look of pure venom that Fergal had given her, thought that she was entitled to feel freaked out, and determined to have a quiet word with Jamie.

'Roz, I'm so sorry,' Kate said.

'What on earth have you got to be sorry about?'

'I don't know, really. I guess because he's a friend of Toby's, I feel guilty.'

'Bloody hell, Kate, I can't be held responsible for Fergal. I have no control over his behaviour,' Toby exclaimed, angry that Kate should bring him into it. He had been shocked by Fergal's behaviour but was not prepared to discuss it or even condemn his friend just yet. 'He'd had a bit too much to drink, that's all,' he said, conscious that he sounded rather lame.

Kate looked furious that Toby could even think of defending Fergal.

'Let's just forget it,' Roz said sensing the atmosphere. She turned to Liz and Carol. 'I hear you two are getting married How exciting. What sort of thing have you got in mind?'

'Don't know yet, we haven't really worked out the logistics. We need to find out how much Mum and Dad are prepared to spend.' She dug her father in the ribs. 'We fancy a flamboyant lesbian wedding, very over the top, no expense spared. Isn't that right, Carol?' she laughed.

'Oh, absolutely, the bigger the better.'

Clive and Ollie looked at each other in mock horror.

'Can't you just elope?' Clive ventured. 'Wouldn't that be more romantic? We'd stump up for the wedding night.'

'Not a chance, Dad, we want something big and flashy, just like us.'

Roz giggled. These two were great fun.

'One more, Roz, before we head home?' Jamie asked. 'What can I get anyone?'

He glanced over to include Kate and Toby but they were making their way to their table. He's a bit of an odd fish, thought Jamie, can't quite make him out, but she seems sweet.

'Let it be the last, Jamie. You have lines to learn.'

'Anything exciting, Jamie?' Ollie asked.

'Sadly no, Ollie. It's a shite part in a shite series but it's much-needed dosh. Only a couple of days filming. Actually, there's a thought. George, when is this big village meeting?'

'Wednesday night.'

'Bugger, I won't be back in time. I doubt I'll get home before about nine. Roz. you'll have to argue the case for the drag contest.'

'You'll be back in time for the important discussions which always take place here after the official meeting,' George said. 'But I have to say it's not looking good. These days the community council seems to be run by corrupt council members, city boys like Fergal and pious do-gooders. Anyone genuine seems to have been nudged out.' George was not normally so indiscreet but he was angry at the way people were trying to change the village.

'I remain optimistic, George,' Jamie said. 'It's not over till the fat lady sings.'

'I promise to keep quiet then,' Liz laughed.

CHAPTER 17

Suffolk

Roz stood at the back door gazing down the garden. The sun was just rising and there was an early morning mist hanging over the river. The sky was pearly pink, bathing the whole countryside in a rosy glow. No wonder so many artists liked this part of the world, thought Roz, and she went to get her camera.

She'd always enjoyed photography, but since moving to the village she had become obsessed with taking pictures. She really ought to make the effort to get up early more often.

'Coffee and orange juice? This is above and beyond your wifely duty. You could have stayed in bed, you know.'

'I was just thinking that I should do this more often, the light is fantastic at this time of the morning.'

'Aye, it's splendid, but on balance I'd rather be in bed.'

'Listen, Jamie, I've been thinking.'

'Always makes me nervous when you say that.'

'Be serious, I've had an idea.'

'Roz, sweetheart, can this wait?' Jamie was searching for stuff in the kitchen. 'I'm running late, I've lost my wallet and I need to focus on my part. I have to mentally prepare for my role.'

'You're playing a down-and-out with a drink problem, how much mental preparation do you need?' she asked wryly.

'You know just how to make me feel good about myself, darling.'

'It was just something about the drag contest, but if you're too busy …'

'I'm all ears.'

'It really sounds like they are going to veto the competition at the fete. No, let me finish …' He had opened his mouth to protest. 'I bumped into Kate again yesterday and we got chatting. I think she feels really bad about all that Fergal business, not that it was her fault. Anyway, we got onto the village hall and she said that, according to Toby, there are plans for a new health club to replace it. It would be a tragedy if that went ahead. She doesn't really believe the hall is in as bad a condition as they're making out. Apparently her dad is an architect and he thought, oh alright, stop jigging around. Here's my idea.' She paused and smiled sweetly at Jamie who looked pointedly at his watch. 'Why don't we put the drag contest on in the village hall? We could make a real evening of it and more importantly help raise money to save it. Maybe that would encourage others to come up with other fund-raising ideas. We really need to stop this health club plan. They're trying to rush it through before anyone grasps what's happening. No one can stop us holding the contest in the hall. We don't need the permission of the committee. If they don't want the competition during their precious fete then that's their loss, we'll simply have it somewhere else.'

'Well, what do you think?' Roz was disconcerted by Jamie's silence.

'Rosalind Forsyth, I love you very much,' he said slowly. 'You are a genius. This is brilliant. I'm going to sit on the train and make plans.'

'I thought you had to get mentally prepared? '

'As you said yourself, darling, how much preparation do I really need?'

'Do you want to go to the village council meeting tonight?' Toby asked Kate that morning as they were drinking their tea. 'Can we get Meg to babysit?'

'Will you be home in time?'

'Yes, I'll catch the early train.' He smiled at her but she didn't reply. 'What's wrong now? What the hell have I done wrong now?'

'It just strikes me as sad that you're able to get away early in order to put the kibosh on a harmless drag competition, and yet you never seem able to get home early to attend the parents' evening or sports day, or any other event come to think of it.'

'And it strikes me as sad that nothing I do at the moment pleases you. I happen to feel strongly about the drag contest, as you well know, and you also know why. I think it is demeaning for the village and thought I could count on your support.'

'Well, you can't. Don't you think it's about time you let the past go, Toby, and concentrated instead on the present and on your children?'

'What the hell do you think I'm doing?' he yelled at her. 'I flog my guts out for you and the bloody kids. I'm in the office before everyone else and I'm always the last to leave. Have you any idea how many people are being made redundant at the moment, Kate? Do you know how many of my colleagues are going home to tell their families that they no longer have a job, that they can no longer afford nice holidays or a nice school?'

'They've already got a nice school, Toby, they don't want to go to a different one.' She tried to remain calm. 'They just want their father. I wish you'd listen to them.' She had a sudden idea. 'Toby, why don't you get the later train? Let's have breakfast with them and you can talk to them. They can tell you what they're going to do at school today and you can see how much they love it there.'

'Don't be so god damn stupid, Kate. I haven't got time to talk to them. Christ almighty, they're only bloody kids. They don't know what they want. It's you who encourages them in this stupid village-school nonsense. I'm telling you I've had just about as much as I can take. I'm not killing myself at work for nothing, they're going to The Lodge and that is final.'

He hurled his cup into the sink, shattering it into pieces, and stormed out of the house, never noticing the white face of his little daughter who had been listening to every word outside the kitchen.

Jamie watched Toby crash onto the train, slamming the door behind him. That man seems to be permanently angry, he thought. He was someone heading rapidly towards an early grave or a nervous breakdown.

He knew that Toby had seen him and was intent on pretending he hadn't, and Jamie was more than happy to keep up the charade. He couldn't contemplate the idea of a few minutes' conversation with him, let alone a ninety-minute train journey. Fergal and another partner-in-crime leapt on just as the train was about to pull out, clearly timing their daily commute down to the last second. They seemed an arrogant bunch, bellowing at the top of their voices with no consideration for fellow passengers. Each trying to outdo the other with their anecdotes and hearty laughter.

Jamie felt nothing but pity for them. When he and Roz were not acting, which was a large percentage of the time these days, they earned their bread and butter by corporate training. He'd never left those companies without feeling relieved that he didn't have to work there. The idea of a nine-to-five job and a daily commute filled him with dread. He may not have the money that these guys had but he would never, in a million years, swap his life for theirs. He lay back in his seat, trying to block out their racket, and concentrated on the idea of the drag contest in the village hall.

CHAPTER 18

Suffolk

At seven o'clock that evening the doorbell rang. Roz was putting her make-up on, and rushed down the stairs, swinging the door open to find Frank clutching half-a-dozen sausages.

'In Jamie's absence, I'm here to escort you to the meeting.' He thrust the bag towards her. 'Homemade lamb and chilli sausages, it's a new recipe, see what you think.'

'Frank, are you trying to seduce me with your meat?' Roz laughed 'First it was stuffed pork, then ham and now bangers. People will start to talk, you know.'

He turned a rosy red. She wasn't far from the truth; he didn't really want to seduce her, but hadn't quite got over his infatuation.

'Come on in, I'm just finishing my war paint, but I'll be ready in two secs.'

Leon joined them on their way up to the village. 'You're a quick mover, Frank,' he grinned. 'Her husband has only been away for a day. Afraid tonight may be foregone conclusion, you know. Jamie won't be happy, Roz. It's a bloody shame.'

Roz was tempted to tell them her idea but she thought it would be fairer to wait for Jamie. 'What happens? Do we all get to vote?'

'Nothing as democratic as that, Roz. The powers that be talk, we make our feelings known and then they go ahead and do exactly what they want,' Leon shrugged. 'That's really what people are angry about. The drag contest is relatively unimportant. Yes, it's great fun and an old tradition but it's what it stands for that matters. It represents the old village and they want to establish a new village.'

'Why don't people like you and Frank join the council? Or Clive and Ollie?'

'Good question, Roz, and sadly the answer is laziness on my part. Clive is on the council, but he's one man against many. Maybe the time has come to take action.' He turned to Frank, 'What do you say? Time for us to shake off our lethargy and get involved?'

Frank was not especially aware that he had been guilty of lethargy, but nodded his head all the same.

The decision not to include the drag contest in next year's fete was not surprising, but still disappointing. Clive and some of the others had tried their hardest but, with the heavyweights of the committee opposing it, they had little chance of success.

George looked over at them now, sitting in a corner of the pub looking pleased with themselves. The ringleader was a man called Edward Hampshire. He was the local squire who rattled around in an enormous manor house. He owned a large percentage of the farmland and donated generously to both the church and the school and was therefore very influential amongst the villagers and his fellow council members.

He was not an unpleasant man except when it came to the drag contest, which for some reason he had always hated and had campaigned against for many years. While his wife had been alive, he hadn't stood a chance. She had been born and bred in the village and loved the competition. Her family had always taken part; a bit of harmless fun for all the family was how she had viewed it.

It was a shame, thought George, that he couldn't have used his considerable influence towards a better cause.

'So, common sense has prevailed at last, eh George? Common sense and morality,' Hugh said with a smug smile. 'We are no longer the laughing stock of the county and can finally hold our heads up high.'

As a landlord, George prided himself on remaining calm in the face of provocation, but right now he was having great difficulty stopping himself from punching Hugh's bulbous nose.

'I've never had a problem holding my head high, Hugh, and perhaps, if you lost a little more weight, then you wouldn't either. Personally, I think it a great shame for the village, a lovely old tradition gone.' He didn't care if he'd offended him, let him take his custom elsewhere.

'There's nothing lovely about a bunch of grown men prancing around in dresses and making a public exhibition of themselves. The right decision has been made, isn't that so, Toby?' Hugh turned to Toby, who had joined him at the bar.

'I think so,' Toby said, not particularly happy about being put on the spot. 'I think the decision has been taken with everyone's best interest at heart.'

'What a load of horse shit,' a voice from the corner said. It was Jack, a local farmworker. He was never normally so voluble, but he was incensed. 'You've not got my best interests at heart, mate. You don't even know who I am. I see you occasionally, coming in with that stuck-up prick over there,' he indicated a drunken Fergal. 'The two of you never even glance in my direction, so don't you dare try and tell me what my best interests are.'

'Same goes for me,' his friend Angus said. 'You've never made any effort to get to know us. You think it's beneath you to sit and have a beer with us.'

'I thought you'd know better, Edward,' Jack glared at the squire. 'You've lived here for as long as I can remember. Your wife's family were the lifeblood of this village. She must be turning in her grave.'

Edward flushed. 'I'll thank you not to speak ill of my wife, Jack.'

'I'm not speaking ill of your wife, Edward. I'm speaking ill of you. Your wife was a wonderful woman.'

'OK, gentlemen. Let's not get overheated,' George gently intervened.

'Here's Jamie,' Jack said. 'He'll be downhearted, poor lad. He'd set his heart on organising this drag contest.'

George looked up to see Jamie threading his way towards the bar. Surprisingly, he didn't look in the least bit downhearted. 'Jamie, have you heard the news?'

'I have indeed, not totally unexpected, I guess. A pint of the usual for me, George, a glass of white for Roz and can I get you two anything?' he asked Jack and Angus.

'We've just got one in, Jamie lad, but thanks all the same.'

'You seem to be taking this rather well, Jamie,' George commented. 'I thought you'd be furious.'

'Furious? A man of my tranquil temperament?' Jamie smiled. 'No, George, I've had another, much better idea.'

'I beg your pardon?' Roz said, arriving at the bar with the others.

'Alright, sorry, we've had a much better idea.'

'Who had the idea, Jamie?'

'Roz, stop quibbling, the important thing is the idea. I'd have come up with it sooner or later.'

'Spit it out then,' Charlotte said impatiently.

'It's quite simple. We hold the drag contest in the village hall. It will be a separate event from the fete.'

'You can't do that,' Fergal said, horrified.

'Why not? What's to stop us? You've banned it from the fete but there is absolutely nothing to stop us from having it in the hall.'

'Great idea. It solves everything. Good thinking, Jamie.' Leon slapped him on the back. 'And Roz, of course,' he hastily added.

'It doesn't solve anything, it's impossible. We've forbidden the drag contest.' Hugh was incandescent with rage.

'As Jamie pointed out, Hugh, it has been banned it from the fete, and we have to abide by that decision, but you can't ban us from holding it elsewhere,' Clive said with delight.

'The hall isn't safe. It's a condemned building.'

'Oh bollocks, Hugh. The hall is perfectly safe. It just needs some tender loving care,' Ollie said.

'And a huge amount of money. I tell you the hall is unfit for public use. It's a dangerous building,' Hugh was clutching at straws 'There's even a huge wasps' nest in the car park. That can't be safe for the kids.'

'That's a beehive, not a bloody wasps' nest,' Jack said.

'Oh, Jack, is that right? Have the bees come back?' Ollie was beaming. 'There always used to be a beehive there but then for some reason they went away. I'm so pleased they've returned.'

'We'll use the drag contest as a way to raise money for the hall,' Jamie was fired up. 'Make a real evening of it. Frank can organise some food and we can charge for tickets. We'll put on a great show. The stage is huge and we can have lighting and music. What do you think?'

'Over my dead body,' Hugh said.

'We live in hope, Hugh,' Ollie said. 'It gets my vote, Jamie.'

'And mine,' Charlotte said. 'By the way, aren't honey bees a protected species?'

'I'm not sure, but I like the way you're thinking,' Jamie said, immediately cottoning on to the implications that could have.

'You'll never raise the money for the hall, you need thousands and thousands of pounds,' Fergal slurred. 'Who the hell's going to pay to see some drag show? You're making us a laughing stock again.'

'We can set the ball rolling,' Jamie went on. 'Pave the way for other fund-raising events. It's absolutely vital that we keep our village hall. Just think of everything that takes place there. And the memories people have. There must've been hundreds of parties and wedding receptions held there over the years. It's part of the history of the village.'

'I think it's an excellent idea,' Kate said, stepping forward much to Toby's annoyance. 'I agree that the hall is an integral part of the village. So much better than some expensive health club.'

Hugh looked at Fergal and Fergal looked at Toby. His face was like thunder. This was supposed to have been confidential information. Hugh had sworn him to secrecy but Fergal had revealed it to Toby one drunken evening. He shouldn't have said anything, but he hadn't expected him to go blabbing to his prissy wife.

Toby was furious with Kate. She was stirring things up deliberately. She knew that no one else was supposed to be aware of these plans. Hugh had turned a dull red colour and Squire Edward was looking totally bemused. He knew nothing about a health club. He had been listening with interest to what Jamie was saying about raising money for the village hall. He may not approve of the drag show but he certainly approved of trying to preserve the hall.

Everyone was momentarily perplexed by what Kate had said. During the few seconds silence the phone rang. George went to answer it and rushed back minutes later.

'Kate, my love, that was Meg. You have to go home. Belinda has gone missing.'

CHAPTER 19

Suffolk

'Missing?' Kate leapt up. 'What do you mean missing? What does she mean missing? What's she talking about?'

'Is she still on the phone, George?' Toby asked.

'No,' George said. 'I said I'd send you home immediately. We'll find her, Kate, don't worry, she can't have gone far. Meg says she went to make some tea and found the back door open and that's when she realised. She says she can only have been gone for a short while. She's distraught.'

'Tom, where's Tom? Has he gone with her? Oh my God, how can this have happened? Where is she?' Kate was ashen.

'Tom is in bed, Kate. Go home. We'll find her. I promise.'

'Of course, we'll find her,' Clive said firmly. 'As George says, she can't have gone far. We'll split up and take various areas. Toby, take Kate home, and don't worry we'll have her back in no time.'

The pub was suddenly galvanised into action.

'We'll take the truck and go along the top lane towards the old barns. The kids love playing around there, maybe that's where she's headed,' Jack and Angus wasted no time.

'Keep in touch with me,' George shouted after them. 'Everyone keep in touch with me, you've all got the pub number. I'll coordinate from here and that way we'll all know what's going on.'

'Leon, get back to Hannah,' Charlotte said. 'Those two are as thick as thieves, she's bound to know something.'

'I'm on my way.' The thought had already occurred to him that maybe Hannah could have been persuaded to take part in whatever Belinda was up to and his blood was running cold. Not pausing for a second, he ran out of the door.

'Charlotte, come with me, we'll go to the woods at the back of the churchyard. They're always making camps there,' Frank said, grabbing her hand. 'We'll go past my place first and pick up a torch.'

'Makes sense if we do the part of the village we know best,' Jamie said. 'We'll take the footpath by the river at the back of our cottage.'

'Ollie and I will cover the football pitch and playing fields,' Clive said. 'She can't have gone far,' he said again, willing it to be true.

'Don't forget to phone,' said George. 'Keep in touch with me.'

Kate and Toby ran home in silence, each wrapped up in their own thoughts. Meg was waiting for them at the front door, her face crumpled in despair.

'I'm so sorry, I'm so sorry, the back door was open, I just didn't hear, if only I'd heard, I wish I'd ...' She was gulping with sobs.

Kate rushed past her up the stairs. Toby put his arm around the babysitter and guided her back into the kitchen.

'It's alright, Meg. No one's blaming you, Kate's just gone to check on Tom. Now just tell me exactly what happened.' He fought to maintain a composure he was far from feeling.

'I came in from the garden to make a cup of tea and found the back door swinging open. I thought it was strange, so I went up to check on the kids and she had gone. Oh God, I'll never forgive myself. I'm so sorry Toby, so sorry.'

'Deep breath. Meg, tell me what time this was?'

'Fifteen minutes ago, maybe less. I rang the pub straight away. I'd only checked on them a short while before that. I'd heard a noise, so I went upstairs, but they were both fast asleep. Oh God, that was probably her getting out of bed, wasn't it?' she wailed. 'She must have banged into something and then leapt back into bed when she heard me coming up. I should have checked more carefully, she was probably fully dressed. Oh, Toby, I'm so sorry.'

'Meg, calm down, it's not your fault. We know she's not been gone very long, we'll find her, don't you worry.'

Kate appeared in the doorway. She held out a piece of paper to Toby. 'She left this in our bedroom.'

Dear Mum and Dad,

I'm running away becos I am making you angry and you shout at each other all the time and I hate it and I don't want Dad to kill himself at work.

I dont want to go to a new school and Tom doesnt want to, his reeding is much better and his words aren't jumbled and he is going to lern the violin and the cat is going to have kittens and I like my friend Hannah. Maybe if there is only one of us then dad wont have to work so hard.

I love you Bell xxxxx'

They stared at each other as the awful realisation of what was happening sank in.

'I'll find her, Kate. I promise I'll find her.'

Kate nodded, too shocked to be able to articulate.

'Wake Tom up and ask him if he can think of anywhere she might have gone. She may have told him something or they may have a special place we don't know about. I'll take my mobile so you can call me if he comes up with anything.'

'I don't want to frighten him. He'll be terrified if he thinks she's missing.'

'Pretend she's playing hide and seek or whatever, it's important we ask him, Kate.' He grabbed a torch and flung his jacket over his shoulders. 'I'll find her, darling, don't worry. I'll find her.'

Leon burst into his house like a tornado, flinging the door open with tremendous force.

'Jess,' he shouted. 'You there?'

'Of course I'm here.' His younger sister emerged from the lounge. 'Leon, what's the matter?'

'Is Hannah here?' He took the stairs two at a time.

'Of course she's here. Calm down, Leon, you're scaring the living daylights out of me.' Jess followed him up the stairs and into Hannah's bedroom where she lay sleeping peacefully.

Leon gazed at her chubby cheeks and tousled hair and sent up a silent prayer to the man he had always claimed not to believe in. 'Belinda has gone missing,' he whispered, before bending down to wake his daughter. 'She's Hannah's best friend.'

'I know who Belinda is. What do you mean she's gone missing?'

'Just that, the babysitter rang to say that she wasn't in her bed and the back door was open. I've got to wake Hannah and see if she knows anything. I had a terrible fear that she may have gone with her. Thank Christ she hasn't.'

'Not Hannah. She's far too sensible to do anything like that.'

'Hello, darling,' he murmured, gently shaking her. 'Wakey, wakey.'

She opened her eyes and stared at him for a second before a warm smile lit up her face.

'Hello, Dad,' she mumbled blearily, holding out her arms to him.

'Hello, monkey.' He kissed her. 'Sit up for moment, poppet. I'm sorry to wake you but I've got to ask you something. It's very important. Are you awake?'

She sat up, brushing unruly curls away from her face. She looked first at her dad and then at her Aunty Jess and a look of fear came into her eyes. 'It's not Granny or Grandpa? There's nothing wrong with them is there?'

Her aunt hastened to reassure her, 'No sweetheart, they're both fine.'

'Hannah, it's Belinda,' Leon held her hand tightly. 'She's run away from home.'

'Oh no, Dad, that's terrible.'

'I know, poppet, and her mum and dad are frantic with worry. Now, did she say anything to you? Did she ask you to go with her? Have you any idea where she may have gone? Think carefully, it's very important.'

'She was crying a lot today. She's unhappy because her Dad wants her to go to The Lodge and she doesn't want to go. She asked me ages ago if I'd ever thought about running away but I just thought it was because she was upset. I never thought she was serious. I could've stopped her. She hates the dark. Oh, Dad, she'll be so scared.'

'Hush, darling, don't get upset, she hasn't been gone long so I'm sure we'll find her. Can you think of anywhere she may have gone? Any favourite place or camp that you have?'

'Maybe she's gone to her gran, she's always talking about her gran.'

'Where does her gran live? Is it near here?'

'I'm not sure, but I think she lives somewhere near Colchester.'

'OK, you stay here with Aunty Jess. I'm going to help look for her, if you think of anything then Aunty Jess can ring me. Don't worry, I'm sure she'll be fine. She's probably fast asleep in a barn or a shed.' He spoke with more conviction than he actually felt.

He was halfway down the stairs when she came running out of her bedroom.

'Dad, she'll be at the school. The cat's about to have kittens any minute and she's mad about the cat and so is Tom and they really want a kitten. She won't have gone anywhere without saying goodbye to the cat, she really loves that cat. She'll be in the school shed, that's where she'll be.' She hurtled past him on the stairs.

'Hannah, what do you think you're doing?'

'I'm coming with you, she'll want to see me, it'll be nicer if I'm there.'

Leon thought about this for a second. 'OK, you may be right. Put a coat over your pyjamas.'

'Can Mister Carter come, Dad?' Hannah asked, catching sight of their beloved Labrador. 'Bell loves Mister Carter.' He was called Mister Carter after the man who had sold him to them. Hannah had thought that was the polite thing to do and nothing could dissuade her.

'Mister Carter and a pregnant cat is not a match made in heaven, sweetheart, he'd better stay here with Aunty Jess.'

'He can stay here on his own. Aunty Jess is coming too.'

Mister Carter would normally follow his young mistress to the end of the world and back but the lure of a forgotten cheese sandwich lying on the coffee table was proving hard to resist and he was more than happy to miss out on this particular night-time adventure.

Five minutes later, they were pulling into the school car park. Hannah was out before Leon had switched the engine off and was running towards the shed. Leon and Jess followed.

'Dad, the light's on, I told you she'd be there.' And she pushed open the door.

Belinda turned around, startled, as the door opened, but relaxed when she saw it was her friend. 'Hannah, she's had her kittens; she's had eight kittens,' she whispered. 'They're so beautiful. I watched her. I was the first one to see them. Now you can be the second.' Her little face was a picture of wonderment and joy. 'Do you think she's OK?' She asked. 'Should we get her some milk? I've only got fruit juice in my bag.'

'She looks absolutely fine to me,' Leon replied, coming in and bending down to check on the cat. 'Rather tired, but otherwise OK. I expect she was very grateful to have you here.'

'I just came to see if she was alright and to say goodbye, but she was all squirmy and restless so I stroked her for a while and talked to her and then all of a sudden the kittens started to arrive. It was so beautiful. I'll never forget it.'

'Yes, it's a very magical sight,' Leon said crouching down beside her. 'Bell, darling, what's your telephone number? I have to ring your mum and dad, you know that, don't you? They're sick with worry. Do you want to speak to them?'

'I suppose you couldn't pretend not to have seen me?' she asked, rather half-heartedly.

Leon shook his head.

'I didn't really think so,' she said sorrowfully. 'You talk to them.' She punched the number into his phone and he went outside.

'I didn't make a very good job at running away, did I?'

'You did better than me. I only made it to the end of the driveway,' Jess said.

Hannah and Belinda giggled.

'Your Dad made it all the way to the station. That was quite impressive. It was a fair few miles.' Jess was trying to make light of the situation.

'I was always an intrepid adventurer,' Leon smiled as he came back in.

'Were they very cross?' Belinda asked.

'It was your mum I spoke to, and she was very happy and very relieved. In fact, she burst into tears. Your dad is still out looking for you.'

'He'll be so angry.'

Leon, who had never seen anything but anger etched upon Toby's face, was inclined to agree but said instead, 'He might be at first, but that's only because he will have been so worried about you. He'll want to know why you ran away, though. I know I would if it was Hannah.'

'Leon, you don't have to worry,' Belinda said. 'Hannah would never leave you, she told me. She said she loves you too much and that anyway you couldn't manage without her.'

Leon gazed down at his little girl. She smiled up at him, her hair a tangled mess, plump legs protruding from the green anorak which was two sizes too large but which she had sweetly chosen, knowing it was cheaper and would last longer than the pink one she preferred. He was overwhelmed by a surge of love for her and bent down to hug her tightly. I'll go and buy that pink coat with the fake fur first thing tomorrow, he vowed to himself. She'll look like a blancmange but, what the hell, it's what she wants.

'Come on, Belinda, let's get you home. Say goodbye to Cassie. I'll pop up first thing tomorrow to check on her again.'

'You know her name?' Belinda was astonished.

'Of course I know her name,' Leon said. 'I'm her vet.'

'My dad doesn't even know there's a cat.'

'I expect he will after tonight.'

'I'd love to have a kitten, but he'll be so angry with me I don't think he'll let me.'

'I wouldn't rule it out,' Leon said, thinking that if it were his daughter he would promise her twenty kittens. 'You've got a way with animals, Bell. Do you want to come to the surgery with me one Saturday? Hannah's been, haven't you, poppet?'

'Oh, Leon, could I really?' Bell couldn't believe her luck. 'I'd love that. Thank you so much.'

'We'll ask your parents, although maybe not tonight.'

'No, maybe not tonight,' she agreed. She had a suspicion that her dad was not all that keen on Leon, although how anyone could not like him was a mystery to her. Not only was he a vet, which was just about the coolest profession that anyone could have, but he was handsome and funny and wore mad clothes.

Toby hurtled into the house to find Kate making hot chocolate in the kitchen, her face awash with tears and makeup.

'What happened? Where is she? Is she OK?'

'She's getting changed for bed; she's absolutely shattered, poor love, but otherwise fine. Leon and Hannah found her.' Kate filled him in on what Leon had told her.

'I'll take this up to her.'

'Be gentle with her, Toby. She certainly can't cope with an argument tonight.'

'I really have turned into an ogre, haven't I?' he said wretchedly. 'Of course I'm not going to argue with her.'

He stood for a moment in the doorway of her bedroom and watched his daughter lying in bed. Her pretty little face, so like her mother's, was white and pinched. The long dark hair, that Kate normally plaited for bed, was scraped back into an untidy ponytail. She looked scared and vulnerable. He walked into the room with the mug of hot chocolate.

'Dad, are you very angry?' Belinda asked, without looking at him.

'Yes, darling, I am very angry.'

She closed her eyes, sure that this was going to be bad. But to her astonishment, she felt her Dad's strong arms lift her out of bed and onto his lap.

'I am angry, my pet, but not with you.' He kissed the top of her head and hugged her tightly. 'I'm angry at myself. I've been a rotten dad recently, haven't I?'

'We haven't really seen you much,' Belinda replied with difficulty, her head was smothered in his arms.

'That's exactly what I mean. I've been a rotten dad. You do know that I love you very much, don't you?' He stared intently down into her face.

'I think that maybe I'd forgotten,' she murmured.

'Oh God.' His arms tightened around her. 'Well, never forget again, do you hear me? And if you ever feel that you're in danger of forgetting, then come and tell me. Will you promise me to do that?'

'I promise.' She sat up in his arms. 'Dad, did you ever run away? Leon and Jess both did although Jess only made it to the end of the driveway.'

'No, I don't think I did. I probably thought about it, maybe I wasn't brave enough.'

'Did Uncle Ben run away, Dad?' she asked. 'Is that why he isn't here anymore?'

'We'll talk about that another time, darling,' Toby said, totally thrown off balance. 'Now it's time to go to bed and dream about your new kitten.'

Belinda's eyes flew wide open and she flung her arms around him. 'Really, Dad? Do you mean it? Can I have a kitten? Really?'

'Yes, I mean it. But you'll have to look after it. No leaving it up to Mum.'

'Of course I'll look after it,' she said, baffled at the thought of relinquishing care of the kitten to anyone. 'I know which one I want. The last one to be born, it didn't make the same noise as the others, they all mewed but this one could only whisper.'

'Well, Whisper it is then. Now drink your choccie and go to sleep. You've had a long day.'

'Whisper, oh what a beautiful name. Thank you so much, Dad.'

'No, thank you, my darling. Thank you for showing me the way back.'

She wasn't really sure what he meant but something else had occurred to her.

'Dad?'

'Yes?'

'Tom might be upset at not choosing the name for the kitten with me. We've talked about it a lot.'

'Then maybe Tom had better have a kitten of his own.'

Belinda couldn't believe her ears. She'd thought her dad would be furious. She'd thought there would be a huge row but instead here he was offering them two kittens and being nicer than she could ever remember. Grown-ups were very strange people.

'Dad?' she said, once more just as he was walking out of the door.

He turned and waited.

'You know how I said that maybe I had forgotten you loved me?'

'Yes.'

'I think that Tom and Mum have sort of forgotten, too.'

Toby stared at her in silence, tears springing to his eyes. 'I'll just have to make sure I remind them,' he said gruffly. 'I love you, Bell.'

'Love you, too, Daddy.'

Kate was sitting at the kitchen table looking exhausted. She'd poured herself a large glass of red wine but it remained untouched in front of her. Her hair was tucked behind her ears and mascara was smeared beneath her eyes. She somehow managed to look both young and old at the same time and Toby longed to take her in his arms, but knew that if he did so then he would linger there for quite some time and he had one more thing left to do on this strange night.

'I've promised them a kitten each,' he said from the doorway.

'They'll be over the moon. They've talked about nothing else for weeks.'

'I didn't know.'

'No, I know,' she replied. 'Do you want a drink?'

'No, I'm going to go back to the pub to say thank you to everyone.'

She looked startled.

'I imagine they'll probably still be there, it isn't even half ten yet although it feels like the middle of the night,' he said, wrongly interpreting her look. 'It was incredibly kind of them to all go looking for her.'

'It's a kind village,' she said quietly.

He turned to go and then paused. 'Bell said you might have forgotten that I love you, Kate. Is it true? Have you forgotten?'

'I thought it was you who'd forgotten.'

'I think you're right,' he sighed. 'I think I lost sight of how much I loved you all and how much you all meant to me. I lost sight of a lot of things for a while. Can you forgive me?'

'Let's talk about it when you get back.'

'She mentioned Ben. She asked if he'd run away, too. It was very odd because I'd been thinking about him all the time I was searching for her.'

'Of course you were. Of course it brought back memories. Go to the pub now, Toby, before it gets too late.'

George was clearing up the last of the glasses and contemplating a small nightcap. He deserved one, it had really been one hell of a night. He chuckled as he remembered Jamie's earlier comment: 'And I was worried that village life may be too dull. It's like a bloody soap opera here. Every day is a different episode. At this rate, I'll have to go back to Glasgow for some peace and quiet.'

He was right, thought George, ever since their arrival a lot of things had been happening. They seemed to act as a sort of catalyst for the village, stirring up and inspiring people. Personally he was all for it. The pub door opened and Toby walked in. George was surprised to see him.

'I didn't expect to see you back here tonight. Thank heavens Belinda is safe. Let me get you something. What will you have? It's on the house.'

'No, let me get you one, George. I came to thank everyone. Where are they all?'

'You've just missed them. Jack and Angus had a swift half before heading off home; they'd been looking in all the barns. Roz marched Jamie home because he was soaking wet. He swam across the river because he thought he saw something. It turned out to be some sheep's wool hanging off a branch but he said his heart stopped beating for a moment. He cut his leg in the process. Don't worry, it was nothing drastic, but they thought they ought to get it cleaned up. Clive and Ollie found a stray dog. Typical of them, they go out looking for one thing and come back with another. Leon, Jess and Hannah have just this second gone and, if I'm not much mistaken, here's Frank back from walking Charlotte home.'

'Everyone else gone, George?' Frank marched in. He'd been hoping that Jess would still be there. He'd been rather taken with Leon's sister and wasn't sure how she'd managed to slip under his radar before.

'Just Toby here, he's come to say thank you.'

'Bloody hell.'

'Frank, what can I get you to drink? I wanted to say how much we appreciated your help. Everyone was so kind. We're much indebted to you all.'

'Thank you very much. Just the usual, please, George.' That was a nice little speech thought Frank, a touch pompous but well meant. 'Let's drink to your daughter's safe return.' He raised his glass, 'We're all relieved.'

Toby felt overwhelmed. He'd barely exchanged three words with the people who had searched for Belinda, and some of those words hadn't been terribly pleasant, yet everyone had gone off without a second thought to look for her. Jamie had even swum across the river because he thought, well, he didn't want to dwell on what Jamie had thought.

He recalled Jamie's fury when Fergal had been baiting Roz and felt totally embarrassed at being part of that exchange. Talking of Fergal, George hadn't mentioned him or indeed Hugh. He turned to him. 'George, what about Fergal and Hugh?'

'Well, um,' George hesitated. 'I think Hugh was looking on his way home, but as for Fergal …'

'What Hugh actually said was, "that he'd take a quick gander" on his way home.' Frank had no hesitation in telling Toby the truth. 'And Fergal was too pissed to do anything. I have to say, I wouldn't be terribly impressed if they were my mates.'

'Easy, Frank,' George warned him. He felt that Toby had probably gone through enough tonight without having his friends' behaviour dissected.

'It's alright, George. He's right, I'm not impressed.' Toby knocked back his whisky and held it out for a refill. 'I've been behaving like a total arse, recently.'

'You said it.' Frank obviously felt it was the time to clear the air.

George and Toby looked astounded for a moment and then they both began to laugh.

'Blimey, Frank, what has got into you tonight?' George was shaking his head.

'I was only agreeing with him,' Frank grinned.

'You've lived up to your name tonight, Frank, and I appreciate it but I'm not sure just how much more honesty I can take. I can't believe I've got it so wrong for so long,' Toby looked suddenly haggard. 'George, if I leave some money behind the bar, can you make sure those involved in the man hunt get their just rewards?'

'Why don't you come and buy them a drink in person? I really think they'd appreciate that more. Jack and Angus are in most nights around six, the others aren't quite so predictable but they're here pretty often. Bring Kate and the kids and then Belinda can say thank you, too.'

'You know what, George, that's a bloody good idea,' Toby smiled. 'I may even bring them for a meal tomorrow, I'm certainly not going to work so we could come in early.'

'That's settled then. I'll reserve a table for you. You can try some of Frank's new sausages.'

'Lamb and chilli,' Frank said. 'You won't regret it.'

CHAPTER 20

San Francisco

With a large coffee in one hand and a chocolate cookie in the other, Drew sat in front of his computer with Elvis at his feet. He was staring at the screen trying to summon some enthusiasm for the range of exercise bikes displayed. 'Elvis, why has no one yet invented a pill that instantly tones and revitalises you? We can put a man on the moon, we can place a camera on Mars and yet I'm still forced to pedal a stupid machine in a bid to keep my waistline from expanding beyond redemption.'

Elvis nodded sympathetically, he was more than ready now for something inside his own waistline. He eyed the cookie optimistically but, just as he was about to declare his desire, the phone rang.

'Drew, it's Fran here. Am I disturbing you? I knew you'd be up.'

'Fran, I'm sitting here contemplating the merits of an exercise bike versus the merits of a rowing machine. Anything that can distract me from that is more than welcome,' he replied, shoving the last mouthful of cookie into his mouth.

Elvis gazed tragically up at him, unable to believe his master's cruelty.

'I have some news for you about Titty.'

'Awesome, Fran, that was quick work. You must have been up at the crack of dawn.'

'I wanted to get in before the others and do some investigating. It doesn't make very pleasant reading, I'm afraid.'

'Fire away.'

'I'd guessed that she must come from an army background with the amount of travelling she'd done as a kid I looked up the name Forrester in military records. It wasn't that difficult to locate because her father was a very high-ranking officer, a major general,' she paused.

'Carry on, don't leave me in suspense.'

'Major General Forrester committed suicide three years ago. The local newspaper reports that he was found hanging in the garage by his younger son. There's no reason that I can find as to why he did it. It just gives an account of his life, how well respected he was, committed to his job, staunch member of the local community, a devoted father and husband etc. A dreadful shock to everyone and apparently totally out of character. He had two sons. The name you gave me was the youngest son, Drew. Titty was the youngest; she was the one who found him.'

'Jesus, poor Titty.'

'Wait, there's more. In a later article, it says that the youngest son disappeared the day before the funeral and hasn't been seen since. The family are extremely concerned for his safety and the police would be grateful for any information regarding his whereabouts.'

'My God, I wonder what the hell happened? What on earth made him vanish like that?' Drew paced the room. 'It doesn't bear thinking about. Listen, Fran, not a word to anyone about this, I'll tell Elliot and Saul, of course, but nothing to Jason or Corey.'

''Course not, Drew, I wouldn't dream of it. Neither Jason nor Corey have any idea you asked me to find out about anything, which is why I wanted to come in early.'

'Thanks Fran, really appreciate all this, you're a bloody good investigative journalist. Did the other interviews go OK?'

'Yeah, I think we got some great stories, I certainly did. I haven't heard all about Jason's interviews yet, we're swapping notes over coffee this morning.'

'I'll be real interested to hear what they all said. Give me a ring and we can organise to meet up, maybe this afternoon?'

Drew felt the need for some fresh air. Throwing the window wide open, he leant outside and breathed deeply. That kid must have been through hell and back. What on earth could have happened to make her miss her father's funeral? He hadn't known Titty for very long, but she didn't strike him as the running away sort. She was spirited and strong, someone who would face up to things rather than shy away from them. Something very bad must have happened. He felt powerless. There was nothing that he could do other than keep a close eye on her and ask the other two to do the same.

He refilled his coffee mug and resisted the temptation to spice it up with cognac. He had a lot to do today. Someone had donated a load of paint to the homeless centre where Saul worked as a volunteer and today was the day they planned to decorate. He and Elliot had promised that they would lend a hand transforming the drab dining room into something more cheerful. Gone would be the grey walls and in their place a vibrant yellow and purple. Not necessarily a match made in heaven but, as Saul said, beggars could not be choosers.

He had another meeting with Chantal to finalise arrangements for the show next week and now he'd promised to meet up with Fran and Jason. He was looking forward to that; he was curious to see what information they had gathered and who had revealed what.

They wouldn't have had any problems with Diana Dross. She was the drag queen Drew knew most about. She had no qualms about revealing her true identity. The youngest of five and the only boy, she had been cosseted and pampered all her life. It had come as no surprise to her family that she had become a drag queen; as one sister once said, 'she was the most feminine of us all and certainly the most beautiful'. At every opportunity she had begged her sisters to dress her up and would choreograph and perform her own routines to anyone willing to watch. The only thing that held her back from fame, fortune and a career in musicals was a voice like a frog. The life of a drag queen, where lip-synching was the norm, was the perfect platform for her.

The others Drew knew less about. Cherry worked as a telephone engineer, but unlike Diana was very secretive. Drew was certain that no one where Cherry worked had an inkling of her night-time activities. She'd once told him that she only felt happy and fulfilled when she was working at the club, and he'd always thought it such a shame her family and friends couldn't be part of that. He knew that she was an only child and that her mother had died a few years ago.

His own mother was also dead. She had visited the club once with Drew's ex-wife and been amused and enchanted by it. At the end of the trip, she'd said that, although being the owner of a drag club may not have ranked high amongst her chosen professions for him, she now couldn't imagine him doing anything else. She hadn't gone as far as to say his father would have been proud, but she did say he would have been pleased to see Drew so happy.

No one knew anything about Mama Teresa. She was simply Mama Teresa. She had a tiny apartment near Chinatown. She sometimes invited him in for a coffee when he gave her a lift after the late Saturday-night show. He imagined that she must earn just about enough on what he and the other clubs paid her.

Babette was a totally unknown quantity and all that he knew about Titty was the disturbing news that Fran had just revealed. He realised how little they did know about each other. He was proud to claim that they were like a family, but outside those four walls they led very separate lives. Perhaps he should spend more time with them individually, get to know them better outside the context of The Honey Bees Night Club.

The shrill of the phone interrupted his thoughts. He glanced at his watch, still only eight thirty in the morning; it must be Fran again.

'Drew, it's me again.'

'Yes, I rather thought it might be,' he laughed.

'Listen, I came across something real exciting while I was doing some more digging about Titty. I came across an advert for a competition in the UK. It's for the Drag Queen of the Year.' Her words tumbled over each other. 'This could be just the angle you need, Drew. You could enter yourself or maybe you could even enter as a group, and then you could market yourselves as winners of the UK Drag Queen of the Year Award. Surely that would pull the punters in? And we could maybe do another article about it.'

'Fran, honey, calm down and breathe. I love your enthusiasm but you're way ahead of me again. Tell me exactly what the advert says or better still send it to me and I'll look it over.'

'I'll do it right now and then maybe you could phone them. I've just checked and it's only mid-afternoon in the UK. It sure could be interesting, don't you think? It could be awesome publicity, articles in the paper, maybe radio and TV interviews?'

'Jesus, Fran, stop right now, you've gone from nought to ninety in about three seconds. I haven't even seen the article yet, sweetie. Send it over and I'll let you know what I think when we see each other later.'

'OK, sorry, got a bit carried away. I tend to do that.'

'I'd noticed,' he said, smiling.

He would take Elvis for a quick trot around the block and then come and see what this competition was all about before heading off to meet the others at the homeless centre.

Half an hour later he was giggling with amusement at the advertisement in front of him:

'Are you man enough to dress as a lass?

Have you got the balls to shake that ass?

Comb that wig and gloss those lips,

Smooth that frock and sway those hips!

It could be you, the glory could be yours,

Sit back now and imagine the applause!

That coveted crown, Drag Queen of the Year!

Can't you just hear the title ringing in your ear?

Don't cower in a corner, be loud and bright:

Drag Queens of the world unite!'

This has got to be worth a phone call, thought Drew, not only to appease Fran but to satisfy his own curiosity. What the hell was the dialling code for the UK?

CHAPTER 21

Suffolk and San Francisco

Jamie was in the kitchen preparing some tea for himself and Roz. They had just come back from a day in London. The work had been mind-numbingly dull and the capital hot and airless. Afternoon tea in the garden was the perfect antidote. The phone rang as he was buttering toast, licking his fingers he reached for the receiver.

'Hi.'

'Hi there, is that Jamie Forsyth?' The voice was American.

'If you're a film director, the answer is yes. If you're the taxman, then I've never heard of him.'

'Well, I'm neither,' Drew chuckled. 'My name is Drew Berry and I run The Honey Bees Night Club in San Francisco. I just read your advertisement for the Drag Queen of the Year competition. It made me laugh. I wanna know details.'

'Oh, come on now, who is this? Great accent by the way, don't recognize you at all.'

'I'm not sure I follow you.'

'Very funny, very funny indeed. But enough now, spill the beans.

You're keeping me from my afternoon tea.'

'I sure hate to keep a man from his drink but my name truly is Drew Berry and I really am interested in the competition. I've just seen your advert on the net.'

'Is this for real?' Jamie stood stock still in the middle of the kitchen.

'Sure is, buddy. What can I do to convince you? You're welcome to ring me back, save me an international phone call. I'll give you my website if you wanna check me out.'

'No, aye, no, it's just, hell, I wasn't expecting this.'

'Me neither.'

'OK, let's start again. I'm very sorry, I'm rather taken aback. So your name is Drew Berry and you run a nightclub and unbelievably you are interested in our competition.'

'Well, that's about the size of it. And your name is Jamie Forsyth and, despite placing an advert on the worldwide web, you seem dumbfounded that anyone should reply.'

'Put like that, I do seem rather mad.'

Fifteen minutes later, they replaced their respective receivers.

Jamie wandered outside, where an impatient Roz was waiting.

'Who the hell was that?'

'That, my sweetheart, was Drew Berry, sometimes known as Honey Berry, owner of The Honey Bees Night Club, a drag club in San Francisco.'

'You're kidding?'

'Nope, this is for real. I thought it was someone taking the piss at first. In fact the whole conversation nearly never happened.'

'And he wants to take part in our competition?'

'I like the use of the word "our", Roz. Finally you're taking joint ownership.' He grinned at her.

'Jamie, just get on with it.'

'Incredible as it sounds, yes, he was interested in knowing more about *our* competition. Seems some journalist mate found our ad on the net while researching another story.' He poured some tea. 'He read my poem, liked it very much, by the way, so your reservations were unfounded, and wanted to talk more.'

'So what did he say? Is he coming over? Is he bringing others? I can't quite believe this.'

'Well I had to be straight with him, didn't I? I could hardly lie to the guy and pretend this really was the biggest drag competition the world had ever seen.'

'I guess not, so what did you say?'

'I told him the truth. I told him that we were doing it to raise money for a small Suffolk village in danger of losing its hall and its heart and that the drag queens were a motley crew comprising a butcher, a postmaster, a farmer and me. Not exactly the premier league, as it were.' He laughed. 'His club is apparently in the doldrums and he thought the coveted title of "Drag Queen of the Year" may have given it the boost it needs. What a bloody shame. It would have been amazing publicity. I can see the headline now: "The Honey Bees Swarm into Suffolk."' He paused for a moment. 'That's bloody brilliant, I should have been a journalist.'

'No one in San Francisco would ever know that it's just a small village competition. He could still take the title to help the club and help us.'

'I guess there is honour amongst queens. He sounds like a decent man, someone with morals. Someone who wouldn't try to hoodwink his public, unlike you, my darling, who have no principals whatsoever. Not that I'm complaining, in fact it's one of the reasons I married you.'

'You're too kind.'

'How about we wander to the pub after this? We can treat ourselves to a bowl of chips and tell George all about it.'

'God, you know how to treat a woman.'

Drew hurried to the homeless centre. The chat with Jamie had made him late but he had really enjoyed speaking to him. Seemed like a great guy and he was sorry that the competition wasn't going to work out. He'd been captivated by the stories of the village and the village characters. They all seemed eccentric and implausible but, then again, he guessed that his description of the drag queens probably seemed the same to Jamie.

Britain held a fascination for Drew. He'd always longed to go there but the chance had never really presented itself and it didn't look as if it were going to this time either.

He arrived to find Saul and Elliot sipping coffee and supervising three young volunteers. Half of one large wall was already a gaudy yellow and nearby a large paint tin lay open revealing a shocking purple.

'Jesus, I can only hope that no one comes here nursing a hangover. Sorry I'm late guys, it's been one hell of a morning. I've sure got a lot to tell you.' He began to pull on some old dungarees. 'Shall we crack on and then I'll treat you to an early lunch. I've a meeting later on and then Fran and Jason are coming to the club to tell us what the girls disclosed in their interviews. Elliot, please don't tell me that you're gonna paint in those clothes, they're more suited to lunch at the country club.'

'I am here in an advisory capacity only. I will provide encouragement and guidance.'

'Holy Mother of God, you really are something else. Come on, Saul, let's get a move on with this hideous purple while Michelangelo here inspires us.'

* * *

A few hours later in a little Mexican café Drew told them the news about Titty. They were as shocked as he had been.

'Imagine being the one to discover the body. That's something you ain't never gonna get over,' Elliot said. 'Jesus, poor Titty, that image must haunt her. Why the hell did she run away, though, that's what I don't understand.'

'Maybe there was some kind of argument?' Drew replied.

'It would need to be one hell of an argument to make her miss the funeral and leave her mom and her brother,' Saul said slowly. 'She must think that for some reason they don't want her there. Titty don't strike me as someone who would run away because of some angry words, there has to be something else that triggered all this.'

'I agree,' Drew said. 'She ain't the running-away sort. Maybe we'll never know. It's not the sort of thing that comes out in casual conversation.'

'Why was she so worried about being interviewed, though?' Elliot asked.

'I guess she's terrified about being found out, of someone recognising her.'

'It's unlikely anyone from her past will read the *Chronicle*.'

'It's a small world. It only took Fran about forty minutes to discover all this. It's actually rather terrifying how quick and easy it proved to be.'

'Ain't no point in hiding, someone's always gonna find you,' Saul said.

'Right, on that note, I'll head off to "Heavenly Bodies" and my meeting with Chantal.'

'Heavenly Bodies? You gotta be kidding right? Most of the girls are over fifty and look like truck drivers.'

'Elliot, that ain't fair. I admit there have been times when the line-up looked unappetising but that was because Chantal was refusing to pay more than about twenty bucks. No one is gonna work for that. She's upped the pay and there are some half decent acts now. Come with me next Thursday. Saul can hold the fort for an hour or so.'

'I'll see. Listen, Joe's coming over at some point, he wants to chat about a Thanksgiving party at the club.'

'Good for him, we could do with more punters like that. I'll be back mid-afternoon before Fran and Jason arrive. Guys, not a word to anyone about Titty, I'd hate for her to think we've been prying, which of course we have.'

'Sure thing. Thanks for the hard work this morning, Drew, much appreciated.'

'No worries, Saul. I'm not sure it looks better but it certainly looks different.'

'Hey, before you rush off you said there was something else, something about a phone call?'

'No time to go into details but it involves a Scot living in a village where the locals dress in drag. See you later.'

CHAPTER 22

San Francisco

'Coffee and biscuits, or should I say cookies? Can't wait to swap stories. Which of us is going to kick off?' Jason placed two enormous mugs of cappuccino and two equally enormous double chocolate chip cookies on Fran's desk. 'They don't do things by halves over here, do they? You'd never get a coffee or biscuit this big in the UK. I shall return home twice my size.'

'Oh no,' Fran wailed. 'How am I ever going to lose weight? Every day I start with good intentions. The other day Drew enticed me with a highly calorific bagel and now here you are tempting me with this. I can't resist, there's no point in even attempting to try. I'll have to resign myself to being a life-long chubby. You start, you had three interviews.'

'OK, well I'll start with the one who gave the least away and that's Babette. I don't think you're chubby, by the way.' Jason sat down and got out his notebook. 'Grew up in Tennessee, lived with her mother in a trailer park, sounded like a fairly tough childhood. No mention of a father or any siblings. Loves country music, especially Dolly Parton and Emmylou Harris. Money was tight, work was infrequent and, reading between the lines, Mum was not averse to the odd tipple.'

'And apparently neither is Babette.'

'Ah well, that's often the case. History repeating itself. You're shapely, you know, not chubby. Anyway, she hasn't been in San Francisco for long and has only recently joined The Honey Bees. She thinks the world of Drew, says he gives people a second chance but didn't elaborate further. When she's not performing at the club, she works in a restaurant and during the day she does whatever else she can. I tried to probe further but she wasn't playing ball. She doesn't work at any other club because she knows that although Drew would never demand it he likes "his girls" to be exclusive to him.'

'I don't think he would mind if anyone worked for anyone else,' Fran said, springing to his defence, 'I mean, he knows they have to make a living. He's not unreasonable. He hosts other shows himself sometimes.'

'I don't think she was saying he was unreasonable, Fran. She was just saying how she saw it. She also said he pays much better than anyone else.'

'Yeah, I heard that too.'

'I guess the most telling thing really was when I asked her what her dreams were.' Jason sipped his coffee. 'She said that every morning she woke up wishing she were a woman. I found that incredibly sad.'

'Did she say she wanted to have a sex change? She must be on hormones already. You don't get tits like hers without help.'

'I asked her if she thought that would be possible one day, and she said not on what she was earning. Imagine knowing you're in the wrong body, must be a terrible feeling. She said that only when she was dressed up did she feel complete.'

'Weird, Titty said exactly the same to me. She said that only when she was in drag did her outside match what she felt inside, but she never said anything about wanting to become a woman.'

'Maybe she doesn't, not all of them do. Drew doesn't for a start. Anyway, tell me more about Titty. I love her act.'

'It originated when she was at college. She was starring in some revue. She said she never imagined for a moment that it would become her career.'

'No, I'll bet she didn't. Where was she at college?'

'She was reluctant to say, but it was an art college.' Fran gave in to temptation and bit into the cookie. 'I think you did really well with Babette, by the way, I didn't do half as well with Titty.'

'I'm sure you did fine. What else did she say?'

'Well, like Babette, she's not been here very long and also only recently joined The Honey Bees. Didn't say much about her childhood other than that they travelled around a lot. She's a bit of a closed book, really, but very nice. She adores San Francisco, says it is one of the friendliest cities she knows, and feel very at home here. She's passionate about art and plays the piano really well. That's about it, I'm afraid.'

'If they don't want to talk, Fran, you can't push them. You got a fair amount there. I'll move onto Diana Dross – unlike Babette and Titty, she has no qualms whatsoever about telling you everything.'

'I'm all ears,' Fran said, reaching over to the giant cookie once more. 'The first thing that she told me is that by day, and I'm pausing here for dramatic effect, she is a gynaecologist.'

Fran giggled.

'I thought that was funny, too,' Jason smiled. 'In fact it struck me as bloody hilarious. She has no problems about her patients knowing that she's a drag queen; in fact, she says in some ways it actually helps, they often feel more relaxed and reassured, almost as if she's one of them. She says they open up to her, sorry, no pun intended.' He laughed. 'I love this story. You couldn't make it up and it just gets better. She's known as Doctor Drag and her patients and colleagues often go to see her perform. She's become something of a cult figure in the medical world.'

'She sounds a real character.'

'She and her sisters loved Motown, especially The Supremes, and when they were playing it particularly loudly her father used to shout, "What the hell's all that dross you're listening to?" hence the name Diana Dross.' He grinned at her. 'Her father is a preacher by the way. He often cites her in his sermons as an example of how different we all are and how tolerant we should be towards each other.'

'Wow, that's an awesome story. It's strange to think a week ago I didn't know any of these people existed.'

'Yes, they get under your skin very quickly, don't they? Your turn again, the mysterious Mama Teresa.'

'She seems real kind and gentle, almost too good to be true. She was born in New York and was abandoned at the door of a Catholic church. She can't remember too much about her early years but it was basically one care home after another until she was able to escape. Some priest gave her a book about the teachings of Mother Teresa and she says they helped her throughout her life. She lives in Chinatown above a restaurant, teaches English to the staff and looks after their children during the daytime. In return she gets free meals every day, and there you have it.'

'I've got something to add to her story,' Jason said. 'I was talking to her at the bar and she asked how I came to be in San Francisco. I told her about my degree and how my dad had once worked here.' He paused to sip his coffee. 'She asked if my parents were still alive and I said yes. She asked if we were a close family and I said yes.' He turned to look at Fran. 'What she said next just broke my heart.

She said that every night she goes to bed and dreams that she is someone like me.'

'You're right, that is kinda heartbreaking. Jason, there's so much going on with these guys. So much happening behind their facade.'

'And we're only just scratching at the surface here, imagine the stuff we would find if we dug a little deeper. I know we're only giving a very general overview in this article, but it's fascinating, isn't it?'

'Sure is,' Fran agreed. 'OK, the last one, let's hear the Cherry story.'

'Again, not too forthcoming. She's a telephone engineer but only wants me to put engineer in the article. She's been with Drew almost since he began; she and Diana were amongst some of the first acts he employed. Apparently her act is about to change but she wouldn't say any more.' He finished his coffee. 'No one knows that she's a drag queen and she's terrified of anyone finding out. Apparently Drew keeps telling her that she should bite the bullet and not hide away, that by keeping it secret she's saying she's ashamed of who she is, when really she should be proud of herself. But she says she's not ready for that. She clearly worships Drew. So there we have it: the loves and lives of the drag queens.'

'The lives and the loves of the drag queens.' Corey stood above them smiling at their enthusiasm. 'The interviews went well, then?'

'We think so. It's real amazing to hear their stories and to learn something about their background. Some of them are real open and others secretive. They're all so different, it's so cool.' Fran had leapt up.

'Just be careful you don't lose sight of what the article is about,' Corey advised. 'Don't get too sidetracked by what constitutes a drag queen, save that for a follow up piece? When are you next going to the club? There are a few things I'd like to chat over with Drew. '

'I said we'd go along later this afternoon, do you wanna come along?'

'Yeah, I may do.' He stole the last piece of their giant cookie and wandered into his office. He was pleased that they were both so fired up about this. It had all the makings of a great story. He was aware that Fran had been less than passionate about some of her recent assignments but you had to take the rough with the smooth and it had spurred her on to come up with The Honey Bees article.

He flicked through his diary, nothing this afternoon that couldn't be altered. He would go along with them, it would be interesting to hear some of the stories and then he could also chat to Drew about his latest plan. He had three big family birthdays coming up. His youngest son would be twenty-one, his brother fifty and his mother eighty, and all of them in the same month. He'd been racking his brains for ages now trying to think of somewhere they could all celebrate together, somewhere memorable. The Honey Bees night club might just fit the bill.

'I'm sure impressed,' Drew said, leaning back in his chair several hours later. 'You got more information than I ever thought you would. Well done, the pair of you.'

'Thank you,' Fran beamed. 'It was neat, we really loved it.'

'The girls were very kind to us,' Jason agreed. 'The most difficult were Saul and Elliot.'

'They're hard nuts to crack, but don't worry, the others are much more interesting.'

'That may be true about Saul,' Elliot said. 'But I'm fascinating.'

Saul shook his head in disbelief and Fran giggled. They were sitting around a table in Elliot's beloved garden surrounded by his exotic plant collection. Nicotiana intermingled with orchids and gardenia. Large ferns grew amongst wild grasses and vibrant coral vine and jasmine crept up the walls. A large palm tree dominated one corner where Elvis slept contentedly in the shade. It was a true oasis and a labour of love.

Corey looked around appreciatively. 'This sure is one hell of a garden. Who takes responsibility?'

'This is my baby, Corey.' Elliot said proudly.

'I'm impressed.' Corey stood up to take a closer look. 'What the hell is that huge daisy-like plant over there besides the orchids?'

'That is a Yucatan Daisy, or to give it the real name, *Montanoa atriplicifolia*.' Elliot went to join him. 'A few initial teething problems but now thriving beautifully.'

'Can I spend some time out here with you at some point? This really is something else.'

'Corey, he will willingly spend every hour of every day discussing the garden with you,' Drew said getting up.

'Drew, before you go, please tell me what happened about the advert for the drag competition?' Fran asked. 'Did you phone them?'

'Is this the mysterious phone call?' Saul asked.

Drew sat down again and recounted his conversation with Jamie. 'So there you have it, Fran,' he said at the end. 'Sadly not the competition for us. He's a great a guy and the village sounds like something out of a storybook. I wish we could help them out. I liked what they were trying to do.'

'Gee, that's a shame. I really thought that may have helped you.'

'How would it have helped you?' Corey asked.

'Fran thought that winning the title of "Drag Queen of the Year" in the UK, and bless her she never doubted that we would win, would generate some publicity and attract some much-needed punters.' He smiled, 'You ain't allowed to print this, Corey, but I don't mind telling you we're kinda struggling at the moment, so any publicity would be welcome. Winning a competition in the UK could have been good marketing.'

Corey leant back in his chair looking thoughtful. 'Let's have a drink, Drew, courtesy of the *Chronicle*. Let's not dismiss this idea without exploring everything. In my experience, these things never come up without a reason.'

The drinks were poured and Corey and Elliot lit their cigarettes.

'You never smoke, Drew?' Corey asked.

'A cigar in the evenings and, very occasionally, in the morning if things are bad.'

'And very occasionally at lunch,' Elliot added.

'And occasionally in the afternoon,' Saul finished.

Drew laughed. 'So, what thoughts do we all have on this competition?'

'They need some drag queens and you need an angle,' Jason said. 'By the way, where is this village?'

'Some place called Suffolk.'

'You're joking?' Jason was surprised. 'I know that part of the world really well, my grandparents used to live there. Do you know the name of the village?'

'Can't remember off hand, Jason. I've got it jotted down upstairs somewhere.'

'God, what a small world,' Jason smiled. 'Suffolk is a gorgeous county.'

'Where exactly is it, Jason? East or west, north or south?'

'It's in East Anglia, Drew. The bubble that sticks out on the east coast.'

'Small world, indeed,' Drew said, glancing at Saul, Elliot and Fran.

'OK,' Corey continued. 'So these guys are putting on a drag show to raise money to save a village hall which plays a large part in their community. You want something that will attract more customers to your club which also plays a large part in this community. Already, we have a common theme.'

'The loss of community is a big deal in the UK at the moment. Pubs, shops and post offices are closing every day. It's a shame, but I think that finally people are beginning to sit up and take notice, like your man in Suffolk,' Jason said.

'Right, so it stands to reason that a village trying to restore its heart and soul will attract attention. Local newspapers, local TV station, radio and so on,' Corey could see the outline of a story here.

'Even more attention if their competition has some real live San Franciscan drag queens,' Fran was quick to catch on.

'So, what's the *quid pro quo*?' Corey asked.

'That they come and perform here,' Drew said slowly, as the penny began to drop.

'Sure, but they're only amateurs,' Elliot said.

'But they're British amateurs, and therefore very interesting. Imagine the publicity if you announced that some real-life farmers, firemen, postmen and so forth all from a small English village were coming to perform here.'

'We help them with their community and they help us with ours.'

'Exactly, Saul,' Corey said smiling. 'Guys, I think we're on to something here.'

'And you'd run this in the *Chronicle*?' Drew turned to Corey.

'You kiddin'? This could be dynamite. We'll follow you every step of the way.' He helped himself to champagne. 'Folk are fed up with politics and the economic downturn, they want something positive, something to feel good about, and this might just be the answer.'

'What do you guys think?' Drew turned to Saul and Elliot.

'Give them a call tomorrow, see what young Scottie has to say and take it from there.'

'Saul, what are your thoughts?'
'New day, new fate.'
'I'll take that as a yes, then.'

CHAPTER 23

San Francisco and Suffolk

'Gina, if a bunch of British farmers, firemen and postmen came to perform at the club would you be interested?' Drew was seated at his usual table in the Paws Café with Elvis at his side.

'Wow. Would they be in uniform?'

'No, Gina, they would be in drag,' he replied, shaking his head in despair. 'It's a drag club, remember?'

She thought about that for a moment. 'Would they be in uniform after the show?' She wasn't willing to relinquish the wonderful image she had in her head. 'Or perhaps when they first arrive?'

'Would who be in uniform when who first arrives?' Her sister Antonia arrived on the scene.

'Drew has a team of firemen arriving from the UK.'

'I don't have a team of firemen arriving. Well, I may have some, but they won't all be firemen.' Drew was wishing he'd never started this conversation.

'Will there be any policemen?' Antonia enquired.' I just love those big helmets.'

'Jesus, you're both obsessed. Forget I said anything.'

'You can't tease us like that,' Gina said indignantly. 'You can't stroll in here and get our juices flowing with talk of firemen and farmers at eight in the morning without telling us more. When are these guys coming over? How many of them?'

'She's right, Drew, you can't leave us dangling like that?'

'OK, there's this guy called Jamie who lives in a small village. The village is in England, although Jamie is Scottish.'

'A man in a kilt. Now I've really died and gone to heaven.'

'Tell me he has a brother,' Antonia said.

'You both need medical help.'

'The sooner the better. Are there any doctors coming over?' Gina said giggling.

'Holy Mother of God, I give up. You're crazy women.'

'Says the man who wears a dress every night.'

Drew hooted with laughter. 'You win. Another coffee, please, and then if you promise to listen seriously, I'll fill you in.'

'Toni made some pecan nut and maple syrup cake. You wanna try some? Sure is good.'

'Sadly not good for the waistline, though. Just the coffee thanks.' He bent down to pat Elvis and reconsidered. 'Maybe just a small slice,' he shouted after her.

Back in his office, Drew settled back in his chair and reached for the phone. He checked his watch. It was nine o'clock his time, which would make it late afternoon in the UK.

Jamie was sitting in the study staring at the computer, when the phone rang.

'Jamie here. How can I help you?'

'Jamie, Drew Berry from The Honey Bees Club in San Francisco.'

'My God, how bizarre.'

'Is it?' Drew laughed, conversations with Jamie never seemed to be straightforward.

'It is. Here I am staring at a computer screen doing some research on honey bees and then suddenly you pop up. Serendipity. Did you know that honey bees can't see the colour red?'

'Actually I did know that. My aunt used to keep bees. In fact the club is named in her honour.'

'Another piece of serendipity then. My wife also has an Aunt Honey.'

'Except that my aunt was called Glenda.'

Jamie said nothing and Drew laughed into the puzzled silence. 'I meant that I called it The Honey Bees because she loved them. She left me some money, which enabled me to buy the club so it seemed a good idea at the time.'

'You lost me for a moment there.'

'I should maybe go back to bed, this is the second mad conversation I've had this morning. I've clearly woken up speaking a different language from the rest of the world.'

'Happens to me all the time, pal. In my case it's called Scottish.'

Drew chuckled. 'There was a point to this phone call other than to chat about honey bees. Why are you researching them, by the way?'

'I need to know if they're protected or not.'

'My honey bees are certainly protected, our barman Saul sees to that. Why do you need to know?'

'There's a beehive in the grounds of the village hall. If it's protected then it may thwart plans to pull the hall down and build a swanky health club that no one wants and no one can afford.'

'Why do they want to build a health club if no one wants it?'

'I assume they'll be well rewarded, someone is undoubtedly greasing their palms.'

'That's what I wanted to talk to you about.'

'You want to grease my palm?'

'Jamie, you're impossible. No, I want to talk to you about my Honey Bees coming to help protect your hall. Take me to your fridge and pour yourself a large gin while I outline our ideas.'

Jamie had almost reached the bottom of his gin and tonic by the time Drew had finished talking. 'Drew, that's pure genius. I've so many ideas I don't know where to start. I'd better run it past the powers that be first, but I can't imagine they'll be anything other than thrilled.'

'Who are your powers that be?'

'My wife, the barman and a freestyle butcher. Who are yours?'

'My barman, a freestyle accountant and Elvis.'

'Elvis is alive and well? I knew it. What's he up to?'

'He's lying at my feet begging for a biscuit.'

'How the mighty are fallen. He was always over fond of his food. Is he still performing?'

'No, he's getting on a bit these days, and you know what they say, you can't teach an old dog new tricks.' They both burst into peals of laughter.

'Ring me back after you've chatted to your powers that be, Jamie. I sure hope we can pull this thing off. I can't wait to meet you.'

'The feeling is mutual, Drew. I'll be in touch very soon.' And unable to resist he added, 'Give the hound dog a bone from me.'

CHAPTER 24

San Francisco

Drew threw open the window and, stepping onto the fire escape, breathed in the San Francisco air. He loved this city. There was a vibrancy and energy about it that stirred him. He remembered how liberated he had felt when he arrived, able to start afresh in a place where no one knew him and no one was going to judge him. It had been powerful and scary in equal measure.

He gazed down the familiar street, his eyes following the road as it descended sharply then rose steeply up the other side and beyond to the bay. Across the road in the Mexican café, Lena was polishing the tables. She was singing to herself and dancing, her huge ass swinging rhythmically from side to side. Putting his fingers in his mouth, he whistled. She looked up, waved and jiggled her tits. He grinned and gave her the thumbs up. Looking up the street, he saw the distinctive figure of Saul strolling down. He had a unique walk, relaxed and easy with long strides. Elliot called it the 'Saul swing'.

Drew watched Saul greet Lena, kissing her firmly on the lips and squeezing her ass. Elliot and he had always harboured a suspicion that they may be having an affair and, watching them now, Drew was pretty sure they'd been correct.

Lena said something to Saul and pointed towards Drew. He looked up and grinned. Saul had a smile that could eclipse the sun; it split his face in two. No one could resist Saul when he smiled. On the flip side he had a scowl that made you recoil. A single glare and you ran for cover.

They made a good team, the three of them. Drew thought how lucky he was to have such friends. He was in the process of miming for an orange juice when the phone rang.

'Drew, it's Joe here. Is this a good time to talk?'

'I'm not sure. I already had two crazy conversations this morning, one of them with your sex-starved sisters.'

'It's about time we married them off.'

'You'll need men of steel, with a sex drive that rivals Valentino's.'

'They come with a large dowry and a government health warning. So, do I fire ahead or ring back?'

'Fire ahead, let's hope for third time lucky. Elliot said you wanted to talk about your office party?'

'Yeah, for Thanksgiving. For the last few years we've been to the same restaurant and the most thankful I've ever felt is when the meal was over. Dried turkey and mediocre wine.'

'Sounds a blast.'

'This year I want to give the guys something special. It's been a real tough year. They've worked damn hard without their usual bonus and I want to say thank you. We want a night to remember, Drew, somewhere we can all let our hair down and have fun.'

'Leave it with me, Joe. I've been wondering what we should do about Thanksgiving so this gives me the excuse to go wild without Elliot throwing the accounts book at me.'

'When have you ever needed an excuse to go wild, Drew? And when have you ever taken any notice of Elliot's attempts to rein you in?'

'What sort of numbers are we talking? Do you want food?'

'I'm throwing it open to everyone. I imagine we're talking around forty. As for food, I'm not sure, maybe just some canapés?'

'Joe, your crew are all fairly young, they'll need more than canapés to soak up the alcohol. How about Mexican? I'll get Lena from across the road to do a special Mexican buffet, how does that sound?'

'Sounds perfect, Drew, I knew I could rely on you.'

'I'll get working on it and we can go over details nearer the time. How's young Bobby, any more thoughts on the wedding date?'

'He's fine, Drew, but no date set yet.' There was a slight hesitation. 'Actually, he's not fine. I don't know why I'm lying to you. He told his parents about the wedding and they've disowned him. I warned him but he wouldn't listen. He was convinced he could make them understand. They're San Francisco old money, there was never going to be a chance they'd give it their blessing.'

'Don't they know who they're dealing with?'

'Drew, I've told you a thousand times. We're not the mob.'

'You belong to an Italian family who own half of San Francisco. I sure wouldn't mess with you,' he laughed. 'Seriously, Joe, I'm sorry. What did they say to him?'

'I think the gist was "the day you marry that greasy eyetie is the day you can wave your family goodbye",' Joe paused. 'His father told him not to be a fool, to get married and if he still had these unnatural predilections then to be discreet. Bobby blew up and said that he could never deceive a woman like that, his father may be able to but he wasn't prepared to live his whole life as a lie. His mother screamed that his father had never deceived anyone and he screamed back saying that even his sister's friends hadn't been safe and that she was the only person in the whole of San Francisco not to know.'

'Oh gee, poor Bobby, but brave Bobby for trying.'

'Yeah, beneath the outrageous flamboyance, he's gritty and determined.'

'He clearly has more honesty and integrity than his old-money family. I take it the wedding is still going ahead?'

'He's more determined than ever now. If it was up to him, we'd be married tomorrow, but I think we'll hold fire until next year.'

It must be terrible to have your family turn on you like that, thought Drew, as he replaced the receiver. He'd never really lived a lie but he hadn't been exactly true to himself. He shouldn't have married Melissa, but at least he'd loved her and had never once been unfaithful.

He'd joined his father in the law firm out of a sense of duty but also because he didn't really know what else to do. He'd loved his father and had grieved when he died but he was candid enough to recognise that he'd been released by his death – well, that and his Aunt Glenda's money.

Saul strolled in to the office bearing a large orange juice.

'So you did understand what I was miming.'

'Only because I can read you like a book. The mime was terrible. You looked kinda serious just now. Who was on the phone?'

'That was Joe. Apparently Bobby's family went into meltdown when he announced their wedding plans.'

'No surprise there. They're the Beresford family, very wealthy, very traditional and very superior. They entertain presidents, they ain't never gonna entertain a gay marriage.'

'How do you know everything, Saul? You never cease to amaze me. You should be working for the CIA.'

'Maybe I am,' he grinned. 'What else did he want?'

'He wants us to throw a Thanksgiving party here for his office, about forty of them. I thought we'd get Lena to cook up a Mexican feast, put on a special show, really go to town. What do you think?'

'What does he think about what?' Elliot asked, arriving in the doorway.

'Thanksgiving. Joe wants his office do here.'

'Why not invite Corey along? He said he wanted to bring his family to see if they approve his choice of birthday venue; that would be an ideal opportunity.'

'Good idea. We'll have a word with the girls tonight. Maybe this could be the time to unveil the new Cherie. She should be ready by then if we get moving.'

'Has she got some new numbers in mind, or have you?'

'We have but we need to get some music recorded. I really want her to sing in her own voice.'

'And she's always been crap at lip synching, so that makes sense,' Saul laughed.

'What about Titty? That might work.'

'What about Titty? What might work?' Drew was lost.

'Titty would be fantastic, yeah I'm with you.' Saul smiled.

'I'm nowhere near you, I'm miles away and, guys, I've had my fill of weird conversations today, so spell it out.'

'Titty plays the piano real well,' Elliot explained. 'That's what Fran found out during the interview.'

The penny began to drop and Drew started smiling. 'I'm liking it, live accompaniment, yeah, I'm lovin' it. Where would I be without you?'

'We often ask ourselves the same thing.' Elliot moved over to the fire escape to have a cigarette. 'So what of young Scotty? I imagine you must have phoned him by now.'

'Jamie's real cool with the idea and he's talking to his powers that be.'

'Where we gonna find the money to fly us all over? We'll have to close the club and that's gonna cost us.'

'We'll work something out, Elliot. Maybe Chantal can open the club in the evenings. We'll cross that bridge when we get to it. Let's not mention it to the girls just yet, though, we don't want to build up hopes.'

CHAPTER 25

San Francisco

It was late and most of the girls had gone home. They'd all been enthusiastic about the Thanksgiving party, as Drew had known they would be.

He'd approached Cherry with the idea that she make her debut as Cherie that night but she hadn't been as keen as he'd hoped. She was apprehensive and still clinging to the comfort of her gingham. Patience was not Drew's middle name but he forced himself to be tolerant. It was a big step for Cherry and he didn't want to frighten her. They'd arranged a day to go shopping and he was hoping that the new outfits and wig would get her into the mood.

Saul was clearing up the bar. The club was empty, as it had been most of the night. Drew noticed Titty sitting on the stage staring at the back wall.

'Everything OK, Titty? Fancy a nightcap?'

She never normally stayed late, so he was startled at her warm response.

'Honey, I would simply love one.' She leapt off the stage, 'You know what I fancy? I'd love a whisky and coke, short whisky, long coke and plenty of ice. Would that be possible?'

'Sure thing. Saul, you heard the lady?'

'Whisky and coke coming right up.'

'Honey, are you particularly fond of that gold curtain?' Titty asked, indicating the shabby curtain that hung over the back wall she had been staring at.

'Gee, I just love the way you Brits speak. Am I particularly fond of the curtain? The short answer is no. It serves a purpose in that it covers a large ugly wall but my feelings towards it are fairly indifferent. Why the hell are you asking?'

'Would you like me to paint a mural there? It's the perfect place.' She ran back across to it. 'We could reposition some of your huge mirrors so that it reflects in them. I've been thinking about it for ages. I have some wonderful ideas.' Her face had lit up. 'It could really look quite stunning.'

Drew and Saul looked at each other in surprise and then turned to look at the wall.

'Well that's the door locked and ...' Elliot stopped mid-sentence and gazed at the three of them gazing at the curtain. 'Have you found the missing audience?'

'Titty has offered to paint a stunning mural there.'

'And what's the cost of a large stunning mural these days, Titty?' Elliot asked sharply.

'I don't know, um, I hadn't really thought about cost. I just thought it might be a good idea.'

'Which it sure is,' Drew glared at Elliot.

Elliot glared back for a second and then shrugged. 'Hell, I'm sorry, Titty,' he said, throwing an arm around her shoulder. 'You gotta forgive me. I'm a little preoccupied with money at the moment.'

She smiled at him but it was half-hearted.

'Let's go outside for a cigarette and you can tell me the sort of thing you have in mind. A large cognac for me, if you'd be so kind, Saul,' he said, turning around and blowing them both a kiss.

'What was that about?'

'He's worried, Saul. He's got the same nervous tick in his left eye he had as a kid in fourth grade and he's drinking way too much.'

Saul raised his eyebrows at Drew.

'I always drink too much,' Drew said in response. 'Elliot don't, that's the point. I guess the truth is, we're both real worried, the facts and figures ain't looking great. It's only you who manages to remain sanguine. I wish I knew your secret.'

'If there is no solution to the problem, then don't waste time worrying about it. If there is a solution to the problem, then don't waste time worrying about it. There is no benefit in worrying whatsoever.'

'My God.'

'No, but close, it's the Dalai Lama.'

'You happy here, Titty?'

'Yes, why do you ask?'

'Sometimes you look a little sad. Kinda lost.'

Her pretty face clouded over and Elliot cursed himself silently. Then she turned and smiled. 'You know, Elliot, you're right. I have been lost, but today I made a few decisions. I've decided it's time to move on.'

'Shit, move on where?' Drew demanded in horror, coming into the garden.

'It's OK, Honey,' she laughed. 'I don't mean move on physically. I meant move on mentally. I've been travelling about a fair bit these last few years and now I think it's about time I settled. I love it here. In fact, I don't think I've ever felt so at home as I do in this city.'

'That's funny. I was only thinking that very same thing this morning.'

'It's a good place to be,' Elliot agreed.

'It's the only place to be,' Saul raised his glass. 'To San Francisco.'

'I'll drink to that,' Drew said.

'You'll drink to anything.'

CHAPTER 26

Suffolk

'These are really good, Roz, really good,' Jamie said, looking at the photographs she'd laid out in front of him.

'Thanks, darling, but take the amazement out of your voice.'

'I'm slightly surprised, sweetheart. I'm not being rude but I didn't know you could do anything as good as this.'

'To be honest, neither did I. This village has inspired me. Do you really like them?'

'Honestly, I really like them. I'm a bit out of focus here, though.' He said, pointing to one taken on the day of the village fete.

'You're supposed to be out of focus, Jamie, everything is slightly blurred. I just wanted to capture the movement and madness of the whole day.'

'But I was the winner of the drag contest. I should be distinct and centre stage, not fuzzy and dim.'

'It's not all about you, my darling.'

'It should be,' he smiled. 'This one of the early morning mist is magical. You could sell these, you know, why don't you think about selling these in the village shop?'

'Oh Jamie, don't be so absurd. They're not good enough to sell. I'm not a professional.'

'I think they're good enough to sell. We should get them into some nice frames and see what everyone thinks. Maybe George would exhibit them in the pub? I'm serious, Roz,' he said, laughing at her startled expression. 'They're fabulous. Maybe not this strange indistinct one, but the others are all great. I love this one of Ollie standing on her head.'

'Idiot,' Roz said, turning the photograph around. 'No, on second thoughts, maybe you're right. Perhaps it does look better upside down.'

'I think we should ask George this evening.'

'We will do no such thing. He may feel he has to say yes and I'd be mortified,' Roz said firmly. 'What time are we going this evening? Did you manage to get hold of everyone? I saw Kate in the farm shop this morning. She said she and Toby would be there.' She smiled remembering the conversation that had taken place at the farm shop.

She and Kate had been standing in the queue when Patricia approached them.

'Kate, my dear, I heard about your naughty little girl running off. All a bit of a storm in a teacup, Hugh said, but nonetheless I imagine it must have been worrying for you. Ours never did that, thankfully. Hugh was a stickler for discipline.'

'You must thank Hugh from me. Apparently he kept his eyes peeled for her during his three-minute walk home,' Kate replied, smiling sweetly.

'The very least he could do,' Patricia said, unsure why all the other women in the queue were smiling.

'As you say, Pat,' Kate deliberately used the hated abbreviation. 'He did, indeed, do the very least he could.'

'You are most welcome, I'm sure. Well, I must hurry, I want to get some tongue from Frank before he drives off. A treat for Hugh, he loves a bit of tongue.'

Jamie snorted with laughter as Roz recounted the story

'Och, that's priceless. I wish I'd been there.'

'It was a moment to treasure. Anyway I told Kate around seven. I wasn't too sure what time you'd said to the others.'

'I didn't really specify a time but I'm sure they'll rock up around then. And Toby is gracing us with his presence, eh? Did you tell Kate it was to discuss the drag competition?'

'Why are you still so against him? He was very charming and sincere when he bought us all a drink the other night. I think you should give him another chance.'

'I just don't believe a leopard can change his spots so quickly.'

'Don't be so mean. Kate said he's ashamed at how badly he's behaved. Apparently he told Fergal what he thought of him in no uncertain terms and has undergone a complete change of heart. She hinted that life's been tough for him during the last few years. She didn't say much, but I think they've had some family trouble. I think it's rather brave of him to admit he got it so wrong and I think you're being very uncharitable.'

'Point taken,' Jamie said, holding up his hands in surrender. 'Tonight I promise to be all smiles. Ollie and Clive are coming with their daughter Liz. Frank said he'd tell Leon, so that just leaves Charlotte. I'll go up to the school later.'

'No, I'll go, I want to see her about these reading afternoons.'

'It's all quite exciting, isn't it?'

'I don't know about that, it's just one afternoon a week helping the kids to read, but I'm looking forward to it certainly,' she grinned at him.

'You know exactly what I mean. I'm talking about The Honey Bees.'

'Yes, it's quite exciting. But don't get carried away, Jamie. There are still a few problems to overcome.'

Roz was right; Toby had undergone some sort of sea change. It was a cliché he knew, but it really did seem as if the scales had suddenly fallen from his eyes. He had taken the rest of the week off work and was devoting himself to the kids and to Kate.

He didn't try to excuse his behaviour. There had been reasons for it, but they were no justification. His daughter had taught him a lesson and not before time. New resolutions had been made, the two most important being to spend more time with his family and to find his brother. He vowed to himself and to his mother that he would leave no stone unturned in his efforts to locate him.

He was walking up to the school to collect the kids but was so deep in thought that he didn't hear Roz until she tapped him on the shoulder.

'Toby, you're away with the fairies,' she laughed 'I've been calling you for the last five minutes.'

'Sorry Roz, I was miles away, totally self-absorbed, something I've been guilty of rather a lot recently.'

'Oh Toby, don't be so hard on yourself. No one's perfect, you can't beat yourself up for ever.'

'You're very forgiving, Roz,' he smiled. 'But I've a feeling that it's going to take longer to convince your husband, not that I can really blame him.'

'Don't worry about Jamie, he'll come around. Are you here to pick up the kids?'

'Yes, for the first time ever. Can you believe that?'

'Toby, stop it, or I'll start to think you're enjoying all this self-chastisement.'

'And why are you here?'

'I want to have a word with Charlotte about helping the kids with their reading.' She couldn't resist a sly dig. 'Surely you remember, Toby? "How the mighty are fallen." Wasn't that how your mate, Fergal, phrased it?'

'Roz, don't rub it in. Fergal is no longer a mate of mine, I can assure you.'

'No loss there,' she grinned to show there were no hard feelings. 'Here they come. See you later in the pub, Toby.'

She kissed him briefly on the cheek before running up the school path.

What a lovely person, Toby thought. He very much hoped that she was right and that Jamie would come around. He'd like to think that the four of them could become friends. He imagined that evenings spent in their company would be a lot of fun; unlike the evenings they had recently spent with Vicki and Steve.

How on earth had he been so blind? Kate had said earlier that she believed he might have been heading towards some sort of breakdown. Maybe she was right, it would certainly go some way towards explaining his behaviour.

'Dad! You came?' Belinda hurtled into his arms.

'Of course I came. I said I would.'

'We thought you might have had to go to work, but we weren't sure,' his son said uncertainly.

'No work for the rest of the week. I told you that.' He could tell by their faces that although they wanted to believe him, they found it hard. 'Come on, let's go and see this cat you've been telling me about.'

'Dad, can Hannah come back for tea?' Belinda asked, reaching out to her friend.

'Of course she can, but we'd better tell her mum.'

There was a pause before Hannah replied, 'I haven't really got a mum but Dad says that it's fine if it's OK with you. He rang to say he had an emergency; some horse what's got its legs tangled up in barbed wire. If it's not alright then I'm to stay with Miss Cornish at school.'

Toby looked down into her earnest little face. 'We'd love to have you for tea, Hannah. Now take me to meet this famous school cat. I need to shake her paw and thank her for having her kittens the night my daughter decided to run away.'

The girls giggled and scampered off hand in hand. They made quite a contrast: one dark and petite and the other fair and sturdy.

'Tom, what happened to Hannah's mum? Did she die?' he asked his son once they were out of earshot.

'No, she's not dead, she's just not there. Hannah says her dad says she wasn't made of the same material that other mothers are made of. Bell says that makes her sound like a pair of trousers.'

Jesus, thought Toby, I really do have one hell of a lot of catching up to do.

CHAPTER 27

Suffolk

Toby and Kate strolled up to the pub arm in arm. Despite feeling drained with the emotions of the last few days, Kate was feeling happier than she had done in a very long while.

'I wonder what Jamie has got up his sleeve now? Roz said it was something exciting.'

'Whatever it is, he's got my vote.'

Kate stopped in amazement and wheeled around to face him. She studied him for a few seconds and then reaching up she kissed him full on the mouth. 'Welcome back,' she whispered.

From the other end of the village, Jamie and Roz were also making their way towards the pub.

'I wonder what everyone's reaction will be?' Roz said. 'You didn't tell them about the first time Drew rang, did you?'

'No, I didn't. I meant to but for some reason I never did. I told George the gist of things earlier but not the whole story.'

'So this will be a complete surprise to the rest of them?'

'It will. From one single, quite brilliant poem, that you had the temerity to laugh at, we have a world-famous drag club wanting to visit us.'

'Hardly world-famous, Jamie, otherwise they wouldn't be struggling,' Roz replied dryly. 'Look, there's Kate and Toby, remember what I said.'

'Roz, I will be charm personified.'

'There's no need to go over the top.'

'I am an actor capable of great subtlety.'

'That must have passed me by,' she grinned.

'Hi, you two, we were just wondering what surprise Jamie had in store for us tonight.'

'A million quid says you'll never guess.'

'Even if I had a million quid, I wouldn't bet against a canny Scot,' Toby laughed.

'Hi Jamie,' he held out his hand.

There was the very briefest of pauses as their eyes met, before Jamie shook his hand enthusiastically. 'Great to see you, pal, glad you could make it. Now what can I get you both to drink?'

Toby smiled to himself. He would certainly bet a million pounds that Roz had told Jamie to be pleasant.

Fergal was, as usual, slouched against the bar when they walked in. 'Toby mate, over here, whad'ya drinking?' He had either forgotten or ignored the phone conversation that had taken place the previous evening. He was very drunk, it had been a long lunch in the city and he'd come straight from the station.

'Thanks, Fergal, but Jamie is getting one in for me.'

'Jamie, the bloody Jock, what the bloody hell ya doin' drinking with him?' Fergal slurred.

'Mind your manners please, Fergal,' George said quietly.

'Toby, stop being such an arsehole. Come over and have a drink with me!'

'As I said, Fergal, I'm having a drink with Jamie and Roz. We're just about to have a meeting to discuss the drag contest.' He knew it would be red rag to a bull but he couldn't resist it. A second later he wished he had.

'The drag contest? You joining the nancy boys? Must run in your family, Toby,' Fergal sniggered spitefully.

'A pint of Adnams please, Jamie, that would be great,' he said, ignoring Fergal and remaining outwardly calm.

Despite himself, Jamie was impressed. 'Coming right up, Toby.'

'Why on earth was he ever friends with him?' Roz whispered to Kate.

'They went to school together. I guess that creates a certain bond. We never really saw him when we lived in London but, of course, when we moved here it was difficult not to. Well, difficult for Toby, but not for me, I've always loathed him.'

'And with reason.' Roz was curious as to what Fergal had meant by his comment about things running in the family, but didn't want to pry. 'The rest of the troops are arriving,' she said, as the door opened.

Fergal looked up from his beer and saw Ollie and Clive walk in with their daughter.

'Christ Almighty, the lesbian's here as well, what the fuck's going on? Is this queers' night?'

'Right, that's enough, Fergal. I'd like you to leave immediately, please,' said George.

'Are you barring me? You can't fucking bar me ...'

'It's my pub. I think you'll find I can do whatever I like. Now get out.'

'Bloody faggot, I've always had my doubts about what you were.'

'Well, I've never had my doubts about you. I've always known exactly what you are. Now, will you please leave these premises immediately, before someone escorts you.' He could see violence written across several faces.

A round of applause followed Fergal's exit. George let out an uncharacteristic whoop of joy and to the delight and immense surprise of everyone broke into 'I Feel Good.' He was soon joined by the rest of the pub.

Charlotte arrived in the midst. 'Why the clapping? Why the singing? What have I missed?'

'George just threw Fergal out of the pub, showed him the red card.'

'And I missed it. Bugger, bugger, bugger.'

'Spoken like a true headmistress. What do you want to drink?'

'White wine, please,' she replied, looking him up and down. 'Apart from the shoes you look almost normal tonight, Leon.'

'What have you got against these?' he said, looking down at bright red baseball boots with multi-coloured laces. 'They're cool. Hannah loves them, she calls them my play shoes.'

'You've brainwashed the poor girl, she'll grow up with no fashion sense,' Charlotte laughed. 'She adores that pink coat, by the way. It's hard to prise it off her.'

'She looks like a pink jelly, but she loves it and that's the main thing. George, when you've stopped dancing around, could I have a glass of white wine for the headmistress and the usual for me.'

'Well done, George,' Charlotte blew him a kiss. 'Evil little toad.'

'It's been brewing for a long time. He just kept getting worse and worse. Tonight was the final straw.'

'I've said it before but I'll say it again, there's never a dull moment around here,' Jamie was smiling broadly. 'It's a mad world, my Master,'

'Thomas Middleton,' George said.

'The one and only.'

'What the hell are they talking about?' Frank asked Roz.

'It's a play by Thomas Middleton. Jamie's always quoting it.'

'I've obviously not got around to reading that one yet,' Frank scratched his head. 'So Jamie, are you going to spill the beans? What's the big story?'

'Are we all here?' Jamie looked around. He could see Jack and Angus at their usual table and Billy was standing at the end of the bar, slightly out of the action as always. 'Right then, hold onto your hats, here goes.'

He launched into the story of Drew and The Honey Bees Night Club and how they could help each other. The others listened with increasing incredulity.

George watched them all from behind the bar. Jamie was good storyteller and they were hanging on his every word. He was charismatic, enthusiastic and full of energy. He noticed that even Edward Hampshire, sitting quietly in the corner on his own, had given up all pretence of reading and was listing avidly to every word.

The very idea of a bunch of San Franciscan drag queens coming to perform in a small Suffolk village was crazy, and for them to want the villagers to go over there was mind-boggling, but if anyone could make it happen then it would be Jamie and Roz.

He glanced across to where Roz sat, watching her husband take centre stage. They complemented each other very well, thought George. Sensing his attention, she looked up and winked.

'Right, that's just about everything. Roz, did I leave anything out?' She shook her head, smiling. 'So, what do you all think?'

There was a moment of silence before everyone spoke at once. Jamie let them all gabble on for a moment taking the opportunity to sip his pint. 'That's certainly got them talking, George.'

'Certainly has,' George replied. 'Even Squire Hampshire was taking notice.'

'Yeah, I saw him earlier. I thought he may have something to say. He hates the drag contest, doesn't he?'

'He's always campaigned against having it in the fete, but I'd say he was definitely looking more interested than angry.'

'So George, what's your view on all this?' Frank yelled over the noise and the rest of the company stopped to listen.

George thought for a moment. 'To be honest, I think the whole plan is preposterous. It's possibly the most ridiculous idea I have heard in a long time.' He looked around at their shocked faces before carrying on. 'And for that reason I have to say that I am one hundred and fifty percent behind it. I love it.'

'Hear, hear.' Frank shouted. 'It's incredible. I don't know quite how you've managed it, Jamie, but I, for one, can't wait to welcome the Honey Bees into our midst.'

'Hold your horses, Frank, it's not absolutely definite,' Roz was trying to be the voice of reason.

'Why not? What's to stop us?'

'Money for one thing, I imagine,' Clive replied. 'Don't look so ferocious, Frank. I think it's an excellent idea. I'm totally for it, but I guess we have to look at the practicalities.'

'Such as?' Frank growled.

Clive laughed. 'Such as, how are we going to pay for the air fares? Flights to San Francisco don't come cheap. We have to budget for marketing and publicity. I don't know what drag queens need, but presumably they want decent lighting and sound and music. This all costs money and I don't imagine we can expect any help from the village council. I agree with Jamie that it would be great publicity and a great way to raise money for the hall, but it would defeat the object if we used the profit for air fares. I'm not saying that there isn't a way around it; I'm just pointing out some of the issues.'

'May I make a suggestion?' Toby asked.

'Of course, that's what this meeting is about,' Jamie replied.

'Firstly, as regards the hall, I think we should get someone in to assess exactly how much the renovations are going to cost. We need to have an idea of how much money we have to raise. I know the village council have organised for someone to look around, but I think a second opinion would be no bad thing. In fact, I think it's essential.'

'What do you know that we don't?' Leon said. 'What was all this talk about a health club? Events took over before we could ever get to the bottom of that one.'

Edward Hampshire leant forward. He was very keen to know the answer to this.

'I don't know very much,' Toby replied. 'But I do know that they were hoping that their surveyor or their architect would condemn the building. I wouldn't go so far as to say that it would be in his best interests to declare it unfit, but I think you all get my drift ...'

'Bloody hell,' Leon said.

'I guess the idea after that would be to pull the building down and build a health club which would benefit, if not all of the village, then certainly some of its members,' Toby concluded.

'The little shits,' Ollie said. 'This was going on under our noses and we knew nothing about it.' She looked across at Edward.

'This is as much of a surprise to me as to you, Olivia,' he said quietly.

'Sorry, Edward, I believe you. I know you care about this village. But what about these other bastards, eh? Trying to pull the wool over our eyes.'

'Trying to pull the hall down more like,' Charlotte said. 'Jamie did you ever find out about the bees?'

'I was on the case when Drew rang me. Then it went out of my mind. Blast.'

'What bees?' Frank asked.

'They're talking about the hive in the car park,' Jack said. 'The bees have returned, they've been away for a long while, it's rare when that happens.'

'And if that hive were protected, then the hall would be safe,' Jamie said.

'It may be safe anyway. It may not be condemned. We need to find out, but it's a good back-up plan,' Toby said.

'Sorry Toby, we digressed, what was your second thing?'

'Let's organize a meeting for next week. I agree that money may potentially be an issue but I have some ideas. I'm sure we all do. Let's mull it over for a week and then reconvene to pool our thoughts.'

'Spoken like a true businessman.'

Toby flushed and started to speak.

'Toby, I meant it as a compliment, I'm not getting at you, pal,' Jamie smiled at him. 'So everyone, same time next week, then. Get your brains into gear and let's come up with some ideas.'

'Listen, Jamie, can we have a word in private?' Clive whispered.

'I'm a happily married man, Clive,' Jamie whispered back, as he followed him into the garden. 'I hope all this talk of drag queens isn't going to your head.'

'It's about the dog we found the other night,' Clive laughed.

'Oh God, I'd completely forgotten about that. How is he or she?'

'It's a he and he's adorable. But we can't keep him, Jamie. He's plaguing the living daylights out of our old lady. She's almost blind and very cantankerous. It's not really fair on either of them.'

'He's talking about the dog, not my mother,' Liz had joined them in the garden for a cigarette. 'Didn't want there to be any confusion.'

Jamie laughed. 'Are you asking me if we want him?'

'Just a thought. I know that you want one and I wondered if you wanted to surprise Roz. Actually it was Ollie who thought of the surprise element.'

'She'll be knocked for six. She's talked about nothing else since moving here.'

'Do you want to come and see him tomorrow? No obligation, Leon says he can find a home for him if you don't want him, but I thought I'd give you first refusal.'

'You won't be able to refuse him, Jamie, he's gorgeous. Carol and I would have him in a heartbeat, but we live in London, we're out all day and we have no garden. It wouldn't be fair.'

'I'll come over tomorrow. Roz has an audition so she won't be here. It couldn't be better timing.'

'What for? Anything exciting?'

'Can't say. She told me not to say anything, she's superstitious like that.'

'Mum's the word,' Clive said.

'It certainly is in our household,' Liz agreed and Jamie chuckled.

'Jamie, do excuse me, but could I have a quick word in private?' Edward Hampshire stopped him as he was making his way back indoors.

'Must be the new aftershave, you're the second one tonight,' Jamie smiled and Edward looked confused.

'I've something I want to talk to you about, but I'd rather not discuss it here. I wonder, would you be free to pop over tomorrow?'

'I have to see a man about a dog, but I'm sure I could squeeze you in.'

'Jolly good. Let's say midday for a sherry? That suit you?'

Jamie nodded.

'Splendid, I'll see you then,' Edward shook his hand. 'It's the manor house,' he added unnecessarily.

'Curiouser and curiouser,' Jamie thought. I'm beginning to know exactly how Alice felt.

CHAPTER 28

Suffolk

'So what are your plans for today?' Roz asked, as she was getting ready to leave the house.

'I have sherry with the squire at midday, after which I imagine I'll be employed as his butler, so I guess the rest of the day will be spent sorting out my uniform.'

'You're not posh enough to be a butler, it'll be the head gardener for you, my lad.'

'Ah well, less money but less pressure.' He came over to give her a kiss. 'Good luck, Rosalind, sock it to them. Give me a buzz when you've finished. I'll cook something for tonight.'

'Go easy on the chilli.'

'You don't even know what I'm going to make.'

'Everything you make has chilli in it,' she grinned. 'Have a fun day. I wish I was coming to the squire's with you.'

'He didn't invite you, my love, it's a male-only bonding session.'

Roz didn't seem particularly excited at the thought of her audition, he thought as he waved her goodbye. In days gone by she would have read the whole play and rehearsed scenes with him. Today, she seemed detached and indifferent, more interested in his meeting with the squire than in her meeting with the director. Maybe she would be more excited after the audition. She would certainly be excited if she arrived home and found a puppy waiting for her, and he smiled at the thought.

Roz drove towards the station with a heavy heart. She just couldn't manage to summon any enthusiasm and she didn't understand why. She knew that Jamie was puzzled and she couldn't really blame him. Acting was what they both lived for. She'd moaned about not hearing from her agent, and yet the moment Jean had phoned, she'd responded with a distinct lack of excitement or joy.

She shook herself mentally. *Come on, Roz; what's the matter with you? Perhaps I've been cocooned in our new village for too long. I bet as soon as I get into London and feel the buzz I'll be back to my normal self.* Cheered, she parked the car and checked her watch. There was plenty of time to buy a coffee before the train arrived.

She wasn't the only one occupied in self-examination that morning. Edward Hampshire was pouring himself a coffee and pondering what had prompted the decision he had made last night. He opened the kitchen door to let the dogs out and stood looking at the garden which had been Beth's pride and joy and wished, as he did every morning, that she was still with him.

He had known he was lonely but until last night hadn't realised just how bored he was. Jamie had a passion and an energy that Edward admired. His tales of the Californian drag queens were amusing and vivid and Edward had been carried away. Like the rest of them, he had felt hugely disappointed when Clive pointed out the financial concerns.

He couldn't really remember now why he'd always been so against the village drag competition. Recently it had provided a focus for him, a campaign for him to get his teeth into, and he was ashamed at how petty that now seemed.

The underhand plans for a health club had horrified him. The hall and all that it meant to the village was something that he cared deeply about. Beth had spent her life there, always involved in some society or other. In fact, if he wasn't much mistaken, it was Beth's grandfather who had donated money to build the hall in the first place. It had been a focal point of the village for so long, and yet it had taken a stranger to make them realise how important it was. He had lain awake for a long while last night thinking things through and had come to a decision in the early hours of the morning.

Now, despite the lack of sleep, he was feeling more energised and happier than he had done in a long while. Beth would approve, he knew she would, and he could hear her saying, 'Teddy, finally you've come to your senses.' She was right, maybe finally he had.

Toby and Jamie crossed paths in the paper shop.

'I had you down as a *Telegraph* man,' Jamie said as they both reached for the last copy of the *Guardian*.'

'I had you down as *The Sun*.'

Jamie snorted with laughter. 'I guess it turns out we've more in common than we thought. Go on, take the last copy, you were here first. I'll be *Independent* today.'

'Believe it or not, I was going to come and see you,' Toby said. 'About getting someone in to look over the hall. My father-in-law is an architect, quite an eminent one actually. He's semi-retired these days, but he still does some consultation work and the odd private commission.

He only lives an hour away. I wondered if we should get him over and show him the hall.'

'Good plan, when were you thinking?'

'I'll give him a ring this morning.' He paused for a moment. 'Jamie, do you fancy a coffee?'

'Yeah, why not?'

'Jamie, what a lovely surprise,' Kate greeted him as they walked into the kitchen. 'You're just the antidote I need.'

'Am I really? Antidote to what? I'm usually the cause of problems, rarely the cure.'

'I've just had Vicki on the phone. Do you know Vicki, as in Steve and Vicki?'

'Never heard of them, friends of yours?'

'Not bloody likely, not anymore.' She was fuming.

'What on earth has happened?' Toby asked, putting the kettle on for coffee.

'She's just spent the last ten minutes telling me that I'm an unfit mother.'

'Did she really say that?'

'Not in so many words but it's what she implied. She said how naughty Belinda was for running away, that I had always been too soft on her and the sooner she went to the new school the better.'

'Did you tell her that she wasn't going to the new school?'

'I did, and she said we'd taken leave of our senses. She said they wouldn't be mixing with the right sort of people and we were selfish not to give them a good start in life.'

'She sounds a monster. Who the hell is this woman?' Jamie asked.

'Wait, there's more. She also said that she'd heard that I had been "gossiping" in the village pub about the possibility of the health club. Steve, apparently, is speechless with rage.'

'So they were in on this health club scam,' Toby said. 'I did wonder. How did the conversation end?'

'I said I was overjoyed to hear that Steve was incapable of speech and long may it last as he was one of the most boring men I had ever met.'

'That's my girl.' Toby gave her a kiss.

'Sounds like you gave as good as you got, Kate, but what a bitch.' Jamie smiled, 'We adore your daughter, by the way, she's a gorgeous wee thing and so is Hannah. Just the sort of daughters we'd like, if we had them. You've done a great job.'

'Oh Jamie, what a lovely thing to say.' Kate threw her arms around him and burst into tears.

'Hey hey, don't upset yourself, hen, she's not worth getting in a state over.'

'She most certainly isn't,' Toby agreed, reaching over to disentangle Kate.

'I'm so sorry. I'm more angry than upset, but she was just so vicious it took me by surprise.' She wiped her nose with the back of her hand, looking for a moment just like her young daughter. 'Listen, I've an idea.' She grinned at them. 'Is Roz at home? Why don't we all go out to lunch and get wickedly pissed?'

'My wife doesn't usually behave like this,' Toby shook his head.

'Doesn't she? Mine does. Normally we'd leap at the opportunity, but Roz is in London and I have several things to do today. Not least is going to meet a new puppy.'

'How exciting. What sort?' Kate asked.

'No idea. It's a stray that Clive and Ollie found when they were looking for Belinda. They tell me he's adorable and that's all I know. It's a surprise for Roz.' He glanced at his watch. 'In fact, I'd better make a move before too long, I've also promised to cook tonight so I've got some shopping to do.'

'What's on the menu tonight then, Jamie?'

'Thai curry, Kate, it's my speciality.'

'Sounds gorgeous. Thai food is one of our favourites.'

'Is it? Why not come over on Saturday night? Roz and I will do a Thai feast and I'll cook something else tonight.'

'Are you sure? Don't you want to check with Roz first?'

'No, she'll love it, she loves having people over. Besides which, she'll be desperate to show off the new dog.'

CHAPTER 29

Suffolk

At midday precisely Jamie knocked on the door of the manor house. Edward opened it immediately, as if he'd been hovering behind.

'Jamie, good to see you. Come on in.'

'Thank you. Do I call you my Lord or will a simple Mr Hampshire do? I don't want to make a social gaffe.'

'A simple Edward will suffice,' he replied, laughing. 'Come on through, what can I get you?'

'Well, you did promise me a sherry,'

Jamie followed Edward through the hallway into an elegant room with French windows leading onto a large garden. 'Wow, this is some place you have here. I've just been to Toby and Kate's. I thought their house was big but it's nothing compared to this. I'm definitely starting to feel like the poor relation.'

'I didn't always have money,' Edward said unexpectedly, as he handed him a sherry. 'I married into it.'

'Did you? Roz's folk are reasonably well off but sadly not quite in this league.'

'It's too big for me. It was too big for two people, really, but now there's just me, it's faintly ridiculous. It was Beth's family home, though, so I'm loath to sell it.'

'When did she die?' Jamie asked. 'If you don't mind me asking?'

'Three years ago. I miss her very much.' Edward hadn't opened up so much to someone in a long while. He was surprising himself.

'Aye, I bet you do, I can't imagine life without Roz.' Jamie wandered around the room slowly taking in the beautiful furniture and the pictures. He stopped by the grand piano.

'Is this her?' He asked, pointing at a black-and-white photograph of a young couple dancing. Edward nodded.

'Wow, she was a little firecracker, wasn't she?'

'Yes, she was indeed a little firecracker,' Edward chuckled. 'It's not a term I've ever used before but it describes her to a T.'

'No kids, Edward?' Jamie asked looking around at the photographs for signs of children.

'No, Jamie, sadly no kids.' Edward shrugged, 'It just wasn't to be.'

'No, it's not to be in our household either. Real bugger, isn't it?'

'I'm sorry to hear that, Jamie.'

'My fault, not Roz's,' Jamie continued. 'It appears I'm firing blanks. I feel so damned guilty all the time, somehow it makes it more difficult that it's me.'

'Yes, I imagine it would. You're not able to be magnanimous and forgiving, you have to rely on the other party for that.'

'You're right, I'd never really thought about it like that,' Jamie said gulping at his sherry.

'Of course in our day we didn't know where the fault lay. One assumed rather unfairly that it was probably the woman, but we didn't have the luxury of knowing. Not that I would consider it a luxury, better off remaining ignorant, I think.'

197

'I think so too, but it's a bit late now,' Jamie replied, draining his glass and wincing.

Edward watched his face and smiled. 'Jamie, would you like a proper drink? I don't know why I persist in serving sherry, just a habit left over from the old days, I guess. How about a beer or a whisky?'

'Little too early for whisky, even for me, but I could be tempted by a beer.'

'Beer it is, then,' Edward said, making his way to the door. 'I'll go and retrieve one from the fridge and be right back with you.'

He's a nice old boy, thought Jamie. Not at all what I was expecting, very easy to talk to and very down to earth. I must ask him if I can bring Roz over, she'd love to see this place. He looked out into the garden where two dogs were lying in the autumn sunshine. The immaculate lawn sloped down to a small wood and beyond that to meadows. He wondered how many acres belonged to the manor house.

'Jamie, I've had a better idea.'

Jamie spun around.

'Why don't we go to the pub for a bite to eat? It will be my treat. I've just caught sight of a most depressing salad in the fridge that my housekeeper has left me for lunch. It didn't fill me with delight. What do you say? It will certainly get tongues wagging.' He smiled broadly.

'I say yes,' Jamie replied. 'I like you Edward, you're not what I was expecting.'

'I like you too, Jamie,' Edward replied, charmed by his disingenuous manner.

Roz sat on the crowded train trying to make sense of her depression. The audition had gone well, as they so often do when you don't really want the job. She knew her reading had impressed the director. He'd already implied that the job was hers. But her best piece of acting by far was managing to sound enthusiastic about the project.

Instead of the buzz and adrenalin she normally felt in the capital she'd felt tired and dispirited. She hadn't been in the mood for an art gallery or exhibition, so had trailed around the shops before giving in and catching an earlier train.

If she did take this job, it would mean spending weeks away on tour. The rehearsals were in London, which meant a daily commute, which wouldn't come cheap and the money on offer wasn't great. She'd promised Charlotte that she would help with reading every week at the school and she'd even contemplated doing a photographic course or an evening class. She wouldn't be able to do any of it if she took the job.

She knew that Charlotte would understand if she couldn't help and she knew she could take photographs any time but that wasn't the point, and neither was the money or being away from Jamie. No, the point was that she really didn't want this job. She didn't want to be part of some tired old comedy doing the rounds of regional theatre.

She felt worried. Was it this particular job or did this mean that she no longer wanted to act at all? And if she didn't want to act anymore, what the hell did she want? Being an actress defined her. What would she be if she weren't an actress?

The pub lunch with Edward had taken longer than expected but had been fun and very productive. Jamie had been amazed that Edward wanted to help out and even more amazed at the rather generous figure he was offering. At first, he told Jamie that he wanted to remain anonymous, but Jamie had persuaded him that the village needed to know that the contest had his full support, and also that people would like to know who had helped them.

Still thinking that he had plenty of time, Jamie strolled across the village green to Clive and Ollie at the post office. Nothing could have prepared him for what he felt when he met the dog. His heart melted at the sight of the scruffy pup that came scampering out to greet him. Jamie knew instantly that this was the dog for them.

He was black with a white bib, bushy eyebrows and beard. Ludicrously long legs and enormous paws contributed to his total lack of coordination. Jamie picked him up and nuzzled him. The little fellow excitedly licked his face, experimenting with his smell and taste until, reassured that this was someone he could trust, he lay back contentedly in his arms, staring up at him with liquid brown eyes. It was the start of a mutual love affair.

'Leon reckons he must be about four months old. He still limps a little from a damaged leg but apparently that will heal. No idea what he is, somewhere between a lurcher and a collie. Judging by his paws, he isn't going to be a small dog.'

'He could grow to the size of a small horse for all I care,' Jamie said, besotted by the floppy creature in his arms.

'I thought this puppy was for Roz,' Clive laughed.

'I've changed my mind, he's all mine,' Jamie grinned back. 'No, seriously, she'll love him, can I take him now?'

Roz drove back from the station deliberating whether to tell Jamie about her decision not to take the job. On balance, she thought perhaps not. She needed a little more time to get her thoughts in order before attempting to explain herself to anyone else. Besides, she hadn't actually been offered the job yet, despite what the director had implied, so maybe she was being a bit too presumptuous. It had been a strange day and she felt very unsettled.

Jamie had been thrown by her early train. Abandoning all thoughts of cooking when he received her call, he'd rushed to the farm shop and bought cheeses and pâtés. If she wanted anything hot then it would have to be a takeaway. He was hiding the pup in the study when he heard the car draw up.

'Keep quiet, my wee fella, don't go giving the game away too soon.' He patted his new friend on the head and went running out to greet Roz.

'You look happy,' Roz said.

'You don't. But we'll soon fix that. Come this way into the garden, milady, where a large gin and tonic awaits you.' He was desperate to keep her out of the house. He wanted the puppy to be a total surprise.

'Kick off your heels, tuck into these olives and get that gin down your neck.'

She eyed him suspiciously. 'Did you get the job of butler? Is this what this is all about? Are you brushing up on your butlering skills?'

'I am being kind to my beloved wife who, from her tense and abrupt phone call, sounded like she needed pampering.'

'My phone call was abrupt because we went through a tunnel but you're right, some pampering is exactly what I need. What's for supper?'

'We have various options. Today sort of ran away with me.'

'You mean you went to the pub?'

'No need to take that tone, Roz, I did go to the pub, as it happens. My new best friend the squire treated me to lunch. It was purely business and I drank only one pint, as George will testify.'

'The squire took you to the pub? Bloody hell. Sit down and tell me all about it, I want to know every last detail. Sit down, Jamie, you're leaping around like a grasshopper.'

'OK, but first I have a surprise for you, stay here and close your eyes. Don't open them no matter what you hear. Do you promise?'

'I promise. What on earth is going on? I knew you were acting strange.'

'I'll be two minutes, don't cheat.'

He ran into the house and into the study. The pup was contentedly gnawing the chair leg but he leapt up, yelping with joy as Jamie came in, and promptly peed with excitement.

'Oh dear, only to be expected, I guess,' Jamie grinned ruefully at the mess. 'We'll clear that up later, little fella, but first let's go and meet the mistress.' He picked him up, went into the lounge, pressed play on the CD player and marched outside to Elvis Presley singing 'Hound Dog'.

'Eyes closed until I tell you.' He sat on the chair opposite and placed the puppy on his knee to face her. 'OK, you can look now.'

She opened her eyes and gasped. 'Oh my God. Oh, Jamie. He's gorgeous. What is he?'

'He's a puppy,' Jamie said, delighted at her reaction.

'I know he's a puppy but what's he doing here? Is he ours?'

Jamie nodded.

Roz reached out for the puppy. 'Oh, you're just too cute for words. Look at you, with your big brown eyes and funny white bib. He looks like he's wearing the butler uniform you thought you'd be trying on, Jamie.'

'Butler, that's a good name for him. Butler, yeah, I like that.'

'Where did he come from?'

'He's the dog that Clive and Ollie found the night we were searching for Belinda. He'd been put in a plastic bag and dumped on the side of the road. I know, hard to believe, isn't it?'

'And he's really ours? Don't they don't want him?'

'Their dog is old and cranky and can't cope with a youngster. He's really ours if we want him. '

'Of course we want him, who wouldn't want him? He's the most adorable thing I've ever seen.' And she burst into noisy tears. Butler leapt from her lap and went to take refuge behind Jamie.

'Hey sweetheart, don't cry. Roz, darling, don't get so upset, what's up?'

'I can't go on tour now,' she wailed. 'That's final. This is the last straw.'

'What are you talking about? Of course, you can go on tour. I can look after Butler. What do you mean this is the last straw?'

'I mean this is another reason not to go.'

'Shush, sweetheart it's alright, everything's alright.' Tears were streaming down her face and she was shaking. Jamie held her tightly. He had no idea what had prompted this outburst but something had clearly rattled her. He kissed the top of her head.

'It's not alright,' she gulped. 'You don't understand, I don't want to go on tour.'

'Well, if you don't want to go then don't go.' Jamie was at a loss.

'It's not as simple as that.'

'Why is it not simple?.'

'Why don't I want to go on tour? What's the matter with me?'

'First things first. Have you been offered the job?

'Not in so many words. But I think I will be.'

'Right, so at the moment you're getting all wound up over something that may not happen. And even if it does … no, let me finish. Even if you do get offered the job, you don't have to accept it if you don't want to. Either way, it's not a problem.'

'Everything's always so black and white with you, Jamie. It's not that straightforward.'

'Sometimes it is, Roz, sometimes you just overcomplicate things. It's best to start with black and white before you move onto the colour.' He hugged her. 'Right, I'm going to feed Butler. Clive and Ollie gave me some puppy food.' He smiled at her. 'Happy with the name Butler?'

'Happy with the name, happy with the dog, just unhappy with myself.'

'Well, don't be.'

The phone rang just as he went into the kitchen. 'Hi, Jamie here.'

'Hi Jamie, it's Drew. I'm guessing it's gin and tonic time?'

'Pouring the second large one as we speak.'

'I love it that you're so predictable.'

'Trust me, Drew, nothing about today has been predictable. Oh no, no don't do that,' he cried as Butler peed against the table leg.

'Everything OK?' Drew asked.

'I'll have to ring you back, Drew. It's not a great time, my wife is having a breakdown in the garden and Butler has just peed on the kitchen floor. On the plus side, everyone loved your idea, a few monetary problems to sort out but the squire has given us the thumbs up, so I think it's all systems go. Council of war meeting here on Saturday night.'

There was a moment of silence as Drew struggled with the image of a butler pissing on the kitchen floor while the squire held his thumbs up.

'Are you like this all the time, Jamie, or do you put on this act for me?'

'All will be revealed, Drew. I'll call later.'

'That was Drew on the phone and I'm afraid that Butler has disgraced himself on the table leg.' Jamie announced as he walked back outside with the drinks.

'Yes, so I gathered.' Roz was looking much calmer. 'What was that I heard about Saturday night?'

'You may want to take a deep breath, Roz. I'm afraid I got carried away and invited a few people over for a Thai meal.'

'How many people?'

'It started with Toby and Kate. Originally it was going to be just the four of us, but then I kept bumping into people. After Kate and Toby I saw Edward and then we went to the pub and I saw Clive and Ollie and …'

'Cut to the chase, Jamie, how many?'

'Fourteen,' he said.

'Butler, could you live up to your name by then?' she asked, as the large pup came trotting out of the kitchen. He lolloped over to her and licked her hand, pleased that the sobs had subsided.

'I'll take that as a yes, then,' Roz patted his head and smiled.

CHAPTER 30

San Francisco and Suffolk

Joe stared wide-eyed at Elliot. 'Well if that don't beat all. Only you three could come up with a madcap idea like this.' He chuckled.

'Don't go putting me in that bracket, I had nothing to do with it.'

'Drew may have had the initial idea but he wouldn't go ahead without the full agreement of you and Saul.'

'So you think it's nuts, then?'

'Sure, I think it's nuts. I think it's insane and therefore very likely to work. The craziest ideas are often the ones that work best. When exactly is it all taking place?'

'Who knows? There's a lot of things to be sorted out before then. One of which is how the hell are we gonna finance a trip over to the UK?'

'How are they financing it their end?' Joe enquired. 'Are you gonna have to pay for their guys to come out here?'

'I don't know but I sure hope not. Drew's gonna have another long talk with Jamie. He said he couldn't understand the last conversation, it was all about squires and butlers, but the general gist was that it was going ahead.'

'You're kidding me, right? Squires and butlers. Just wait till Bobby hears about this.' Joe finished his coffee. 'He already believes that England is a cross between P.G. Wodehouse and Agatha Christie and this will confirm it. We may just have to come along for the ride.'

'Is he alright?' Elliot asked, motioning to the waiter for more coffee. 'Drew told me about his folks. Poor Bobby, I know how he feels, my mother was an absolute monster.'

'Was she? I never knew that, you never said.'

'I try not to talk about her or even think about her very much. No, I'm serious,' he said as Joe began to smile. 'She made my life hell. She was evil personified. I'm not kidding.'

'Sorry to hear that, buddy,' Joe said, gently taking his hand, disturbed to see the haunted look in Elliot's eyes.

'Water under the bridge now. Bobby's lucky he's got you, I was lucky I had Drew.' Elliot shook his head. 'OK, let's move onto a pleasanter topic. Have you seen our article in the *Chronicle*?'

'Sure have, and it's excellent, those two kids have done a great job. I showed it to the guys in the office, they think it's awesome, and can't wait to have Thanksgiving there. You must all be pleased, should be good publicity.'

'Hope so. We sure as hell need it. In fact Corey is coming over with Fran and Jason later on this afternoon to talk about the next piece, well, that's what he says, personally I just think he wants so look at my garden.'

'And he thinks this British venture is a good idea?'

'One hundred percent. He says it's a great story and just the sort of thing the public want. He's the newspaper man, so if he says it's cool then I guess it's cool.' Elliot shrugged, 'I'm not entirely convinced but everyone else seems to be so let's hope they're right.'

'I think Corey is smart,' Joe said slowly. 'It's a good story and if the articles continue to be as interesting as this then it could be the saving of The Honey Bees. I'm betting that already you'll see a few fresh faces in the club.'

'I'll drink to that,' Elliot raised his coffee mug. 'Will you be up for lunch next week? Will things in the office have calmed down by then? Coffee and muffins ain't really a substitute for wine and pasta.'

'Lunch next week for sure,' Joe smiled. 'I may even drop by later on, we need to talk money for Thanksgiving.'

'Music to my ears.'

Roz heard the phone while she was in the garden playing with Butler. She hurtled into the kitchen, took a deep breath and picked up the receiver.

'Hello,' she said hesitantly.

'Hi there,' a deep American voice replied. 'I guess you must be Roz. It's Drew Berry here from The Honey Bees in San Francisco.'

'Oh, Drew, how wonderful to hear from you. I thought you may be my agent, I'm so glad you aren't.'

'Well, sweetie, I feel a little offended, I'm sure I would make a great agent.'

'I'm sure you would too,' Roz laughed. 'Better than mine probably, no, actually that's not fair, my agent is a lovely lady and has looked after me very well for many years.'

'So why don't you want to speak to her?'

'Because I'm going to have to tell her that I'm turning down a job I've just been offered. In fact I'm going to have to tell her that I may be about to turn my back on my whole acting career and it's not going to be an easy conversation.'

'And why are you turning your back on your acting career?'

'Drew, I'm not really sure. It just doesn't feel like something I want to do right now, but I'm not really sure what it is I *do* want to do and I'm not really sure how to explain that to my agent.'

'Why do you have to explain yourself, Roz? It's your life, it's your decision and if you don't want to do it then you don't have to do it.'

'You sound just like Jamie. It must be a man thing, you make it sound so simple whereas I agonise for hours over it.'

'If your mind is made up, then there's no point in agonising.'

'That's the trouble, you see, I think that my mind is made up, in fact I'm almost sure, but then I think that maybe I should give it one more shot. Jamie wants us to go to Los Angeles, I was offered a part in a film there once and he thinks I should see if anyone remembers me.'

'If that's gonna help clarify your decision then go with that. You only live life once, you gotta be sure to get the most out of it.'

'I can see why Jamie always comes off the phone smiling, you're a great person to talk to, Drew.'

'He always comes off the phone smiling because he's been drinking gin and tonic.'

'Maybe that's what I need right now, some Dutch courage before Jean rings.'

'Always works for me,' Drew smiled. 'Is Jamie around, Roz?'

'Drew, I'm so sorry. I've been rabbiting on about things that cannot possibly interest you, costing you an absolute fortune on the phone and, no, Jamie isn't here. He's with an architect looking around the village hall. Shall I get him to ring you back?'

'It's been a pleasure talking to you, Roz. You, your husband and your village fascinate me. Tell Jamie I'll ring back another time. I was only phoning to chat and to see what the latest news was. He had to rush off last time, something about your butler peeing?'

'Yes, I'm afraid there've been quite a few accidents. He's not house-trained yet, but I'm sure it won't take too long.' There was a pause at the other end.

'Drew?' Roz giggled. 'You do know that Butler is a dog, don't you?'

'I'm mighty relieved to hear that, Roz.'

'You can't seriously have thought that Butler was a person?'

'Hard to know what to think with you two. Anything seems possible. For all I know everyone in your mad village could have a butler.'

'No one in our village has a butler, Drew.' She laughed, 'It may have become more middle-class in the last few years but trust me no one has servants. Not even the local squire.'

'Ah yes, he was someone else who Jamie mentioned, something about giving us the thumbs up.'

'He's been a staunch supporter of the anti-drag campaign for years but somehow Jamie has managed to get him on board and he's now our new best friend, which is great news as he's the big cheese in the village.'

'I think your husband could convert the Pope to paganism if he had a mind to,' Drew grinned. 'Anyway I'll get off the phone in case your agent is trying to ring, good luck with everything and speak soon.'

'Bye, Drew, great to talk to you.'

She was just walking out of the door when the phone rang. Once again, she took a deep breath and picked up the receiver.

'Hello.'

'Roz, it's Drew again.'

'Hello, Drew again.'

'I've had a brainwave. When you come to Los Angeles, you must come to San Francisco. It's just down the road.'

'I had no idea they were so close. How long would it take?'

'A one-hour flight or an eight-hour drive. What do you think?'

'You have the audacity to call us mad and yet you think an eight-hour drive is just down the road. I love the idea, it's certainly something worth thinking about.'

'Great, well think about it and then book it. Bye again.'

This time she was halfway through mixing her drink when the phone rang.

'Hello.'

'Another brainwave.'

'Drew, you're making me a nervous wreck, this is the third time that I've thought you were my agent.'

'Sorry honey, this will be the last time, I promise. Have you thought about dates for Los Angeles?'

'Not in the few seconds since your last call.'

'What do you think about Thanksgiving?'

'I don't think about it that often, Drew. In fact I don't think about it at all, should I?'

'Yes, you should, because that's when you should come over to San Francisco. We're having the mother of all parties here at the club and it's vital that you and Jamie be present. Talk to Jamie and let me know what you think. Bye.'

Another transatlantic phone conversation was also taking place that day. Jason was talking to his father in London, eager to hear what he thought of the article he had emailed to him.

'It's great, Jay,' he was saying. 'I'm impressed, it's witty, sharp and well-written. It would have been all too easy to have taken the piss but you haven't, you've made it very real and thought-provoking.'

'What do you think about the interviews?' Jason was delighted with the praise.

'Fascinating, they're all fascinating, especially the ones who won't reveal anything. And I tell you what I really loved,' he paused, and Jamie could imagine him reaching for his pipe. 'I loved the social comment about how society should take responsibility for the shame some people feel about who they are.'

'I can't take much credit for that bit,' Jason admitted. 'That was Fran. In fact this whole article came about because of Fran. She's really very good.'

'She obviously has a nose for a good story. You've worked well together, though, and sometimes that's not easy, one person usually wants to grab the limelight.'

'I guess she got the lion's share, which was fair because it was her story to begin with. She was the one who first met Honey.'

'He sounds an amazing character. I'm tempted to leap on a plane and come and see for myself.'

'Strangely enough they're planning a trip to the UK, and even more bizarrely it's in a village somewhere not far from where Gran and Grandpa lived. Just wait till you hear this, Dad, this is crazy.' Jason proceeded to tell his father about the fundraising idea.

'I love it, I just love it.' His dad was laughing when he'd finished. 'It's unbelievable, and the *Chronicle* is going to cover the whole story?'

'That's what they say.'

'I'll definitely come to the village, wherever it is, but I'm still tempted to come to San Francisco. If only your sister would hurry up and have her baby. Your mother will never allow me to leave the country before the birth of the century.'

'Who are you trying to kid?' Jason laughed. 'You're every bit as excited as Mum. You'd never dream of leaving the country before the birth.'

'Guilty as charged.'

'How are they all?'

'Fine, just fine. They miss you. We all miss you.'

'I miss you all, too, give them my love and tell them I'll see them at Christmas.' He waved at Fran who was loitering outside. 'Bye, Dad, and let me know the instant the baby arrives.'

'It'll be headline news, son, trust me. Take care, and well done again.'

'You look like the cat that got the cream,' Fran said, plonking a coffee in front of him.

'That was my dad. He loved the article, although I have to say that the bits he singled out for special praise were the bits you had done, which was a touch galling.'

'He's obviously a man of great intelligence who knows his stuff.'

'Actually, he is.'

'You're clearly very close. His praise must mean a lot to you.'

'It does, especially as it's not easily come by.'

'Whose baby is arriving?'

'My sister Sasha's, actually she's my twin sister.'

'You have a twin? How fantastic. Are you identical?'

'There is one major difference,' Jason smiled. 'In that, she's ready to pop any minute.'

'Terrible expression.' Fran shuddered.

'Yes, I agree,' Jason said. 'I don't know why I used it. But you get the general picture.'

'Is it her first child?'

'Yes, it's her first child, their first grandchild and my first nephew or niece. We're all idiotically excited about it.'

'How lovely to have such a close-knit family.'

'Not the case with you then?'

'Not the case with me.' She changed the subject. 'I just met Corey, he says he's going over to The Honey Bees later this afternoon and would we like to go with him and talk about our follow-up piece?'

'I certainly would. I'm buzzing with ideas.'

'Me too,' she smiled broadly at him.

God, she has a gorgeous smile, he thought to himself, as he grudgingly turned back to his computer.

I must stop grinning like a bloody baboon every time he speaks to me, she thought to herself, as she reluctantly left the room.

CHAPTER 31

Suffolk and San Francisco

Toby stood silently in the doorway watching Kate prepare the evening meal. He still couldn't believe how forgiving she had been and he uttered up a silent prayer of gratitude to whoever was looking down. It frightened him when he thought of how close he had come to losing them all. How close he had come to losing himself.

'I'm going into the office tomorrow, why don't you bring the kids up to London after school and we can go and see a show. How does that sound?'

'Sounds lovely but it's not necessary you know. We're your family not your firm, you don't have to pay us damages.'

'I know that, darling, I just feel that I have a lot of catching up to do.' He gave her a squeeze. 'I'll go up in the morning. I want to be sure I see Gerry and he has a habit of sloping off early on a Friday, which is just what I'll be doing from now on.'

'What will you be doing from now on?' a curious little voice asked.

'Leaving work early on a Friday, Tom.' Toby looked down at his small son. 'Do you fancy coming to see my office tomorrow and then going to see a show? Does that sound like fun?'

'Why are you going to work, Daddy? You said you weren't going this week.' Belinda stared up at him accusingly.

'Sweetheart, I have to ask my boss something very important, actually it's something for the village.'

'I thought you were the boss.' Tom was surprised.

'Not quite, Tom.' Toby smiled. 'I'm the boss of quite a lot of people but I also have a boss.'

'What are you going to ask your boss?'

'Well, remember when I ran the London marathon earlier this year?' Tom and Belinda nodded.

'Well, I want to know if I can put the money I raised towards saving our village hall. I think I probably can but I need to check with my boss.'

'Toby, what a brilliant idea, will that be OK with Gerry?' Kate handed him a glass of wine.

'But I told everyone in class that you were the big boss.' Tom was disconcerted about this latest revelation. 'Mrs Jenkins said that you must be a very clever man. I said you was clever at work but not at home.'

'Why did you say that?' Kate asked.

'Cos you said he was bloody useless in the house.' Kate gasped. 'Only I didn't say the word bloody coz I know it's a bad word.' He quickly added, pleased at his thoughtfulness.

Belinda looked at them anxiously. 'He didn't do anything wrong, did he?'

'No sweetheart.' Toby was laughing. 'He just told the truth, I guess.'

'We have to go to.' Jamie said when Roz told him Drew's idea. 'When exactly is Thanksgiving?'

'I'm not sure, sometime in November I think.'

'Well I'll phone him and find out.'

'Jamie, isn't it a bit sudden? I haven't even spoken to Jean yet. She may think it a terrible idea to go to Los Angeles.'

'Darling, that's not really the point. If you want to give LA one last shot then it's up to you. We could stay with Seb, it would be fantastic to see him. He's flavour of the month at the moment. He may even have some contacts for you, or indeed for me.' Jamie said, referring to their drama schoolmate who had really hit the big time in Hollywood.

'Do we have the money to go?'

'No, but when did that ever stop us?' Jamie picked up the phone. 'We haven't had a holiday in ages. A week in LA followed by a week in San Francisco is sounding bloody good to me.'

'Well, don't actually commit ourselves, say we're thinking about it. What about Butler?'

'Jesus, Roz, stop trying to find excuses. Someone will look after Butler. This is a perfect opportunity. Jean has plenty of time to try and organise auditions for you. I'll get my agent to try to get some auditions for me. We get to see Seb, and we get to meet Drew and The Honey Bees. I'm going to ring him right now.'

'Great news, guys.' Drew said joining the others at the bar. 'That was Jamie on the phone, he says that he and Roz are coming over for the Thanksgiving party.'

'He's certainly keen.' Elliot said.

'Well actually I suggested it. They're going to LA first and so I told them to come here after for Thanksgiving. I thought it would be fun for us all to meet.'

'Wow, that's so cool, Jason and I could interview them and get the British angle going on the story.' Fran leapt off her stool. 'Get some photos, see what they think of The Honey Bees, see how they compare with the drag queens in their village and talk more about saving their hall, maybe even …'

'Fran, sweetie, slow down, you exhaust me.' Corey smiled at her. 'But you're right, this is good publicity.'

'What are they doing in LA?' Elliot asked.

'They're going to try and line up some auditions, apparently Roz wants to give her career one last whirl before calling it a day.' He paused for a second before casually adding. 'They're staying with their mate Sebastian Cooke. He was at drama school with them.'

There was a general intake of breath. They stared at him in shock.

'Wow, no way, oh my God that's just amazing.' Fran sat back down abruptly.

'Well maybe he'd like to come to the Thanksgiving Show.' Elliot grinned. 'He'd sure be welcome any time.'

Fran giggled. 'Join the queue, Elliot.'

'Now that really would be some publicity coup.' Corey said looking at Drew.

'We may be jumping the gun here.' Drew laughed. 'They only said they were staying with him, nothing at all about him coming here, so calm down everyone.'

'Did Jamie say any more about the actual drag show?' Jason was keen to steer the conversation away from the sexy film star.

'Only that nearly everyone loved the idea and that the local squire, yeah they really do have a local squire, has donated some cash. They're having a further pow wow tomorrow night.'

'Well we don't have a local squire or a fairy godmother so we still have to find the funds to take five drag queens and ourselves to the UK.' Elliot was suddenly serious.

'We'll find a way, don't you worry.' Drew threw an arm over his shoulders.

'It's my job to worry, I'm the accountant. That's what accountants do, they worry.'

'What do you say, Saul? Something will turn up, eh?' Drew turned to the third amigo.

'Success don't come to you, you go to it.'

'These endless life quotes are not always what I want to hear, Saul.' Elliot groaned.

'Maybe the *Chronicle* can help out, Elliot.' Corey said.

'That, on the other hand, is exactly the sort of thing I want to hear.' He winked at Corey. 'Come into my garden and let's talk money.'

Joe and Bobby came in a few minutes after the other two had disappeared outside.

'Hey guys, great to see you. You've met Fran and Jason, haven't you?' Drew asked.

'Sure have, good to see you again, awesome article by the way.' Joe turned to Drew. 'You must be pleased, it's bound to generate some more punters, my lot can't wait to come for Thanksgiving.'

'Talking of which, we have the Mexican feast in place, the girls are excited and we're starting rehearsals for a new show. We've a few surprises up our sleeves and slightly against my better judgement your sisters are on board for extra help so you best warn your guys in advance.'

'Will do.' Joe laughed. 'Sounds neat, Drew, so much better than the dreary affairs we've had the last couple of years.'

'Elliot and Saul are in charge of the decorations although I'm not sure how wise that is. Last year Saul bought indoor fireworks and Elliot wanted to dress Elvis up as a turkey. The combination could have been lethal.'

He bent down to pat the little dog whose ears had pricked up at the sound of his name. Frankly he would have put on a mongoose outfit had any of his three masters wished him to do so.

'We've also just heard that Roz and Jamie are coming from the UK which will be great. It's gonna be one hell of a night.'

'Joe was just telling me about your British friends, they all sound awesome with their butlers and lords and everything, man I sure want to meet them.' Bobby said.

'Well apparently Butler is a dog.' Bobby's face fell. 'But they do have a genuine squire' He quickly added.

'So cool.'

'And this from the boy who has grown up with hot and cold running servants.' Joe raised his eyebrows.

'That's different.'

Joe wasn't sure how but he refrained from comment.

'Sorry to hear about your folks' reaction to the wedding, Bobby.' Drew said. 'It sounded terrible.'

'Yeah well, shit happens,' Bobby shrugged. 'I've got all the family I need right here.' He squeezed Joe's hand and smiled around the rest of the room.

'And they don't come much better than this.' Saul said.

'Where's Elliot?' Joe asked looking around.

'Talking money to Corey.'

'He was talking about his mother this morning.'

'Was he really? Not normally his favourite topic of conversation.'

'She sounded pretty mean.'

'She was a she-devil, one of the wickedest women ever to walk this earth.'

'When did she die?' Joe was intrigued.

'Not a moment too soon.' Drew grinned. 'The funeral was attended by two people, Elliot and myself, and the only reason we were there was to make sure the bitch was actually dead. There was an obituary in the local newspaper, which read;

"One should only speak good of the dead. She's dead. Good." He smiled. 'It's a great line from Bette Davis but Elliot always suspected me of putting it in the paper and I always suspected him. Whoever was responsible sure hit the nail on the head.'

'There was a hell of a lot of excitement backstage tonight,' Elliot said later that night as the three of them plus Joe and Bobby sat out in the garden. 'They're all buzzing about the proposed trip to England.'

'They all looked pretty shell-shocked,' Drew smiled.

'Of course they are. Most of them consider crossing the Golden Gate Bridge an adventure, in fact apart from Diana I ain't sure any of them have ever left the country. They probably all need passports.'

'I think they're all so lucky,' Bobby said. Joe looked at him thoughtfully.

'There's one person who ain't thrilled and that's Titty. Did you see her face?' Saul asked. 'She was sheet white.'

'Yeah, that's a worry. We'll have to work on her. We can't leave her behind, she's one of our best acts.' Drew said.

'Why isn't she keen to go?' Bobby asked. 'She's British, surely she'd want to go back for a visit.'

'Maybe she knows it's not all changing the guards and cucumber sandwiches, Bobby,' Joe laughed. 'Maybe she came out here to escape from all that.'

'Why would anyone want to escape from that?'

'Did you see Mama Teresa?' Elliot asked. 'She became real animated, I didn't think she'd be that keen.'

'Life is a game so play it.'

'Oh, Saul, quit with your bloody philosophy,' Elliot said.

'Not my bloody philosophy but Mother Teresa's.'

CHAPTER 32

Suffolk

Coincidently the next day Toby met Gerry in the lift going up to his office. 'Gerry, just the man I wanted to meet.'

'Toby, I thought you were taking the week off? How's your daughter? Hope it was nothing too serious.'

'She's fine, thanks, Gerry. It was nothing serious, well it was at the time, I just meant that she wasn't ill, she ran away.'

'Well in my book that's serious.'

'It certainly scared the living daylights out of us.'

'I imagine that it would. I remember when our two ran away. Luckily for us Jason left a note telling us where they were going and what time they would like picking up. His sister was furious with him.' Gerry laughed at the memory.

'How are they both? Is Sasha still pregnant or have I missed the birth?'

'Not yet, could be any minute. Rose is on tenterhooks and so am I although of course I pretend not to be. Even Jason seemed a little anxious when I spoke to him yesterday. Sasha's on her own, perhaps you know that?'

'I had heard something.' Toby replied carefully.

'Yes I'm sure you have.' Gerry smiled. 'It's no secret, the father has scarpered. Frankly we were all relieved, he was a complete bastard as this has proved but obviously Sasha's been through a tough time. It makes us all a little overprotective, ridiculous really, she is an adult.'

'Not ridiculous at all. Belinda running away has taught me just how precious they are.' Not to mention my brother, he thought to himself. 'What's Jason doing these days? Is it still journalism?'

'Very much so. He's in San Francisco right now working at the *Chronicle*. I worked there once, in another lifetime,' he said wistfully. 'In fact Toby, if you've got time I'd like to show you an article he wrote the other day. I'm rather proud of it, a piece about a drag club. The story is that they're planning a trip to the UK, to Suffolk. That's your neck of the woods, isn't it? Listen, come into my office, we'll have a drink and you can read it.' The doors opened and they stepped out of the lift.

'Gerry, I don't believe this,' Toby stared at him open-mouthed.

'The sun is over the yardarm somewhere in the world, it's not that outrageous.'

'Not about the drink, about the drag club. This is very weird,' he paused. 'Are they called The Honey Bees by any chance?'

It was Gerry's turn to stare. 'How the hell did you know that?'

'Let's go into your office and have that drink. It's a bloody small world, Gerry.'

An hour later Toby strolled out of the office building into the bright sunlight. He still couldn't believe the coincidence. Who on earth could have imagined that Gerry's son was writing a column about the very drag club who were coming over to their village?

For obvious reasons Gerry had been enthusiastic about the village hall project and saw no reason why the money Toby had raised shouldn't go to a local cause. Funds raised by employees for charitable concerns were matched by the firm and Gerry was of the opinion that the village hall qualified as a charitable concern. It wasn't his decision alone but he promised Toby to do all he could to influence it in his favour.

Toby was over the moon, not only did he wish to redeem himself in the eyes of the village but also it suddenly seemed very important that the lifeblood of a community be saved. He couldn't wait to tell Kate but first he had another important meeting.

He looked at the name and address he had scribbled down. Black's Investigation Agency, a specialist private detective company providing a professional and discreet service. He had sworn that he would leave no stone unturned in his quest to find Ben and he was determined not to break that promise. Kate had suggested that he go to a private detective and reluctantly he'd realised that it may be his best option. Feeling like a character out of a B-movie he hailed a cab and gave the address.

'Jesus, Roz, how many are you catering for tomorrow?' Frank asked as Roz stood in his van ordering vast amounts of chicken and beef in preparation for the Thai meal.

'Twelve or fourteen,' she replied, desperately trying to calculate how many chicken breasts she needed for a Thai green curry and how many steaks for a spicy beef salad.

'Bloody hell, who have you got coming?'

'Well, there's you and George, Clive and Ollie and their daughter Liz and her partner Carol.' She counted them off on her fingers. 'Toby and Kate and Edward, of course, and oh bugger, I'm not sure if Jamie asked Billy. Do you have his number, Frank? I'd hate him to feel left out. We can't talk about the drag show without including Billy.'

'What about his granny?'

'Do you think I ought to include her too? I hadn't thought of that.'

'Roz, I was teasing. Of course I don't think you should ask her, I don't suppose you've even met her.'

'I saw her in the far distance once, does that count? Anyway I've never really met the squire but he's coming.'

'I still can't believe that he's donating money towards the drag show. How the hell Jamie pulled that one off is beyond me. Did he resort to blackmail?'

'Possibly. But remember to act surprised tomorrow, no one else is supposed to know yet.' Roz laughed. 'Now shut up and let me concentrate.'

'Is there anything I can bring? This is costing you a small fortune. Obviously I'll bring a vat of wine but what else do you need?'

'That's so sweet of you but I think I'm OK. Ollie is bringing home-made ice cream.'

'Did she say what flavour?'

'No, I left it up to her.'

'Prepare to be surprised then,' he winked at her.

Jamie was sitting outside reading when she returned home laden with shopping. Butler was digging a large hole in the middle of the garden.

'Take it easy, sweetheart,' she called. 'I don't want you exhausting yourself.'

'I'm reading an article about The Honey Bees that Drew sent over. Bloody hell, what have you got there?'

'Half a cow and several chickens. Have you asked Butler to build us a pond? If not I'd rather he didn't destroy the lawn before the village descend on us tomorrow.'

'Don't worry, Roz, despite appearances to the contrary everything is under control. Butler, come here at once.' The dog looked up but made no move. Jamie shrugged. 'It's very early days in his training. Go and dump the meat and then come and read this article and I'll show you what else I've been doing.'

She went into the kitchen, shoved the meat into the fridge and stopped in bewilderment at the sight of a large collection of mismatched plates, glasses, bowls and cutlery lying on the table. 'Has the squire been emptying out his cupboards?' she asked as she came outside. 'What the hell is all of that stuff on the table?'

'I bought it this morning while you were out. Got the whole lot for a fiver at the charity shop, bloody brilliant.'

She still looked puzzled.

'Sweetheart, you said we didn't have enough plates and stuff for everyone. Well, now we have, see. I told you everything was under control.' Jamie beamed at her.

'But they don't match.'

'So?'

She stared at him in amazement feeling tears pricking at the back of her eyes.

'Roz, what is it? What's the matter?' He got up and came towards her.

Butler stayed where he was just in case there was another outbreak of noisy sobs.

'No one's going to care if they match. It's just a plate, the food's the important thing and the master of Thai cuisine stands before you.'

'I love you, Jamie.' She flung her arms around him. 'It's not the plates. Of course it doesn't matter if they match. I mean it would be nice if they did, but it doesn't really matter if they don't. I don't know what's the matter with me. I just want to get this conversation with Jean over with, I feel completely discombobulated.'

He smiled at her use of their favourite word. 'Sit down, darling, and read the article. I'll make a cup of coffee and then you can ring Jean and have a proper conversation with her. What exactly did she say yesterday?'

'Not a lot, she was on her mobile on a train.'

'Well, you can talk to her later, I'm sure she'll understand. You didn't sign up to be an actress for life, sweetheart, and as Drew and I both said, it's entirely your decision.'

'Jesus, it's beginning to feel like I have two husbands. Pass me this amazing article and make me a comforting coffee with cream and sugar.'

Jamie raised his eyebrows; she normally drank it strong and black with neither milk nor sugar. He wandered into the kitchen with Butler at his side. 'Women are weird,' he whispered to the dog. 'And none more so than your mistress, but keep that to yourself.'

'You're right, this is an extraordinary article,' Roz said when Jamie returned with her coffee. 'It's fascinating stuff. This drag queen who is a gynaecologist is hysterical.'

'The one they call Doctor Drag? It's mad, isn't it? My favourite was Miss Titty Titty Bang Bang, that's pure genius.'

'But what about the one who wakes up every morning wishing she was a woman? They don't say who it is so I guess she doesn't want anyone to know that. It's just so sad.' She shuddered and Butler took a couple of wary paces back. 'Who was on the phone?'

'George – wanting to know if we want to borrow some plastic chairs and tables?'

'We most certainly do. Keep your fingers crossed that this Indian summer lasts until after tomorrow night. We can't fit them all inside that's for sure.'

'I'm sorry, Roz, I wasn't thinking. It's a lot of trouble, isn't it?'

'Not at all, I was just being a wimp before. It will be great fun.'

She got up and kissed him. 'Now I'm going to ring Jean and tell her to organise auditions for LA and then we can go to San Francisco. This article has me all fired up. I'm longing to meet them all.'

CHAPTER 33

Suffolk

Luckily Roz's prayers for the continuation of the Indian summer were answered. Saturday was a glorious day. She was feeling much better. The conversation with Jean had gone well. She had been very understanding and hadn't actually seemed that surprised. Unfortunately she didn't hold out too much hope for LA, 'the industry is on its knees, darling' but was prepared to give it a try.

She and Jamie had spent a wonderful afternoon cooking Thai curry and looking at travel options from LA to San Francisco. They had drunk too much champagne, got the giggles badly and had gone to bed helpless with laughter and horny as hell.

She stood now in the early evening sun looking around the courtyard. The plastic tables were covered with yards of red material over which she'd scattered rose petals. Brightly coloured chopsticks lay amongst bowls of fresh herbs and chillies. Chinese lanterns hung from the trees in the garden beyond and tea lights had been placed in every nook and cranny ready to sparkle when night fell.

'It looks stunning, Roz, well done.' Jamie came into the garden.

'Well done yourself.' She turned towards him. 'Jesus Christ, what on earth are you wearing?' She stared at a strange pair of shapeless, pea-green trousers that tied around his waist and ended just below his knee.

'These are my Thai fisherman's trousers. We bought them in Krabi, remember?'

She was dumbstruck.

'I bargained with the little fella on the beach for ages. I think I bought a couple of pairs but I could only find these. I've never worn them before.'

'Why?'

'Why what? Why have I never worn them before?'

'No, that's obvious. I mean why everything else. Why did you buy two pairs? Why did you pay money for them? And why the hell are you wearing them tonight?'

'We're having a Thai evening. You've got your Thai kaftan on.'

'My kaftan is pretty and it fits.'

'These fit.'

'Jamie, they barely reach your knees.'

'Well I'm obviously taller that most Thai fishermen. I think you're being very mean. I was delighted to find them and no,' he said, correctly anticipating her next question. 'I am not going to change.'

Their conversation was cut short by the arrival of Clive, Ollie, Liz and Carol.

'Wow, it all looks beautiful,' Ollie said, gazing around.

'It certainly does,' Clive agreed. 'And so do you Roz. Jamie, you look bizarre.'

'I've made you ice cream,' Ollie handed Roz three huge containers. 'They need to go into the freezer right away. You have three flavours:

liquorice and toffee, marshmallow and mint, and green tea and ginger.'

'My God,' Jamie said.

'Trust me, they do taste nicer than they sound,' Liz laughed. 'We didn't dress up, I'm afraid. Our figures aren't really suited to tiny Thai clothes. Frankly the less flesh we show the better, but we've bought flowers for everyone to wear in their hair.' And she and Carol opened a box full of beautiful orchids.

'In my opinion a woman can never show enough flesh.' Leon appeared with his sister Jess. They were both wearing brightly coloured sarongs, silk scarves and strings of beads.

'Leon, you never disappoint,' Ollie smiled. 'Lovely to see you, Jess. I didn't realise you were coming.'

'I sort of gatecrashed. I was going to babysit but Hannah has gone to stay with Belinda so Leon rang and asked if I could come.'

'A most welcome gatecrasher,' Jamie said giving her a kiss and taking an orchid for his hair. 'Now what can I get you all to drink? Thai beer, wine or Roz's rum punch, which is probably more Caribbean than Thai but damn good and very strong.'

'Strong rum punch sounds good to me,' Carol said, fixing the flower in Jamie's curls. 'Beautiful hair, Jamie. Why do men always seem to get the most beautiful hair? Same in our family, my brother has thick luscious locks and I have this fine mousy rubbish,' she laughed. 'My mother says it doesn't really matter, given how I've turned out. She's not quite accepted my sexuality as you can tell.'

'I can tell a party is going to be good when the first word I hear is sexuality.' Frank strolled into the garden clutching two large carrier bags. His eyes lit up at the sight of Jess but he went straight towards his hostess. 'Roz, I went to the Thai restaurant in town and bought thousands of spring rolls, I wasn't sure if you had a starter or not but I thought ... Jesus, Jamie, what the hell are you wearing?'

'Frank, what a fantastic idea, I adore spring rolls.' Roz gave him a kiss. 'Let's have them now with drinks. Jamie, pour everyone a rum punch. Let's get the party started.'

'In answer to your question, Frank, what I have on is a pair of genuine Thai fishermen's trousers which I bargained for and ...'

'Punch, Jamie,' Roz ordered.

'Why, what's he done?' Toby asked, as he and Kate arrived laden with bottles. 'We have beer, we have wine and we have bubbles, wasn't sure what we were drinking so we brought the lot.' Toby was really looking forward to this party. He couldn't wait to tell them the news about the sponsorship money. He'd been feeling on a real high all day.

They'd had a great evening the previous night in London and he had made the first step towards finding his brother. He hadn't really known what to expect when he arrived at the private detective agency. He had images of a sexy secretary and a chain-smoking man in a trilby. But Gary Leonard had been polite and professional. It had been a relief to unburden the facts in front of a total stranger and not to feel that he was being judged. Toby had left the office feeling happier and more relaxed than he had in a long time.

'I didn't realise it was fancy dress,' Edward said, arriving with an enormous bouquet of flowers in one hand and a bottle of seriously good-looking wine in the other.

'Every day is fancy dress for Leon,' Frank replied.

'I look positively normal compared to Jamie.'

'You do look quite unusual, Jamie, I have to say,' Kate giggled.

'There are not many men who could carry off this outfit,' Jamie was stung.

'There aren't many who would want to.' Charlotte joined the group in the garden. She was wearing a pair of silk pyjamas and looked stunning.

'Charlotte, I shall ignore that remark because you look dazzling.'

'And because I have two bottles of very expensive champagne which were donated by a grateful parent although I can't now remember what they were grateful for. I wasn't sure whether to dress up or not but I've never worn these pyjamas before and it seemed the perfect opportunity.'

'If I looked like that in pyjamas I'd never take them off,' Roz said.

'Cheers, everyone,' Ollie said raising her glass. 'This is bloody fantastic, Roz, hits the spot beautifully.'

'Certainly starting to hit yours,' Clive grinned.

'We're still missing George and Billy and possibly Billy's granny.'

'You invited Billy's granny?' Frank laughed.

'Well, it seemed mean not to.'

'Are you referring to Billy Thomas?' Edward asked.

'Yes, do you know him?'

'I don't know him very well but I do know his grandmother. Louisa Thomas and I go back a long way.'

Roz waited for further information but Edward was giving nothing more away.

'I'm sure they'll be here soon. George has probably been caught up in something, it's difficult for a landlord to get an evening off,' Frank said.

George had indeed been caught up with various things. Firstly a phone call from his niece, who owned the pub, to say that she was coming over soon to see him and have a chat. Something about this phone call had unsettled him. He couldn't quite put his finger on it but a sixth sense told him that all was not right.

Secondly, his normally reliable staff were late and he was feeling uncharacteristically annoyed. On another evening he may have been tempted to cancel his plans but he rarely got a chance to go out and Jamie had been so insistent that tonight he was determined to go. He poured himself a small vodka and took a few deep breaths.

Billy and his grandmother arrived and were greeted by their hosts.

'How lovely to see you, I'm so glad you could both make it.'

'It was very kind of you to include me in your invitation.' Billy's grandmother said. 'I wasn't entirely sure you meant it but this sounded much more appealing than another evening in front of reality TV so here I am.'

Roz, who had been expecting a grey-haired old lady similar to her own granny, was taken aback. Louisa Thomas was tall and glamorous. Her white hair was swept back into an elegant chignon, her lips and nails were painted scarlet and she was wearing an exquisite white linen trouser suit.

'I'm so pleased you could come. Do you know everyone? I'm sure you do.'

Louisa gazed around the courtyard, her eyes finally alighting on Edward. 'Good God, Edward, what are you doing here?'

'I was invited.'

'Yes, but why?'

Roz watched this interchange with amusement. There was clearly some history here and she couldn't wait to find out more.

'Sorry I'm late. Let down by everyone at the last minute.' George grabbed the glass of punch that Jamie was holding out. 'Tonight I'm off duty and I feel a craziness coursing through my veins. Beware, folks, George the dragon is out tonight and he's breathing fire.'

'It's shaping up to be a bloody good evening,' Ollie held out her glass for a refill.

A few hours later Jamie came out of the kitchen and paused for a moment to regard the scene in front of him. Darkness had fallen, the candles were twinkling, the Chinese lanterns were glowing and around the table there was laughter and happiness. Roz was behind him with the ice cream.

'It looks lovely, doesn't it? When are you going to tell them about Edward's donation?'

'Now, I shall tell them right now. I shall make the announcement as you hand out the ice cream. It may distract them from the weird flavours.'

'I have a small announcement to make, too. Butler ate the rest of the spring rolls.'

'Yes, I know,' Jamie replied as he walked back into the garden. 'Ladies and gentlemen, if I may have your attention for a moment please, I have something I want to say.'

'And I have something I want to say,' Ollie leapt to her feet. 'This is a fucking gorgeous evening and gorgeous food. Let's raise a glass to our host and hostess.'

'I second that, Olivia, only without the swear words,' Edward raised his glass too.

'Stop being such a bloody pompous ass, Edward, and please call me Ollie like everyone else.'

There was a collective intake of breath and everyone turned to look at Edward. He looked around the room in silence and then howled with laughter. 'You are right, Ollie, I am a bloody pompous ass and it is a fucking lovely night.'

The assembled company broke into a round of applause.

'My God, you've changed,' Louisa was disbelieving.

'Do you like the new me?'

'Huge improvement.'

'OK, your attention once again, please, ladies and gentlemen.' Jamie was banging on the table. 'I have an announcement to make regarding our forthcoming drag competition involving the Honey Bees from San Francisco. As you know there was some concern regarding money, or rather the lack of it. Tonight I have great pleasure in announcing that Edward here, who wishes to remain anonymous, has been kind enough to make a very generous donation which goes a long way to relieving our financial concerns.'

Kate glanced over towards Toby, anxious to see if he was looking disappointed at someone stealing his thunder. He wasn't, he was looking as delighted and surprised as the rest of them.

'But you've always loathed the drag competition, Edward.' For the second time that night Louisa looked astonished.

'But I have always loved the village hall.'

'Beth would have been so proud of you,' she smiled gently.

'Yes, I rather think she would,' he said, and was not ashamed of the tear that ran down his cheek.

'Three cheers for Edward,' Frank yelled leaping to his feet and grabbing Jess's hand. 'Hip hip hurrah.'

Edward smiled at the group a little uncertainly. He couldn't remember when he had last felt so valued and appreciated. It was a good feeling. He caught Jamie watching him and raised his glass in a silent gesture of gratitude for showing him the way.

'Ladies and gentlemen, if I may also have your attention for a moment,' Toby stood up, tapping his glass. 'I have something which I would, um, also like to say.' He suddenly felt ridiculously nervous and looked across at Kate. She nodded her head encouragingly. 'We have a policy at work which enables employees to raise money for various charities. Some people climb Everest or cross the Sahara. I was a little more modest and ran the London marathon.'

'Hell, Toby, that's some achievement,' Leon interrupted and there were murmurs of agreement.

'Thank you, I won't pretend it wasn't hard work. Anyway the point of all this is to say that yesterday I asked my boss if I could use the money for a charity close to home. There's still some red tape to go through but I would be delighted if you would accept the money I raised and put it towards the drag show to save the village hall.'

'Another three cheers.' This time it was George who started them off. 'Let's hear it for Edward and Toby.' He began to clap loudly.

'Wait, there's more,' Toby said.

'I'm not sure I can take much more,' Charlotte said.

'You'll like this. It is just the most amazing coincidence,' Toby quickly told them about Gerry's son Jason working for the *San Francisco Chronicle*.

'This evening just gets better and better,' Jamie said when he'd finished. 'Toby, I have the very article you're talking about. Drew emailed it over so that I could send it to the *East Anglian Times* to generate publicity this end. It's excellent.'

'Go and get it, Jamie, read it out to us,' Leon said.

'OK,' Jamie jumped up.

'That didn't take much persuasion,' Roz laughed.

'Biggest audience I've had in a while, sweetheart.'

'Shall I fetch the expensive champagne, Jamie?' Charlotte enquired.

'Go, girl.'

'OK, I've done the lanterns and candles, the rest of the glasses are all on the tray and here are the tablecloths, let's leave the rest until the morning,' Jamie suggested.

'Sounds good to me, I'm bushed.'

'Quick nightcap in the garden?'

'Of course. But just a small one otherwise you'll have to carry me to bed.'

'It wouldn't be the first time. Go and sit outside and I'll bring the drinks.'

Roz sat out under the stars with Butler by her side. The consumption of several spring rolls didn't seem to have had an adverse effect on him.

'You must have a cast-iron stomach, monster puppy dog.'

'Cast iron is right. He's also chewed my glasses case and a flip-flop of yours,' Jamie said, coming out with two glasses of champagne. 'Wasn't it a great night?'

'It certainly was. I think we can safely say the evening was a huge success. Cheers, big boy.'

'Cheers. You looked very lovely tonight by the way, you were positively glowing.'

'That sounds like I was sweating but I'll take it as a compliment, thank you.'

'Don't feel you have to compliment me,' Jamie said after a few minutes silence.

'I couldn't if I tried. You look like a freak but your cooking was superb.'

'I don't know what everyone has against these trousers?'

'I'm too tired to even begin to answer.'

'George made a nice speech about us, didn't he?'

'God yes, I was nearly in tears.'

'Nothing new there then,' he grinned at her.

'I've been very weepy, I agree. Don't know what's the matter? Well no, that's not true, I do,' she slurped her champagne noisily.

'Care to share it?'

'It's just sort of everything and nothing.'

'That's made it much clearer, thanks.'

'I'm sorry, I mean that we had a couple of very stressful years before coming here, then there was the stress of moving and now there's the stress of not acting.' She paused trying to find the right words. 'I think that I'm finding it hard to define myself. I always thought that I'd be a mother and I'm not and I thought I'd always be an actress and I'm not sure about that anymore.' Jamie remained silent. It was important to hear Roz out. 'Our old life seems to have faded away and we are surrounded by new friends who feel like very old friends which is fantastic but surreal at the same time and one of the most important people in our lives right now is a drag queen called Honey Berry who lives in California and who we've never met.' She drained her glass and looked over at Jamie for his reaction.

He looked back at her and his lips began to twitch. His shoulders started shaking and tears began to roll down his cheeks. He clutched at his stomach and suddenly howled with laughter.

'Jamie, stop it, I'm serious.' But it was no good, his laughter was infectious and before long she too was helpless.

'I'm so sorry, I was listening and I do understand and it's not funny but that last bit just sounded so ridiculous.'

'It is mad, isn't it? We're mad, the whole bloody village is mad.'

'Mad but wonderful,' he kissed her. 'It's a bit scary because we're starting on a new phase of our lives but we've got each other and that's all that counts.' Butler barked, alarmed at the hysteria.

'Make that each other plus one.'

CHAPTER 34

San Francisco and Suffolk

'Fantastic, Cherie.' Drew clapped enthusiastically. 'Saul, what do you think?'

'Coming along nicely, Cherie, but sweetie you need to smoulder a bit more, move your body, sway with the music. You're looking hot, act sexy.'

'Do you really thing I'm looking hot?' Cherie giggled self-consciously.

'Sizzling, ain't she, Titty?'

'Absolutely,' Titty replied. 'Cherie, why don't you use the piano more? Come over and lean on it or sort of glide around it.' She got up to demonstrate her point. 'It's just a suggestion,' she added quickly, in case Cherie should think she was interfering. But Cherie seemed to love the idea.

'Yeah, I'll try it, thanks, Titty.'

Drew looked at Titty. She really was very talented, she played the piano exquisitely and she was a gifted artist. The mural on the back wall, although unfinished, was looking excellent. And yet at times she seemed so vulnerable and lacking in confidence.

'How goes it, girls?' Elliot strolled into the bar.

'Great timing, Elliot. We're just going to go through the number one more time. Sit down and tell us what you think.'

'Bring it on, I'm all yours.' He sat down at the bar. 'Looking swell, Cherie.' He winked at her and she blushed. She'd always had a bit of a thing for this tall handsome man.

'But then you'll have to call it a day, Drew, tea dance in about an hour.'

'OK, from the top again, Cherie, and remember what Saul said, we want smouldering sex. Think Marilyn. Take it away, Titty.'

Titty struck the chords for the opening bars of 'Diamonds are a Girl's Best Friend.'

'She's very good,' Elliot whispered to Saul.

'Which one?'

'I was talking about Titty but Cherie is shaping up nicely too.'

'Yeah, Drew picked a good number.'

'How is he?'

'Pretty cut up, there were some tears earlier, he's not really looking forward to this afternoon.'

'No, we'll all miss her but eighty-seven years of age ain't bad.'

They had received news this morning that one of the old ladies in the home had died.

Martha Ellis had been Drew's particular favourite; she was a feisty woman with a wicked sense of humour and had reminded him of his Aunt Glenda. They had become good friends over the years and she'd never missed a single tea dance. He had been very upset to learn the news. It had been a heart attack during the night, very sudden but not entirely unexpected.

'Cherie, my love, that was something else, you'll knock 'em dead. The regular punters won't recognise you. Are you going to make an announcement, Drew?' Elliot leapt up to applaud.

'I think that's a good idea. Cheerio to Cherry Pye and bonjour to Cherie, What do you think?' he turned to Cherie.

Cherie, whose real name was Greg, was basking in all the attention. He was a bit of a loner at work, popular enough but kept himself to himself. He went out for the occasional drink with his colleagues but never really felt at ease. He lived in constant fear of them finding out about his secret life. He wished he didn't feel this way, he wished he could be as courageous as Diana and had told her so. Diana had been typically upfront.

'Sweetie, I'm not courageous, I'm just me. I'm not ashamed of who I am and neither should you be. We're not murderers, Cherry, we're not paedophiles or drug dealers, we just like performing as women and that ain't nothing to be ashamed of. Hell, Cherry, that's been going on since Shakespeare, that's where the freakin' word drag comes from, "dressed as girl".'

What she had said made sense but he still had reservations. The only place he felt at ease was here at The Honey Bees. Here there were no judgements, no malicious remarks or looks of repulsion. The person inside, the person he'd been attempting to hide all his life, was welcome here. He suddenly realised that they were all watching and waiting for a reply.

'I'm not sure, Honey. Maybe a big announcement would kinda make me more nervous.'

Drew was disappointed, he'd been looking forward to making something of it, but it had to be Cherie's decision.

'May I make a suggestion?' Titty asked.

'Sweetie, you don't stand on ceremony here, go right ahead. I just love it that the Brits are so god-damn polite.'

'Maybe you could make the announcement at the end, perhaps at the curtain call. That way Cherie wouldn't be nervous, but everyone could applaud her new character.'

This girl is bright, thought Drew, bright and perceptive, and for the umpteenth time he wondered what she had run away from.

'Roz, I've found some for £425 each,' Jamie yelled from the study. They had spent the best part of two days trying to get the cheapest flight to Los Angeles.

Roz came running into the study and tripped over Butler who yelped in indignation. 'You're not a Butler at all. Butlers are discreet and silent and don't lie in doorways. We should have called you Matt,' she giggled weakly at the terrible joke and looked over Jamie's shoulder at the computer screen. 'For that price it must be going via Mongolia.'

'Not exactly, but it does have two stops, one of which is in Madrid for six hours.'

'Jamie, I think we're just going to have to bite the bullet and go for the more expensive one. We're not going for very long and we don't want to spend the best part of the holiday recovering from twenty hours of travelling, it's just false economy.'

'I tend to agree but I'll have one last shot and then we'll make our minds up. It's all becoming rather real isn't it? I can't quite believe it.'

Since the Thai evening things had certainly happened fast. Jamie had spoken to Drew and told him of the latest developments regarding the money; they were now definitely in a position to go ahead with the proposed Honey Bees visit.

The *East Anglian Times*, inspired by the article that the *San Francisco Chronicle* had done, had agreed to come and do a piece on them. They'd spoken to Seb, who had been overjoyed to hear of their proposed visit.

He wasn't sure what his work schedule was but they were welcome to stay in his place for as long as they liked. Drew had said they could stay with him in San Francisco and Roz's agent was pulling out all stops to get some casting auditions.

Edward was prepared to take Butler on for two weeks although Roz had severe misgivings. Visions of half-bitten grand piano legs and priceless Persian rugs in shreds kept floating through her head. Edward had assured her that all would be OK. The garden was huge; Butler would have a ball and hopefully inject some life into his old girls who had become rather fat and lazy.

Jamie told her to stop worrying, Edward knew what he was doing and was used to dogs. No one is used to a dog like Butler, she responded, mentally totting up what sort of bill for damages they might expect on their return.

CHAPTER 35

Suffolk

Kate wheeled her trolley out of the supermarket and into the car park. She stopped with a cry of dismay in front of her car. Both sides had deep scratches gouged out of the bodywork. Someone had obviously gone along with a set of keys. She bent down to inspect it. A car beeped, she looked up and realised that her trolley was blocking the way. As she ran to retrieve it she saw that the person in the car was Vicki. Forgetting their last frosty phone conversation in her agitation she rushed over to explain what had happened.

'Someone obviously has it in for you, Kate,' Vicki didn't look displeased at the thought.

'You mean someone deliberately targeted me? But why?'

'You've obviously made a few enemies in the village. A lot of people wanted a health club, you know, Kate, which you ruined by spilling the beans.'

'I didn't think anyone was supposed to know about the possibility of a health club, so how could a lot of people want one?'

'Well, you know how it is, word gets out.'

'No, I don't know how it is. All I knew was that it was a tightly guarded secret. You were desperate to rush plans through before anyone could have a chance to object.'

'And who in their right mind would have objected?' Vicki suddenly screeched. 'A modern health club with all the facilities versus a freezing, mouldy village hall that the experts say should be pulled down.'

'We've had our own experts look at it and they have a very different opinion.'

'And is that so-called expert your bloody father?' she sneered.

'As well as my bloody father, we also got someone independent in.'

'I always said to Steve that I didn't think you were one of us,' Vicki spat the words out. 'Now I've been proved right.'

'Thank God for that.'

'You better be careful, Kate,' Vicki hissed. 'You, your husband and your damn kids. A lot of people have lost money; a lot of people are very pissed off.'

'Is that a threat, Vicki? Maybe I should go to the police, show them my car and recount our conversation.'

'I'm warning you, Kate …' Vicki began, but got no further as an impatient driver began to honk his horn.

Kate hurled the shopping into the car boot. How dare she? Who the hell did she think she was, threatening her like that? And it had been a threat; there was no doubt about that.

She was halfway home before the shock set in. She pulled into a lay-by and opened the car door for some fresh air. She was shaking like a leaf. She reached for a bottle of water from her shopping bag and, taking a few sips, tried to calm herself down.

It had been the inclusion of the word kids that had scared her. She thought about ringing Toby but she knew he had a big meeting today and anyway what could he do? Taking a few deep breaths she got back into the car and carefully pulled away.

She didn't want to go back to an empty house. She drove slowly past Roz and Jamie's cottage but their car wasn't parked outside and she couldn't see any sign of life. Bugger, she really needed to talk to someone. Turning the corner she saw the pub on the right and immediately pulled into the car park. She would go and have a chat with George.

'Kate, that's horrible.' George said handing her a coffee. 'I'm not surprised you look so shocked, what a dreadful woman. Do you want something stronger?'

'I'd love something stronger but I'm driving and I'd better keep my wits about me in case someone tries to run me off the road,' she laughed but George could see that she was still distressed.

'You poor love, but try not to worry, I can't imagine that she will actually do anything.'

'I'm sure you're right. I'm sure the scratches were just coincidence.'

'Yes, but then again you do have a very distinctive car,' George looked out of the window at Kate's bright yellow Beetle. 'You know what? I think you should go to the police, Kate. They won't be able to do much but at least you'll have reported it in case there's any further incident.'

'I don't know, George. I know I said that to Vicki but it sounds a bit dramatic doesn't it? They'll just think it's some stupid cat fight in a Waitrose car park.'

'I'm not sure. Threatening you and your family is a little more than a stupid cat fight.'

'I'll see what Toby says when he comes home. He's got a big meeting today so I don't really want to disturb him at work.'

'Do you want a top up?'

'I'd love one and then I'd better gird my loins and get back home.'

'I don't think you should be alone. You've had a shock and you'll spend all afternoon worrying about it.'

'I'll be fine, George, honestly. I'm making a mountain out of a molehill; it was just so unexpected.'

'No, you're staying here,' George said firmly. 'Jamie and Roz are coming for lunch. They nipped in to book a table just before you arrived. They're driving up to the woods for a walk with Butler and Edward and his dogs and then they're all coming back here, so you can join them.'

'It does sound nice. But I've got a million things to do this afternoon and all the shopping is in the car.'

'Go home, unpack the shopping and then walk back here. The million things can wait. If you're not back in half an hour then I will come and get you myself.'

'OK, you win,' she smiled at him. 'Thank you, George.'

'Kate is joining you for lunch,' George told the three of them when they walked in later.

'Is she? How lovely, is Toby coming too?' Roz replied.

'No, just Kate, she's had a bad morning.' George told them about her argument with Vicki.

'Who is this Vicki woman?' Jamie wanted to know. 'This is the second time she's upset Kate, last time she'd been on the phone lecturing her about something or other.'

'I don't think we've ever met her, have we, George?'

'No, they rarely deign to come into the pub. They're mates with the bulbous Hugh and his wife Patricia. You know them, don't you?' George turned to Edward.

'I know Hugh and Patricia. He's on the committee with me. He helped put an end to the drag show, I'm afraid,' Edward shrugged. 'But I have to say I never particularly liked them.'

'Thank goodness you did put a stop to it, Edward. If you hadn't we'd never be putting on a show with The Honey Bees,' Roz laughed.

'She's right, you did us a favour. I remember Hugh. He's friends with Fergal. They're all in this health club scheme together,' Jamie said. 'They must have been promised a very nice backhander from someone for them all to be so angry about it.'

'Here's Kate now,' Roz said. 'Let's have a bottle of wine. I bet she could do with a drink.'

'This is my treat,' Edward said. 'Jamie, do you want a beer first?'

'I like the use of the word "first" in that sentence.'

'Kate, over here,' Roz waved. 'George has just been telling us about Vicki. She sounds like a nightmare.'

'Yes, she was fairly ferocious. It just came out of the blue.'

'Have you told Toby?'

'I was going to wait until he came home but actually he phoned just now so I put him in the picture. He can't believe that they're all so fired up about it.'

'Just what I was saying,' Jamie said. 'They must all have lost face big time.'

'Let's forget about them and have a nice lunch.' Roz said. 'We've booked our tickets, Kate. California here we come.'

'I'm so jealous. And you'll really be going to see The Honey Bees Night Club?'

'We certainly will. '

'Talking of honey bees, I had a word with a mate of mine who's something of an authority on the subject.' George said. 'He's going to drop by and take a look at the hive in the hall car park. He's of the opinion that they may well be protected.'

'One more nail in the coffin for the health club then,' Jamie said.

'I'll raise a glass to that,' Edward responded.

'That was a fun lunch,' Roz said as they strolled back up the village. 'How lovely of Edward to treat us.'

'He's a good guy, the more I get to know him the more I like him.'

'I think he's very lonely. He doesn't seem to have many friends. I get the impression that he relied on his wife for most of their social life and without her he's been left a bit high and dry.'

'As I would be without you, my love.'

'You might be high but you certainly wouldn't be left dry.'

'If by that remark you are referring to my alcoholic intake then I take exception. I was remarkably abstemious at lunch, we all were.'

'It always seems wicked to be drinking at all at lunchtime.'

'Well it's certainly a vice that I could become used to,' Jamie grinned. 'If only we didn't have to go out and earn an honest crust.'

'We're not earning much of a crust at the moment. And if I give up acting we'll be earning even less.'

'Don't fret, I've got another bit of filming coming up, we've still got something left from your last commercial, not a lot admittedly, but enough to keep the wolf from the door, and who knows what LA may bring?'

'I can't quite believe we're actually going. It all seems to have happened in a heartbeat.'

'Well it won't be long, just a few more weeks.'

'I keep forgetting that we're already in October.'

'It's this glorious weather, we're not used to it in the UK,' Jamie laughed. 'I can't wait to tell Drew we've booked the tickets, he'll be so thrilled.'

Roz giggled weakly.

'Why are you giggling?'

'Just that everything seems so dreamlike at the moment.'

CHAPTER 36

San Francisco and Suffolk

Roz was not the only one thinking that. Drew was experiencing his very own dreamlike moment. He'd just received the extraordinary news that Martha Ellis, his friend and late resident of the old people's home, had bequeathed him a substantial amount of money.

He sat staring at Blossom Adler, matron of the home, and at Mr Gregory the solicitor.

'Is this for real?' He asked for the fifth time in as many minutes.

'Sure is, Drew,' Blossom grinned. 'And no one deserves it more than you.' She waddled over to the cupboard. 'Feeling the need for something medicinal?' She waved a bottle at him and Drew nodded without even looking to see what it was. 'Always keep something in the office for emergencies, although it's usually grieving relatives.' Blossom looked over towards Mr. Gregory enquiringly,

'No, not for me, thank you all the same.'

'You deserve it more than me.' Drew announced. 'We must share this.'

'Typical of your generosity, Drew, but Martha didn't forget us either.'

'I just had no idea that she was so rich.' Drew shook his head and knocked back his drink. 'What about family? Doesn't she have any family?'

'You were her family, Drew, you and Elliot and Saul. You meant the world to her.'

Half an hour later back at the club Drew sat in front of his two astounded business partners.

'Eighty thousand?' Elliot stared at Drew

'Eighty thousand,' Drew confirmed.

'Eighty thousand?' Saul echoed. 'Eighty thousand bloody dollars.'

They all sat and stared at each other in complete silence for a couple of minutes before Elliot leapt to his feet with a loud war cry.

'Martha Ellis, you little beauty.' He punched the air and danced around the room whooping with joy. Drew and Saul immediately joined him and Elvis sought refuge behind the bar.

Titty, arriving at that moment to continue work on the mural, stood in the doorway and watched in amazement as three grown men cavorted around the bar performing a sort of tribal dance. Saul was the first to spot her and held out his hands in invitation. She went towards him hesitantly and found herself being whirled gracefully around the room.

'Is this a workout you do most mornings or are we celebrating something?' she asked when they had all finally collapsed.

'We sure are celebrating, Titty,' Drew said. 'One of our old ladies died the other day and I just found out that she's left us a whole lotta money.'

'Was that the old lady you made a speech about at the tea dance?'

'The same. I'd forgotten you were there.'

'Oh, Drew, how amazing for you. I'm so thrilled.'

'Not just amazing for me but for all of us.' He put his arm around her. 'For starters we can pay you a decent whack for your mural.'

'What you're paying me is fine. I'm enjoying doing it, I really am.'

They both stood looking at the image in front of them. The wall had been painted black and on top she had imposed images of the drag queens in silver, white and grey. The effect was very dramatic and very distinctive.

'It's one hell of a mural, Titty,' Elliot said coming up behind them. 'It's like looking at a black-and-white photograph.'

'You sure have talent, lady,' Saul said.

'She sure does,' Drew agreed. 'It's given me an idea for the rest of the place. I've been wanting to change the décor for ages and now thanks to Martha we can.'

'It's gonna be great to be able to throw some serious money at the club, give it a real overhaul,' Saul was grinning in anticipation.

'I think we need a new image,' Drew continued. 'We need glamour and elegance, at the moment we have garish and gaudy.'

'It doesn't exactly scream sophistication, I agree.' Elliot looked around at the glitter ball and gold walls.

'We won't have time to do it before Thanksgiving but after that we'll shut down for a couple of weeks and tart the whole place up. Titty can be our resident advisor.'

'One thing we could do before Thanksgiving is invest in a new sound system,' Saul said. 'That really would make a heck of a difference.'

'Holy Mary Mother of God, we are gonna have one hell of a party,' Drew laughed.

'Listen, before we get too carried away we need to talk about the best way to invest the money, we need to –' Elliot got no further.

'Elliot, I know that you want to be sensible, and rightly so, but can we just have one wild night of extravagance?' Drew pleaded. 'I want to throw caution to the wind and have the best Thanksgiving party ever.'

He got down on bended knee and Saul did the same. 'Elliot, we faithfully promise that we will be responsible for ever after but allow us this one night of unrestrained indulgence.'

'Amen,' Saul said.

'When did anything I ever said stop you two anyway?' Elliot threw up his hands. 'You win, let's go mad, we deserve it. Let's have the motherfucker of all parties.'

The three of them gave a cheer. Even Titty applauded, their happiness was infectious. These three guys never failed to amaze her. They were all so different and yet all so close. She thought it must be fantastic to have a friendship like that.

'Early lunch to celebrate?' Drew asked. 'Shall we go somewhere wickedly upmarket or Mexican at Lena's?'

'Lena's,' Elliot and Saul replied without hesitation.

'Good call,' Drew agreed. 'You coming, Titty?'

'I still have some work to do on the mural.'

'You can do that after lunch,' Elliot said. 'We don't have a show tonight, we can all get merrily drunk.'

'I don't want to intrude on your celebration.'

'Titty, you're family, you couldn't possibly intrude,' Drew replied. 'Tell you what, let's make it a real celebration, we'll phone Joe and Bobby and the crew from the *Chronicle*.'

'Any of the girls free?' Saul enquired.

'You phone them, Saul, I'll phone the others and Elliot can go and buy an expensive bottle of champagne.'

* * *

Elliot bought an expensive case of champagne and after guzzling a couple of bottles the four of them danced across the road to Lena's.

Fran was on the lookout. 'They're here,' she yelled to the others.

'Sorry we're late, guys, we had some celebrating to do,' Drew grinned at them all.

'Drew, put us out of our misery and tell us what the hell's going on,' Fran exploded. 'We've been sitting here patiently but I can't take much more.'

'Two more seconds, sugar, let me pour everyone a drink. You're sure gonna need a drink when you hear what I've got to say.'

Lunch lasted all afternoon, everyone was in a festive mood. Drew, Saul and Elliot couldn't stop smiling, every time they looked at each other their faces lit up. They had worked so hard to create the club and now it looked like it would live to see another day.

'We've no show tonight,' Drew said to them. 'How about we close the club and continue the party?'

'With you all the way, buddy,' Saul agreed. 'Everyone's on a real high, seems a shame to break the spell.' He turned to Elliot. 'What do you say?'

'Days like this only come along once in a blue moon, let's make the most of it.' He grabbed their hands and the three of them gazed at each other, unashamed of the tears that rolled down their cheeks. A shout from Fran broke the moment.

'Come and listen to this, it's the most amazing coincidence. Jason, start your story again.'

'I was just saying that one of the guys who works with my old man lives in the same village as Roz and Jamie. Apparently this guy, I've forgotten his name, wants to put some money he raised for charity into their village hall appeal.' He looked at their bemused expressions. 'It's all part of something called Corporate Social Responsibility, you've been doing it over here for years. Anyway this guy ran the London marathon and has asked Dad if the money can go towards the drag show, *your* drag show, to help save the hall.'

'Isn't that so bizarre?' Fran said.

'It's a small world,' Drew agreed.

'Where is the village?' Titty asked.

'It's in a county called Suffolk, not far from Bury St Edmunds. Is that an area you know, Titty?'

Titty turned sheet-white and rushed outside. Drew followed immediately. 'Titty, you look as if you've seen a ghost. What the hell's up, sweetheart?'

There was no reply. She just stood there shaking. Drew put an arm around her thin shoulders and drew her to him.

'Titty, you're scaring me, what is it, sugar? What's so bad?'

'I can't go back to the UK, Honey, not back to there. I'm sorry, anywhere else maybe but not there. I can't run the risk of them seeing me, I can't destroy them again.'

'Who are you talking about? Tell me what's the matter.' Drew led her gently to the seat.

'They're ashamed of me, terribly ashamed of me.'

'Why would anyone be ashamed of you?' He said taking the cigarette from her shaking hands and lighting it.

'Because of who I am.'

'You are beautiful, kind and very talented. Who could possibly be ashamed of that?'

'My family, or what remains of them. I've destroyed them.' The floodgates had opened and tears were streaming down her face.

'Titty, how have you destroyed them? Why do you think that?'

'Because my father is dead,' she whispered. 'He was so ashamed of me he took his own life. That's how I destroyed them.'

Drew reeled back. 'No, Titty, I can't believe that. How do you know that's true?'

'I heard her on the phone. I overheard my mum on the phone.' She paused for a moment as she struggled to control herself. 'She said that he could no longer live with the shame and that no one else must know.' She turned to Drew her eyes full of hurt and torment. 'Those were her exact words, Honey, that's why I had to leave. Because of me he died. Because he was so ashamed I was gay, so ashamed of his own son. Have you any idea what that feels like?'

She sobbed onto his shirt and Drew held her tightly, murmuring endearments until gradually her tears began to subside.

'Were they very angry when you told them you were gay?'

'No, not at all. They didn't even seem that shocked,' she gulped. 'Obviously they were just putting on an act. Or maybe it was delayed reaction. Doesn't really matter now.'

'No Titty, the first reaction is usually the true one. It just doesn't make sense. Something else is going on here.'

A small glimmer of hope suddenly burst into life inside Titty but just as suddenly she crushed it. That way madness lies, she told herself firmly.

'Honey, you're being very kind but I've got to face facts.' She was calmer now, desperately trying to distance herself from any hope, which worried Drew more than the tears. 'What else could it have been? I heard it with my own ears. She had no idea I was listening and those were her exact words.' She stood up. 'Because of me my father died. They hate me and the best thing I can do is to stay out of their lives.'

She said as if chanting an oft-repeated mantra. 'Let's go back inside, Honey. I don't wanna ruin your party.' She smiled a little too brightly and ground her cigarette out.

CHAPTER 37

Suffolk and San Francisco

'That was Kate on the phone,' Roz said, walking into the kitchen. 'Apparently Toby's car has also been scratched and his windscreen smashed. She just wanted to warn us in case they targeted us next.'

'I doubt we'd notice any extra scratches on our car but I guess we would pay attention to a smashed window.'

'It's a bit worrying isn't it, with us going away and everything.'

'There you go again, Roz, worrying about things that don't exist. No one has done anything to us yet and everyone will keep an eye on the place for us.'

'I wonder who it is?'

'Someone like that tosser Fergal, probably.'

The phone started ringing again.

'My agent, no doubt,' Jamie laughed. 'With a thousand film auditions.'

That would be nice, Roz thought. So far her agent had only managed to line up two auditions. Roz was going along with the 'let's give it a last shot theory' but her heart wasn't really in it. It was far more important that Jamie got seen for something, acting had really taken a back seat for her. What was disturbing her, though, was what else she could do.

She shrugged: as Jamie said, there was no point in constantly worrying, something would turn up and she could always ask George if he needed extra bar staff. Jamie was still talking on the phone so she grabbed her camera and went outside to take some photos of Butler. He was, as usual digging holes in the garden but he bounded over as soon as he saw her and leapt up enthusiastically, placing muddy paws on her thighs.

'You are a nightmare puppy dog,' she said, looking down at her filthy jeans. He growled in agreement and looked up at her lovingly.

'But you're the cutest dog that ever lived.' She laughed. 'Come on, let's capture that dopey face on camera.'

Jamie came out as Butler was posing on the garden table. Butler was a natural model, staring up at the camera without a hint of shyness, totally at ease and unselfconscious.

'That was Drew on the phone,' Jamie clambered onto the table beside Butler. 'He's offered to pay our airfare to San Francisco.'

'He's what?' Roz exclaimed, putting the camera down and looking at him in amazement. 'We can't possibly let him pay, that's just ridiculous.'

'That's what I said, and he said we could argue about it when we went over.'

'But what on earth has prompted all this? Why's he suddenly wanting to pay?'

'He's just come into a fair amount of money. Someone has left him eighty thousand dollars in their will.'

'Bloody hell, I wish someone would leave us eighty thousand dollars.'

'I wish someone would leave us eight.'

'Yeah that would do,' Roz agreed. 'But surely he can't be serious, anyway we couldn't possibly accept.'

'He seems quite determined.'

'Was he drunk?'

'Roz, it's about ten in the morning there. But then again he did say that they had been partying pretty hard yesterday so maybe he is.'

Drew wasn't still drunk but he did still feel as high as a kite. Yesterday had been an extraordinary day. There had been tears, there had been laughter and there had been a huge amount of champagne.

He was finding it hard to come to terms with this sudden turn of events. All three of them had admitted that recently they'd been feeling under a lot pressure. The Honey Bees had been their life for a number of years and each of them was worried it may be coming to an end.

The party had carried on at the club until the early hours. Everyone had been riding high on a wave of emotion and the air had been thick with schmaltz and emotion. When Drew had got up to make a poignant speech about friendship and family there hadn't been a dry eye in the house. Only Titty had stood apart looking lost and fragile and Drew's heart had gone out her.

The shrill of the phone broke into Drew's reverie. He glanced at his watch. It could only be two people at this time of the morning, Jamie or Fran and he'd already spoken to Jamie.

'Highly calorific bagel or chocolate muffin?' He smiled into the phone.

'Do I have to give you a decision right now? We're not coming out for a couple of weeks, how long does a highly calorific bagel take to prepare?'

'Well I want to make sure everything is to your satisfaction.' Drew laughed. 'I just don't wanna leave anything to chance.'

'Who did you think it was? Who do you have early morning bagel and muffin assignations with?'

'My journalist friend Fran. We're both early risers. Are you ringing to accept my offer of flights?'

'No I'm not. Roz won't countenance the idea.'

'Why the hell not?'

'She says it's far too generous of you considering we haven't even met you yet. You may hate us.'

'I don't think so, Jamie. Something tells me we're gonna be very important to each other. Our souls and future are connected, buddy.'

'No, Drew, we don't go in for all that psychobabble touchy-feely Californian twaddle over here. I'm a stalwart Scot. We barely hug. The only time we're allowed to show emotion is at a football match.'

'Gee Jamie, I just can't wait to meet you.' Drew was laughing. 'You sure crack me up, my friend. Tell Roz to swallow her bloody British pride and allow me to pay. It would give me a lot of pleasure and I know you'd do the same for me.'

'I certainly would, Drew, like a shot, but Roz is mean. She can't bear to part with money. Tight as a duck's arse, that's my wife.' Jamie winked at his wife who was just walking into the kitchen. She grabbed the phone.

'Don't listen to a bloody word he says, Drew,' she shouted.

'Accept my bloody offer then,' he yelled back.

'We'll think about it, Drew, I promise,' she said, handing the phone back to Jamie.

'So, what were you phoning about?' Drew asked.

'We got a bit worried that having come into this small fortune you may not want to, or indeed may not need to carry on with our joint venture.'

'Jamie this is a much-needed injection of cash, but, buddy, we still need to promote the club.' Drew hastened to reassure him. 'We've been running at a loss for quite some time now. We need new sound equipment, we need new lighting and we need to decorate the whole place, trust me we still need this publicity.'

'Good, that's what we wanted to hear. Just needed to check that you didn't feel duty bound to go ahead with something you didn't want to do.'

'We're all looking forward to it big time, Jamie. The girls would lynch me if we backed out now.'

'That's great. In that case I'll opt for the highly calorific bagel and Roz will go for the muffin.'

CHAPTER 38

San Francisco

Half an hour later Drew and Elvis arrived at the Paws Café to find Fran had beaten them to it. She leapt up on their arrival.

'What an incredible day yesterday.' She said flinging her arms around Drew. 'It was awesome. Thank you so much.'

'Well we sure had a lot to celebrate,' Drew said, eyeing her low fat blueberry muffin in astonishment. 'What the hell are you eating?'

'I'm trying to shed some weight, Drew.'

'Why?'

'Because I'm too chubby.'

'You're not chubby, you're shapely and gorgeous.'

'I don't want to be shapely. I want to be stick thin.'

'Oh God, no you don't.'

'Oh God, yes I do.'

'Fran, you look like a woman, it's beautiful to see a woman looking like a woman.'

'Well I'd like folk to see a lot less of this particular woman.'

'Don't you dare change a bloody thing. You're curvaceous and sexy and feminine and I'm not the only one who thinks like that.'

'Who else?' she said blushing.

'You know exactly who else, Jason of course, couldn't take his eyes off you all day yesterday.'

'Couldn't he?' she asked hopefully. 'But then again he was pretty drunk.'

'Fran, you need to start believing in yourself a bit more. Why have you no self-esteem?'

'I once overheard my dad describe me as the frizzy haired, pigeon-toed plump kid. Don't you dare laugh,' she said as Drew began to chuckle. 'It scarred me for life.'

'Well you need to get over it. You're not plump and I've never noticed the pigeon toes. Sure your hair is a touch frizzy but nothing that a decent cut couldn't sort out. You have a smile that would light up the night sky, you are bright and beautiful and here ends the lesson for today.' He beckoned the waitress over. 'Toni, two large full-fat cappuccinos and two large full-fat chocolate muffins please.'

Saul cleaning up the bar after yesterday's excesses was amazed when the door opened and Titty walked in. Drew had told them about their conversation and Saul certainly hadn't anticipated seeing her this morning.

'Titty, you're up bright and early, didn't really expect to see you today.'

'I've got a job to do, Saul,' she said sharply. 'I've promised Drew that the mural will be finished by Thanksgiving and I'm not going to let him down.'

'Looks pretty finished to me right now.'

'Some finishing touches, Saul, it's the finishing touches that make the difference,' she said, marching over to the wall.

There was something different about her today, Saul thought. She was brittle and snappy. Her face was pale and her eyes were ringed with dark circles. They worked together in silence for a while until she suddenly uttered an exclamation and throwing the paint brush onto the floor sank back into a chair. Saul poured a large coffee and went over to her.

'Titty, you look exhausted.' He handed her the coffee.

'I've fucked up Babette's hair.'

Saul looked at the mural but could see nothing wrong. 'Leave it for today, Titty. Go home and get some rest. You had a tough day yesterday.'

'Drew told you, didn't he?'

'Yes he did, do you mind?'

'Not really, I imagine that there are no secrets between the three of you.'

'Oh, we can keep secrets, trust me, but we were concerned about you. We wanted to know if you were OK.'

'I'm fine thanks, Saul.'

'That's not how it looks from here.'

'Saul, I'd really rather not talk about it. I just need to get on with my life.'

'Sometimes you have to face the past before you can face the future,' Saul replied.

'What the hell is that supposed to mean?' she snarled.

'It means that you need to try one more time with your mom and brother. Suppose you misread the situation?'

'I didn't misread the situation, Saul, I know exactly what I heard.'

'I'm with Drew here, Titty. There's much more to this than you think and I think you need to find out what. No, baby, hear me out,' he said as she rose to go. 'Listen, what have you got to lose? If you go back and you find you're right then you ain't no worse off, but on the other hand if you go back and find you're wrong then …?' He left the question dangling on the air.

'I'm not sure I can go through all that again, Saul. I'm not sure I can face the rejection all over again. I'm frightened.'

'You don't strike me as a coward, Titty. And this time you won't be facing the rejection alone. You have another family now; you have us.' He patted her shoulder. 'Just think about it, that's all I ask. Now scoot home and get some damn sleep before you collapse.'

Drew came back into the club a few minutes after Titty had left. Saul reported the conversation back.

'I just wish we could do something else, try and find out more. Should I ask Fran to do some more digging?'

'No, Drew, we can't interfere. It's Titty's life, it's up to her.'

'But maybe we could help her on the way. I think she's read it wrong, I don't know what her father was ashamed of but I don't think it was her.'

'Saul's right, Drew,' Elliot said, strolling into the club. 'You can't go charging around like a bull elephant into affairs that don't concern you.'

'I'm not a bull elephant and it does concern me and what the hell are you doing up so early? You ain't seen this side of midday for some time.'

'I was afraid you'd both be hatching plans to spend the money. I know what you two are like, I need to be here to curb your excesses.' He grinned. 'No, seriously I think we need to sit down sensibly and discuss everything.'

'No time like the present. Let the coffee and cognac meeting commence. Where's Elvis?'

Jason was waiting impatiently for Fran as she arrived back at the office. 'I've been searching everywhere for you, where have you been?'

'Early morning coffee with Drew.'

'I'm beginning to get a little jealous of Drew.'

Fran turned away to hide her smile. 'You're never usually in at this time,' she said. 'I wasn't expecting to see you for another hour or so, especially after yesterday.'

'Fantastic day, wasn't it?'

'It was ace, but why the early start?'

'I was woken up by an important phone call,' he stood grinning at her. 'I have a new title. I'm now officially Uncle Jason.'

'Oh, Jason, how cool. Tell me all about it, boy or girl?'

'Girl: Tansy Jay Rose, seven pounds and eight ounces. Mother and child doing great, grandparents and uncle ecstatic.'

'What beautiful names, unusual but lovely. Is Jay after you?'

'Yes, Jay is after me and Rose after my Mum. God knows where she got Tansy from. Sasha is not what you would call conventional.'

'Did you feel the birth pains with her? Isn't that what twins are supposed to do?'

'I can thankfully say that I felt no twinge of anything remotely resembling a birth pain, for which I am enormously grateful.' He sank down onto a chair. 'Mind you the state I was in last night it's possible I wouldn't have noticed if I'd gone through labour.'

'Oh I imagine you would,' she laughed. 'Have they sent pictures?'

'Yes, but only a terribly blurry one sent from Sasha's phone. I think they were all so emotional no one was capable of holding the camera still.' He looked wistful.

'Are you missing not being there?'

'Very much. It's strange not being with them at such an important time.'

'When are you gonna see them all?'

'I'll go back for Christmas but my dad is threatening to come over for Thanksgiving which, as you yanks say, would be awesome.' He smiled. 'Fran, do you fancy going somewhere tonight to wet the baby's head with me?'

'I think I probably drank enough last night to wet a thousand babies' heads.'

'Oh, well in that case …' His face clouded over.

'Jason, that wasn't a no. I'd love to raise a glass to Tansy. I know the perfect cocktail bar, pricey but worth it.' She beamed at him.

There goes that smile again, he thought. I'm a lost man when she smiles at me like that.

CHAPTER 39

Suffolk and Los Angeles and San Francisco

The evening before their departure Roz and Jamie settled Butler with Edward and then went for a drink at the pub. Everyone turned out to wish them well and to have a final chat about The Honey Bees. They had yet to decide upon a date for them to come over for the show and ideas were being tossed around.

'We'll talk to Drew but I've a feeling that sooner rather than later may be preferable. The sooner they come over here to help us then the sooner we can go back there and help them. Despite the sudden windfall I've a feeling that they still need the publicity as much as ever,' Jamie said.

'I think that it should be for a theme like Easter or Valentine's Day,' George volunteered.

'A lot of people tend to go away for Easter, or they have family events,' Charlotte said. 'That could be a problem.'

'I'm liking the sound of Valentine's Day myself, a Valentine's party with a difference,' Frank said. 'Honey Bees have hearts. I can picture the poster now.'

'Frank, that's genius,' Jamie grinned. 'Drew will love that.'

'Let's put that to them then,' Leon said. 'I guess it depends on how big Valentine's Day is over there. They may not want to close the club over a busy period.'

'Yeah, you have a point there. Well, we'll see what they think,' Jamie drained his glass. 'Come on, Roz, early start for us. Cheers folks, we'll keep emailing George and he can keep you up to date.'

'Before you go we have a card that Belinda and Hannah made for you.' Kate handed them a large envelope.

'How sweet of them,' Roz tore it open. It was a large card wishing them happy holiday and decorated with honey bees, but honey bees with a difference. The bees were all dressed as women, long eyelashes, big pouty lips, high heels and jewellery. It was witty, imaginative and beautifully drawn. 'Wow, this is fantastic,' Roz said showing it around. 'This is really stunning.'

'They spent hours doing it,' Kate said. 'Our kitchen table is covered in glue and glitter.'

'There is some real talent here. Who is the artist between them or are they both budding Picassos?'

'I think Belinda is the artist,' Leon laughed. 'Glue and glitter are Hannah's speciality.'

'They both came up with the idea for the picture,' Kate said, keen to give equal credit.

'Kiss them from us and tell them that we'll show it to the real Honey Bees.'

'I have a mate at work who compiled something for you,' Toby handed them a piece of paper. 'It's a list of all the things you shouldn't visit while in Los Angeles. He says it will save you a lot of time and disappointment.'

'What a cheery creature he must be,' Roz said laughing.

'Life and soul of the office,' Toby grinned.

'I've put together some of the photos from last year,' Frank said. 'Let them see the competition from across the pond.'

'I doubt they'll be too worried,' Jamie said, glancing down at the top photo of Frank resplendent in his tutu. 'But I guess it will give them an idea of what to expect.'

Their plane landed at ten past five in the afternoon and by six thirty they were following the chauffeur Seb had sent to collect them.

'This is so nice of him,' Roz whispered. 'We could easily have taken a … bloody hell.' They had stopped in front of a large limousine and the chauffeur was opening the door for them.

'You will find a bottle of champagne inside courtesy of Mr Cooke,' the chauffeur said, smiling at the look on their faces.

As they settled into the cool, luxurious interior Roz had to pinch herself several times.

'Am I still asleep or has jet lag kicked in early? When he said he was sending a car I certainly didn't expect this.' She gazed around. 'This is amazing. What a way to travel!'

'It's typical of Seb: extravagant, ostentatious and incredibly generous.' Jamie popped the cork on the champagne bottle.

'This can't belong to him surely? He must have hired it just for us. It must have cost a bloody fortune. We could easily have taken a taxi, or got the bus.'

'Speak for yourself. I wouldn't have missed this for the world.' Jamie leant back contentedly. 'This is the life. Did you remember to do the lotto for the weeks we are away?'

Roz smiled and gave herself up to the sumptuousness of her surroundings. The last few days had been fairly full on and she was shattered, but full of anticipation.

Seb was out at a meeting when they arrived at his house in Beverly Hills. His housekeeper let them in and showed them to their bedroom where tumblers of iced water stood on a glass table beside a vase full of exotic flowers. The bed was the size of Wales and covered in piles of snowy white pillows. The whole house was astounding, white marble, minimalist and immaculate.

'Either Seb has paid a fortune for an interior decorator or his tastes have changed beyond recognition,' Jamie said, remembering the clutter and chaos of the flat they'd shared during drama school.

'It really is something else, isn't it?' Roz opened sliding doors to reveal palm trees surrounding a glittering swimming pool. 'I knew he'd hit the big time out here but I didn't imagine anything like this.'

'Starting to change your mind about giving up on your acting career?'

'Maybe, just maybe.'

'So, do you fancy another glass?' Jamie waved the remainder of the bottle of champagne.

'God no, I feel quite woozy. Not sure if it's the journey, the bubbles or the excitement. But I tell you what I do fancy. I fancy leaping straight into that pool.'

'Go on then. The housekeeper said he wouldn't be back for about another hour. Was her name Minty? I think I heard Minty. Did you hear Minty?'

'I heard Minty,' Roz replied. 'OK, pool, here I come. Are you game, Jamie?'

'Always, darling, you know that.'

Roz was just clambering out of the pool when Seb arrived back home. He came charging across the terrace and, oblivious to the fact that she was dripping wet, enveloped her in an all-embracing bear hug.

'Seb, I'm soaking you,' Roz laughed.

'I don't care. I'm just so bloody excited to see you. I've been in a fever of anticipation these last few days.' He held her at arm's length. 'Roz, you glorious creature, did you come alone or did you have to drag that tiresome husband with you?'

'Tiresome husband present and correct,' Jamie said emerging from the bedroom with a towel around his waist.

Seb hurtled over and the two men hugged each other enthusiastically.

'Did you enjoy the limo?' Seb demanded. 'Couldn't resist. I knew you'd think it hideously flashy and ostentatious but welcome to Los Angeles.'

'It was a wonderful gesture, Seb, but wildly extravagant,' Roz said.

'I am getting an obscene amount of money, Roz, my love, and if I can't spend it on two great mates then what's the point?' He threw his arms around them both. 'We're staying in tonight. I want you all to myself. Drinks on the terrace followed by the best Italian meal in the world delivered straight to our door. And then, before you go to bed, I'll give you a sleeping pill and you can pass out till morning and wake without a hint of jet lag.' He grinned at them. 'It's just so good to see you guys. I didn't realise how much I missed you until you told me you were coming out. Go and get some clothes on and then I want to hear all your gossip, including this crazy story about a San Franciscan drag club. Sound like a plan?'

'One of the best,' Jamie replied.

'I don't normally like mozzarella,' Roz said helping herself to the last piece.

'One would never guess,' Jamie commented dryly.

'Seb is right, this is the best Italian meal I have ever eaten.' She lay back on her chair. 'I feel kind of muzzy and mellow. I may not last much longer.'

'Long enough to have a refill?' Seb asked.

'Oh yes!'

They chatted on for a while catching up on all the news. The air was balmy. Giant pots of jasmine surrounded them and their smell was intoxicating. A faint breeze stirred the palm trees. Seb had lit the candles and turned the pool lights on. The water sparkled in the twilight and Roz was almost tempted to leap in again but tiredness suddenly overtook her.

'I have to go to bed, guys,' she announced. 'I am suddenly feeling most peculiar. I feel very wobbly, like a tightrope walker about to fall off.' She stood up and swayed.

'Whoa there, darling. Let's get you to bed.' Jamie put his arm around her.

'Night, Seb,' she bent to kiss him.

'Night, Roz, you'll find a sleeping tablet beside your bed. Take it, sleep like a baby and you'll feel like Bambi in the morning.' Seb watched them walk across the terrace. Roz was pretending that she was on a tightrope and Jamie was struggling to hold her up. They were giggling like children and suddenly Seb felt a slight twinge of envy.

Jamie strolled back across the terrace a short while later.

'Can you manage one more or are you about to fall off the rope, too?'

'I think I can hold my balance for a while longer,' Jamie grinned.

'That's my boy,' Seb jumped up. 'I'll go grab another bottle then.'

Jamie stood gazing around him. He couldn't quite take it in. 'This really is some place you've got here, pal. I wasn't expecting anything quite like this,' he said as Seb returned with the bottle.

'Jamie, can I ask you something?'

'Of course you can.'

'Are you jealous of me at all?' Seb said quietly.

Jamie took the glass Seb was offering him and looked at his friend in surprise.

'No Seb, I'm not jealous,' he replied slowly. 'I have to admit I wouldn't mind having a pad like this and I guess that I wouldn't mind the lifestyle that goes with it. I'd love to be offered the work that you're offered and to have the choice of scripts that you have.' He paused for a second. 'And I certainly wouldn't mind a fraction of what I imagine must be in your bank account. So, there is maybe a touch of envy but never jealousy.' He raised his glass. 'It couldn't have happened to a nicer bloke. Well, obviously it could, it could have happened to me.' He grinned. 'But if it wasn't going to happen to me then I would rather it happen to you than anyone else. There's no one deserves it more.'

Seb let out a breath he hadn't realised he'd been holding. He slugged back a large mouthful of wine. 'Thanks Jamie, that's just so good to hear.'

'What's brought all this on?'

'I don't know really. I guess it's something I've wondered from time to time,' Seb smiled. 'And then watching you and Roz just now I felt a touch envious.'

'Really?'

'Really,' Seb laughed. 'What you have is real, Jamie. What I have is transient.'

Jamie raised his eyebrows.

'I'm on the crest of a wave at the moment but I don't kid myself it will last for ever,' Seb explained.

'It shows no sign of letting up at the moment, mate.'

'No, that's true,' Seb agreed. 'Long may it last, and while it does I'm making the most of it.' He took another slurp of wine. 'I'm not really sure what I'm trying to say except that you're a lucky bastard, too. I know you've both been through hell and back recently but nonetheless you've still got what a lot of people dream of.'

'I feel pretty bloody lucky right now, that's for sure,' Jamie said looking around him. 'Great mate, great place and great wine. Who could ask for more?'

CHAPTER 40

Los Angeles and San Francisco

Nothing about Los Angeles was as they had anticipated or imagined, as Roz said in an email to George.

It's a bizarre place, George. I don't quite know how to describe it. There doesn't seem to be any real centre or heart – it's just a series of different areas linked by what they call 'boulevards' but which are really six-lane highways. There is so much traffic: it makes the M25 look like a country lane. Everyone drives everywhere. Apparently you simply have to have a car – no one ever uses public transport, so guess what? You know what I'm going to say, don't you?

Yes – Jamie has risen to the challenge and, despite being offered a car by Seb, we are attempting to go everywhere by bus and train!

Actually, it's great fun. Sometimes – OK most times – we get completely lost but everyone is incredibly friendly. We've met a few whacky weirdos but, for the most part, people have been pretty sane and we've had some fantastic experiences. Jamie is inclined towards Venice Beach where he struck up a friendship with a man on roller skates giving away free hash cookies – I kid you not!

You asked about auditions. They've not been a great success for me – I could tell that they weren't exactly bowled over. But I tell you what, George – they're a damn sight more polite about it here than their British counterparts!

Anyway, I'm not that fussed – as you know I've sort of given up on the idea. It's more important for Jamie and they seemed to love *him (or so he says) although they did say that 'Scottish is not really happening over here!'*

Is it happening anywhere, I ask myself?????

So we're not holding our breath but it was worth a go!

Seb's house is incredible and I mean incredible *– palm trees, pool, the works. He is being wonderfully generous and we feel like royalty. In fact his current girlfriend – a curvaceous blonde called Fenella, cute as a button and very Californian – has just come to inform me that cocktails are being served on the terrace … it's a tough life!*

Love to everyone – will mail from SF!

R & J xxxxx

P.S. Have you heard from Edward? Is Butler behaving?

Fenella was chatting animatedly on her phone while she waited for Roz outside. She ended her call as soon as Roz appeared. 'That was my folks. They wanna visit us next weekend. I'll go tell Seb.'

She ran excitedly over to Seb, waving her mobile, her tits dangerously out of control beneath a tiny bikini top. Roz followed more demurely.

'Seb, honey, that was Pops. He and Mom are coming here this weekend along with my baby sister and Nanna. You'll get to meet them all. How cool is that? You'll all get along just fine, I just know you will.' She stooped to kiss him almost smothering him in the process. 'They said they'd stay in a motel but, honey, I was wondering if they could come here?'

Seb didn't miss a beat. 'Sweetie, of course they can. But I won't be here. I'm heading off to San Francisco with these two rascals. We planned it last night.'

Roz choked on her wine but Jamie had not spent three years at drama school with his mate for nothing. He stepped manfully up to the mark.

'Listen, pal,' he said to Seb with a totally straight face. 'We're dead excited about you coming with us, and the hotel you're going to book us into sounds out of this world but we totally understand if you want to back out, don't we, Roz?'

'Oh, totally. It's much more important that you meet Fenella's parents. And don't you worry about that splendid hotel.' She smiled sweetly. 'Another time, maybe?'

It was Jamie's turn to choke on his wine.

'No, a promise is a promise,' Seb said, looking at them both through narrowed eyes. 'Fenella understands, don't you, sweetie? I can't just abandon my old mates like that.' He reached up and pulled Fenella onto his lap. 'It's not a problem, is it? If only we'd known a day earlier, before I'd made plans with these two.'

Fenella looked utterly bewildered. 'Maybe I could ask Pops to put it off. Perhaps they could come another time, then I could come along to San Francisco, too.'

'Don't even think of it,' Seb said hastily. 'Let's go and make the arrangements with Minty right now and then you can ring them back and offer them this place. It will be much nicer than staying in a motel. Minty will look after you all.' He stood up and practically dragged her into the house, throwing them a desperate look as he went.

'He's so rotten,' Roz said. 'And so are you, what's all this about a hotel?'

'Just keeping it real, sweetheart. Remember improvisation classes, accept and build, that's all I was doing.'

'Poor Fenella, he's not being fair to her.'

'I don't think he treats her too badly,' Jamie laughed. 'She's never allowed to pay for anything, he showers her with gifts and now her family are staying here at his expense with acres of wine and food thrown in, I imagine. No, I think on the whole she does OK. '

'You know exactly what I mean. He's leading her up the garden path.'

'Stop being so old fashioned, Roz. She's a little dizzy but certainly not stupid. I imagine she knows exactly what she's doing. She's probably more than happy to be led up the garden path for a short while. Maybe she doesn't want anything more serious, neither of them do. And if they're happy just having fun and fantastic sex then what's the problem? Don't be so judgemental.'

'You sound almost envious.'

'It has a certain appeal.' He winked at her and reached for the wine bottle.

Seb came strolling back across the terrace.

'All sorted with Minty?' Roz enquired. 'Such a shame we'd made all these previous arrangements and you have to miss the family get-together.'

'All sorted,' Seb replied ignoring her sarcasm. 'As we speak Minty is booking the Fairmount Hotel in San Francisco for a couple of nights.' He grinned at them.

'Seb, no,' they both exclaimed.

'That was a joke,' Roz said. 'Jamie was accepting and building.'

'Just as I am doing now,' Seb laughed.

'Seb, mate, absolutely no way,' Jamie was adamant. 'You've done so much already, there's no way you're paying for a hotel in San Francisco.'

'Not just any old hotel, Jamie, but *the* hotel in San Francisco.' He smiled at their expressions. 'Listen, you two, for the umpteenth time I am making oodles of dosh out here. My accountant is being sensible with most of it but the rest I am blowing by having a fucking marvellous time and if that marvellous time includes treating you to a couple of nights in San Francisco then so be it.'

'But, Seb,' Roz began but was interrupted.

'No, Roz, I'm serious. I've barged in unexpectedly on your time in San Francisco so it's only fair that I recompense you. Minty will be cutting a good deal with the hotel, don't you worry. They'll get some pictures of me, I'll say some nice things, it's all part of the business.' He chuckled. 'Actually I can't wait. This drag queen business has me fascinated. I want to see the Honey Bees for myself and as a bonus I get to spend more time with you.'

Roz threw her arms around him. 'I don't know what to say. It will be wonderful going to San Francisco with you. You're unbelievably generous, please let us pay for pizza tonight.'

Jamie and Seb both roared with laughter.

'OK, Roz, but I warn you, my taste in pizza is expensive. Not for me the humble margherita, I want the house extravaganza with all the trimmings.'

'You're kidding me?' Elliot stood stock still. 'Is he really coming to The Honey Bees? I know we joked about it but I never thought it would happen. Is this for real?'

'He's really coming,' Drew laughed at the look on Elliot's face. 'Apparently he's putting them up at the Fairmount and then they want to come to us as planned.'

'Sebastian Cooke is coming here?' Elliot couldn't take it in. 'Wait until the girls find out. They'll be hysterical. Does Saul know?'

'Does Saul know what?' Saul asked, walking in.

'Sebastian Cooke, *the* Sebastian Cooke, the one and only divinely gorgeous Sebastian Cooke is coming to The Honey Bees. What do you say to that?'

'Not quite as much as you do,' Saul chuckled. 'But you're right, the girls will be beside themselves.'

'Not sure we should mention it to anyone just yet,' Drew said. 'I doubt he'll want the paparazzi outside. He may not want to be seen in a drag club, it may not be good for his image.'

'Well it sure as hell would be good for ours,' Elliot retorted.

'I know, but let's just see what happens. Jamie says he's a great bloke so if there's a way he can help us then I'm sure he will, but until we know the score let's keep it under wraps, agreed?'

'Agreed,' Saul replied.

'Agreed,' Elliot echoed, somewhat more reluctantly.

CHAPTER 41

San Francisco

'Drew, we're here. We're actually here in San Francisco, can you believe that?' Jamie shouted into the phone

'Where are you now?'

'Standing in the grand foyer of the Fairmount Hotel. We arrived about an hour ago, it took us that long to get to our room.'

'It's pretty awesome, ain't it?'

'It's ridiculously over the top and ornate. We feel overwhelmed.'

'I can't imagine you being overwhelmed by anything.' Drew laughed. 'So what are your plans?' He was desperate to meet up with them but was hesitant to suggest anything in case he interfered with any arrangements they had made with Sebastian. This was their holiday after all.

Jamie had no such reluctance. 'We're both chomping at the bit to see you, Drew.'

'And I you.'

'Sebastian insists on a cocktail at somewhere called the Top of the Mark rooftop bar. He says it's the best place to watch the sun go down.'

'He's not wrong.'

'And then we thought we'd head on over to join you. Is that OK? Do you want to come and have a cocktail first? Do you have a show tonight?'

'No show tonight, we've been rehearsing all afternoon for Thanksgiving so I'm giving them the night off and we …'

'Get yourselves over for a drink then,' Jamie interrupted.

'Nothing would please me more, it's one of our favourite places. But madness ensues here. Saul has bought a new sound system which cost a fortune, looks like the flight deck of a Boeing 747 and has him totally defeated.'

'Sebastian's his man. He's a technical genius, used to do all the sound at drama school. Do you mind if he tags along with us?'

'If he must,' Drew chuckled, delighted at the thought of the famous film star tagging along like a little kid.

'He's like a child, can't bear to be left out of anything and he's dying to meet you all.'

'Jamie, of course he must tag along. Elliot would never forgive me if he didn't. Warn your friend to expect some fawning.'

'Oh he's well used to that. Frankly the more fawns the better,' Jamie paused. 'Drew, I'm ludicrously excited.'

'So am I, buddy, so am I. Have a mojito for me.'

The Top of the Mark bar was sensational and Roz and Jamie ran from window to window with Seb giving them a running commentary.

'Fisherman's Wharf, Golden Gate Bridge, Alcatraz in the distance, Sausalito beyond, no idea what that building is but somewhere in that direction is Coit Tower.'

'Seb, I didn't know you knew San Francisco so well.'

'Don't really know it that well but I've spent a fair amount of time in here. Can we stop disturbing the other punters now and sit and get a drink?'

'I'm having a mojito, Drew's orders.'

'Let's all have something different then we can try each other's.' Roz suggested.

'You add a touch of class wherever you go, Roz,' Seb grinned. 'I'm all for mutual slurping, let's have some nibbles as well.'

'It's just as I imagined,' Jamie said, stepping out of the taxi at the front of The Honey Bees Club.

'Of course it is, you clown, Drew sent you loads of photos,' Roz laughed.

'Fair point,' Jamie conceded. 'He didn't send me photos of him though, or only of him as Honey.'

'Will he be Honey or Drew tonight?' Seb asked.

'Never thought to ask,' Jamie replied. 'There's no show so I imagine he'll be Drew but I'm not sure. Only one way to find out.' And he lead the way in.

Drew spotted them immediately, he had been on the look-out for the last half hour. 'They're here,' he yelled to Elliot who had taken over as temporary barman while Saul floundered with the flight deck of the Boeing 747.

'Right, I'll grab the bubbles,' Elliot said, reaching inside the fridge for the bottles Drew had put there in readiness.

Drew was halfway across the floor before Jamie spotted him waving. He abandoned Roz and Seb and raced towards him. The two men embraced enthusiastically.

'Good to see you, Jamie,' Drew looked him up and down. 'I was expecting flaming red hair and a kilt.'

'I was expecting false tits and a tight dress.'

'You have to wait until Thanksgiving for that.'

'As do you for the kilt but there's no way I'm dyeing my hair.'

They grinned at each other delighted to be face to face at last.

'Drew, this is Roz,' Jamie said as the other two approached.

'Hi sweetie, welcome to the Honey Bees,' Drew threw his arms around her.

'And this is Sebastian.'

'Hi, Drew, pleased to meet you. Thanks for letting me barge in like this. These two have talked about you non-stop so I had to come and see what the fuss was all about.'

'You're welcome, Sebastian.'

'And Drew has talked non-stop about you two as well.' Elliot joined the group. 'Jamie and Roz, I feel I know you intimately, you're part of the family.'

'You must be Elliot, how wonderful to meet you.' Jamie held out his hand but instead felt himself being pulled into an embrace.

'If you're family you get hugged. Come here, Roz.' Elliot reached out for her. 'And obviously you need no introduction at all,' he said turning to Seb. 'Boy, you're even more glorious in the flesh than on the screen.' He gazed in frank admiration at the strong jawline, the slow charismatic smile and the clear hazel eyes that had melted a thousand hearts.

There was no doubt that Seb was a showstopper but Drew preferred the more characterful face of Jamie with his shaggy locks and bright blue eyes.

'I told you there would be fawning.'

'Oh come on, look at the man,' Elliot exclaimed 'How could you not fawn? He is a god.'

'You're not so bad yourself,' Seb smiled.

'I can die a happy man.'

'Before you do, would you pour the champagne?' Drew laughed. 'Saul, right on cue, how goes it?' he asked as Saul emerged from backstage.

Saul wasn't listening. He was seriously worried about his sound system which he had purchased with such enthusiasm and confidence and which now lay in a tangle of wires, speakers and microphones all of which had to be connected and assembled by Thursday.

'Saul?' Drew broke into his thoughts.

Saul's frown disappeared at the sight of the three visitors. 'Roz and Jamie, I presume, and none other than Mr Sebastian Cooke.' He shook their hands heartily and embraced Roz. 'Good to see you here guys, we've sure been looking forward to this.'

Roz thought he was wonderful. Deep soulful eyes, braided hair and a smile that rivalled Louis Armstrong's. Not a tall man but a powerful one, impossible to guess his age, he had remarkably few wrinkles but those eyes had certainly been places.

'Jamie says you have a new sound system,' Sebastian had a gleam in his eyes. 'Mind if I take a look? I don't pretend to be an expert but ...'

'He's good,' Jamie said.

'Very good,' Roz echoed.

Saul looked at Seb with interest and more than a hint of desperation. 'Really?' he asked. Was it possible that his salvation lay in the unlikely form of Sebastian Cooke? 'Hell, I sure could use another opinion. Drew just says read the manual and Elliot says for that price I should have an army of men to install it.' He glared at his partners who stared back unrepentant.

'Lead the way then, let's take a look at this beauty.' Seb started to move towards the stage.

'Finish your champagne first,' Drew ordered. 'This is celebration time.'

'Sorry, Drew, a toast to new friends,' Seb raised his glass and knocked the drink back in one. He smiled at everyone. 'Won't be long, just going to have a quick peek.'

'We won't see them for the rest of the evening,' Jamie laughed. 'He's as happy as a pig in shit. Don't worry, Drew, if anyone can sort the system out Seb can.'

'Aren't we missing someone?' Roz asked. 'Where's the other member of your team?'

Drew smiled and whistled and a few minutes later Elvis padded in.

'Oh, he's adorable,' Roz said, bending down to stroke him.

'He really does look as if he's wearing shades, it's quite unnerving,' Jamie said, looking down at the shaggy white dog with black eyes.

'Don't be so rude, Jamie, he's simply gorgeous. Don't you listen to him, Elvis.'

'It's OK, little fella, I'm only joking – you're sweet, odd looking, but sweet.'

'Drew, this place is fantastic,' Roz said looking around. 'I still can't quite believe we're here. Wow, who did this wall? It's incredible.' She walked over for a closer inspection.

'One of our girls did that, it's awesome ain't it.'

'I've never seen anything like it. When you say girls you mean one of your drag queens?'

'Yeah, that work of art is by Miss Titty, or Miss Titty Titty Bang Bang to be precise. Talented lady, she also plays the piano.'

'I read about her. I love the name, it's priceless. Titty Titty Bang Bang,' Jamie was laughing. 'Roz is right, Drew. This place is great.'

'You're not really seeing it at its best. It comes to life when we have a show and a full house. Tonight's gonna be dead, I don't expect many punters a couple of days before Thanksgiving.'

'Here come a couple,' Elliot said, spotting Joe and Bobby in the doorway.

'Just about to open a fresh bottle, guys, come over and meet Jamie and Roz.'

'You're always about to open a fresh bottle,' Joe laughed.

'This is Joe and his partner Bobby. And this gorgeous couple are Roz and Jamie.'

'My God, that's some shirt,' Jamie stared in amazement at the psychedelic patterns Bobby was sporting.

'Glad you like it,' Bobby smiled, completely misinterpreting Jamie's comment.

'Pleased to meet you both. Drew's mentioned you. You're getting married, right?'

'We are indeed. No date set but sometime next year,' Joe replied.

'How exciting,' Roz said shaking their hands. 'A couple of girlfriends of ours are also getting married next year.'

'Gee, I love the sound of that town of yours,' Bobby said. 'Drag queens, lords and ladies and now a lesbian wedding.'

'It seems to have it all,' Joe agreed, smiling.

'I'm not entirely sure about the lords and ladies,' Roz said amused.

'Don't disillusion the poor lad. He's convinced that behind every front door in Britain there lurks a duke or duchess taking afternoon tea.'

'Talking of tea, we have some presents from the UK for you all,' Roz said, delving into a large plastic bag. 'Tea selection from England,' she handed a large tin to Drew.

'Whisky from Scotland,' Jamie said handing him a bottle. 'It's a fifteen-year-old single malt called Glenfarclas, from the last family-run distillery in Scotland. Pure nectar.'

'Gee, thanks guys.'

'Elliot, you probably have every book on gardening known to man but we bought you one on cottage gardens along with some seeds. I think there are foxgloves, hollyhocks, lupins and hyacinth. Not being gardeners, we have no idea if they'll thrive here, or even if they'll grow at all, so it could be a useless present,' Jamie grinned.

'Nothing to do with gardening could ever be useless. This is neat. Thanks, guys.'

'For Saul, we have a bizarre book called *Cocktails Through The Ages* which was chosen by our local landlord. Some of them seem pretty weird but he loves them.'

'Where is Saul?' Joe enquired.

'Closeted away backstage with a rather special guest. They're sorting out the new sound system but I'll give him a yell, we need him behind the bar,' Drew said walking towards the stage.

'We also have some photos of our village drag queens which I suggest you only look at once we have consumed a lot more alcohol.' Jamie produced the album that Frank had put together. 'In fact I'm not sure that you should look at them at all.'

'And I wanted to show you this. It's a card that our friends' children made. I think it's incredible, they're only nine years old.' Roz handed the card to Elliot and turned to Bobby and Joe. 'I'm so sorry we don't have gifts for you two, but Drew could share his tea and whisky.'

'Maybe the tea but I draw the line at whisky,' Drew said coming back. 'I've shouted to Saul. They're coming in a moment. I said he couldn't monopolise our guest for too long.'

'Who is the guest?' Bobby asked but Drew merely smiled.

'Drew take a look at this, it's wicked.' Elliot handed him Hannah and Belinda's card.

'This is spot on,' Drew said, impressed. 'Look, that's me in the middle, the big fat Queen bee with too much make-up. I love it. Who did this?' Drew handed it over to Joe. 'We could do something with this, don't you think? Maybe design a new logo?'

'It was made by two nine-year-olds,' Roz said.

'Get away. You're kiddin' me? Nine-year-olds?'

Joe was impressed. 'You're right, Drew, we could do something with this for sure.'

'Joe's a graphic designer, he's …'

But Drew was interrupted by a high-pitched screech from Bobby who was staring open mouthed at Sebastian Cooke coming into the room, chatting with Saul.

'It's Sebastian Cooke,' he announced unnecessarily. 'It's Sebastian Cooke.' His eyes were like saucers. 'Joe turn around. It's Sebastian Cooke.'

Joe turned around. 'Jesus Christ.'

'You're Sebastian Cooke,' Bobby said.

'Certainly was last time I looked,' Seb smiled at the young man staring up at him. 'Holy shit, that's some shirt you have on.'

'Gee, do you like it?' Bobby smiled triumphantly. 'See, Joe, everyone likes it. Even Sebastian Cooke. You said it was hideous.'

'How could I have got it so badly wrong?' Joe rolled his eyes.

'The young man with the shirt is Bobby and this is his partner Joe, graphic designer, local mafia, owns half of San Francisco,' Drew announced.

'The first bit is true, the rest is bullshit.' Joe shook his head in despair.

'How's it going?' Roz asked. 'Have you managed to switch it on yet?'

'Roz, darling, it's not a bloody ghetto blaster,' Seb replied in amusement. 'It's not a question of just switching it on or off. This is precision engineering. It has to be handled gently. It requires skill and dexterity.'

'In other words you still haven't got it working,' she laughed.

'We were called away too soon. But by the end of tomorrow we'll have the best sound system in San Francisco, won't we Saul?'

'It's gonna be awesome.'

'It better be,' Elliot muttered.

'You're coming over tomorrow?' Drew asked. 'That seems unfair. Don't you want to spend time with Roz and Jamie?'

'I've just spent a week with them, there's only so much I can take,' Seb grinned. 'Tomorrow they're all yours.'

'Trust me, Drew, he's much happier playing with the sound system. He has no interest in doing the touristy things we want to do and neither, I imagine, do you. Listen we're quite happy on our own. Tomorrow we're taking a tram and visiting Fisherman's Wharf.'

Saul and Elliot smiled at each other.

'Fisherman's Wharf is one of Drew's guilty pleasures,' Elliot laughed. 'He loves it, there's no way he's gonna let you go and watch the seals on your own.'

'Sure, I'm coming with you, me and Elvis, whether you want us to or not.'

'We want,' Roz assured him.

'Guys, why don't you go into the garden?' Saul suggested. 'Elliot's been polishing the plants all morning.'

'Drew?' Seb took him surreptitiously to one side. 'I need to have word with you alone,' he whispered.

'OK,' Drew said. 'Elliot, take them to your garden and I'll follow with the drinks. Seb, do you want to give me a hand?'

'Beautifully executed,' Seb said when they'd all left. 'Now listen, Saul says that you won't be open tomorrow night. Is that right?'

Drew nodded.

'That's great,' Seb beamed. 'Before we left Los Angeles I had my assistant find out about hiring a boat for a sunset dinner cruise around the bay. She's come back saying that she can organise it for tomorrow night so I've told her to go ahead. The boat holds about twenty people, so I want you three to join us. I've already mentioned it to Saul. Shall we ask Joe and the shirt? And who else do you think? Would your girls like to come or will they be resting up before the big night? It's your call.'

'What a fantastic idea, Seb. We'd love to come on one condition.'

'No, this is my treat, you're not paying anything,' Seb interrupted, rightly anticipating what Drew was going to say.

'But I was going to take you all out for a meal anyway. Let's at least go halves, Seb.'

'Absolutely not. You're doing Thanksgiving and you're providing champagne tonight so tomorrow evening is on me.'

'I'll surrender the evening then but lunch is on me if you and Saul can tear yourselves away.'

'Lunch is on Elliot and me, buddy, you've lucked out there,' Saul said, emerging from behind the bar with a couple more bottles of champagne. 'We want to welcome Roz and Jamie too and I'd like to thank my technical genius here.'

'I give up,' Drew said.

CHAPTER 42

San Francisco

Everything about San Francisco exceeded expectations. They were the only passengers on their first-ever tram ride and the driver took delight in explaining the mechanics to Jamie. Roz was more interested in gazing at the architecture. She had known that San Francisco was hilly but she hadn't expected the hills to be quite so steep or the scenery to be so dramatic.

They met Drew and Elvis at Fisherman's Wharf. 'Seb is already hard at it with Saul,' Drew said.

'We know, we didn't even see him at our delicious breakfast.'

'I hope you left plenty for room for lunch. Saul and Elliot are treating us. They wanted to go Italian but I persuaded them that they had to come here and we would eat crab, which is what this place is famous for.'

'We're costing everyone a fortune,' Roz frowned. 'When do we get to treat you?'

'Plenty of time for that, don't worry,' Drew said, although he had absolutely no intention of letting them pay for anything. 'You've already earned your keep by bringing Seb along. I can't tell you how grateful Saul is. We'd be kinda lost without music for tomorrow's show.'

They spent a glorious morning wandering around Fisherman's Wharf and despite the gargantuan breakfast managed a small bowl of clam chowder served in a sour-dough bread bowl.

'That's got to be one of the nicest things I've ever tasted,' Roz said, spooning out the last few drops. 'I'd be happy to have that again for lunch and dinner.'

'Wait until you see the menu at Scoma's restaurant, you'll be spoilt for choice.' Drew said.

'I simply never knew crab could be cooked in so many ways,' Jamie sat looking in amazement at the food laden on the table at Scoma's.

Roz was tucking into risotto balls stuffed with sweet crab; Saul and Drew were eating crab ravioli; Elliot had a sort of crab and seafood soup called Cioppino, and Jamie and Seb sat with half a garlic-roasted Dungeness crab in front of them.

'I'll be walking sideways up the bloody hills after this lot.'

'As long as we are walking,' Roz said. 'Christ knows we need the exercise, we haven't stopped eating or drinking since we got here. Please tell me that your evening surprise doesn't involve an eighteen-course meal, Seb.'

'It doesn't,' he replied, giving nothing away.

'Can't we just have one tiny clue?' Roz begged. 'Just a little something to whet our appetite.'

'You just said that was the last thing you needed,' Seb refused to be drawn. He had told them to present themselves in the foyer of the hotel at seven thirty on the dot and was saying nothing more.

They were left to their own devices after lunch and wandered for miles arriving back at their hotel around four in the afternoon absolutely shattered but both in agreement that San Francisco was simply one of the best cities they had ever visited. They had a much-needed siesta and as commanded were waiting in the foyer at seven thirty precisely.

Roz was worried about the amount that everyone was spending on them.

'Sweetheart, stop fretting,' Jamie told her. 'We'll do exactly the same for them when they come over to the UK. Remember, Roz, Seb is a millionaire and Drew has just inherited eighty thousand dollars whereas we can barely pay the mortgage.'

Seb was ready for them and ushered them into a taxi which sped towards the bay.

'I can't take the suspense much longer, Seb. Where are we going?' Roz demanded.

'All will be revealed shortly. Did you have a good afternoon?'

'Wonderful, how about you?'

'Yep, we finally got the sound system up and running. It's a beauty. I'm helping Saul operate it tomorrow night. After that he's on his own.'

'Were you there all afternoon?' Jamie asked.

'Pretty much,' Seb grinned. 'No worries, I loved every minute of it.'

The taxi pulled up not far from where they'd been in the morning. Roz looked around but couldn't see any sign of a restaurant or bar.

'Where to now, Seb?'

'Mr and Mrs Forsyth, your ship awaits you,' Seb said, motioning towards a beautiful boat moored up nearby.

'You've got to be joking,' Jamie said, as they walked towards it.

The captain was standing on the deck to greet them. 'Welcome aboard *The Dolphin*,' he announced as they stepped across. 'It sure is a pleasure to have you here and we hope you enjoy your cruise with us.'

'Seb, you've never hired this boat just for us.'

'Hell no, he invited a few mates along too,' Drew said, coming to greet them. 'Come on into the bar, cocktails are being served.'

Roz burst into tears and Seb put his arms around her. 'Roz, darling, don't cry. It's supposed to be a fantastic surprise.'

'It's a fantastic surprise,' she gulped. 'I'm just so overwhelmed. I can't believe it. Why are you all being so nice?'

'Why not?' Drew laughed. 'Come on sweetie, come and get a drink, there are a few people I want you to meet.' He led her into the bar.

Jamie stopped Seb before he followed. 'Seb, you're doing way too much pal.'

'I'm doing exactly what I want to do, Jamie,' he smiled at his friend. 'You've both been through a rough time, you deserve to be spoilt and I'm in a position to do it. To be fair, Drew wanted to go halves but I wouldn't let him.' He pulled Jamie towards him in a tight embrace. 'Humour me, mate. You and Roz mean a lot to me. I'm having the best time ever being with you and meeting the Honey Bees. I mean it, I can't remember when I last had such fun.'

They walked into the bar together. Roz had recovered herself and was chatting animatedly. She waved them over.

'Jamie, this is Jason. Jason works for the *San Francisco Chronicle*, as does Fran and this is Corey the editor, and you won't believe this, but this is Jason's dad, Gerry,' she pulled Gerry over. 'And Gerry is Toby's boss who said yes to Toby donating his sponsorship money towards our drag competition. Isn't that incredible?'

'I don't know, Roz. Frankly, I've not followed a single word you've said,' Jamie laughed, shaking hands with everyone.

Drew had asked Seb earlier if it would be OK to invite the guys from the *Chronicle*. He'd explained how they were helping the cause with their articles about The Honey Bees and the proposed UK trip. He'd promised Seb that they wouldn't breathe a word about him being here for Thanksgiving. There would be no paparazzi waiting for him at The Honey Bees. Seb hadn't been fussed at all, even promising to let them have an exclusive if it would help.

'This has been one of the best nights of my life,' Roz said as they sailed under the Golden Gate Bridge. 'This is the stuff that dreams are made of. It's like a fairy tale; I feel like the beautiful princess.'

'Good, that makes me the handsome prince then,' Jamie said.

CHAPTER 43

San Francisco

Drew was busy with rehearsals the following morning, and Seb was helping Saul with the music, so Jamie and Roz were left on their own. They had volunteered to help decorate the club in the afternoon but Drew had turned them down, saying that there would be enough people to help and that they should make the most of their time in San Francisco.

They arranged to meet Seb for afternoon tea at the hotel and spent a very relaxed morning mooching around Union Square and Chinatown. The shops were mostly closed and everyone was in holiday mood. Drew had told them that there would be a turkey trail trot around Golden Gate Park with live music and market stalls but, tempting as it sounded, so much had been happening over the last few days they were more than happy to drink endless cups of coffee, watch the world go by and soak up the ambience.

The next day would be Black Friday, the biggest shopping day of the year when the whole of Union Square would be in chaos, so it made sense to see it while it was quiet.

Seb rang around lunch time to say rehearsals were going well, the sound system was a triumph and that he and Saul were off to the local community centre where Saul worked to wish them Happy Thanksgiving and deliver pumpkin fritters made by the Mexican cook who was responsible for the meal tonight.

'He's having a great time, isn't he?' Roz said.

'He's loving it all. He said he couldn't remember when he last felt so happy and relaxed. It's good to see.'

'I guess this is a complete change from his normal routine.'

'Let's face it, it would be a complete change from anyone's routine,' Jamie laughed. 'Hanging around drag clubs and then taking fritters to a community centre. It's hardly your average day.'

The phone rang again. It was Seb. 'I completely forgot the other reason I was ringing. The hotel asked if I or my guests wanted a spa treatment courtesy of the Fairmount as a Thanksgiving gift. I said it was not for me but thought that maybe you would like one. So guys, if you want to pamper yourselves, go ahead.'

'Seb, did they really say that or is this another one of your treats?' Jamie was suspicious.

'Mate, they really said that, just one of the perks of being a star. Like getting fresh flowers delivered to my room, best tables at restaurants, complimentary cocktails, the list is endless. You should try it one day, it's not a bad life. See you later, have fun.'

'How are we ever going to return to normal?' Roz asked.

'Maybe we never will. I've a feeling that once you've met the Honey Bees nothing will ever be the same again.'

'Our lives have changed beyond recognition since moving from London. It seems a different world. I can't believe that this time last year we were still living there.'

'It's strange, I agree.' Jamie was bent over the camera. 'Roz, these pictures are very good. I know I'm probably biased but they are excellent. The ones on the boat are so natural, you've captured the atmosphere completely.' He smiled at her. 'You've a real talent, sweetheart.'

'Listen to this, you two.' Roz was reading the afternoon tea menu.

Seb had been talking them through the morning rehearsals. He hadn't shut up since he'd arrived. It sounded like they had a real treat in store for them that night.

'And then we went to the community centre. Honestly I think that every café and restaurant within a radius of three miles had donated some food. You'd have loved it, guys, and everyone worships Saul. The local school helped decorate and the place looked totally mad. Drew and Saul painted the walls yellow and purple.'

'Are they symbolic Thanksgiving colours?' Roz asked.

'No, it was a while back,' Seb laughed. 'Some paint someone had donated. They didn't have much choice. Sorry Roz, what was it you were trying to say?'

'It says here that in 2010 four honey beehives were installed in the hotel's culinary kitchen garden in order to help support the bee population. Just seems a strange coincidence, don't you think.'

They looked back, not grasping the connection.

'We're trying to protect the honey bees in Suffolk. There's The Honey Bees nightclub and now the hotel is muscling in on the act,' she explained. 'We should get the girls to come and perform here.'

'Actually we should,' Seb was serious. 'I'll mention it to the manager. Good idea, good publicity for them.'

'It doesn't really seem a natural venue for drag queens,' Roz had been joking.

'No, it doesn't and that's why it would have more of the wow factor.'

'Jesus Christ,' Jamie exclaimed as the waiter placed huge tiers of tiny sandwiches, pastries and scones in front of them. 'I thought we were having something light so as not to spoil our appetite for the Mexican feast later on.'

'They don't know the meaning of the word light over here,' Roz said.

A few hours later Jamie and Seb were once again installed in the foyer, only this time instead of tea they were drinking Honey Saison beer courtesy of the beehives from the hotel's culinary garden. They were waiting for Roz to finish getting ready.

'Not bad, not bad at all.' Jamie took an experimental swig. He was resplendent in his kilt and his arrival had caused quite a stir in the foyer.

'It's OK,' Seb agreed, equally splendid in a light pink linen suit. 'Wouldn't drink more than four pints but it's OK. Ah, here comes Roz.'

She crossed the room, turning a few heads as she did so. She was wearing an antique cream and white lace dress with fresh flowers in her hair.

'Roz, you look stunning.'

'You sure do, sweetheart,' Jamie agreed, gazing at her with pride.

'Do you think the flowers in the hair may be over the top?'

'Roz, remember where we're going,' Seb laughed. 'Nothing could ever be over the top.'

'You look beautiful, Roz, rather like a virginal bride,' Jamie said.

'Jesus, how much of this beer have you had?'

'What a divine trio you make.' Elliot strode across the club to greet them. 'Jamie, I'm lovin' the skirt,' he winked at Roz knowing full well it wasn't called a skirt.

'Elliot, you must all have worked flat out, this place looks amazing.'

Huge orange balloons covered the ceiling, ribbons of gold fluttered beneath them. The walls were draped in red and gold streamers. Each table was decorated with brightly coloured gourds and tea lights. A huge wooden effigy of a pilgrim stood in one corner of the room and an enormous papier maché turkey in another.

'This is breathtaking. I've never seen anything like it,' Roz said, looking around the room. 'Jamie, don't you think this is incredible?'

He wasn't listening, he was staring in admiration as a voluptuous woman in a striking fishtail dress walked towards them. She shone and glittered as a medley of gold and silver sequins caught the light. Perched on top of a tangle of gleaming curls sat a diamanté tiara. Her long golden gloves were bedecked with jewelled rings and she trailed a shimmering boa nonchalantly behind her. She was a radiant, sparkling coruscation and Jamie was struck dumb.

'I don't believe you've met our Queen Bee,' Elliot laughed at the look on their faces. 'Allow me to introduce you to the one and only Miss Honey Berry.'

'Fuck me,' Jamie said. 'I don't believe it.'

'Drew, sorry, Honey, you look, well, you look unbelievable,' Roz was as taken aback as Jamie.

Even Seb, who had seen the dress during rehearsals, could only gaze open mouthed.

'Thanks, guys, good to get the thumbs up,' Honey laughed at their surprise. 'But you've seen pictures of me as Honey before. I sent you photos right?'

'Nothing could prepare us for this,' Jamie said. 'You looked nothing like this in the photos. This is sensational. I'm not sure if I fancy you or if I'm frightened of you.'

'I'm not sure which I'd prefer,' Honey laughed. 'Come on over and meet the rest of the girls, they're longing to meet you. You all look pretty sensational yourselves, by the way.'

'Are the rest of the girls as glamorous as you, Honey? I'm not sure I can take much more,' Jamie asked.

'Frankly I'm not sure how much more I can take either. Under this dress I'm boned and trussed like a chicken.'

'It's worth it,' Seb said.

'I bloody hope so, I'm in agony.' He grinned and lead them towards the bar where the girls were waiting. 'Jamie and Roz meet the Honey Bees.'

Drew threw his arms out dramatically.

'Introducing, from the left: our country-and-western flame, the beautiful Babette; the divine Diana Dross, specialising, of course, in The Supremes; Miss Titty specialising in just about everything; Cherie is backstage having a panic attack; and last but by no means least our very own Mama Teresa.'

'Hi, everyone,' Roz smiled uncertainly. 'I feel a little tongue-tied, you all look so wonderful.'

It was true, she did suddenly feel strangely nervous in front of these extraordinary, larger than life characters. Jamie however suffered no such sensitivity.

'Hello, Honey Bees, how lovely to meet you. We've been looking forward to this for such a long time. You all look incredibly exotic and sexy, can't wait to see the show. Seb here has been singing your praises.'

It was absolutely the right note to hit and they all buzzed around him, living up to their name, fluttering their false eyelashes, exclaiming over his kilt, adoring his accent and asking about the village. Only Titty stood slightly apart and Roz tried to draw her in.

'Miss Titty, you're from the UK, aren't you? Whereabouts did you live?'

'Oh, all around really, but I haven't been there in a while.' She wasn't very forthcoming and Roz tried again.

'I understand that you're responsible for the mural. It's stunning. I've never seen anything like it before.'

'Thank you very much,' Titty smiled. 'I really enjoyed doing it.'

Roz was relieved, this was clearly a subject she enjoyed talking about. 'Did you study art somewhere?'

'Yeah, I studied it.' The guarded look had come back and Titty moved away as if to signify the conversation was at an end. Roz didn't know how she'd offended her.

'Roz, try one of my cocktails, from the chapter entitled "Parties and Celebrations".' Saul handed her a glass. 'Don't worry about Titty,' he said in an aside. 'She just ain't that keen on talking about the past.'

Roz smiled at him gratefully and took a sip. 'Saul, this is gorgeous, what's in it?'

'Champagne with mint, a hint of cointreau, spoonful of sugar and a splash of orange. Taste OK?'

'Tastes divine,' Seb said, coming over to join them. 'I'll take another, please.'

'Hey buddy, I want you fully operational for the show.'

'Last one, I promise, and anyway I'll soak it up with the Mexican food which is smelling superb.'

Roz looked over towards the buffet table. It was certainly shaping up to be some feast. Drew had said that Lena was the best Mexican cook in the whole of San Francisco and without even tasting the food Roz felt inclined to agree. The room was filling up. Joe and Bobby had arrived and most of Joe's work colleagues and she could see Fran, Jason and Gerry threading their way towards the bar. She waved them over.

'Come and try Saul's lethal cocktail,' she cried. 'We've all got to have at least one so that we all get as drunk as each other.'

'Your man clearly hates being the centre of attention.' Gerry laughed, looking over at Jamie who was standing in the centre of the girls.

'I think he's even overshadowed Seb for once in his life.'

'They met me this afternoon. I'm yesterday's news and anyway who can compete with a man in a kilt,' Seb smiled.

'Your husband sure is something else,' Babette drawled, coming over to Roz.

'Isn't he just.'

'He's so cute. I adore his furry sack.'

'She's talking about his sporran,' Roz said quickly to Fran, who was choking on her drink.

'Roz, my child, it's a joy to have you amongst us,' Mama Teresa appeared at Roz's side. 'Honey has been looking forward to this for a long while, as we all have.' She smiled a beatific smile and softly stroked Roz's cheek. 'You have good energy the pair of you, you bring happiness and luck.'

'Ease off with your talk of karmas, energy and auras,' Diana laughed, overhearing the conversation. She came dancing over to Roz's side, a beautiful vision, vibrant in red and gold. 'We don't want to scare them off with your mumbo jumbo.'

'I don't think Mama Teresa is capable of scaring anyone,' Roz replied, looking at her gentle and serene face.

'You say that now, just you wait till you see her striptease later tonight. She's an absolute minx,' Diana and Babette broke into gales of laughter and Mama T. smiled indulgently.

Roz loved them, she had never witnessed anything like this before. Their energy and joie de vivre was contagious. 'Do you all lip synch?' she asked.

'Babette and I sure do but Titty has an awesome voice. Mama T, you sing occasionally don't you? I can't reveal anything about Cherie, and Honey bellows outrageously.'

'I resent that,' Drew said coming to join them and catching the last remark. 'I have a strong, resonant voice.'

'OK, Honey has a strong, resonant voice, but sadly we've only ever heard her bellow outrageously.'

CHAPTER 44

San Francisco

'Ladies and gentlemen, if I may have your attention for a moment.' Elliot was on stage with the microphone. 'I'd like to welcome you all to The Honey Bees. It's wonderful to have you here to help us celebrate.' There was a roar of applause. 'We're sure gonna have one hell of a night. We have a mouth-watering Mexican feast followed by a mouth-watering show. Let your hair down, folks. Let yourselves go. Forget your troubles. Let the party begin and let's make this a Thanksgiving night to remember forever.'

'Right, that's our cue to go backstage,' Drew said. 'And your cue to find your table.'

'Catch ya later, enjoy the show.'

The girls blew them a kiss.

'They're something else, ain't they?' Fran said to Jamie and Roz.

'They certainly are. They take your breath away.'

'They're such a close knit team,' Roz said. 'I somehow wasn't expecting that.'

'Drew's responsible for that,' Fran said firmly.

'Let's go and grab our table,' Jamie suggested. 'Corey is over there, waving at us.'

He threaded his way towards him. 'Corey, hello there, good to see you again.'

'Hi, Jamie, you're looking incredible.'

'Ah, we Scots scrub up well.'

'You certainly do. May I introduce my ma, Grace, and this is my son Eric.'

'Delighted to meet you. Is this your first time here?'

'It sure is,' Grace replied. 'Corey suggested it as a venue for some big birthdays we have coming up next year.'

'And what better place than here to celebrate.'

'I'm inclined to agree,' Grace said.

'It's too cool for words,' Eric said, looking around. 'I'm impressed, Pa. There's life in the old dog yet, eh? Who would have thought you'd come up with a drag club as a venue for my twenty-first?' He gave his father a high five.

Jamie laughed. 'It'll be a twenty-first party you won't ever forget. Mine was held in a pub in Glasgow called 'The Muscular Arms' and I've been trying to forget it for years.'

'This dress fitted me when I came in,' Roz said a few hours later. 'Now I'm bursting at the seams. I can't believe how much I've eaten.'

'You certainly didn't hold back,' Jamie grinned.

'I was overwhelmed. I had to try everything.' The Mexican feast had been impressive and the choice of food startling. Roz had tried to do justice to it all. She lay back in the chair, stroking her stomach. 'I look about eight months' pregnant. Why didn't someone stop me?'

'You were on a mission,' Jason laughed. 'We didn't want to stand in the way.'

'Do you and Jamie want kids?' Fran asked, laughing at her discomfort.

Roz was totally unprepared for the question and to her humiliation was unable to stop her eyes welling up. Fran was mortified.

'Not … not that it's any of my business. I'm so sorry I asked,' she stammered.

'We wanted kids very much, Fran,' Jamie said gently. 'But sadly we were unable. My fault, I appear to be firing blanks.'

'No one's fault,' Roz corrected him, wiping her eyes. 'Just one of those things.'

'I'm so sorry,' Fran said. 'That was so insensitive of me and I'm supposed to be a bloody journalist.'

'Fran, you weren't to know,' Roz smiled.

'I should have some sixth sense or something instead of barging in like a bullfrog. Now I've upset you which I never meant to do, especially over Thanksgiving which seems to make it worse. You better fire me, Corey, I'm the worst journalist in the world.'

'Oh Fran, you're priceless. Of course you haven't upset me, please don't worry.'

'Girls, shush now, Elliot is back on stage.'

'Ladies and gentlemen, was the food good?' Elliot asked. There was a roar of approval and Elliot held up his hands to quieten them down. 'Well folks, now is the time you've all been waiting for, so let the lights go dim and let the show begin.'

Again there was a huge roar from the audience who were obeying his previous instructions to the letter and letting their hair well and truly down.

'Ladies and gentlemen, please welcome our first act. She's beyond compare, beyond repair and beyond the curtain, so put your hands together to give her the clap she so richly deserves. Presenting the one and only, the incomparable Queen of the Bees, Miss Honey Berry.'

'Oh he's very good,' Jamie whispered to Roz.

Drew belted out one of his favourite Liza Minnelli numbers from *Cabaret*.

He was in his element. He no longer had to worry about money. For the first time in a long while the fate of his beloved night club seemed reasonably secure and sitting out in the audience were his friends and family. He stretched out his arms as if to envelop them all. They were singing along with him now, enjoying it every bit as much as he was. He was ludicrously over the top, flamboyant and fantastic. Roz and Jamie were on their feet at the end whooping and cheering.

'He's bloody brilliant,' Jamie said to Roz. 'I'd no idea he would be so brilliant. Did you think he'd be that brilliant? Honey, you're bloody brilliant,' he yelled across to the stage. Drew turned and winked at them both before sweeping theatrically off the stage ignoring the calls for an encore.

The lights went dim once more and the audience settled down. A spotlight came up on Titty in a bowler hat, cami-knickers, suspenders and boots. She looked stunning.

'Look at those legs,' Fran wailed. 'They go on for ever, why can't I have legs like that?'

'Your legs are fine as they are,' Jason replied, squeezing her hand.

Fran blushed ferociously and Gerry and Roz exchanged an amused look.

Titty was carrying on the cabaret theme singing 'Bye Bye, *Mein Leiber Herr.*'

She was joined by Babette and Diana. It was a witty and clever parody of the Liza Minnelli original.

'Who's responsible for the choreography?' Roz asked as she watched the three of them whirling the chairs around their heads. 'It's superb.'

'It's genius.' Jamie had tears rolling down his cheek. 'Titty is incredibly talented and my God she can sing. She really reminds me of someone, can't think who.'

'That's funny, I've been thinking the same thing.'

'I think that Saul is responsible for most of the choreography,' Fran said. 'So it was probably a combination of him and Titty. Saul's an awesome dancer, you'd be surprised.'

'Fran, if you said he was a nude tight-rope walker it wouldn't surprise me,' Roz laughed. 'Nothing about this place or its people surprises me anymore.'

'I know what you mean. After a while everything seems normal,' Fran smiled. 'They all kinda get under your skin.'

The routine came to an end, the girls threw their hats into the crowd and the audience went wild.

'And now, ladies and gentlemen, something a little more elegant and sophisticated to raise the tone. She's sexy, she's seductive and she's making her debut here tonight. Please give a loud cheer for Cherie.'

They had decided that a low-key announcement would be best. Cherie made her way nervously onto the stage. She was wearing a strapless pink dress, her wig was a nod to Marilyn and diamanté sparkled and glistened around her throat and wrists.

Drew had insisted on paying for her outfit and hadn't given a thought to the cost. It had been his idea to change her image and he wanted her to feel fabulous.

'Wow,' Jason said as she stepped into the spotlight. 'If that's the same woman I think it is, then that is some transformation.'

'What did she look like before?'

'Judy Garland in *The Wizard of Oz*, pigtails and pinafore.'

'She's pretty gorgeous now,' Jamie gave a loud wolf whistle.

Cherie glanced anxiously over to Titty who gave her an encouraging smile and struck up the opening chords to 'Diamonds are a Girl's Best Friend'. The first few bars were nervous and shaky. Cherie stood petrified in the middle of the stage. Drew, watching from the wings, willed her to get into her stride. He saw Titty beckon her over to the piano. It was the right thing to do, the act of walking across the stage seemed to free her up and the proximity of Titty calmed her down.

She started to flirt with the audience who responded with whistles and catcalls and, by the second chorus, Drew could breathe a sigh of relief. The new Cherie had emerged and was a triumph.

Babette, the lass from Tennessee, was next, our very own Blue Grass Belle as Elliot put it. She bounded onto stage in leather tassels, cowboy boots and blonde ringlets.

'Sometimes it's hard to be a woman,' she mimed the opening lines of her favourite song.

'Tell me about it, baby,' someone from the audience yelled.

The evening went from strength to strength. Mama Teresa sang 'One Day at a Time' which made Roz want to weep. Diana Dross followed with an energetic performance of 'Baby Love' and a saucy number called 'Slide Some Oil Onto Me.'

Titty and Babette sporting the obligatory Abba catsuits and platform boots gave their version of 'Thank You for the Music' which brought the house down and then, all too soon, Elliot was back on stage announcing the finale.

'Ladies and gentlemen, we're now arriving at the climax of the show.'

'It's too soon,' someone yelled.

'Too soon? Hey buddy, we've been going for nearly an hour. I don't know about you but my climax normally comes way before that.' The audience roared. 'Now please welcome back onto the stage The Queen Bee herself, her honey bees and a couple of their workers.'

Roz and Jamie looked at each other eyebrows raised. They had a sneaking suspicion who the workers were going to be.

The spotlight came up on the girls in a tableau holding luminous orange umbrellas and as Honey sang the first few lines of 'It's Raining Men' gold glitter fell from the ceiling.

The audience cheered and when Saul, Seb and Elliot joined them on stage, Roz thought they would raise the roof. The guys were wearing white flares, shirts undone to the navel, high platform boots and all three looked as if they were having the time of their lives.

'He's outrageous,' Roz laughed. 'Who does he think he is, Tom Jones?' she asked as Seb unashamedly thrust his hips towards the audience.

'There are a few here who would throw their knickers at him,' Grace chuckled.

'Jamie where are you going?' Roz said in alarm as Jamie suddenly leapt to his feet.

'On stage, I'm not having him hogging all the limelight.'

'Jamie, it's their finale, you can't just barge in.'

'Watch me. Anyone else coming?'

'You bet,' Gerry said.

'With you all the way,' Corey stood up to join them leaving Eric and Jason completely dumbfounded.

'Get up there guys, you can't let the old guys go on their own,' Grace shouted at them.

'Fran, get some good shots,' Jason said, throwing his phone at her. 'My mother will never believe this.'

'Gee, they didn't take much persuading.' Fran laughed.

'Certainly didn't, oh no, Jamie no,' Roz squealed as Jamie lifted his kilt and treated the audience to a glimpse of his bare arse. 'God, that man has no shame.'

'With an arse like that he doesn't need to be ashamed,' Grace grinned.

There was a stampede as the rest of the men fought to perform with the girls. It was chaos on stage and chaos in the audience. The men were dancing and the women were craning to get a better look at Seb. Most of them couldn't believe their eyes.

'Ladies and gentlemen,' Drew was yelling into the microphone. 'My thanks to my wonderful Honey Bees, and to Elliot, Saul and Sebastian.' A huge cheer went up. 'And last but not least, my thanks to you, the audience, for helping make tonight's Thanksgiving so very special. The night is yet young folks, let the party continue.'

CHAPTER 45

San Francisco and Suffolk

'I don't want to go, I can't believe everything has finished,' Roz wailed as they stood waiting for their taxi to the airport.

'Nothing has finished Roz, quite the opposite. I've a strong feeling that everything is about to begin for you,' Saul said smiling. 'The only joy in the world is to begin. No idea who said that but he's kinda right.'

'Give us a hug then, honey,' Drew pulled Roz towards him.

Roz flung her arms around him. 'I'm going to miss you all so much, it's been out of this world, I can't thank you enough.' She turned to embrace Saul and Elliot. 'We've just had the best time ever.' She felt very close to crying again. She'd never cried as much in her life as she had done recently.

'We'll be with you soon sweetie,' Drew put his arm around her. 'We'll be in the UK in two months, that's no time at all.'

'You're right, that makes me feel better. Jesus, we've a hell of a lot of things to organise before then.' She turned around. 'Now, where's Elvis? Where's my joint favourite dog in the whole world?'

'He's here, waiting for a goodbye kiss and I'll take another one too.' Elliot stood beside the dog with his arms outstretched.

'Taxi's here, guys.' Saul announced, looking out of the window.

Drew and Jamie turned to each other.

'Drew, what can I say?' Jamie held out his arms. 'A thousand thank yous for everything. You're one of the best, pal.'

'I knew I'd love you, I just wasn't prepared for how much,' Drew said gruffly holding him tight.

'Don't hog him, Drew. Saul and I want our turn.'

'I can't believe how perfect everything has been.' Roz said as they sped towards the airport. 'Seb's fantastic house, the Fairmont Hotel, the boat trip, the Thanksgiving, it's just all been too good to be true.'

'The trip of a lifetime, sweetheart, and it's not over yet,' he winked at her.

'Jamie, what's going on?'

'Drew swore me to secrecy but I guess it's safe to tell you now,' he paused for dramatic effect.

'Don't tease me.'

'He was cross that we wouldn't let him pay for our airfares so he's upgraded our flights.' He leant over to kiss her. 'We're turning left when we get into the plane.'

Roz stared at him for a moment before bursting into tears yet again.

Jamie laughed. 'I felt like doing that myself when he told me,' he admitted. 'He really is an extraordinarily generous man.'

'They all are,' she gulped. 'We must make sure that we give them a fantastic time when they come to us.'

'We'll give them the time of their lives. It's certainly been the time of our lives, but you know what? I'm actually quite looking forward to walking through our own front door.'

* * *

At the time they were speaking their own front door was in the process of being painted. There had been an escalation of vandalism in the village. After Kate and Toby's cars had been scratched, the tyres on Frank's van had been slashed and the plants ripped out of the tubs in the pub garden.

The following week 'Death to the Drag Queens' had been daubed over the walls of the village hall and most recently 'Go back to Glasgow' had been painted on Jamie and Roz's front door.

Now Frank and George stood back and admired their handiwork.

'Do you think they'll notice it's a different shade of blue?' Frank asked.

'Depends on how jet-lagged they are, I guess,' George grinned. 'OK, job well done. Drink on the house, Frank? Thanks for your help.'

'No problem, we couldn't let them come home to "Go back to Glasgow". When exactly do they arrive back?'

'Roz said in her email that they'd be arriving late tonight and would be in the pub tomorrow evening.'

'Can't wait to hear all about it.'

'Certainly sounds like they've had a ball.'

Jamie and Roz arrived home bleary-eyed in the early hours. Neither of them commented on the front door although Roz did have a notion that it looked smarter than it had in her memory.

'Sleeping tablet and bed?' Jamie asked heading to the kitchen.

'Sounds good. Jesus, look at all this mail.'

'Nothing that can't wait until the morning. George has left us some bread and cheese and one of Frank's pork pies, do you fancy anything?' he asked.

'That's kind of him, but I think food will only wake me up.'

'Nothing will wake you up after one of Seb's heavy-duty sleeping pills, but I know what you mean,' Jamie said.

'It's nice to be back in our little cottage,' said Roz. 'And I can't wait to see Butler.'

CHAPTER 46

Suffolk

The sleeping tablets did the trick and Jamie woke the next morning feeling bright and rested. Roz was still in a deep coma so he eased himself out of bed and headed for the shower.

He was about to make himself a coffee but then had a better idea. He would nip to the village shop, grab a couple of pastries and head over to Edward's to pick up Butler. Scribbling a note to Roz he threw on his jacket and headed off into the cool autumnal sunshine.

Butler was beside himself at seeing Jamie. He'd had a great time at the big house but nothing could match the joy he felt at being with his master.

'So let's get this straight,' Jamie said, accepting a coffee. 'One of your welly boots, the remote control, a garden trowel, two cushions and a box of Frank's Cornish pasties including the box itself. Are you sure that's all, Edward? Don't lie to me, if he ate anything else we really want to know.' He took a bite from his Danish pastry.

'The pasties weren't really his fault, I stupidly left them on the table, they were just too hard to resist. The same with the loo roll,' Edward smiled.

'You didn't mention loo roll.'

'Ah well, add loo roll to the list then.' He could also have added certain articles of Louisa's clothing but that would have begged the question of why her clothes had been in his house and he wasn't ready to reveal to Jamie exactly what he and Billy's grandmother had been getting up to. Jamie would make a good audience though, he thought, maybe one day over a few beers.

He and Louisa had bumped into each other by chance a couple of times after the Thai evening at Jamie and Roz's. He'd been surprised by how much he enjoyed her company. His wife had known Louisa for years and had adored her but Edward had always found her cold and aloof and he knew she disapproved of him.

Unexpectedly she'd offered to come and help walk the three dogs with him and equally unexpectedly he'd agreed.

She turned up one morning and he had made them both a coffee. He thought how well she looked, a tall, slim figure in jeans and shirt, seeming far younger than her years. She bent over to pat one of the dogs and he caught a glimpse of her white lacy bra.

His wife Beth had always favoured plain, functional underwear so he was totally unprepared for the effect the fancy lingerie had on him. He wondered whether her knickers matched. The thought aroused sensations in him that had lain dormant for a long while. She stood up and looked at him, he found himself blushing.

'Edward, you look positively foxy, what on earth are you thinking?'

'I was wondering whether you had matching panties and bra,' he replied before he could stop himself.

She stared at him for a second then threw back her head and laughed, a wonderful deep throaty laugh. 'Well, Edward Hampshire, why don't you come here and find out?'

They had made love with a passion that had amazed them both. Abandoning caution along with clothes, they hadn't given a second thought to Butler.

'Still it was worth it,' Louisa had said later on, holding up her half-eaten shoes and scarf.

Edward emerged from his reverie to find Jamie staring quizzically at him. He blushed again.

'Sorry Jamie, miles away.'

'You certainly were, Edward. You look like the cat that's got the cream. What on earth have you been up to while we've been away?'

'It's been fun having Butler around.' Edward ignored the question. 'He is one of the most affectionate and loving dogs I have ever encountered.'

Roz was in her dressing gown making coffee when Jamie returned. 'Butler, you've grown another foot,' she said as the dog leapt up. He was ecstatic to see her too and raced around the kitchen chasing his tail. 'Shouldn't he have grown out of that by now?'

'It's a lot of tail to grow out of.'

'Has he been good? Do we owe Edward for any damages?'

'A couple of cushions, some of Frank's pasties, garden equipment, the usual,' Jamie replied. 'But I've a feeling that he was being economical with the truth.'

'Oh no, do you think he ate something really precious?'

'No, I don't think so but there was certainly something he wasn't telling me. He looked rather self-satisfied. In fact if I'm not much mistaken I'd say that Mr Edward Hampshire has been misbehaving while we've been away.'

'Misbehaving? Who with?'

'That I don't know, but I'm determined to find out.'

'Jamie, these are excellent,' Charlotte said, looking at the photos he had printed off.

'Roz took most of them. I can't take the credit.'

Everyone was crowded around the table in the pub where he had lain the photos out. They had all been fascinated by the tales of San Francisco and Roz and Jamie had enjoyed recounting them.

'Drew looks pretty damn gorgeous,' Leon said.

'Not half as gorgeous as Sebastian Cooke.' Ollie was drooling over a photo of Seb and Jamie on the boat.

'I'll second that,' Kate said.

'I'm also in that photo,' Jamie said, looking over their shoulder.

'Are you? Hadn't noticed.'

'And is he really going to be here for the drag contest?' Frank asked.

'It depends on his filming schedule, but he's certainly very keen.'

'We'll have no trouble selling tickets once word gets out about that,' George said.

'Once word gets out about what?' Louisa and Billy walked into the pub. 'Hi everyone, sorry we're a bit late. Welcome home, you two.'

As Jamie was standing up to say hello he caught a look on Edward's face that told him all he needed to know. The man was devouring her with his eyes and in response Louisa winked at him slowly. No one else appeared to have noticed.

'Edward, you old goat,' he whispered in his ear.

Edward gave a guilty start and a red flush crept up on his face.

'You're blushing like a teenager.'

'Keep it to yourself, Jamie,' Edward implored.

'Something you've clearly not been able to do,' he chuckled.

'Who is this glorious long-legged lady?' Clive asked pointing at a photo of Titty in her cabaret outfit. 'I can't see her face because her hat is covering it but she looks sensational. Is she in drag?'

'She certainly is. That is Miss Titty Titty Bang Bang.'

Clive hooted with laughter. 'Titty Bang Bang, bloody wonderful. Please tell me she's coming over.'

'Hope so, although I have to say she's the only one who doesn't seem that keen,' Jamie said.

'She's very talented,' Roz said. 'She plays the piano, she sings and she's a superb artist. Here's a picture of the mural she drew on the wall. It's incredible. I've never seen anything like it.' She held out the photo to them all.

'Oh my God,' Toby said slowly, staring at the photograph. 'Who did you say did this?'

'Miss Titty,' Roz replied. 'Are you alright, Toby? You look as if you've seen a ghost.'

'I think maybe I have. Kate take a look at this.' He grabbed the picture and passed it to his wife.

'Jesus Christ.'

Toby was shaking like a leaf as he examined the photo once more. 'Tell me about Titty. What more do you know? Tell me everything.' His voice was hoarse.

'We don't know too much Toby, she kept herself to herself,' Jamie said, wondering what the hell was going on.

'Is she British?'

'Yes, as a matter of fact, she is British.'

'Do you have any photos of her?' Kate asked, gently taking Toby's hand.

'Here are a couple of photos but you can't really see her face.' Roz handed them over.

'I don't need to see photos. No one else paints like this. It's Ben. Jesus Christ, Kate, it's Ben. We've found him.' He put his head in his hands.

George silently handed over a large glass of brandy while the others stared in utter astonishment.

'Ben was, sorry, is, Toby's younger brother.' Kate realised an explanation was necessary. 'He ran away from home three years ago just after, um …' she hesitated for a moment.

'Just after my father died,' Toby raised his head and took up the tale. 'My father committed suicide and Ben ran away before the funeral. We've been searching for him ever since.' He stood up. 'This is unbelievable, this is fucking unbelievable. I'm on the first plane to San Francisco.'

'Drew will know her real name. Do you want us to ring him to make sure?'

'No, Jamie, I'm absolutely sure it's him. Drew sounds like a great guy but his loyalty will lie with Ben. He may feel obliged to say something and I can't risk Ben taking off again. I'd rather you didn't breathe a word.'

'I understand, no problem. Drew's one of the best, he'll help all he can once you're there, that much I can promise you.'

'Thank you for everything, Jamie.'

'Christ, I've done nothing mate.'

'You have, you both have you, just don't realise it.' He grabbed Kate's hand and they headed towards the door.

'Keep us posted.' Jamie yelled after them.

'Will do.'

They all stared at each other.

'My God, that was some revelation, what an incredible coincidence.' Ollie finally broke the silence.

'Certainly was,' Clive agreed. 'It calls for another round of drinks, please, George.'

'She really is gorgeous,' Billy gazed reverently at the photo of Titty.

'Yes, Billy, I guess she is,' Roz looked at him curiously.

'You two certainly know how to stir things up,' George grinned at Jamie and Roz.

'It's been an uneventful couple of weeks and then the moment you arrive back all hell breaks loose.'

'Oh come on, I would hardly call the last two weeks uneventful,' Jamie said mischievously glancing at Edward, who looked alarmed. 'What about all the vandalism and graffiti?'

'OK, not totally uneventful then.'

'Hang on a moment, those pale into insignificance compared to this,' Leon exclaimed.

'This is absolutely extraordinary. Young brother disappears without trace after father's untimely death and three years later turns up in a San Francisco nightclub under the guise of Miss Titty Titty Bang Bang. You couldn't make this up if you tried. I feel like I'm in the middle of a film.'

'What part are you playing?' Charlotte laughed.

'I'm the sex interest, of course, isn't that obvious?' Leon grinned.

CHAPTER 47

San Francisco

Toby arrived at San Francisco airport with no real plan of action. He was tempted to just get a taxi straight to The Honey Bees Club but common sense told him that was probably not a good option. He phoned Kate as he queued in passport control. She was about to go to bed but had been waiting up to hear from him.

'Toby, just go straight to the hotel I booked for you and try and get a few hours' sleep. You hardly slept a wink last night and I'll bet you didn't get much on the plane.'

'A bit,' he lied.

'The show doesn't start until the evening so Ben is unlikely to be there anyway.'

'That's true,' he said. 'It's just that now I'm here I can't bear to wait any longer.'

'Darling, you're very tired and, not surprisingly, very emotional. Ben is not going anywhere, just go and get some rest, watch TV, have a shower and go along to the club later. Why don't you ring and find out exactly what time the show starts.'

'Good thinking. I could even make sure that Ben is performing.'

'I'd be careful, if you start asking about Ben or Miss Titty in an English accent they may get suspicious and the last thing you want to do is scare him away.'

'Yeah, you're right. OK, I'm heading to the hotel. I'll ring you in the morning your time.'

'Ring me anytime, let me know as soon as you've spoken to him,'

'OK. I love you, Kate.'

'I love you too, sweetheart, and Toby, be gentle with him. No more anger.'

He gave the address of the hotel to the taxi driver, grinning childishly at the name Nob Hill. His emotions swung between utter joy at being so near to Ben and utter terror and he felt alarmingly close to tears most of the time. Not a feeling he was used to.

He leant back and allowed memories of his brother to come floating to the surface. Holding him for the first time in hospital, this longed-for younger child. His mother saying to him, 'He'll look up to you, Toby. You'll be his big brother, his hero. You'll have to look after him.'

She'd been right. Ben hero-worshipped Toby and Toby had secretly revelled in the attentions of his young sibling. He had always looked out for him. He remembered taking him to school on his very first day, a beautiful blond five-year-old proud in his new school uniform, his little face awash with joy and anticipation. And he remembered the same little face awash with terror and tears as, time and time again, he became the easy prey for the school bullies.

Toby told him that he had to stand up for himself and then secretly went to seek out the bully boys in question. Toby was tall, muscular and a good deal older, it hadn't taken him long to persuade them never to pick on Ben again. The next day a delighted Ben reported that he'd plucked up the courage to tell them to stop and unbelievably they had slunk away. Toby had hugged his bony frame and to this day Ben believed that he'd ended his torture by himself.

He gave him his first pint and his first cigarette, although had he realised Ben would become such a nicotine addict he may have had second thoughts. He encouraged his love for art and music, inwardly awed and a touch jealous of his talent.

He always knew Ben was gay and it never bothered him. That was Ben, that was part of who he was. He sat with Ben when he told their parents. His mother showed no surprise at all. His father would have preferred him not to be but accepted the fact that he was. There had been no family row and no huge arguments, which was what had made his disappearance all the more strange.

Toby knew that the shock at being the one to find their father hanging in the garage had been unbelievably horrific for Ben. He would have given anything for that not to have happened but even that didn't explain why Ben had run away. Perhaps tonight would reveal all and the thought made his heart beat faster. The taxi pulled up at the hotel.

He was welcomed and checked in by a youngster who introduced himself as Chuck.

Chuck informed him that there was a wine tasting every evening in the hotel foyer from five until seven.

'Is there really?' Toby was impressed. 'How incredibly civilised.'

'Surely is.'

'Chuck, do you know of a club called The Honey Bees?'

'Surely do.'

'Could you ring them to ask what time the show is tonight?'

'Surely can.'

'That's very kind of you,' Toby said holding his breath for the reply. He was disappointed.

'You're welcome.'

He went to his room stripped off and lay on the bed. He was surviving on a combination of adrenalin and alcohol topped up with copious amounts of caffeine. Kate was right, he needed to get some sleep, but his dreams were haunted by images of his father and Ben who then merged into his son Tom. He woke up feeling anxious and far from rested.

He made his way down to the foyer where the wine tasting was nearing the end. There were about half a dozen people sitting around slurping Californian red. Toby was not in the mood for small talk so decided to head straight to the hotel restaurant. Chuck however had other ideas.

'Mister Forrester, you've surely time for a glass before you go, your drag show ain't gonna kick off till around ten o'clock.'

The half-dozen people turned to look at Toby with renewed interest. He smiled back weakly and accepted a warm red from Chuck.

'Surely gonna like that, Mister Forrester.'

'Surely am, Chuck.'

CHAPTER 48

San Francisco

Toby was nervous, his mouth was dry and his heart was pounding. He alternated between keeping his head fixed to the ground for fear of being spotted by Ben and looking wildly around hoping to catch sight of him. He arrived at the club a complete wreck and stood outside taking a few deep breaths. The temperature was cool but he felt hot and clammy.

'Come on, Toby, get a grip,' he chided himself out loud and resolutely opened the door.

He stood gazing around for a few minutes. It fitted Roz and Jamie's description exactly but he wasn't really taking in the décor. He scanned the room but he couldn't see any drag queens. They were probably all getting ready for the show. He was terrified that Ben would somehow spot him and do a runner. His eye was caught by the mural and he walked slowly towards it.

It was incredible. There was no signature but he didn't need one to know that it had been done by Ben. He was in no doubt whatsoever and he slowly put his hands on it as if by doing so he could touch his brother.

Saul watched Toby from the bar with interest. The guy stuck out like a sore thumb. Tall and good-looking but clearly desperately ill at ease. He kept running his hands through his hair in a gesture that was oddly familiar. The man stood gazing at Titty's mural for quite some time and Saul swore he wiped a tear away from his eyes.

Saul glanced around to see where Drew and Elliot were but they were deep in conversation at the other end of the bar and hadn't noticed a thing. He checked his watch, Drew should really be going to get ready. The other girls had long since disappeared.

The tall guy was making his way towards him. His eyes were nervously sliding from side to side and he kept licking his lips as if he had a dry mouth.

In the past there had been the occasional drug deal made in the club but it hadn't happened in a while and Saul was usually able to spot them immediately. This guy was behaving strangely but he didn't look like a drug dealer.

'Good evening. What beer do you have?'

So the tall guy was English, the mystery thickened. Saul went through the list but he could see he wasn't really listening.

'I'll have a bottle of San Miguel, please, Saul.'

Saul stared at him. 'How the hell do you know my name ?'

'Must have overheard it,' Toby stammered, caught out.

The black guy was regarding him with suspicion and looked pointedly around. There was no one else within earshot.

'What brings you to The Honey Bees?' Saul asked quietly, sure that this man spelt trouble.

'The, um … the concierge at the hotel recommended it to me.' That didn't ring true and they both knew it. Toby tried a new tack. 'The mural over there is wonderful. Who painted it? Was it one of the girls?'

Now Saul was on red alert. Why was this guy so interested in Titty's mural and how had he known or even suspected that one of the girls had drawn it? He looked over to Drew and Elliot. Drew glanced up and Saul motioned him over.

Toby knew things weren't going well. He sensed two men walking towards him and his heart started pounding.

'This gentleman is real interested in the mural we have.' Saul said.

'Is he now? Is this gentleman interested in art then?' Drew asked.

'He seems more interested in the artist.'

Drew was looking at Toby.

'I, er, it's very unusual, it reminded me of something, well, um, someone.' Toby could feel beads of sweat trickling down his face.

'Who did it remind you of?' Elliot asked coming to stand the other side of Toby.

'Someone I used to know.' Toby was shaking. Christ this was terrible. 'It's someone I've been looking for you see, someone I badly want to find.' He could see the hostility in their faces.

'We're not that keen on strangers asking questions about our girls,' Saul said.

'Makes us kinda suspicious,' Elliot added.

'And I'm not keen on people bullying me,' Toby was suddenly angry. 'I've come a bloody long way to find this person so don't you dare try and stop me.'

'You'd best calm down, buddy, or you're out,' Saul said.

'Look is Drew around?' Toby asked desperately 'I really need to speak to Drew.'

'How the hell do you know all our names?' Saul asked.

'Jamie and Roz told me. Jesus Christ, could you just please fetch Drew?'

'You know Jamie and Roz?' Drew asked.

'They never said they had a friend coming,' Saul said quietly.

'I asked them not to mention it.' This was fast becoming an absolute nightmare.

'Why would you do that?' Elliot asked.

'Because I didn't want it known that I was looking for this person. I recognised the mural but I couldn't risk you knowing and saying anything in case he ran away.' He knew he was making no sense. He licked his dry lips and took a deep breath ready to try again.

'Saul, I think the gentleman could use a drink,' Drew said and Saul passed the beer over. Drew laid a hand on Toby's shoulder. 'OK, buddy, I'm Drew.'

'Thank God.'

'Take your time, let's have the whole story. What's your name?'

'My name's Toby Forrester.' He took a long swig of his drink and squared his shoulders as if making his mind up about something. 'I'm Ben's brother but you know him … her as Miss Titty. When Roz showed me the photo of the mural I knew immediately it was Ben's work, and that I'd finally found him.'

'Have you been searching for him then?' Elliot enquired.

'I've been searching for three years.'

'And what do you intend to do now?'

'I intend to see him, of course, why the hell else do you think I'm here?'

'And what if Ben doesn't want to see you?'

'Then I imagine he'll be able to tell me that to my face and give me the reasons why.' Toby glared at the tall, elegant man, who looked unrepentant.

'Do you know why Ben disappeared?' Drew took over.

'No, I have absolutely no bloody idea. Do you?' He was beginning to feel like a criminal.

'Yes, it happens I do,' Drew said softly.

CHAPTER 49

San Francisco

Toby was taken aback. He hadn't expected this. He waited for Drew to elaborate but Drew remained silent, as if debating how much to reveal

'Well, buddy?' he said in a direct parody of Drew. 'Do you feel like enlightening me?'

Drew regarded him for a moment. 'Ben ran away because he thought you were all ashamed of who he was.'

'Why? Why the hell should he think we were ashamed of him?'

'He overheard your mother on the phone saying that your father couldn't live with the shame. And that was why he'd killed himself. That's why your brother ran away.'

Toby reeled backwards as if he had been punched. 'No, Jesus Christ, no.' His legs turned to jelly and the colour drained from his face.

Drew and Elliot quickly guided him to a seat and pushed his head between his legs. Saul sprinted over with a cold towel and a cognac.

'Easy, buddy, deep breaths now,' Drew said, pressing the cold towel on the back of Toby's neck. 'Take it nice and easy.'

After a few minutes, Toby lifted his head. He still looked shaken but

340

at least some colour was beginning to return to his face. Drew handed him the brandy. 'So I take it that's not the truth.'

'Christ, no,' Toby replied. 'Ben could never do anything to make me ashamed of him. Our father was a high-ranking army officer and admittedly he wasn't particularly keen on Ben's sexuality becoming public knowledge within the ranks, but that wasn't the reason he took his own life.'

He paused and put his head in his hands. The others waited in silence. Finally he looked up at them. 'Trust me, my father did not commit suicide because of Ben. There was another reason but it doesn't feel fair to tell you before I tell Ben.' He gulped his brandy. 'There's been the most terrible bloody misunderstanding. Ben had no reason to run away, no reason at all. Christ, what a mess, what a fucking mess.' Toby's eyes were streaming and his nose running.

'The most important thing is that you're here now,' Elliot said, handing him a silk handkerchief.

'Thanks,' Toby blew his nose loudly. 'Sorry, guys, I'm not normally like this.'

'You've had a hell of a shock, you're jet lagged, you've had too much alcohol and too little sleep. Frankly I'm amazed you're still standing,' Drew smiled at him gently. 'Now Elliot's gonna take you upstairs to the office. You've about an hour and a half before the show, it'll take me that long to get ready. I take it you want to see the show?' he added as an afterthought.

'I certainly do.'

'OK, well go and lie on the couch, make yourself at home and Elliot will come and get you before the show starts. We'll put you in a dark corner where no one can see you and I'll bring Titty straight up afterwards.'

'Thanks.' He smiled weakly at them. 'Jamie said you were great guys, I had a moment of doubt back there but he was right.'

Toby lay down on the huge couch in Drew's office, put the TV on and within seconds was fast asleep. Elliot woke him ninety minutes later.

'You look better,' he remarked, placing a large tumbler on the table. 'No idea what's in this. Saul has a new cocktail book that Roz and Jamie bought for him. It's become his bible, apparently there's a drink for every occasion.'

'What's this occasion called?'

'The reunion, I guess.'

'It's doing the trick whatever it is,' Toby said taking a large swig. 'I feel almost human again, guess the sleep has helped.'

'That and finding out the truth,' Elliot said. 'Now you know what's been going on you can stop torturing yourself.'

'Are all Californians this wise or is it just you three?' Toby asked. 'Hang on, it must be just you three, there was a guy in the hotel who thought Lake Como was in Paris.'

'Isn't it?'

Toby looked up in consternation but saw that Elliot was smiling. 'Whenever you're ready, Toby.' He headed out the door. 'Saul has a stool at the end of the bar furthest from the stage. You'll be safe there. I won't start the show until I see you in position.'

The show was a blur for Toby. He thought the girls and Drew were excellent but he only had eyes for Ben. When Elliot introduced Miss Titty Titty Bang Bang and Ben walked onto the stage he was afraid he may faint again.

He was completely blown away by her performance. She looked

amazing and her talent shone out. He had no idea he was crying until Saul handed him a box of tissues.

'Christ, I'm supposed to be inconspicuous and yet here I am sobbing like a girl. Everyone will be wondering who's the crazy cry baby in the corner.'

'No one was looking at you, Toby, they only had eyes for Titty. She's a class act, ain't she?'

'She's down right disgusting. I love it.'

'You should see her encore of "Truly Scrumptious".' Saul chuckled. 'I doubt she'll do it tonight though, it's too quiet and I know Drew wants to keep the show short for you.

'Thank heavens for small mercies, that may just have sent me right over the edge.'

Drew brought Titty upstairs straight after the show as he had promised. She had no idea why he was so insistent on taking her to his office and could only assume that she'd done something wrong. He paused outside the door and laid his arm gently on her shoulder.

'There's someone here to see you, Titty.' He opened the door. 'In you go, sweetie.'

Toby was standing there more nervous than he had ever been in his life. Titty screamed when she saw him and started backing out of the door. Drew blocked her way. 'He's come a long way to find you, Titty, hear what he has to say.' He pushed her back inside and quietly closed the door.

CHAPTER 50

San Francisco

The two brothers stood stock still staring at each other. Neither seemed capable of speech. Ben was paralysed with fear and tears were once again streaming down Toby's cheeks as he faced his sibling at long last.

Toby finally broke the silence. 'Why on earth did you think we were ashamed of you, Ben?'

'I heard Mum on the phone,' Ben whispered. 'I heard her say that Dad couldn't live with the shame any more, that he couldn't bear for it to be public knowledge.'

'Why did you think she was talking about you?'

'What else could she have been talking about? What else could he have been ashamed of if not me?'

Toby took a deep breath. 'Ben, sit down, I've something to tell you.'

Ben sank onto the sofa and Toby moved to the window trying to find the right words.

'There's no easy way to say this,' he finally said, turning round to his brother. 'Dad had a terrible secret, Ben. He was an addict. He was addicted to gambling.'

Ben gazed at him uncomprehending.

'He'd been gambling for years and he'd run up mountainous debts that threatened to ruin us, did ruin us in fact. He knew that is was only a matter of time before he was found out and then his reputation, his career, his marriage, everything he had worked so hard for would be ruined.' He paused. 'That was what he was ashamed of Ben, not you. This was what he couldn't bear to become public knowledge.'

Ben started shaking uncontrollably as a tide of emotion swept over him. Huge relief that he was not responsible for his father's death but incredulity to hear of what was. It was inconceivable that his father had been a gambler and nothing could have prepared him for the shock he felt.

'Dad was never ashamed of you Ben,' Toby said gently. 'He loved you very much, so does Mum and so do I.'

Ben let out a cry that pierced Toby to the heart. He rushed over to the sofa and held onto his brother as Ben howled like a wounded animal. He rocked him in his arms letting their tears mingle.

'I'm so sorry, Ben, so very sorry,' he wept. 'We should have told you. We were going to but we thought you'd been through enough, we thought it best to wait until after the funeral. It was the wrong thing to do, I'm so sorry.'

'Every night I've gone to bed with the image of how I found Dad and with the knowledge that I killed him,' Ben sobbed.

'And every night I've been torturing myself wondering what I'd done to make you disappear without trace,' Toby replied. 'Wondering if you were alright, if you were even alive and whether I would ever see you again.'

'How did you find me?' Ben suddenly asked.

'Because of your painting.' And Toby recounted the story to him.

'I never gave up, Ben, I was very angry with you for a long while but I never gave up. I even hired a private detective.' This made Ben smile as Toby had known it would. 'I missed you so much; I couldn't believe that you had just walked out on us.'

'I honestly thought no one wanted me,' Ben hung his head. 'These last three years have been absolute hell for me.'

'For all of us.'

'How is Mum?' Ben looked up. 'What happened? How did you clear the debts.'

'We didn't really. We sold Mum and Dad's house of course but it was mortgaged up to the hilt, the same with the Norfolk cottage. We sold pretty much everything we could get our hands on but it wasn't enough. Mum was officially bankrupt. Kate and I sold our London house and that, together with our savings, gave us just enough money to buy a tiny cottage for Mum and somewhere for Kate and me.'

'Your savings were for Belinda and Tom's education.'

'I know, and for a while I nearly killed myself working every hour I could in order to be able to recoup them. But they don't want to go to a private school and something happened recently to teach me they were right. It's a long story, I'll tell you another time.'

'Jesus, what a nightmare.'

'Things went from bad to worse. Kate had a miscarriage when she was six months' pregnant. She was very ill for a long while.'

'Christ, Toby, you've been through hell and I wasn't there for you.'

'You're here now,' Toby said, reaching out for him. 'And I'm never letting you go again.'

'I can't believe you're here.'

'Me neither. You were excellent tonight by the way.'

'Really?'

'Really. Although if I'd known the effect *Chitty Chitty Bang Bang* was going to have on you I may have stopped you watching it so often,' he grinned. 'It's a wickedly filthy routine, Ben, and Saul tells me "Truly Scrumptious" is even worse.'

'Wait till you see what I've got in mind for "Toot Sweets".' Ben said and the two of them collapsed into gales of laughter that had more than a hint of hysteria.

The door opened and Drew stuck his head in. 'I hear laughter so I assume it's safe to enter.'

'Oh, Honey, I got it so badly wrong.' Titty said. 'Dad was never ashamed of me.'

'I never thought he could be. No one who knows you could ever be ashamed of you, Titty.' He looked from one to the other. They both looked drained. Drew was desperate to know what had happened but he knew that Titty would tell him everything in time. Right now he was just delighted that they'd found each other and that Titty was no longer haunted by the awful fear that she'd been responsible for her father's death.

He shuddered, what a dreadful thing for her to have lived with. 'The girls are anxious, sweetie, they know something is up but I haven't told them what. Elliot has lit the heaters and we're all waiting in the garden.'

'Are they really worried?'

'Sure they are, Titty. They care about you a lot, we all do.'

'Honey has been simply wonderful,' Ben said to Toby.

'I can see that, and I am eternally grateful,' Toby smiled at him.

'They've all been wonderful,' Titty said in a rush of emotion. 'They're like family.'

347

'Well come on then, we'd better go and meet the rest of my sisters.'

The girls were delighted with Toby.

'Three sexy Englishmen in one week, y'all know how lucky we are?' Babette was beside herself. 'I sure can't wait to visit this village full of these cute guys.'

'Jamie would have a fit if you called him English,' Toby laughed.

'Gee, Titty, where've you been hiding this brother?' Diana asked. 'How come we ain't seen him before? If I had a brother like this I'd stick to him like glue.'

'Trust me that is what I'll be doing from now on.' Titty smiled and turned to Drew.

'Honey, I'm going home. I'm going back to England, I'm sorry to let you down but I've got a lot of catching up to do.'

'Of course, you wanna go home to be with your mom and your family. Of course you do, sweetie, I totally understand.'

He did understand but that didn't stop him from being devastated. Not only was Titty a real asset to the club but he had come to care deeply for her and he knew the others felt much the same way. He gave her a hug.

'We're all gonna miss you very much, Titty. It sure won't be the same without you. Thank you for all you've done. You're welcome back anytime.'

The rest of them looked totally shocked and Cherie burst into tears. Titty looked at their faces. She'd had no idea that they would be so upset by her departure and she felt overwhelmed at the depth of their feeling.

'No, you don't understand,' she cried. 'Of course I'm going home but only for a couple of weeks. You don't think I'm seriously going to leave you all, do you? We've got Christmas coming up and Saul and I have some great ideas for a new number.'

She smiled and held her hands out to them.

'You're family. I deserted one family and I regretted it. I'm certainly not about to desert another.'

CHAPTER 51

Suffolk

Kate was waiting for them at the airport. She kissed Toby as if she hadn't seen him for a month and then turned her attention to Ben. She held out her arms.

'Welcome home, Ben. We've missed you so very much.'

'And I you,' he said. 'It's good to see you, Kate. You're more beautiful than ever.' He glanced over her shoulder as if searching for someone.

'Your mum is at home, Ben,' Kate smiled. 'She decided not to come, she said she'd get too emotional and she'd rather make a fool of herself in private, her words not mine.'

She put her arms around them both. 'Have you had a wonderful time?'

At her insistence they had spent a few days together in San Francisco before returning. Toby had wanted to come home straight away but Kate had persuaded him to delay for a short while. 'Have some time together, Toby, there's no need to rush back. Get to know each other again. You'll have to relinquish Ben to your mum and to me and the kids when you get back so why don't you spend some time just the two of you.'

She'd been right. They had spent a marvellous few days putting the past behind them and relaxing into each other's company.

Toby did have to relinquish Ben, not only to his mother and family, but to the whole village.

Ben adored meeting everyone and Toby adored showing him off. He particularly liked spending time in the pub and struck up a firm friendship with George.

'We don't have pubs in California and I miss the atmosphere. We have plenty of bars but nothing beats a British pub. You've a great community here,' he said gazing around one evening in the pub. 'Such wonderful people, such characters.'

'Not quite as colourful as the ones you have in San Francisco, I imagine.'

'Oh I don't know. I'd say you've got your fair share of colour here.' Ben glanced around the pub, his gaze taking in Leon vibrant in orange and purple and Ollie swearing at the top of her voice.

Roz and Jamie of course were delighted to see Titty again.

'Isn't this fantastic?' Roz exclaimed. 'I'm so pleased everything worked out, we were stunned when Toby suddenly took flight.'

'Thank you for being the ones to find me,' Ben flung his arms around them both.

'It was our pleasure, although it was totally unintentional,' Jamie laughed. 'We had no idea anyone was searching for you.'

'I felt so bad when you were out in San Francisco, you must have thought me so cagey and hostile.'

'Not at all. You were understandably reticent about certain things but never hostile,' Roz said. 'I really miss everyone, I can't wait until February.'

351

'Talking of which, I wondered whether I could design a poster for you,' he looked around at everyone. 'I mean, only if you want, you may have done something already. I don't want to tread on toes.'

'I don't think you'd be treading on anyone's toes, I think it would be a brilliant idea.' Jamie said. 'What sort of thing do you have in mind?'

'I loved the bees that Belinda and Hannah came up with and Frank's logo "Honey Bees have Hearts".' Frank puffed out his chest. 'I'll play around with some ideas.'

'I'd like to help you,' Billy said unexpectedly. He had been lurking on the outside of the group as usual but now edged forward. 'I'm working from home for the next couple of days, we could maybe try some images on the computer.'

'Do you work in graphic design?'

'Our new boss prefers the term Visual Arts,' Billy grinned. 'Actually, Roz, I also had an idea about some of the photos you took of the drag queens. I thought it might be an idea to alter them to black and white, enlarge them to poster size and hang them on the walls. It would sort of match Titty's mural back at The Honey Bees.' Billy loved the name Titty, it suited her better than Ben. 'What do you think?'

'I think it sounds great,' Roz was stunned by Billy's sudden animation.

'Our new management team are getting rid of all the office furniture,' Billy continued. 'It's black and chrome. I rather like it. We could create a 1920s black-and-white Art Deco theme for the evening.'

'That's the sort of thing Drew has in mind for The Honey Bees,' Ben said smiling at him. 'How bizarre that you should have the same idea. That's exactly why I did the mural in that style.'

'I'll ask the manager what they intend doing with the old stuff then.'

'It might be an idea for Ben to cast his eye over the whole village hall,' Frank said. 'Let us know what else we need in terms of music, lights, props etc.'

'We do need a piano,' Ben replied. 'What's this one like?' He indicated the old upright in the corner.

'It's certainly seen better days,' George laughed. 'No one's played it for ages, no idea if it's even in tune.'

'Have a go, Titty,' Jamie said. 'Let's have a sing-song.'

Ben glanced over towards Toby who smiled encouragingly.

'She's bloody good, isn't she, or is it he? I'm not really sure what to call her?' Frank said to George as they watched Titty create magic from the old tuneless piano.

'You're not the only one who thinks so,' George nodded towards Billy who was watching Titty with a look of naked adoration on his face. 'I'd say he was fairly smitten.'

There was no response, Frank wasn't listening. He'd just spotted Leon walk through the door with his sister Jess and was sprinting over to greet them. Billy clearly wasn't the only one who was smitten. Cupid appears to be working overtime, thought George, and chuckled to himself.

'Telling yourself jokes again, George?' Jamie asked.

'Sure sign of madness,' Leon was right behind him. 'Carry on like this and we'll have you committed.'

'Where I go you follow,' George smiled.

'Any requests?' Ben asked the room

'"Love Me Tender"', Leon yelled.

'Are you sure that's only a song request, Leon?' Ben grinned wickedly.

The room was in uproar and it was the final straw for Steve who had been sitting in the far corner with a German business colleague who was staying the night.

He hadn't wanted to come to the pub. He would have much preferred to be impressing his associate with both his new conservatory and his latest wine delivery but Ulrich had been very keen that they visit the local pub for a beer and Steve's boss had told him to keep him sweet at all costs.

He was mortified that he should have been exposed to this impromptu show. He threw back his beer. 'Time to head off, old boy, before they get too rowdy. They're all getting a bit carried away.' He tried to make light of it but inside he was seething.

Ulrich Schnickman from Bonn was reluctant to leave. This was exactly the sort of thing he loved, British eccentricity at its best. 'Maybe one more, Stefan?'

'I think not, old boy. She who must be obeyed said to be back for seven.' Steve gave a false laugh. Why the hell does he insist on calling me Stefan, he wondered? He knows my name is Steve.

Ulrich was amused at Steve's irritation with the way he pronounced his name. It had been deliberate, he was perfectly capable of saying Steve but this man was beginning to annoy him. He hated the way Steve spoke, like some character from an old war film. He slowly drained his glass and stood up. The crowd around the piano were cheering and dancing, it looked like such fun.

He smiled politely and thanked the barman on his way out, in contrast to Steve who marched out slamming the door behind him in a petulant manner. Ulrich was startled and began to question whether they really wanted to do business with this sort of person.

'Honestly, it was humiliating to witness,' Steve was saying to his wife Vicki a short while later while their guest was upstairs changing. 'The nancy at the piano is Toby's brother, imagine that.' He reached for the wine. 'Apparently that Scottish git Jamie found him in some drag club in the States and Toby went to rescue him. Personally I'd have left him there but Toby is unashamedly parading the poofter around the village.'

'It does seem that the whole village has become obsessed with drag queens,' Vicki stirred the sauce vehemently. 'Rumour has it there's a whole bunch of them coming over from San Francisco for this bloody show in February.'

'It's all down to that fucking Jock. We had things pretty much sewn up before he arrived on the scene. I don't know who wrote "Go back to Glasgow" but I agree wholeheartedly.'

Allegra and Archie doing their homework at the far end of the kitchen table exchanged a secret smile.

'We should start a campaign, "Say No to the Faggots from San Francisco".' He felt rather pleased with that. It had a nice ring to it.

Allegra and Archie giggled.

Ulrich coming down the stairs overheard the last remark and was horrified. He stood unseen outside the door uncertain whether to go in or not.

'I thought we'd have a drink in the conservatory,' Steve was saying.

'Won't it be rather chilly?' Vicki replied. 'We haven't had any heating on.'

'No, it'll be fine. Besides, he's German, he's used to the cold.'

Ulrich thought longingly of the roaring fire in the pub.

'Are the kids eating with us, they could practice their German.' He wandered over to them and Allegra quickly covered the piece of paper on which she had written, 'Say no to the faggots from San Francisco.'

'Does he have any kids?' Vicki asked.

'God knows, never thought to ask,' Steve replied in a careless fashion.

It was those dismissive words which finally sealed his fate. Ulrich decided there and then that he would give Steve his decision in the morning. There would be no business deal between their two companies. He wished with all his heart that he were back in the pub enjoying the fun and laughter.

'That was a great evening,' Jamie said to Roz back at home.

'It certainly was. What the hell are you doing?'

'Trying to get this bloody fire back to life,' he replied red faced and choking. 'I told you we should have bought a wood burner.'

'No you didn't, you told me that a wood burner was unnecessary and too expensive,' Roz replied. 'Oh, Jamie, get that wood away from Butler, he's making an unholy mess.'

'Yes but as long as he's chewing that log he isn't chewing anything else.'

'Point taken,' Roz said, looking over to where Butler lay in the corner surrounded by shards of wood.

Butler heard his name mentioned and saw them staring at him. This wood was fine but a meaty treat would be so much nicer. He gave them what he thought was his winning look.

'Look at him, he looks demented. He's positively barking.' It took a couple of seconds before she realised what she had said and then she collapsed into giggles. 'Barking! Did you hear me, Jamie? I said the dog was barking.'

'That makes two of you,' he grinned at her. 'OK I give up, this fire does not want to come back to life.'

Butler remained optimistic but sadly the meaty treat didn't materialise. Still at least he'd made them happy and that's what counted.

'Titty really is talented,' Roz said. 'I mean we knew she was in San Francisco but watching her tonight playing song after song with no music was incredible.'

'Toby said it had been a toss-up between art college or music college, both were keen to have her.'

'How lovely to have people fighting over you.'

'I fought for you, my love.'

'No you didn't.'

'Well I would have done had anyone else shown any interest.'

CHAPTER 52

Suffolk

Titty's two weeks flew by in no time at all. The poster was designed with the help of Billy and also Belinda and Hannah, who were overjoyed at being asked.

'You're very good, Bell. Keep practising. Take a sketch book everywhere you go, it's important. Tell you what, darling, I'll send you a special one from America.'

Bell smiled up at him. She idolised her uncle. In fact Ben had made an impact on the village as a whole. Not only had he designed the poster but he had inspected the hall as Frank had suggested, drawn up a list of things to be bought or borrowed and most importantly he'd promised to help the Suffolk drag queens with their acts before the final show.

'We know we're going to look pretty shabby besides the real McCoy but it would be great if you could spend some time with us,' Frank said.

'I'm flattered to be asked. Of course I'll help you.'

'Won't that give us an unfair advantage over the others who enter?' Leon questioned.

'Don't care. I want to get to San Francisco by fair means or foul.'

'Why do you use the word "us" Leon?' Charlotte challenged. 'You're not entering the competition are you?'

'Of course I am. I thought we needed as many men as possible. Besides, I want to go to San Francisco.'

'But, Daddy you can't sing.' Hannah was horrified. Her father couldn't do much wrong in her eyes but his singing was truly terrible. Perhaps he didn't realise how bad he was. She couldn't bear the thought of people laughing at him.

'Poppet, I shall mime,' he said putting his arms around her. 'Don't worry, your old dad won't let you down.'

She smiled but remained unconvinced. Still maybe if Ben was going to help all may not be lost. Like the rest of the village she had been captivated by Bell's uncle. He had come into school to give an art class, he was a fantastic teacher and every kid had gone home inspired. She crossed over to Belinda.

'Is your Dad going to do something?' she whispered.

'Not sure, I've never really heard him sing and I don't think he can dance,' Belinda giggled. 'Maybe they should do a duet.'

'Maybe they should just sell tickets,' Hannah replied and the two of them began laughing.

Toby smiled at his daughter. It was great to see her so happy. He would never forget the terrible fear that had overtaken him when she'd run away. It had brought back ghastly memories and he glanced over at Ben. To think that he'd nearly lost them both, he shuddered at the thought.

Kate took his hand. 'Are you OK, sweetheart?'

'Just thinking how lucky I am and how much I'm going to miss Ben. It's all gone too fast.'

'He'll be back in a couple of months. Everyone will miss him, everyone adores him.'

'He's been a bit of a hit, hasn't he?'

'He certainly has and rightly so. You sound surprised, did you think there would be problems?'

'No, not really. I think I was the only one with a problem. I was just so bloody angry with him after he left, I sort of blamed the whole gay population for his disappearance. Not exactly fair or rational but then I wasn't behaving like a rational human being.'

'You'd been through one hell of a lot, Toby, don't be so hard on yourself.'

'You're very forgiving, Kate, I know I was an absolute monster.'

'Well there's no denying that but at least you were my monster.' She squeezed his hand.

Billy was also looking at Titty and thinking how much he was going to miss her. He had connected with her in a way that he'd never connected with anyone else. He found her exotic and extremely sexy. She was also kind and compassionate and there was a frailty about her that touched his heart. Other people may think he was besotted but he knew beyond doubt that it was love. He just didn't know if it was reciprocated and he was far too shy to ask.

Titty knew that he was watching her and wondered what the hell was in his mind? She'd never felt like this about anyone before and it excited and confused her. She knew there was a real spark between them but nothing had been said and she was too insecure to be the first one to make a move.

Louisa watched her grandson watch Ben and wondered if either of them would ever pluck up the courage to reveal their feelings. She loved her grandson dearly and had always known that he was gay. It had never bothered her but she knew that it had bothered him. He had struggled with his sexuality and had always felt ill at ease in social situations. She'd watched him come alive before Ben with delight. Nothing would please her more than to see him in a secure relationship. Maybe when Ben returned in two months the time would be right. Maybe then would also be the right time to disclose her own new-found happiness and she glanced across at Edward and smiled.

In the early hours of the morning a few days later the two brothers stood staring awkwardly at one another in Heathrow's Terminal Three.

'I'm crap at saying goodbye,' Toby said.

'I know,' Ben grinned. 'You always used to ruffle my hair and whack me hard on the shoulders.'

'I think that's what I'm about to do now,' Toby said, but made no move.

'Thank you for finding me.'

'Would you have come home eventually?' Toby asked the question that had been praying on his mind.

'I'm not sure, but yes I think so, eventually.'

'Well I'm pleased we didn't have to wait until eventually.'

'Me too.' Ben reached out and clasped Toby in a tight embrace. They hugged each other for a few minutes neither speaking and then Toby broke away. 'Right I'm going to whack you on the shoulder and walk away before I break down completely. Take care, kiddo. Phone when you get back and see you in a couple of months.' He strode away without looking back.

Watching him go, Ben felt bereft. He resisted an urge to run after him and turned purposefully away. He felt very tired, it had been an emotional few weeks and he was ready to go back home. He smiled as he realised that San Francisco really did feel like home.

He'd missed Drew and the Honey Bees. He'd never forget the support they had given him when Toby had arrived and he suddenly felt excited about returning. He would of course miss his family and he would also miss the village and one person in particular but he knew he would be going back.

CHAPTER 53

Suffolk

It had been an emotional few weeks for them both and Toby also felt suddenly exhausted. He decided to ditch the car at the garage where it needed a service and walk the couple of miles back home. It would save another trip later and the fresh air and the exercise would do him good.

He set off briskly across the fields and had worked up quite a sweat by the time he reached the football pitch behind the village hall. He spotted a familiar figure in the distance and shouted and waved.

Roz turned around, surprised to see him. Butler hurtled over and Toby braced himself for the impact but the big dog managed to skid to a halt inches away and looked up mischievously.

'I swear that bloody dog is laughing at me,' he said when Roz had caught up.

'Yes, it's a new habit he's got into, scares the living daylights out of people. One of these days he'll misjudge it and there will be an almighty collision.' She reached up to kiss him. 'What on earth are you doing up so early?'

'Just come back from taking Ben to the airport and I needed some air and exercise. What about yourself?'

'Early morning photographs.' She waved the camera at him. 'The light is amazing first thing, it's bloody cold but beautiful.'

'I'd love to see your photos of the village, Roz. You know you should have an exhibition, ask George to put them up at the pub.'

'That's what Jamie said but I don't think they're good enough.'

'If they're anything like the ones you took of San Francisco they most certainly are. Ben was terribly impressed.'

'It's always strange to hear you call him Ben. I'm sorry but he'll always be Titty to me. I guess that name must sound totally bizarre to you?'

'I must admit I haven't quite got my head around it yet. Ah, there goes Butler again.'

The dog galloped towards the village hall where he could see a couple of people. He slid to a halt just before them and then yelped in pain and surprise as a stone came whizzing through the air, cutting him just above his right eye.

'What the hell are you doing?' Roz yelled running towards the dazed puppy. She was amazed to see two youngsters there. 'How dare you throw stones at him.' She knelt down beside Butler. 'Jesus, you could have blinded him, what the hell were you thinking of?'

Allegra and Archie turned to flee but found their path blocked by Toby. He grabbed them by their arms. 'You're not going anywhere,' he said, taking in the paint pot and brush beside them. He turned and looked at the doorway of the hall. 'Roz, how's Butler?'

'Bleeding, he's going to need stitches. I'll ring Leon. I can't believe these kids.'

'Well, there's more to it. Come and have quick look.'

She patted Butler and went to see what Toby was pointing at.

'Say No to the Faggots from San Francisco.' She read out loud. She turned to the children and looked them up and down contemptuously. 'My God, you two really are something else aren't you? Do you know these kids, Toby?'

'Their names are Allegra and Archie and they belong to Steve and Vicki.'

'And are you responsible for all the other things that have happened recently?' Roz asked in an icy voice.

Archie nodded, tears starting to run down his cheeks. Allegra stood completely still, paralysed by fear as the enormity of what they'd done began to dawn on her for the first time. She glanced towards the dog, she hadn't really meant to hurt him, she just wanted to frighten him away and now he lay bleeding. Toby's next words turned her insides to jelly.

'Well, the police will have a field day with this. I'm tempted to take you straight there but first let's see what your parents have to say.'

'You can tell your parents that they'll be receiving a vet's bill from me,' Roz said going back to Butler. She was using her scarf to stem the flow of blood. 'Haven't you got anything to say? No apology or anything?'

Archie muttered something through his tears but Allegra just stared sullenly at the ground, she knew she should say something but couldn't find the words.

Toby marched them through the village and up to their house. Vicki was astonished to see them.

'What on earth is going on?' She looked at everyone. 'I thought you two were going in early for your new project, what's happened?'

'They were certainly involved in a project but nothing to do with

365

the school. Do you two want to tell your mum what you've been up to or shall I?'

Vicki listened in horror as they stumbled through their explanation. 'There must be someone else, someone must have put them up to this. They'd never have thought of this themselves.' She turned to them. 'Who was it, who was behind all this?'

'We thought Dad would be pleased,' Archie gulped.

'Dad?' Vicki screamed. 'Dad never asked you to do all this, don't lie to me.' She grabbed his arm and shook him.

'I think he means that he heard Steve say all these things, Vicki,' Toby said quickly intervening.

'Steve never said anything like this.'

'Oh come on, Vicki,' Toby was exasperated. 'They'd never have come up with a slogan like that. "Say No to the Faggots from San Francisco". That has Steve written all over it.' One look at her flushed face told him he'd hit the mark.

'Will we go to prison?' Allegra asked in a small voice.

'No, of course not,' Vicki turned to Toby. 'I mean this isn't a police matter, is it? No need to involve them, I'm sure we can sort it all out between ourselves.'

'I think it's very much a police matter, Vicki,' Toby replied and Archie started to sob again. 'On the other hand it may just be possible to sort it out in the village, it rather depends what the other people involved think.'

'They must realise it's just a childish prank. Just kids messing around,' she said, clutching at straws.

'I don't think anyone will see it as a childish prank, Vicki. They've just wounded a defenceless animal. Frank's tyres cost a fortune, as did George's garden. They had to repaint Jamie's front door and scrub off all the graffiti from the hall. Kate and I had our cars scratched, as you know'

'We didn't scratch your cars,' Allegra suddenly found her voice. 'But you sounded so pleased, Mum, you said that someone needed to teach her a lesson, you said you wished you'd thought of it first.'

'Just shut up, the pair of you,' Vicki screeched. 'Shut your bloody mouths and get out of my sight.'

The kids fled and Toby began to feel almost sorry for them. No wonder they behaved like they did with this as a role model. He was seeing the true Vicki here, the veneer had cracked; this was not the Vicki she usually presented to the world.

'Obviously we will make good the damages. I really can't see the need to involve the police at all,' Vicki turned to Toby.

'I don't know, Vicki, everyone's very angry about what has happened. I'm very angry.'

'But they just said they didn't do your car.'

'No, but they wrote about my brother on the village hall today.'

'So, what else can we do?'

'I think if people hear that they are genuinely sorry that would go a long way.'

'Oh, but they are sorry, or they certainly will be after Steve has talked to them,' Vicki replied. 'We'll tell all the people involved how sorry they are when we pay them the money.' She smiled, money was always the solution.

'No, Vicki, it needs something more than that. The whole village has been affected, everyone has been worried about what has been happening.'

'What the hell do you suggest?'

'For starters they need to apologise themselves to the people involved and then I think a few words from them in the parish magazine wouldn't go amiss, something along the lines of how sorry they are for all the trouble they've caused.'

'No way,' she was outraged. 'That would be such a public humiliation.'

'Up to you, of course, but I'm just thinking of ways to avoid bringing the police in,' he smiled sweetly. 'I really think that people would appreciate a public apology and as well as paying damages you might consider donating some money into a village fund, the village hall fund for example. People would certainly see how sorry you were then.'

He bid her goodbye and walked out of her house chuckling to himself.

There was a lot of chatter in the pub that night.

Butler was the centre of attention and was lapping it up, showing everyone the three stitches above his eye. Frank had made him a special Butler sausage and Edward had bought him a new squeaky toy guaranteed to drive Roz and Jamie mad but then, as he pointed out, it wouldn't be for long. Butler would soon make short work of it.

'I'd like to have seen her face when you mentioned putting the money into the village hall fund,' George was over the moon.

'It wasn't a pretty picture I can tell you. She's an absolute monster, they both are, no wonder the kids behave as they do.'

'There was a time when you didn't think like that,' Frank observed wryly.

'In my dim and distant past, Frank. I've grown up since then,' Toby grinned, not rising to the bait.

'You certainly have,' Frank said. 'Who wants one for the road?'

There was a clamour of voices.

'Whenever it's my round no one ever says no,' he grumbled as he turned to the bar.

'You've a persuasive manner, Frank. It's not everyone who has that talent,' Jamie laughed.

CHAPTER 54

Mainly Suffolk

Christmas was fast approaching and Roz and Jamie were busy decorating their little cottage, but not everything was going according to plan.

Butler was having a field day with the Christmas tree. He just couldn't understand that they hadn't bought it purely for his pleasure. Why else would they bring a tree into the sitting room and dangle brightly coloured baubles from it if not for him? It drove him wild, he couldn't leave it alone. He knew he was doing something wrong but the temptation was simply too great to resist. It attracted him like a magnet.

They gave up in the end and compromised by hanging the baubles from the ceiling and wrapping holly and tinsel around the beams. Huge bunches of mistletoe were suspended from the doors and coloured lights were strung in the courtyard outside.

'Why do people always send us such tasteless cards?' Roz asked as she put them up on the mantelpiece. 'I notice in other people's houses that they have picturesque snow scenes with robins and angels whereas we get Santa peeing down a chimney and a couple of cherubs having a shag. What does that say about us, I wonder?'

'Says more about our friends than us I think,' Jamie grinned. 'Frankly I find shagging cherubs more interesting than a robin perched on a rake, and talking of such things are you free for an hour or so, Mrs Forsyth?' He gave her a saucy smile.

'I'm not sure about an hour or so but I could manage thirty minutes before I tackle the ironing.'

'And who said romance was dead?' He looked at her in despair. 'Thirty minutes it is then but you'll never know what I had in mind for the full hour had the ironing not taken precedence.'

'You'll just have to give me the abridged version,' she laughed, racing up the stairs.

Roughly forty minutes later Jamie was on the phone to Drew while Roz was busy with her ironing.

'Butler kept eating the bloody Christmas tree so we've had to be creative with decorations on the ceiling.'

Roz raised her eyebrows at the use of the word 'we' but Jamie ignored her.

'Yes, she's fine, she's buried behind a pile of ironing at the moment but she only has herself to blame, I did offer her a much sweeter alternative. Between you and me I don't know why she bothers, it makes her grumpy and she's completely useless at it.' He winked at Roz and then howled with laughter. 'No, Drew, I'm talking about the ironing.' And grabbing a beer he headed into the sitting room.

Roz could hear him laughing and chatting, it was amazing how well those two got on. They could talk for hours. She rescued a pair of her knickers from Butler and looked with loathing at the ironing in front of her. Jamie was right, it was definitely not her forte.

She came to a sudden decision and picking out just a few things that needed attention she pushed the rest into the basket and carted it upstairs. Life was just too bloody short for ironing, she would hang it in the wardrobe in the hope that the creases would somehow magically disappear.

She returned to the kitchen opened a bottle of red, poured two glasses, stripped down to her bra and knickers and went into the sitting room. Jamie was mid-flow.

'I've got an interview with the local radio after New Year and if Seb is able to get here then I'm damned sure the local TV will be interested and … Bloody hell,' he broke off suddenly as Roz appeared in the doorway.

She moved slowly towards him swaying her hips provocatively.

'Drew mate, I'm going to have to continue this conversation another time, a semi-naked woman has just walked into the room,' Jamie said.

Drew replaced the receiver laughing to himself. Those two were such fun, he loved their zest for life and their tremendous energy. He looked at his watch and decided to ring Fran.

It was answered on the second ring. She sounded flat.

'Hi, Fran, how are tricks?'

'OK.'

'I've just been speaking to Jamie, we've had a few ideas about publicity, have you got a minute?'

'Sure, fire away.'

Something was definitely wrong. Drew was worried.

'How about a coffee, Fran? Usual place in about fifteen minutes?'

'Sure, see you there. Order me the calorific bagel if you're first.'

CHAPTER 55

San Francisco

Drew shrugged on his coat and scarf and went to collect Elvis. 'Come on boy.' He said putting his lead on. 'Something is troubling our young reporter, let's go find out what.'

Fran was just getting seated when Drew and Elvis arrived. She smiled warmly but the usual sparkle was missing. They ordered coffee and bagels and Drew told her Jamie's idea about getting in touch with the local newspaper over there.

'It's something like the *East Anglian Chronicle* but I can't quite remember. Anyway he thought that maybe if you spoke to them and sent the articles it would generate some publicity. What do you think honey?'

'Yeah, great idea. Jason's gone over to the UK for Christmas so why don't I get in touch with him and see what he can do from there? I know he was hoping to hook up with Jamie and Roz anyway.'

She sounded wistful. Maybe that was the problem Drew thought, she was missing Jason.

'He sort of invited me to go and spend Christmas with them all,' she said and finally a small sparkle came into her eyes.

'Wow, how cool is that?' Drew grinned. 'Sounds pretty serious when someone invites you to meet their family.'

'I dunno, Drew, I mean nothing has been said really, well, things have been said but not really seriously, maybe they're serious I dunno, I just mean nothing has really happened, not yet, maybe he was just being kind.'

'For a journalist you can be amazingly inarticulate,' Drew smiled and smoothed her wayward hair. 'What stopped you going sweetie?'

'My parents,' she said and her eyes filled with tears.

'Fran what's wrong with them? Are they ill?'

'No, Drew, nothing's wrong with them.' She was crying.

Drew was puzzled but waited patiently for an explanation.

'They're not bad people, Drew, they've done nothing wrong but that's just it, they've done nothing. They do nothing.' She grabbed the napkin and blew her nose. 'I guess they must love me in their own way but they never seem excited to see me and they never seem sad to see me go. They never ask about my job or my life. They spend their lives watching the TV. They go to church once a week, they drive to the giant Walmart on the edge of town every Friday and stop off at the diner on the way back.'

'Different people lead different lives, Fran, what suits one ain't gonna suit another. You should know that.'

'I know Drew and I know I sound selfish. They're my parents at the end of the day and I gotta go and see them. It's just that the thought fills me with dread.'

'Don't you have any old friends left there?'

'The ones who stayed have families of their own now, Drew, we don't have much in common anymore, maybe we never did.' She bit viciously into her bagel.

Drew regarded her. She was a great kid. He didn't know of many others who would turn down an opportunity to go to the UK in order to spend Christmas with folks who didn't seem to care if she was there or not.

'I've an idea, Fran,' he said. 'Why not go early to your folks and then come back and spend Christmas with us. That way you do your duty to your parents and then you can come back and have a fun Christmas, which is what you deserve, which is what everyone deserves.'

'Oh, Drew, could I really?' Her eyes shone. 'Are you sure I wouldn't be butting in? What do you guys do for Christmas?'

'We gather for a late breakfast. Same routine every year.' He drank his coffee. 'Saul does waffles, I do crispy bacon and Elliot lays the Christmas table. We open champagne and we exchange presents. It's always open house and friends drop by. We put in an appearance at the homeless centre and take champagne to Blossom and her mob at the old people's home. In the evening we cook a meal but this year we're going to Lena's. Joe and Bobby will be there too. You'd be more than welcome to join us for the whole day or any particular part of the day you fancy. What do you think? '

'I think I love you very much.' She flung her arms around him. 'I'm gonna ask Corey right now if I can change my dates. I'm sure glad I met you, Drew Berry. It was a lucky day for me.'

'Fran's gonna come and spend Christmas day with us,' Drew told Saul and Elliot later on and he explained what had happened this morning.

'Poor Fran,' Elliot shook his head. 'Christmas should be fun, it sucks when it ain't and I should know.' He poured himself a large coffee. 'When other kids were busy opening their stockings, I was on my knees in a cold, draughty church praying to a god who hated all children and me in particular. Back home my mother would read me horror stories from the Old Testament. The god I grew up with was vindictive and unforgiving, a malevolent, bloodthirsty bully. We had no decorations, no presents and certainly no Christmas feast. I used to torture myself trying to imagine what was going on in other homes. It was the worst day of the year for me.'

Saul and Drew looked at each other in horror.

'Let's go to town this year. Let's lay the ghost of Christmas past once and for all,' Drew said smiling gently at his friend.

'My ghost has already been laid thanks to you two but let's make it one hell of a day for Fran,' he grinned at them both. 'I thought next Tuesday would be our big shopping day, we've no evening show so it kinda makes sense. I've already drawn up a list of presents we need to buy. It's lengthy, we oughta hit the shops early guys.'

His enthusiasm was contagious. He produced his list and he and Saul bent over it together.

Drew stood back and watched them. Elliot didn't often talk about his past and even though Drew knew his had been a ghastly upbringing it always came as a shock to hear about his mother's cruelty. That he had managed to maintain his sense of humour and love for life despite all that had gone on before was a testament to his strength of character and loving nature.

Elliot always said that the years spent here in San Francisco in The Honey Bees had been the happiest of his life. Drew knew that he and Saul felt the same and yet again he sent up a silent prayer to Martha for leaving them the money to enable the club to continue. Elliot broke into his thoughts.

'Drew, buddy, we need your input here,' he waved the list at him.

CHAPTER 56

Suffolk and San Francisco

Jamie and Roz were also planning on making their very first Christmas at the cottage one to remember. Roz's parents were coming over for the day and George and Frank were joining them for a late Christmas lunch.

Roz drove to the farm shop to order her turkey and stood in the queue patiently waiting her turn. Everything in the farm shop looked enticing and by the time she reached the counter she'd added chutney, homemade jam and gingerbread biscuits to her basket. She didn't recognise the old boy behind the counter but smiled brightly.

'Hi there, I'd like to order my Christmas turkey if I'm not too late.'

The old boy didn't look up but began to write in his book.

'White?' he asked.

Roz was taken aback. What other colours did they come in? 'Yeah, white is fine thanks,' she replied hesitantly.

There was a pause and then he repeated his question. 'White?'

'What other choices do I have?' she giggled nervously.

He looked up and regarded her as if she were a simpleton. 'How many people?' he asked very slowly.

She looked confused. 'How many people for what?'

'How many people are going to eat the bloody turkey?' He spelt out each syllable.

Finally the penny dropped. 'Oh weight, you were saying weight. I'm so sorry,' she stammered. 'I thought you were saying white, as in the colour white.'

Jamie was doubled over with laughter when she recounted the conversation later that day.

'Christ, I wish I had been there.'

'You were about the only one who wasn't, half the bloody village were there to witness my humiliation,' she replied. 'As I was parking back here a couple I'd never seen before yelled out to tell me they had a pink turkey for sale.' She kicked him on the shin. 'Stop howling, it's not that bloody funny.'

'Talking of humiliation, I had a visit from Vicki while you were out.'

'Oh really, what did she have to say for herself? Was it just Vicki?'

'Yes just Vicki. She said that the kids were sorry and that if we let her know how much she owed us her then she hoped we could put this childish nonsense behind us.'

'No,' Roz exploded. 'How dare she call all of this childish nonsense. Why the hell couldn't the kids come themselves?'

'My question exactly,' Jamie agreed. 'I said that if her children couldn't be bothered to come and say sorry in person then I very much doubted the sincerity of their apology.'

'Good for you. Did you mention an apology in the parish magazine?'

'I did and she said we were all just trying to publicly humiliate them. I told her that I felt I had been publicly humiliated by the slogan written on my front door and half the village felt the same way after

378

the graffiti on the village hall. I said we'd just have to wait to see what the police said.'

'Christ, what did she say to that?'

'She marched off.' Jamie scratched his head. 'She never even enquired after Butler. Terrible bloody woman.'

Fran had the best Christmas she'd ever had. It surpassed all expectations and was exactly the sort of Christmas she'd always imagined and had always longed for. She spent the whole day with the Honey Bees arriving in time for breakfast and leaving late after dinner at Lena's. Elliot had provided red Santa hats for them all to wear and Fran hadn't taken hers off once. She couldn't thank them enough.

On the other side of the Atlantic the day had also been a huge success. George had opened the pub for a couple of hours, the usual suspects had assembled and it had been a very merry gathering. Roz had cooked the white turkey to perfection and their late lunch had lasted until late evening. They had taken Butler for his night-time pee at the bottom of the garden and had stood hand in hand under the stars feeling mellow and extremely happy.

'Happy New Year, Drew,' Jamie yelled into the phone six days later.

'Happy New Year,' Drew yelled back. There was a slight pause and then Drew said. 'It's not yet midnight in either of our time zones, Jamie.'

'No, but I may not be capable of saying it at midnight,' he replied. 'I wanted to raise a glass to you. Cheers, Drew.'

'Cheers, Jamie.'

'Have you got a drink?'

'No, I haven't.'

'Well take me over to your cognac cupboard and pour one.'

'What are you doing tonight?' Drew enquired, pouring himself for once, quite a conservative cognac.

'Off to Ollie and Clive's for a big bash.'

'Is that the squire's house?' Drew asked. He loved hearing about every detail of their village life.

'No, it's not the squire, although he will of course be there and we've also been promised a Russian count.'

'I want to hear all about it tomorrow. Love to Roz.'

'She's blowing you a kiss as we speak. Love to everyone your end.' Jamie put down the phone. 'Hello, wife, you look rather splendid.'

'Thank you, husband, so do you,' Roz said stealing his glass of wine. 'Is there really going to be a Russian count?'

'So I've been told, an old family friend.'

In fact the Russian count was one of the first people Roz met. He was hard to miss, a great bear of a man with long white hair and a striking silk jacket. He pulled her into a smothering embrace. 'Ah such English aristocratic beauty.' He placed his hands on either side of her face nearly crushing her skull. 'You are vonderful, darlink, the perfect English rose, you remind me of why I defecated.'

Roz spat wine down his shirt front. 'Reminds you of what?'

'Why I defecated, darlink, defecated to the Vest.' He patted her on the head and strode off into the party leaving Roz shaking with laugher. She turned to search for Jamie but found her way blocked by a woman with horn-rimmed glasses and a moustache like a Patagonian fisherman.

'Excuse me,' Roz said.

'Yes, please,' the woman responded. 'A glass of white would be lovely.'

'No. I'm sorry, I didn't mean …'

'Red then, no matter,' she beamed at Roz holding out her glass.

Roz gave up and taking her glass headed towards the kitchen. She found Charlotte and Jamie helping Ollie with a pile of smoked salmon sandwiches.

'You've some mad friends, Ollie,' she remarked grabbing a bottle. 'Some blind hirsute lady mistook me for a waiter and your Russian count just told me he's defecated.'

'Defecated? Not in my fucking lounge,' Ollie cried, rushing off.

The house was decorated from floor to ceiling with balloons, brightly coloured bunting and yards of streamers. A carnival atmosphere pervaded the whole place.

'I feel like I'm in a circus,' Roz confided to Liz and Carol. 'I've met a mad Russian, a bearded lady and now I'm just waiting for the clown and a trapeze artist.'

'Well here's your clown,' Liz said as Leon strode towards them in a bright orange shirt and baggy black trousers.

'I heard that,' Leon said looking aggrieved.

'You look lovely, Leon, and unique as always,' Roz hastened to reassure him. 'I was just saying that I felt like I was taking part in a circus.'

'Clive certainly seems to be playing the part of ringleader,' he said, looking towards the kitchen where their host could be heard loudly issuing instructions. 'Have you girls told Roz your news yet?'

'No, they haven't. Are you pregnant?'

'Roz, we're not even married,' Carol chuckled. 'We do have some standards.'

'Come on then, spill the beans.'

'Well, as you know we wanted something flamboyant and different for our wedding party,' Carol began.

'And now we think we've found it,' Liz butted in. 'We're inviting twenty or so of our mates to come to your Valentine's Drag Show.'

'No way? Really?' Roz clapped her hands in delight. 'That's fantastic.'

'We're planning the marriage for the week before. We thought the drag show would be a perfect way to celebrate. Dad's going to pay for the tickets and we've asked him to donate what he would have spent on our wedding party to the village hall fund.'

'That's incredible. Jamie will be over the moon. That's so kind of you.'

'On the contrary, it's kind of you to provide our perfect wedding festivities,' Carol smiled. 'It's proving to be quite a talking point.'

Roz caught sight of Jamie emerging from the kitchen with a tray full of drinks. She waved at him. 'Jamie, quick,' she shouted. 'Come over here and listen to this.'

He spun around, caught his foot on the rug and landed on the floor with his kilt around his waist and his bare arse exposed to everyone.

'What were you saying about a circus?' Liz said to Roz clutching her sides.

'No, Jamie, don't fucking move,' Ollie's voice could be heard clearly above the rabble. 'I want to take a picture.'

CHAPTER 57

Suffolk and San Francisco

'Great news, folks. Seb is definitely on board for the Valentine's Show.' Drew burst into rehearsals a few weeks later waving a print-out of Jamie's latest email. There was a chorus of delight.

'Honey, I'm in heaven,' Babette drawled, sinking onto the nearest chair.

'What else does Jamie say?' Titty asked, laughing at Babette.

'He says the cracked rib he sustained from falling arse over tit at the New Year's party is marginally less painful but the humiliation and loss of dignity still hurt.'

The girls giggled.

'Then he goes on to talk about the accommodation. Do you want me to read it out? Am I interrupting?' he turned to Saul.

'You are, but we all want to hear so let's stop for a coffee break.'

'OK, here goes. Seb and I are staying with Roz and Jamie. He says it's only a small country cottage, nothing posh and there is a strong chance that Butler will eat everyone's shoes.' He looked up smiling. 'Maybe safer to leave my costume elsewhere.'

'The very words "country cottage" send a thrill though my veins,' Diana said dramatically.

'It's a beautiful cottage,' Titty said. 'Picture perfect, the whole village is.'

'What next?' Elliot demanded.

'OK, well there are five guest rooms at the local pub and Elliot, Saul, Corey, Fran and Jason are booked in there. Jamie says the rooms are charming with low beams, wooden floorboards and chintz. George is a wonderful character who makes a mean cocktail, cooks the best breakfast and sometimes combines the two.'

'George is utterly fantastic,' Titty interrupted once again. 'You guys will love him.'

'Titty, you're obviously staying with Toby, as are Gerry and his wife and their daughter Sasha. Bobby and Joe are ensconced in a converted barn belonging to Clive and Ollie which they let out as a holiday cottage. Secluded and romantic but with all mod cons. Sounds gorgeous.' Drew looked up. 'And the rest of you,' he paused for a second teasing them.

'Honey, I'm gonna strangle you,' Diana squealed.

'As for the rest of you, you're all staying at none other than the squire's house.'

There was a stunned silence; the girls looked at each other in amazement.

Drew laughed at their expressions. 'Jamie says the manor house is absolutely everything an old English manor house should be, with an air of faded elegance, stunning antiques, and majestic gardens running down to the river.'

'Wow,' Cherie gasped. 'We're really going to stay there? I just can't believe it.'

'It's true, baby,' Diana pirouetted around the room. 'We're all gonna live like royalty in a palace.'

'And at some point, he doesn't say when, the squire is hosting a drinks party in our honour,' Drew said looking back at the email.

'Y'all, this is just blowing my mind,' Babette was wide eyed.

'He also says they have rooms on standby should anyone else come along unexpectedly. One with a vet who looks like a scarecrow, one with a headmistress who looks like a goddess and one with a freestyle butcher who is handy with a cleaver. Who the hell would want to stay there? He sure knows how to conjure up an image.'

'Sure does, he should be a writer.' Saul said smiling.

'He ends by saying that he's been on the local radio, the posters are everywhere, there have been articles in the newspaper and the local TV is very keen to get in on the act now that Seb is coming. Ticket sales are going through the roof. He sends each and every one of you a kiss and says the village is in a fever of anticipation.'

'They're not the only ones,' Elliot grinned. 'I can't quite believe it's happening.'

'Believe it buddy, the tickets are booked and the bees are about to swarm across the pond.'

They gave each other a high five.

The village was indeed in a fever of anticipation, heightened now by the news that Sebastian Cooke was coming to take part.

'This time last year we were an unknown village with a condemned hall, a failing drag competition and a rapidly diminishing community spirit,' Frank commented to George. 'Now look at us, we're bloody famous.' He pointed to the article in the newspaper.

'Mainly down to Roz and Jamie. They've been the catalyst for most things which have happened around here,' George replied.

'I agree with that,' Edward said coming to the bar. 'My life has certainly changed for the better and that's partly due to them.' He put his arm around Louisa. Their relationship was now common knowledge, they'd wanted everyone to share in their new-found happiness. 'It's extraordinary how much they've achieved when you think they've been in the village less than a year.'

'They've shaken us up,' Louisa said. 'They've shown us what's important. Sometimes it takes an outsider to do that.'

'It seems odd to think that there was ever a time when they weren't part of village life,' Ollie reflected. 'Did you actually put any bloody gin in this, George?' She pushed her drink towards him.

'The usual amount Ollie, about half a bloody bottle,' he pushed it back.

'Ah, talk of the devil here they are,' Clive said as the pub door burst open. 'Your ears must have been burning we've been talking about you.'

'In glowing terms I trust?' Jamie smiled. 'Sorry we're late guys, I was talking to Seb.'

'When does the movie star arrive?' Louisa asked.

'He's arriving with the Honey Bees. He's going to San Francisco first, says it makes sense for them all to arrive together but I've a feeling that's not the whole story.'

'You think he's planning something with them?' Frank asked.

'I'd put money on it,' Jamie laughed. 'Drew says everyone there is delirious with excitement.'

'I'd say people here feel much the same,' George poured their drinks. 'So, have we got everything under control?'

'Let's go through the list again,' Roz said, producing a battered piece of paper.

'That's seen better days,' Louisa smiled.

'That's seen Butler's mouth.'

'Talking of which, we wondered whether we should hire a butler for our cocktail party?' Edward said.

'Hire Butler? What the hell for?' Jamie stared open-mouthed.

'Hire *a* butler, not your Butler,' Edward laughed.

'Why?'

'Why not? I've a strong suspicion you've built me up,' Edward looked at him. 'I think you know what I mean Jamie, the squire in his manor house. Am I right?'

'Trust me I didn't need to build you up. They've done that all by themselves.'

'My point exactly.' Edward said. 'I don't want to let them down, a butler is exactly the sort of thing they'll expect, added to which we have a movie star in our midst.'

'Seb is the least pretentious man on earth,' Roz said. 'I honestly don't think a butler is necessary.'

'Not necessary but it could be fun,' Louisa said. 'Let's give it some thought. Right, now what's next on the list?'

It was after eleven when they left the pub. It was a frosty night and the air smelt clean and fresh.

'I can't believe that Edward is really thinking of hiring a butler for the night.' Roz was skipping up the pavement. 'He's thrown himself completely into all this. Having the girls to stay in the first place then organising a party, loaning us his beautiful piano and now this mad butler idea.'

'And this from the man who once loathed the idea of drag queens.'

'I still can't quite believe it's all happening.'

'And happening very soon. It's all totally mad. '

Roz giggled and looked up into the heavens. 'Hello up there, what else have you got in mind for us eh?'

'Whatever it is, it certainly won't be weirder than this.'

Across the Atlantic three other people were having much the same conversation.

'In a few days' time we'll be in the UK,' Drew said, drawing heavily on his cigar.

'Performing in a dilapidated hall,' Saul added.

'Hosted by a world famous movie star,' Elliot finished.

They looked at one another and burst out laughing.

'We've sure done some crazy things in our time but this has to be one of the craziest,' Drew said.

'What the hell have we got ourselves into?' Elliot lit another cigarette.

'Well, whatever else it won't be boring,' Saul said smiling. 'Not with Jamie at the helm.'

'To Roz and Jamie,' Drew lifted his glass. 'We've had good luck since we first got in touch with them.'

CHAPTER 58

Suffolk and San Francisco

Finally the big day arrived and Roz and Jamie were standing impatiently in the arrivals hall of the airport. They were waving a bunch of heart-shaped balloons and standing next to them, holding a banner saying 'Welcome Honey Bees' were Frank and Toby.

'They're starting to come through,' Roz said, jumping up and down as she caught sight of the labels on the suitcase of a tired-looking couple. 'This is their flight.'

'They'll be some time yet. Drew said they had more luggage than you could possibly imagine,' Jamie said.

'I believe him. I somehow can't imagine a drag queen would travel light,' Toby laughed.

'I just hope they're not too exhausted.'

'They'll be too excited to be exhausted,' Jamie grinned. 'Drew says this is the first time that most of them have ever been on a plane.'

'I've never been on a plane before either,' Frank suddenly announced.

'Frank, you're kidding?' Roz looked at him in surprise. 'You've been abroad though?'

'Coach to Athens, not something I'd repeat, and the ferry to Ireland and France.'

'If you get to go to San Francisco we'll have to see if the pilot will let you into the cockpit,' Jamie chuckled. 'I'm not sure if they give out lollies anymore but they used to.'

Frank was saved replying by a screech from Roz. 'Here they are, there's Seb.' Roz leapt up and down waving her balloons.

'And he wanted to make a discreet entrance,' Jamie raised his eyebrows in despair at the others.

The Honey Bees came through looking amazingly bright and fresh and, as Drew had predicted, laden down with luggage. They shrieked at the sight of the balloons and banner and for a short while there was total chaos at the Heathrow arrivals hall. Trolleys were abandoned while everyone hugged and kissed. The noise level was astounding and passer's by looked on dumbfounded.

Frank had hung back suddenly feeling shy but was drawn in immediately by Jamie.

'This is Frank, freestyle butcher and fellow drag artist.'

'The freestyle butcher. Delighted to meet you, Frank,' Drew smiled.

Frank was surprised. They all looked like fairly normal guys. He had expected sequins and stilettos. 'I thought you'd be all dressed up.'

'No, Frank, we leave our alter egos in the suitcase. Just wait until the show though, they'll be no holding us back then,' Drew grinned.

A sudden flashbulb halted the celebrations. A couple of journalists were hurtling towards them.

'Sebastian, what brings you to the UK?'

'What can you tell us about your role in the new Bond film?'

'How do they do it?' Seb said. 'I swear they can smell my aftershave.'

'Perhaps they have a sniffer dog trained especially for you,' Roz giggled.

'A quick couple of photos, guys, and then I'm on my way.' He threw his arm around Roz and Jamie. 'Just visiting my mates and absolutely no comment on the Bond film.'

Half an hour later they were all settled in the minicoach Jamie had hired for them.

'Welcome to the UK, guys.' A huge cheer went up. 'It's so good to see you, I can't quite believe this is happening.'

'Neither can we, Jamie. Neither can we,' Elliot shouted back.

'Of course you all know Roz, most of you know Toby and in case you didn't get introduced in the melee this is Frank.'

'Ain't he gorgeous,' Diana cried. 'You're a real cutie.'

Frank blushed rosy red and sat down quickly. Jamie laughed and Roz took over.

'We'll drop you off at your houses. You can meet your hosts, get some rest and then there's a welcome dinner at the pub tonight.' She beamed at them all. 'Everyone is so excited about meeting you. Thank you so much for coming.' She suddenly felt quite emotional and sank down next to Saul.

'You OK, baby?' The big man put his arm around her.

'Just seeing everyone here,' she said snuggling up. 'It doesn't seem real.'

'You're not alone,' he smiled. 'Fran started blubbing on the plane and Drew had us all in tears with a highly emotional speech last night.'

The coach stopped outside the Manor House.

'OK,' Jamie yelled. 'First stop, Babette, Cherie, Mama T. and Diana. Come and meet your host, the squire.' He leapt down from the coach and then stopped in his tracks with his mouth wide open.

Edward appeared at the doorway wearing a three-piece tweed suit comprising jacket, waistcoat and plus fours. A silk necktie, bright yellow socks and brogues completed the picture. Louisa wafted just behind him in flowing chiffon and a floppy straw hat.

'Edward, you old bugger, you really are something else. And you had the temerity to accuse me of building you up,' Jamie was shaking with silent laughter.

'No idea what you're talking about, Jamie. This is my normal daytime attire.' He smiled suddenly, 'Let me introduce you to Hawkins our new butler.'

Hawkins, stepped forward, immaculate in his uniform. 'Pleased to meet you, sir,' he said with a little bow.

'You mad man, you actually went for it,' Jamie looked at Edward with admiration.

'And worth every penny. Look at their faces,' Edward was having a ball. He couldn't remember when he'd last enjoyed himself so much. He was right, everyone looked thunderstruck.

'Ladies and gentleman, may I introduce Edward Hampshire, Lord of the Manor, and the beautiful Lady Louisa,' Jamie said with a flourish. 'You are totally insane, but you look stunning,' he whispered in an aside to Louisa.

'Couldn't wear tweed, it's just not my look at all,' she whispered back.

'Not sure that it's Edward's,' Jamie chuckled.

'Was that an act?' Drew asked Jamie when they were all back on the coach. 'He doesn't seriously have a full-time butler, does he?'

'If it was an act then please keep it from Bobby,' Joe whispered, overhearing them. 'He thinks he's died and gone to heaven. This is exactly his idea of what England is all about.'

'OK, well let's not spoil his illusion,' Jamie said. 'Next stop you two.

Romantic barn conversion complete with wood burner and outdoor hot tub.'

'Sounds glorious,' Joe smiled.

'Owned by Clive and Ollie, mad as a box of frogs but wonderful. You'll love them. It's their daughter and her partner who are celebrating their marriage at the show. Did Drew tell you?'

'He did, what a wonderful idea. Can't wait to meet them.'

The very last stop was of course Jamie and Roz's.

'Welcome to our cottage.' Jamie threw open the door and an ecstatic puppy hurtled out. 'And we too have our own very special Butler, not quite as useful as the squire's but full of love and joy.'

'He's adorable,' Seb said caressing him

'He's sure cute,' Drew agreed as the big puppy leapt up at him.

'Don't leave anything around for him to eat,' Roz said.

'And don't make the mistake of thinking that he wouldn't eat something,' Jamie added.

'Trust me, this dog eats anything and everything, shoes, phones, wallets, glasses, you name it, he'll eat it.'

Butler looked proud of himself.

'This is beautiful,' Drew said stepping inside the cottage.

'Well it's a bit different from either of your places,' Roz said, suddenly feeling a little self-conscious.

'It's enchanting, Rosalind,' Seb said, giving her a hug. 'It's perfect.'

CHAPTER 59

Suffolk

It was perfect for everyone else too.

Elliot, Saul, Jason, Corey and Fran were settling in with George. They were charmed by the quintessential English pub.

'I so hoped it would be like this but I didn't really believe it would be. I kinda thought that places like this only belonged in story books.' Fran looked around at the low beams and the brick fireplace with happiness. 'I feel like I'm in a Dickens novel.'

'Probably more Thomas Hardy than Dickens,' Jason smiled. 'More likely to meet milkmaids and farmworkers around here rather than convicts and criminals.'

'Don't be such a smart arse, Jason, you know exactly what I mean, Fran retorted. 'I just feel like I've been transported into a very different world.'

They weren't the only ones who felt like that. The drag queens in the manor house were bowled over.

'This place is just awesome,' Diana said wandering around her room. 'I feel like a goddamn princess.'

Edward had really gone to town. There were fresh flowers in every room, crystal decanters filled with chilled water, baskets of fruit and boxes of chocolate.

'It sure beats the hell out of my condo,' Babette grinned. 'A girl could kinda get used to this.'

There was a knock on the door and Hawkins entered. 'Drinks will be served downstairs. At your convenience.' He bowed and exited. They all looked at each other in amazement and then collapsed in giggles like a bunch of schoolgirls.

Downstairs Edward and Louisa surveyed the table. There was a sherry decanter and glasses, a plate of cucumber sandwiches and some antique lace napkins.

'Any chance we may have gone over the top?' Louisa laughed.

'Every chance but who cares?'

The door opened and Hawkins announced their visitors.

'Come in everyone, come and have some refreshment.' Edward smiled warmly at them all. 'How are your rooms? Are they OK?'

'Hell, they're divine,' Diana replied.

'I'm so pleased. Now, sherry everyone?' He lifted up the decanter.

There was small pause, the girls were unclear about sherry.

'Is that kinda like bourbon?' Babette asked finally. 'I can't drink bourbon no more on account of the fact that I once drank too much,' she said with unexpected candour.

'Did you?' Edward wasn't quite sure how to respond.

'Well, I was sort of lost and hurt and I guess I thought it would help.' The others looked on amazed.

'Why were you lost and hurt?' Louisa asked gently.

'My mom had died. She weren't the best mom in the world but she was all I had,' Babette shrugged. 'She'd a thirst for bourbon too, it made her kinda mean, she slapped me around some and I wished her dead a fair few times but then when she did die I sure missed her.' There was a long pause while they all digested this new information.

Then Louisa spoke softly. 'My father had a thirst too. A thirst for whisky,' she paused. 'It sometimes made him kind of mean too.'

Babette looked at her with interest. 'Really?'

'Really.'

'Sucks don't it,' she said.

'It sucks,' Louisa replied.

'Sod the sherry,' Edward said, kissing them both. 'Let's have champagne.'

'As you wish, sir,' Hawkins made his way out of the room.

'Gee, he's just too cute for words,' Cherie said, watching Hawkins disappear. 'How cool to have your own butler.'

'Well I'm afraid that I have a confession to make.' Edward said. 'Hawkins isn't actually our butler, we hired him for you.'

They gawped at him.

'You hired him just for us?' Diana asked.

'We thought it would be a bit of fun, we thought you might appreciate it,' Edward shrugged apologetically and looked at Louisa for help.

'You and Lady Louisa hired him for us? Just for us?' Diana couldn't believe it. She looked from one to another. 'Heck, that's gotta be one of the nicest things anyone's ever done for me,' she said in wonderment and the others nodded their agreement.

'Also we're not, strictly speaking, Lord and Lady, just plain Edward and Louisa.' Edward continued.

'I suspect that you'll always be Lord and Lady to us,' Mama Teresa said quietly.

* * *

'Hey, folks, how's it going?' Roz asked, coming into the village hall the next day. 'George says that lunch is ready anytime you are.'

'Give us another fifteen minutes, Roz,' Seb said. 'Is that OK?'

'Of course it's OK, whatever you need,' she replied. 'What are you rehearsing exactly?'

He just smiled enigmatically and waved her away, laughing to himself. He knew they were longing to find out every detail, but Drew had sworn him to secrecy. He had gone to San Francisco to rehearse and, at Saul's insistence, they had hired a professional choreographer for the routines. They had performed it in front of a small audience and it had been a triumph. Seb had forgotten the buzz of live theatre, the rush of adrenalin, the immediacy of the audience, and he had made a promise to himself that he would work on stage more in the future.

'Any clues?' Jamie asked as she came outside.

'Nope, none at all, in fact he waved me away.'

'He's up to something. I'll wheedle it out of him at the drinks party tonight.'

'I just hope they're not too exhausted,' Roz said. 'We didn't go to bed until after midnight, and now they're rehearsing, they must be completely knackered.'

'As Drew said, midnight is an early night for them. They're like vampires, Roz, they exist better in the dark.' He winked at her. 'It was a good night, though, I think they all enjoyed themselves.'

'They had a ball, everyone loves them and we've still got Edward's party tonight and the show tomorrow.' She laughed. 'I'm not a vampire Jamie, I'm planning on a long siesta this afternoon.'

She wasn't the only one who was feeling the effects of a late night. George had sat up with Saul long after the others had gone to bed. They had recognised in each other a kindred spirit, realised that they had a lot in common. As Saul said at one point, 'We've both spent a lot of our lives behind bars.' A sentence which reduced them both to helpless laughter.

George decided to make his special hangover remedy. He reckoned that they'd all appreciate that.

'They're coming in about fifteen minutes, George,' Roz announced walking into the pub. 'And if that's what I think it is then yes please, a very large one for me.'

George smiled and handed her a tumbler. 'Feeling rough Roz?'

'Not rough exactly just slightly jaded. I'm planning on a long sleep before tonight.' She smiled. 'Mind you after a couple of these I may not feel the need for bed.'

'I heard the word bed. I hope you're not trying to seduce my wife, George?' Jamie strolled in behind her.

'You've caught us out. Will a large hangover cocktail make up for it?'

'Make it two and she's all yours,' Jamie laughed. 'Great night, George, everyone had a blast, thanks for making it so special.'

'I loved it, they're fun, more than fun, they're unique. I just can't wait to see the show.' He handed Jamie his drink. 'How many entries for the competition have we got?'

'Off the top of my head about ten. I reckon that will last about an hour, then we'll have the interval and then an hour with the Honey Bees. Does that sound OK?'

'Sounds fantastic. Are you taking part?'

'Wouldn't be fair George, I'm just too good,' Jamie grinned. 'No seriously, I'm going to San Francisco anyway and they couldn't judge me without being biased.'

* * *

'Y'all, which one do you think?' Babette was holding out two dresses. 'Sophisticated and chic or sexy and shimmering?'

'Sexy and shimmering,' Diana said.

'Sophisticated and chic,' Cherie said.

'Go ask Hawkins,' Mama Teresa said.

'I like your thinking, Mama T,' Babette looked at her appraisingly. 'You're one smart bird.' She went off in search of Hawkins and found him in the kitchen with Louisa.

'Gee great, two heads for the price of one,' Babette giggled and held out the dresses.

'We're all dressing up tonight and I wanna do Edward proud, which do you think?'

They both pointed to the same one.

'OK cool, thank you, guys.' She stole some smoked salmon. 'Hawkins, I sure hope you're coming to the show tomorrow.'

'His Lordship has intimated that he has a ticket for me,' Hawkins replied solemnly. 'I look forward to the event with pleasure.'

'You're one cool dude, buddy, you crack me up,' Babette blew him a kiss and went to get changed.

'Hawkins, you do know you don't have to carry on with the act don't you?' Louisa asked.

'I was hired to do a job, my Lady, and that is what I am doing,' he replied. 'Besides which I'm enjoying myself hugely.' He winked at her.

'It is such fun isn't it,' she laughed. 'They all make me feel so alive.'

CHAPTER 60

Suffolk

Edward stood in the sitting room and looked around with pleasure. A large vase of lilies stood on the central table and the air was heady with their perfume. Everything gleamed and sparkled and the candles flickered on the mantelpiece adding their scent to the room.

Outside was no less impressive. He had bought three large Mexican fire pots for the occasion and they stood blazing on the terrace. The outside lights showed off the magnificent garden which Beth had lovingly designed. The huge trees looked very dramatic, Beth had been right to insist on the uplights.

She would have been proud of the way everything looked tonight Edward thought. She would also be proud and amazed at his recent involvement in the village. He could picture her now smiling at him and he raised a glass in a silent salute.

'Thinking of Beth?' Louisa came to his side.

'Indeed I was.' Edward held out his hand to her. 'I was thinking that she would be proud of the house tonight.'

'She would not only be proud of the house Edward, she would be enormously proud of you.' Louisa kissed him softly on the cheek. 'And somewhat surprised I imagine.'

'Not in a million years would she have believed what we're doing tonight.' He burst out laughing. 'Let's face it Louisa, no one could have imagined this scenario. The pompous fart Edward opening his house up to a troupe of San Franciscan drag queens.'

'Not a pompous fart anymore but a warm, sensitive and sexy man.' She took his hand and looking up into the night sky said. 'You were right about your husband, Beth. He's a very special man. I hope you don't mind but I'm falling in love with him.'

Edward turned slowly to look at her. His face radiated happiness. 'And I with you, Louisa, and I with you.' He pulled her to him in a passionate embrace which was how Jamie and Roz found them a few minutes later.

Jamie coughed and Roz giggled.

'Much as I hate to disturb such a beautiful moment your guests are arriving,' Jamie said.

'We're in love.' Edward beamed at his young friend.

'That much is clear.' Jamie smiled back.

It was an enchanting evening. Edward and Louisa's happiness seemed to infect everyone and the non-stop flow of champagne certainly went a long way to help.

'Seb, will you come and meet my sister,' Jason asked. 'She's longing to meet you but will be too shy to come and see you herself.'

'Lead the way,' Seb smiled.

'Sasha this is Seb, Seb this is my twin sister Sasha.'

A tall girl with long dark brown hair turned around. Seb had completely forgotten that Jason had a twin, he had been expecting a young awkward teenager not this brown-eyed beauty.

'Charmed.' He bent over to kiss her hand.

He was furious with himself. What sort of pretentious greeting was that. He'd never greeted anyone that way in his life before. She must think him a complete tosser.

'Pleased to meet you.' She held out her hand. What a pretentious git she thought.

'Ah, Seb,' Gerry came over to greet him. 'I see you've met my daughter and this is my wife Rose.'

'Pleased to meet you.' Seb smiled at Rose.

'Here you are, darling,' Gerry said, handing over a glass of champagne to Sasha.

'Oh lovely, thank you, Daddy,' she simpered.

Sasha was furious with herself. She couldn't believe what she'd just said. She hadn't used the word Daddy since primary school. She must sound like a spoilt brat. What on earth would he think of her?

What grown up still uses the word Daddy, Seb thought? She sounds like a spoilt brat, what a shame, she was very sexy.

Bobby was in seventh heaven. This was exactly what he had imagined English life to be like. He was actually at a party in a large manor house owned by a lord. There had been some confusion amongst the girls over whether they were a real lord and lady but in Bobby's mind there was no doubt.

'You look like the cat that got the cream,' Joe laughed, giving him a quick peck on the cheek. 'Are you in paradise?'

'I most certainly am.'

'Is this what you imagined, Bobby?' Liz asked, coming over to join them.

Bobby had confided his love of all things British to her and Carol last night and had talked endlessly of going to the manor house.

'This way surpasses all my expectations,' he replied theatrically.

'Having a fun time?' Louisa came over to see them.

'Lady Louisa, I'm having the time of my life,' Bobby said giving a little curtsy.

Louisa looked alarmed.

'He's harmless, I promise,' Joe assured her. 'Just a little overawed at the moment.'

Louisa chuckled. He was a sweet lad. She spotted Billy standing awkwardly at the edge of a group which contained Titty. Poor boy, she thought, he'll have to be braver than that to grab her attention.

She called him over. 'This is my grandson, Billy.' She said. 'Did you all meet last night?'

'Are you the Billy who helped Titty with the posters?' Joe asked.

'Yes I am.'

'Well I'm sure impressed. They're real neat. She tells me that you're a graphic designer. Is that right?'

'He is, and a very talented one too.' Louisa said squeezing Billy's arm.

'She's biased,' Billy smiled at Joe.

'I am biased, it's true, but it's also true that you're extremely talented.'

Bobby had been watching this exchange with interest. 'Gee, every family I've met over here seems real close. It's kinda weird but wonderful.'

'I'm sure your family would seem wonderful to us too, Bobby.' Louisa smiled at the flamboyant young man.

There was a long pause. Bobby had gone pale and Joe looked anxiously at him.

'I'm terribly sorry, Bobby.' Louisa gently laid her hand on Bobby's arm. 'I've obviously said something wrong. I didn't mean to upset you.'

'You haven't upset me at all Lady Louisa.' He knocked back his champagne. 'It's just my family ain't exactly what you'd call real close. My father screws every female in sight, my mother is an uptight, racist bitch and the only thing they have in common is that they both hate me. I'm unnatural apparently, a freak of nature whom they wish to disown.'

Joe looked astounded. Bobby never revealed this much to anyone.

Edward coming to join them caught this last speech and looked at Louisa with amazement. What was it about this woman that made people reveal their secrets? First Babette and now Bobby.'

'It's their loss, Bobby,' Billy said unexpectedly. 'It's absolutely their loss.'

Jamie went off in search of his wife. It was getting late and it was time to go home. Tomorrow was a big day for them all. If he were being truthful he was actually a little nervous. They'd all gone to so much trouble and he was desperate for it to be a success. He fancied a quick nightcap and then bed. Unusually for him he had gone easy on the champagne.

He saw Roz deep in conversation with the butler. One look at her flushed face and sparkling eyes told him that she had not been as cautious with the champagne as he had. He wondered if George had any leftover hangover cure for the morning.

'You could become a permanent resident of the village, Hawkins,' Roz was saying to him. 'We could all take it in turns to have you and that way you would be available for all the major events.' Hawkins merely smiled and offered her another glass of champagne. 'See, that's what I mean. You're invaluable, you're a mind reader,' she said.

'It doesn't take much talent to read your mind, Roz,' Jamie smiled. 'Has she been bothering you, Hawkins? I'm afraid she's always drawn to a man with an open bottle in his hand.' He took Roz's arm. 'Time to go home, darling.'

'Really? Is it time already? Where's the evening gone?'

'And this from the girl who wasn't going to drink tonight.'

'It would have been very rude not to have drunk Edward's champagne.'

'No one's going to accuse you of rudeness tonight, Roz,' he said putting his arm around her.

'Nightcap anyone?' Jamie asked once they'd got home.

'Not for me. I'm going to bed,' Roz said.

'Wise decision.' Jamie blew her a kiss which she returned with a scowl.

The rest of them settled in the sitting room and each lit a cigar.

'Looking forward to tomorrow, Jamie?' Drew asked. 'You seem uncharacteristically stressed.'

'Not stressed at all, well not really, well OK, maybe a bit.' He smiled ruefully, 'Not really sure why? As you say, it's unlike me.'

'You've done so much work, you and Roz and the rest of this crazy village. Of course you're worried,' Drew said. 'But trust me, buddy, there's no need. It's going to be a huge success.'

'No doubting that,' Seb agreed. 'Relax, Jamie, you've done your bit, now let us do ours.' He inhaled deeply on his cigar. 'You've got the dream team, mate, what could go wrong with me and Drew at the helm?'

CHAPTER 61

Suffolk

Roz woke up the next morning feeling surprisingly bright. 'I'm not sure whether to be relieved or worried,' she announced at breakfast.

'Take the relief any day.' Drew said. 'Look, is anyone else going to eat that last bacon roll or can I have it?'

Roz pushed the plate towards him. 'It's your third but who's counting?' she smiled.

The village hall was a hive of activity. Titty was playing the beautiful baby grand piano loaned to them for the occasion by Edward. Frank and a team of helpers were busy in the kitchen preparing his slow roast pork and sausages, George was setting up the bar and Saul was trying to sort the music out. He looked delighted to see Seb. 'Over here Seb. I need you.' Seb needed no further encouragement and soon the two of them were busy programming the computer.

'You've worked wonders with the hall, Roz. It looks amazing,' Drew said.

'Wait till you see it tonight,' she smiled. 'It needs lights to give it some real atmosphere.'

'I just adore this wall. These pictures are good, Roz,' Drew went up close to examine the poster-sized photos of the drag queens.

'I keep telling her they're amazing. She never believes me,' Jamie said.

'Where's Billy?' Joe asked coming to join them. 'I want to ask him how he kept such amazing definition. He's a clever lad.'

'He's over there, hovering in the corner watching Titty play,' Roz said. 'In fact he spends most of his time watching Titty.'

Joe grinned. 'I'd noticed.'

'Roz?' Drew suddenly shouted.

Roz jumped out of her skin.

'I've had an idea,' Drew continued. 'I'm going to buy these from you. Can I buy these?'

'I don't know. I guess so. Do you really want them? I'm not sure they're for sale.'

'Of course they're for bloody sale,' Jamie said. 'Roz, darling, you've just sold your first photographs. This is only the beginning, sweetheart.' He danced around her.

'You're right, Jamie. It sure is just the beginning because I'm also gonna give you your first commission, Roz.' Drew was grinning. 'Take some more tonight. Some of the Suffolk drag queens and some of us and we'll get Billy to give them the same treatment. What do you say, honey?'

Roz didn't say anything – she was speechless.

Enormous heart-shaped balloons were in place in each corner of the hall and red roses and chocolates adorned every table. The lighting was soft and subdued and Titty was playing mood music on the piano. The evening was about to begin.

Roz and Jamie stood at the door ready to welcome the audience.

'I know we've said it before but …' Roz began.

'I can't believe it's really happening,' Jamie finished. 'Come here and give me a Valentine's kiss before all hell breaks loose.'

'What if no one comes?' Roz whispered. 'It's like that awful feeling you get before a party. What if no one turns up?'

'Then we'll all look like right chumps, but that's not going to happen, darling.'

He was right, that didn't happen. The hall was packed to the rafters. There was a real buzz in the air, an air of anticipation. Nobody knew quite what to expect. The drinks were flowing. George and Saul's Valentine cocktail was proving a hit.

'Ladies and gentlemen, could you please take your seats. This evening's show will begin in three minutes.' Jamie's voice boomed loud and clear over the microphone.

Roz leant against the bar beside George. 'Fingers crossed.'

'Fingers crossed.' He put his hand over hers.

'Ladies and gentlemen,' Jamie's voice boomed out once again. 'Would you please welcome to the stage, all the way from Hollywood, the one and only, the incomparable, the unmatchable, the unrivalled, the legend that is … Mr Sebastian Cooke.'

The noise was deafening. Roz heard people exclaiming as Seb made his way to the stage. Despite all the publicity some people hadn't really believed that he would actually be there.

Seb leapt up onto the stage and grabbed the microphone from Jamie. 'Ladies and gentlemen, boys and girls and those of you not yet sure,' he winked at a couple sitting nearby. 'Welcome to The Honey Bees Have Hearts Valentine's Drag Show.'

The applause was rapturous. He really did have charisma by the bucket load, thought Roz.

'What a spectacle we have for you tonight, ladies and gentlemen. What tremendous treats we have in store …' He waited for the clapping to die down.

'It's fantastic to see so many of you here tonight to celebrate Valentine's Day with us, and, talking of celebrations, I understand that we have a wedding party here this evening.' He looked out across the audience. 'Will you please be upstanding and raise a glass to the brides. To Liz and to Carol.'

Encouraged by their friends, Liz and Carol leapt to their feet and took the applause.

'Ladies and gentlemen …' Seb continued. 'Tonight we have the talented and frankly the not so talented. We have glitz and glamour, we have comedy and tragedy. We have wenches, weirdos, tarts and treasures, we have maids, we have mamas and we have one thing in common, we're *men.*' There was a huge round of applause. 'Ladies and gentlemen, we're going to kick off this evening with our own drag competition. Be kind to them, folks, it takes balls to put on a frock. Clearly something not all of you are endowed with.' He grinned down at two lads sitting near the stage who, luckily, grinned back.

Where did he learn all this patter from, Roz wondered? Where does he get the confidence from?

'But first, ladies and gentlemen, I want you to welcome our judges.' There was a large cheer from the village. 'From all the way across the pond I bring you, the world-famous, the world-class, the outrageous talent that is Miss Honey Berry and her Honey Bees.'

The music blared out playing 'Mambo Number Five' and Seb started singing:

A little bit of Honey in my life,

A little bit of Titty by my side,
A little bit of Cherie's all I need.
A little bit of Mama's all I see,
A little bit of Babette in the sun,
A little bit of Diana all night long.
A little bit of Honey, here I am.
A little bit of you makes me your man.

It was clever, it was funny and Seb was excellent.

'So this is what they've been rehearsing,' Jamie whispered to Roz. 'I knew he was up to something.'

'He's so good,' Roz whispered back. 'I wonder whose idea this was? It's brilliant.'

The routine finished to a standing ovation. The audience were clearly here to enjoy themselves.

'Thank you, ladies and gentlemen, you're too kind. And now, put your hands together to welcome the first of our amateur drag queens hoping for glory. Ladies and gentlemen, we have a duet, we have Bernadette and Cynthia singing from the musical *Chess*: "I Knew Him So Well".'

The lights went up on the stage and the music started. Frank and Clive walked on stage. It was a wonderful parody, with Frank playing Elaine Paige and Clive taking the part of Barbara Dickson. The guys were superb, the lip-synching was a little out at times but that didn't matter. The comedy was there and the audience loved them.

'Obviously Titty has had a hand in this,' Jamie said to George and Roz.

The next act was Leon spinning around to 'The Hills are Alive with the Sound of Music'. He was like a whirling dervish, energy and enthusiasm making up for his total lack of coordination and musicality. Obviously Titty had not helped out here but Hannah had. She and her aunt had spent the last few evenings sewing his costume. She sat bolt upright beside Aunty Jess willing her dad on.

'He's alright, isn't he, Aunty Jess? He's doing OK, isn't he?' She was desperate for people to like him.

'He's doing fine, darling. He's completely mad and I'm not sure the pinafore will hold up to many more spins but he's doing well. Come on, let's give him some encouragement.' And grabbing her niece's hand she proceeded to whistle and whoop.

Next, someone called 'Lady Boy' performed a bizarre routine to 'Wannabe' by the Spice Girls.

'Not much of a lady, not much of a boy, and singing a song meant for five,' Seb commented in amusement after the number. 'Still, apart from those flaws, we loved him, didn't we, ladies and gentlemen?'

Gerry was next up and gave a spirited version of Nancy's 'Oom Pah Pah' from the musical *Oliver!*.

'I'd lay money this isn't the first time he's sung this,' George said to Roz and Jamie. 'I've a suspicion that this is his party piece. Am I correct, Jason?'

Jason merely smiled.

'And what a fantastic Nancy Boy you make, Sir,' Seb laughed. 'Your family must be so proud.' He glanced into the audience and locked eyes with Sasha who was cheering her father with unrestrained delight. It was with great difficulty that he managed to look away.

There were a couple of others and then Seb was announcing the last of the competition entrants. 'And last but certainly not least, we have Miss Fit. Clever word play there, I'm loving it, and I'm loving the song choice. Put your hands together to welcome Miss Fit, singing Lady Gaga's 'Born This Way'.'

Billy stepped on stage looking sensational with a peroxide blonde

411

wig and exquisite make-up. The audience sat up, sensing something a bit special. The music started and Billy began his routine.

He was stunning, simply stunning.

'My God,' Roz said. 'Did you know he was this good, George?'

'No idea.'

'He's better than good, he's incredible, he's unbelievably talented.' Jamie was taken aback. He wasn't the only one, the faces of the audience said it all. When it got to the chorus, everyone leapt to their feet and chanted along with him. The applause was loud and long. Billy looked ecstatic and the Honey Bees looked astounded.

There was a huge buzz of excitement during the interval. Billy was definitely the hero of the hour and he'd never had so much attention, but there was a great deal of anticipation about the rest of the show.

'Great stuff, Seb,' Jamie slapped him on the back. 'Well done, mate.'

'Loved every single minute.' Seb laughed, glancing around for Sasha. 'It's a superb evening, Jamie, everyone's having a blast.'

Jamie looking around the hall couldn't help but agree. 'And the best is yet to come.'

CHAPTER 62

Suffolk

'Ladies and gentlemen, will you please take your seats, the second half of this evening's performance will commence in three minutes.' Jamie's voice once again boomed out across the hall.

People started making their way back immediately, their appetite had been wetted and they were eager for more.

'My lords, ladies and gentlemen, boys and girls ...' Elliot was resplendent in a red silk jacket and white silk cravat. 'Happy Valentine's Day.'

'Happy Valentine's Day!' the audience screamed back.

'We've crossed borders, we've crossed the pond and we've cross-dressed to be here with you this evening.' Like Seb before him Elliot knew how to work a crowd. 'Ladies and gentleman, her talent knows no bounds and neither does her waistline. No one can beat her, no matter how much she pays them.' Roz looked around at the laughing faces and felt a surge of pure happiness.

'She's a legend in her own lifetime and that of many others, she's unique and she is none other than Miss Honey Berry.'

Honey stepped on to the stage to tumultuous applause and began her signature song: 'Kiss me, Honey, Honey, Kiss Me'. She had been delivering this number for years but tonight was special. Tonight was her first in front of a British audience and she was giving it her all.

'She's on fire tonight,' Jamie whispered to Roz.

'She certainly is. She's wonderful. I think it's a success, Jamie.'

He turned to smile at her. 'It's going rather well, isn't it?'

All the Honey Bees were on fire that night. The audience were ecstatic and extremely loud. The girls were loving it. The atmosphere was like nothing else they had ever experienced.

Cherie came off in tears after her performance of 'I Wanna be Loved by You'.

'It's awesome out there. They were joining in with me, they were whistling me. I'm staying put right here, Honey.'

Honey grinned at her. 'Tempting isn't it? Right, you two, are you ready?' She smiled at Titty and her brother. 'Knock em dead, guys.'

'And now, we have a rather special number.' Elliot paused in anticipation. 'Please welcome back to the stage Miss Titty.' There was a huge round of applause. They had adored her 'Chitty Chitty Bang Bang' routine. 'But this time she's not on her own, tonight, for one night only, ladies and gentlemen, Miss Titty will be joined by someone making their stage debut.'

Roz and Jamie looked puzzled.

'They lost each other for a while but now they're back together. Ladies and gentlemen, I give you the Miss Forresters.'

Titty and Toby stepped out hand in hand to the sound track of Irving Berlin's 'Sisters'.

Roz couldn't believe her eyes. 'Did you know this was going to happen?' she asked Jamie.

'Absolutely no idea, and we weren't the only ones.' He pointed over to where Kate and the kids sat open mouthed as Toby and Titty continued.

Tears streamed down Kate's face. She reached over and grabbed her mother-in-law's hand. 'Isn't this incredible?'

Her mother-in-law was unable to do more than nod her head.

'Mum, are you OK?' Belinda asked, concerned at the tears. 'Dad's good, isn't he?'

'He's more than good, sweetheart, he's bloody marvellous. We should all be so very proud of him.'

Toby was enjoying himself. He'd never done anything like this before and probably never would again but he was loving every second. He couldn't wait to hear the reaction from Kate. The song finished to yet another standing ovation. Titty and Toby hugged each other.

'You know I always wanted a younger sister,' Toby said.

'And I always loved having an older brother. So it seems we both got what we wanted after all,' Titty smiled.

Everyone, even those that didn't know the background, found it emotional

'This audience seems to spend more time on its feet than its arse,' Jamie remarked, as the clapping and cheering continued. 'Christ, that really got to me, look at me, I'm crying like a baby.'

'You're not alone,' George gulped. 'If anyone had told me a few months ago that I would see Toby Forrester in a dress and wig I would have laughed in their faces.'

'That was terrific, guys,' Drew said as they came off stage.

'How the hell are we supposed to follow that?' Diana laughed. 'Go on, Mama T, there's Elliot announcing you now.'

Mama T stepped on stage and smiled serenely at the audience. As always, and without ever really knowing why, the audience felt a peace and calmness in her presence.

She started off with her customary quote from Mother Teresa. 'If you judge people then you have no time to love them.' The audience were bemused. This was not your usual drag act. Nonetheless they loved her rendition of 'Love is the sweetest thing' and clapped her warmly at the end.

Babette, Diana and Titty, wearing magnificent black beehive wigs, leapt onto the stage to the music of The Supremes 'You Can't Hurry Love'. It was wild and upbeat and had the audience once more on their feet dancing and singing along.

'They've rehearsed hard,' Roz said. 'Not only their single numbers but all these new ensemble routines. This one must be so tricky to mime to and they're fantastic.'

'They really are extremely talented,' George agreed. 'I'm not sure what I expected but certainly nothing as professional as this.'

'Ladies and gentlemen, we are nearing the end of our show.' Elliot was back on stage and this announcement was greeted with boos and hisses. 'But we still have a couple of treats for you.' The clapping recommenced. 'For one last time, scream yourselves hoarse to welcome back Sebastian Cooke and The Honey Bees.'

'What the hell's Seb doing now?' Jamie yelled into Roz's ear.

'We're about to find out,' she yelled back over the riotous applause.

There was a moment's silence, before the unmistakeable sounds of Roy Orbison's 'Pretty Woman' came over the speakers. Seb emerged onto the stage in dark glasses, black suit and ridiculous wig and sideboards and launched into the opening lines.

He wasn't miming and Jamie was impressed. 'No wonder he's a Hollywood film star. The boy has real talent.'

The girls sashayed and twirled around the stage as Seb sang. It was a slick piece of choreography and a fabulous end to the show.

'He's such a bloody show off you've gotta love him.' Jamie was grinning from ear to ear. He put his fingers in his mouth and whistled loudly. Seb looked over and Jamie gave him the thumbs up.

Honey stepped forward at the end of the number and held her hands up for silence.

'You've been a wild and crazy audience and we love each and every one of you.'

'You're not so bad yourselves,' someone yelled out. Roz had a feeling it was Clive but couldn't be sure.

'Before we leave you, I've a few things I want to say,' Honey continued. 'I want to thank Mr Sebastian Cooke for his wickedly sexy performance here tonight. He is a star in the true sense of the word and it has been an absolute honour to share the stage with him.' Drew led the applause. Sasha was clapping more than anyone. She had been spellbound by Seb and was starting to revise her original opinion.

'I also want to thank all the folk in this beautiful village for making us so very welcome and for their hard work in helping make this evening an incredible success.' Drew paused until the applause died down. 'Now, ladies and gentlemen, we have the small matter of announcing the winner of the drag contest. As you know, the prize for the lucky top four is the chance to perform with The Honey Bees in San Francisco.' There was a loud cheer. 'Breaking with tradition, I'm gonna announce the winner first, folks. Now, I'm sure you'll all agree, there was one performance that really stood out, one performance which was truly magnificent, one deserved winner, and that winner, ladies and gentlemen is Miss Fit.'

There was a loud roar of approval as Billy stepped up on stage.

'Congratulations, Miss Fit, that was a stunning routine.' Drew gave Billy a hug. 'Is there anything you'd like to say about tonight?'

Drew handed him the microphone.

'This has been the best night of my life,' Billy said quite simply.

Louisa burst into tears. She couldn't have felt prouder of her grandson if he'd won an Olympic gold. He'd finally found the courage to be true to himself and face up to who he really was.

'And now, we come to the runners-up,' Drew paused and glanced across at Seb, who imperceptibly nodded his head. 'You all had verve, you all had nerve, you were audacious and awesome. In other words, you're all winners.'

The audience and competitors looked baffled.

'In an unprecedented act of enormous generosity, Mr. Sebastian Cooke is donating the flights to any competitor wishing to take part in the San Franciscan show.'

There were gasps of surprise and astonishment.

'No, he can't do that,' Roz exclaimed. 'That's just way too generous.'

'That's unbelievable.' George was taken aback.

'That's Seb,' Jamie said.

'I told you he was a star in the true sense of the word,' Drew was saying. 'And this proves that I was right.' He turned to applaud Seb who bowed modestly. 'Now, as you know, this evening was all about saving this magnificent hall which is the heart of this village and of this community. Well, I don't know the exact figure, folks, but I can tell you that this heart is sure gonna carry on beating for a while yet. So, let's raise a glass to the continuation of the village hall.'

The audience stood up and raised their glasses.

'Now, folks, I have one last announcement to make. A very important announcement.'

There was a buzz of expectation. 'In this hall are two very special people. A young couple who have more heart and soul than Otis Redding

418

himself. Without them none of this would have been possible. I know that they've enriched the lives of many people here, and I know for sure they've enriched mine.' He paused a moment and took a deep breath. 'I'm sorry to get all emotional here, but it's that sort of evening, I'm that sort of guy and these sort of people don't come along very often. So put your hands together with your loudest applause yet and welcome onto the stage a couple I am so very proud to call my friends. Ladies and gentlemen, I give you Jamie and Roz Forsyth.'

Jamie and Roz stumbled through the audience, up the stairs and into the arms of Drew. It was hard to say which of them was crying the hardest.

'You bastard, Drew. How dare you suddenly spring that on us!' Jamie said through his tears. 'You've reduced us to blubbering wrecks.'

Roz was incapable of speech. She clung onto Drew's strong arms and was dimly aware of the shouting and screaming behind her.

Drew spoke into the microphone one last time. 'I feel something, ladies and gentlemen. Do you feel it too? I feel happiness and I feel joy.' The audience cheered. 'But what I feel most of all is LOVE.' And the music blared out for the final time, as Drew bellowed the opening lines of 'Love is in the Air.

'If you feel the same, ladies and gentlemen, then show your love. Stand up and sing, dance in the aisles, dance on the tables, come up and dance on stage. It's Valentine's Day folks, and love is most definitely everywhere I look around.'

The audience went wild. Everyone was on their feet and there was a general stampede towards the stage.

Edward and Louisa were already holding hands. Titty beckoned shyly to Billy. Seb scoured the room looking for Sasha and Frank knocked over a few people in a bid to reach Jess.

'Do you want to dance, Jess?' he asked breathlessly.

'OK,' Jess said. He wasn't really her type but he was a sweet guy.

Jason was slowly making his way to where Fran stood at the bar. Joe and Bobby gave each other a kiss, at the same time as Liz reached out for her new bride, Carol.

'Dad, go and ask Charlotte to dance,' Hannah said.

'Why?' Leon was puzzled.

'Because you like her.'

'Well, of course I like her.'

'And she likes you.' Hannah couldn't believe he was being so dim.

'Well, I hope so, and she likes you, too.'

'No, Dad, I don't mean we all just like each other.' Hannah was exasperated. 'I mean you like each other in the sort of kissing type of liking.'

Leon stood for a moment looking down into the earnest face of his young daughter and then without saying a word strode off in search of Charlotte.

'Everyone's crying.' Belinda came to sit by her friend.

'I know, weird isn't it?' Hannah replied, not taking her eyes off her father.

'And everyone's kissing,' Belinda continued.

'I know,' Hannah said, finally turning around with a smile that went from ear to ear.

And in the middle of all this tumult and chaos, Drew, Jamie and Roz stood gazing at the party they had created.

'Elliot is waving a bottle of champagne at us,' Roz said pointing to the bar. 'Let's go and join him.'

Jamie and Drew stood for a moment looking at each other.

'We make a damned good team, don't we?' Jamie said.

'Sure do, buddy, we sure do.' Drew replied, as arm in arm they followed Roz off the stage.

THE END

ACKNOWLEDGEMENTS

Firstly a big thank you to Anita Burgh for starting me off on my writing journey and for her encouragement once I'd taken the first steps.

My thanks also to the lovely Katie Fforde for her support and for awarding me the Katie Fforde Bursary, which gave me a tremendous boost at a time when I needed it most.

Authors Jo Thomas, Jane Wenham-Jones, Judy Astley, Catherine Jones, Veronica Henry, Clare Mackintosh, Jenny Harper, Sue Moorcroft, Rosie Dean and Fiona Fullerton for their laughter and their continued inspiration.

I owe a massive debt of gratitude to my marvellous agent David Headley for showing faith in me from the early days when *Life's A Drag* was still very much in bud. His belief has helped me hugely – and I am honoured and proud to be the first book published by his new company The Dome Press.

Thanks also to my excellent editor Rebecca Lloyd for her positivity and her invaluable advice.

Lucy Borden at the Cinch Saloon and Victoria Secret from the Faux Girls in San Francisco (www.fauxgirls.com) – you introduced me to the wonderful world of drag queens and you were priceless – we loved the time we spent with you.

My very early readers – Kate, Camilla, Stephen and David – cheers for your constructive criticism and enthusiasm.

Thanks and love to my Mum and Dad, to my brother Chris for giving me the germ of the idea and to Bernie, Thomas, Anne and Allan – your massive support means so very much to me.

Rory – our mad hound – for his enthusiastic greeting every morning at 6.00 making it easier for me to get up and write and, of course, for providing me with the role model for Butler!

And lastly, but most importantly, to my husband Mickey for his tireless patience, his humour and his unflagging faith in me. Our gin-and-chapter sessions became a much-valued part of the writing process and long may they continue. I love you.